Unclaimed

laurie wetzel

ISBN 13: 978-1-940014-24-1

LCCN: 2014945331

Printed in the United States of America

First Printing: 2014

18 17 16 15 14   5 4 3 2 1

Cover and Interior design by Tiffany Laschinger

WISE

Wise Ink, Inc.
222 2nd St. N, Ste. 220
Minneapolis, MN 55401

www.wiseinkpub.com

To order, visit www.itascabooks.com or call 1-800-901-3480.
Reseller discounts available.

For Mike
Without your love and support, this would
have stayed a dream—I love you.

CHAPTER 1

Maddy

I FLOAT ON A BREEZE THROUGH MONSTERS, WITCHES, CE-lebrities, and a few costumes I don't recognize. Hundreds of them are on the dance floor, and others are mingling outside the party tent. None of them react to my presence, but they never have any other time I've been here. It's not their fault, though. I'm see-through, and they're frozen like statues. They will remain that way until I find the one who brought me here.

Once I do, the party will begin. Everyone will have the same conversations and dance with the same partners they have all the other times I've visited. But it's never dull. It's better than rereading my favorite book.

The breeze carries me beyond the guests, and I spot her at the top of the terrace. She's alone. It's been a while since this dream has started here.

With ease, my light body glides up the steps and paus-es beside her. She's dressed as an angel in a flowing white satin gown. Her blonde hair is pulled back so it trickles down to her sheer fabric wings. She's frowning while staring at the celebration, but even still, she's beautiful. The rest of her face is hidden behind a silver masquerade mask. All that can be seen is the one thing we have in common: emerald-green eyes.

Hers show she's strong, independent, and confident. I have no doubt in my mind it's because she's loved. I mean, really loved. Like the kind of loved that makes me wish this was my reality and that I, Maddy Page, were loveable ...

We've never spoken, even though I've known her all my life. She's frozen like the others. But she's different. She reacts to me. Once I enter her body, her world reanimates and I sink into the background as she takes control. I see everything through her eyes. I feel her emotions. I hear her thoughts. She's completely in charge, and only when she decides I've seen enough does the night end and I return to my life. Her life is so great I often wish it wouldn't end at all. I ease into her body, falling into my familiar role as the silent observer, and let the Dream Girl take over.

DUSK HAS SETTLED OVER THE BAY, GIVING THE EVENING A sense of magic—as if dreams really could come true tonight. Everyone is enjoying the party, except one. A man in a tux and devil horns has spent the last two hours weaving through the crowd but conversing with no one. I think he's searching for someone.

I don't know why I'm caught up in him. He's handsome, but so is every other man here. After a few more trips around the floor, he leaves the party area and strolls along the pathway to the valet.

At the sight of my entertainment leaving, I lean on the railing and sigh.

He turns, and solid black eyes meet mine. I can't find the will to break away, even when the masked stranger strides across the lawn and up the terrace steps to me.

"Good evening," he says. Deep, soothing tones curl around me. There's a touch of an accent, Old English-sounding, but it suits him.

"Hello." Even though it was just one word, I feel as if I've gained back some control. I lower my gaze in time to catch a smile forming on his lips. "Are you looking for someone?"

"I was."

"Did you find the person you were looking for?"

"Perhaps."

I take a deep breath, and a rich spice, like a burning log over a fire, fills my airways. My body even feels warmer. It's wonderfully calming.

"Do you always spend every party watching from the shadows?" His black eyes hold mine again. There's something oddly comforting about their simplicity. It's as if they're open windows to his soul.

"Not every party. Just … this one."

"Why?"

I open my mouth to tell him it's not his business, but the words disappear when I see the intensity in his eyes. He honestly wants to know my response.

For reasons I can't fathom, I want to tell him not only why I can't make myself go down to the party I have fantasized about for so long, but every other detail of my life too. Even down to the name of my childhood stuffed rabbit: George.

"What if it's not as perfect as I dreamed it would be?"

He leans closer, pursing his lips while narrowing his brows. "I do not understand."

I sigh and resume enviously staring at all the fun taking place nearby. "Ever since I was three, I've had this ... vision of how tonight would go. It's exactly right, except for one thing."

"What?" Heat claims me once more as he leans so close, our bodies nearly touch. This time it's not just from inside me, but it's also radiating from him. It's so hot, I feel as if touching him would burn me.

I focus on a couple dressed as Romeo and Juliet. They dance a waltz on the temporary dance floor set up near the boathouse and shoreline. That. I want that.

"Dance with me," he whispers.

My heart skips a beat, and my cheeks heat. Earlier, he had moved between the crowds of people so easily, as if he knew exactly where their movements would take them before they did. It made me want to watch him dance. But I hadn't expected I would be his dance partner. My lips twitch as I fight a smile. "Why me?"

"Because dancing with me for one dance is better than wasting the evening up here alone."

I turn and stare up into his eyes, trying to figure out why he would care. "Who are you?"

"You may call me the Dark Prince."

Great. I ask for his name, and he tells me his costumed name. "Never heard of him."

"I would know if you did," he states matter-of-factly. "So now that I have responded to your query, what answer do you have for mine?"

At some point, I'll have to go down there. What better way to ensure this night will be unforgettable than by dancing with him? "Okay. You win. I'll dance with you."

My heart skips a beat at the joy radiating from him. All I did was say yes...

He extends his arm, and after a deep breath, I accept. A rush of tranquility spreads through me. I know he said only one dance, but now that's not enough. If I get my way, we'll be the last to leave the dance floor.

"Shall we?"

I nod, and together we join what will surely be the best night of my life.

We navigate through the dancers to the center of the floor. As his hand touches mine, an intense heat rushes through me, causing us both to gasp. It's so much more powerful than before. He is fire, and he could easily consume me. I want him to.

"Are you all right?" he asks.

I nod again, and with that, we begin our dance. He moves with such grace, I forget my previous worries, and everyone on my periphery fades into a blur. It's as if we were the only two people here.

A beam of light hits the horns resting in his sandy-brown hair, and I smile.

"What is it?" he asks.

"Well ... " I pause and try to figure out how much I want to say. "Don't you find it strange that the man now responsible for turning this evening from tragic to utterly perfect is dressed in a costume coordinating mine?" I nod to my angel wings and his devil horns. "I'm not sure if it's fate or a coincidence."

He stiffens, and his mouth sets into a harsh line. "There is no such thing as coincidence—simply a series of unwise decisions made by others that led me here tonight and ultimately to you. Fate, however, does exist. But up until recently, your fate was in your own hands."

"And now?"

"Well, as I am here holding you close, I would say your fate is in my hands."

"Oh." My heart beats wildly against my ribs as if it were trying to push its way out. "So ... what are you going to do with it?"

His hand holding mine tightens, then he sends me twirling across the floor, as far as our outstretched arms will allow. An unexpected, carefree laugh bubbles out of me as I spin back into his waiting arms. For the life of me, I can't remember the last time I've ever laughed like that.

"You have a wonderful laugh." He bends me low so my wings and hair touch the floor, then leans over me—his intentions written all over his face. He's reeling me in for a kiss.

I didn't expect this. I've watched couples kiss like this and I wanted to do the same, but can I kiss him? A kiss is much more complicated than dancing. Kisses are the basis for every tragic love story. If I kiss him ... I'll be hooked. I can't allow myself to fall for him, to fall for a nameless mystery.

Before our lips can meet, I turn my head, and his lips press into my cheek instead.

Even still, my body pulses with euphoric bliss.

What have I done?

I peek at him from under my lashes. His eyes beseech mine, and I know he's disappointed. I am too. He returns me to my feet and starts dancing again.

"I'm sorry, I—" I begin.

"Do not apologize. I got caught up in the moment, though I suspect it would be a common occurrence if I were to spend more time with you."

Never have I wanted something so much than for his statement to come true. Not just a few more dances. I want to see him again, beyond tonight. But before I can respond, something behind me causes him to stiffen. I turn and follow his gaze.

My happiness fades as a familiar couple dressed as Anthony and Cleopatra move toward us. Our time is up. It's not fair. Even Cinderella had until midnight with her prince...

I grab his chin and force him to look at me. "Before they get here, I want to say thank you. No matter how many parties I go to or people I dance with, this one will always be my favorite because of you. Thank you for making my dream come true." I want to say more, but there is no time.

He inhales sharply. "You have—"

"Forgive my interrupting, sir," Anthony says to my Dark Prince. "But I couldn't help notice your enchanting companion."

I turn away, resting my head on his shoulder to allow myself an extra moment to breathe him in and absorb as much of him as possible. There wasn't anger in Anthony's voice, as I would have expected. Instead it was something else. It was tense, with just a dash of hope underneath it. It wasn't for me. Although he had called me "enchanting," it was merely an excuse to get my Dark Prince's attention. Anthony didn't know it was me. So what did he really mean by interrupting us?

With reluctance, I shift my attention to Anthony and Cleopatra to gauge their mood. Anthony's smile is tight, one I know well. He wears it whenever he's nervous about a business deal—hoping it will go his way but unsure of the outcome. Cleopatra rubs the four champagne flutes in her hands while watching the guests around us. This isn't like them. They're always gracious hosts, so why are they acting so differently?

"I do hope this means you've accepted the new terms of our agreement," Anthony says, continuing to stare at him.

They *know* each other?

The Dark Prince's knuckles suddenly graze my cheek. I gasp as the heat overtakes my body again. He closes his eyes and sighs. When his eyes reopen, they lock onto mine. "This gathering is everything you promised, Mr. H. You are a man of your word, as am I. After much deliberation, I agree to your suggested new terms."

"Excellent," Anthony says, though the sentiment lacks any emotion. "A toast, then, to the end of our successful partnership." He takes two glasses from Cleopatra and hands one to my Dark Prince. Reluctantly, he removes his hand from my cheek to accept. I release the breath I didn't know I was holding and accept a glass from Cleopatra. I've had champagne at parties before, but I've always snuck the glass from an unoccupied tray. She doesn't even hesitate handing this to me. Either my secret costume works better than I expected or something else is going on here.

Beneath her shimmering gold mask, her emerald-green eyes meet mine. I'm not sure, but it's as if they're filled with sympathy—or regret. She turns away.

The Dark Prince stares poignantly at me. "To possibilities and hope, things I once thought foolish, but now I see they cannot exist without the other."

Our glasses clink, and I down my glass to avoid Cleopatra. She retrieves our glasses, and Anthony places his arm around her waist. "Come, dear, we must get back to our other guests. Thank you, sir, for all you've done for me over the years. Good luck Miss … " He pauses, extending a hand toward me.

"H.," I respond, copying in their strange greeting style.

Time slows as my father and mother change from distant to angry and frightened as they reexamine my costume and appearance.

"No!" My father and mother gasp and step back in unison. She drops the champagne flutes, and they shatter on the floor. Around us, the party stops as others turn to see the commotion.

"I'm sorry, sir, but this won't do," my father protests. "I won't allow it. Pick anyone else. I invited so many for—"

"We toasted to the new deal. It is set. If you go back on your word, then the next course of action is to honor our original agreement. What say you, Mr. H.?"

My father visibly shakes before me. I've never seen him react like this. Especially not in front of so many people. I turn to my mother to see tears welling up in her eyes. My father turns his attention on me, and his brown eyes are misty too. "But she's my daughter."

I have no idea what is going on, but I get the feeling it goes beyond he and I dancing together. What has he done, and how does he know my father?

"So I gathered," the Dark Prince says. "I will be back in a year's time to collect your decision, whatever it may be." He bows formally to me. "Miss H., thank you for making the evening one that I, too, shall never forget." He rises, turns, and exits the tent into the dark of night.

I rush after him, but there's nothing. It's as if he simply vanished.

As loneliness and desperation claim her, I'm pushed out from her body and out of the dream. I wake up in my own bed. Bright sunlight hits my eyes, and I roll over to escape the intrusion. The soft green light of my alarm clock greets me, telling me it is 9:46 a.m.

After two weeks of nightmares, I finally had a good dream—I even slept through my alarm, which I had set early enough to get in a run before … school. I glance back at the clock again, confirming that I'd read it right the first time. Not only have I missed my run, but also my first two classes.

"Crud," I say.

CHAPTER 2

MJ

I PICK OFF THE CLEAR, JELLY-LIKE SUBSTANCE FROM MY white dress shirt and flick it onto the mist-covered ground. It sizzles, then disintegrates. It's poltergeist residue. Alexander—my second-in-command—shakes himself like a dog, flicking bits and pieces of residue everywhere.

"Was that necessary?" I say.

"Consider it a memento of the time we've spent together," he replies as we head down the main street to the Recordum— our replica of the Great Pyramid. We pass other buildings shaped to resemble famous mortal ones: the Petronas Towers, Buckingham Palace, the Empire State Building, the Colosseum, and the Leaning Tower of Pisa. There are more than thirty all together, all designed to give mortals a sense of familiarity when they arrive here.

I pull open the Recordum's front door and step into the long, white hallway. The walls absorb the ever-shining sunlight, making it just as bright inside.

Alexander shakes his head. "I still can't believe it. MJ, picking up his very last assignment, and I get to bear witness. There should be dancing girls or confetti or whatever mortals do to celebrate milestones nowadays. Cake, for sure. Or better yet, a cake with a dancing girl inside it."

"The Council would never allow that. Once this assignment is finished, I'll be reborn and move on like all the others. No big deal."

"So ... are you looking forward to anything?"

"Aside from not seeing your ugly mug every day?"

"Har, har. I'm serious. There must be something you miss from your old life."

"Hmm ... " We don't get a choice of what our next life will be, so I hadn't thought about it. My old life was so long ago; the majority of it has faded. "I guess ... I miss being surprised by something. It will be nice to sit with people and not know every detail of their lives before they even utter a greeting."

"Touching will be great, too. You'll actually be able to *feel* something from it."

I think back to the last time I touched someone and felt anything. It was a woman, and I held her hand while we ran for our lives. The feel of her skin on mine is gone.

"I have half a mind to transfer now, too," he says.

"Let's not get carried away."

"True. Someone needs to stay here and pick up your slack."

The hallway ends, and we face the Room of Innocence. The glass door opens on its own, as always. On glass shelves sit thousands of files containing information on souls currently tormented by demons or other paranormal entities.

Those are our Charges, and as Protectors, it's our duty to help them.

A gust of wind, neither cold nor warm, swirls around us. Once it identifies us, the wind plucks two files, one a light blue and one a shimmering pink, from the shelves and floats them toward us. Each color pertains to the owner of the soul, not the case itself; it's his or her favorite color. I open the pink one while Alexander opens the blue.

The file's contents transfer to my mind. Even though Charge files are never wrong, one piece of information has me double-checking the pages to ensure its accuracy. The longest an assignment has ever taken is two weeks. When the Archangels asked me to do one last assignment, I agreed. Two weeks is nothing here. This has to be a mistake. On the fourth page, I find the one line that determines how soon my new journey can begin.

Estimated time of completion: Six weeks to one year.

It's true. With that, I close the file and ask, "Trade?"

"You don't even know what I have."

"Fine. What is it?"

"Exorcism."

"Done."

I grab his file before he can protest and leave the room. Exorcisms are simple. Pretend to be a priest, read from the Bible, sprinkle some holy water, then cast the evil spirit out. Memories of the mortals involved are altered, and they go on living as if nothing happened. At most it will take a day.

Unknown to them, the evil spirit enters the empty vial that held the water. Away from prying eyes, we toss it into a fire, which sends him to Hell. In the old days, the demons would stay there. Demon escapes have risen, and we haven't discovered why.

"Wait," Alexander calls. "I've never seen a case like this before. Says here your Charge is the last target of a very selective unknown demon. Well, not *that* selective as he's also murdered 136 bystanders in the last year. Regardless, he's overdue for a one-way ticket back to Hell. As much as I'd like to be the one to send him there, the file was selected for you." He holds out my file and gazes at me expectantly.

"Fine." I snatch my previous file, knowing the trade wouldn't have been accepted anyway. It's against the rules.

For once, I wish that rule didn't exist. I don't want to take this case. It's not because of the timeline. It's too similar to my past. To him—the demon that killed me. His tastes were blonde women with green eyes, all from the same blood line. I died trying to save the first one. I can't beat him. He's an Original. One of the five Archangels that fell from Heaven and now reside in Hell. Thankfully, this demon is targeting brunette teenage girls, so it won't be him.

After collecting clothing for our assignments at the Vestimentum, which is currently shaped like the Petronas Towers, we head through the Pearly Gates. Lines of new arrivals watch on as we enter the Great Divide for one of my last journeys to Mortal Ground in this lifetime.

CHAPTER 3

Maddy

I RODE MY BIKE AS IF I WERE IN THE TOUR DE FRANCE AND made it with twenty minutes remaining in the third period. The ride ruined my hair. It's in a ponytail, but it's a hot, knotted mess. I try fixing it again in my locker mirror before lunch, but give up and shut the door.

"Why does every teacher insist on assigning homework on the weekends?" Kelli, my locker neighbor and friend, asks. "My backpack is full, and we still have three classes left! Don't they realize we have lives?"

I turn and face her. As usual, she's in pajama pants and a Bon Jovi hoodie. Most people think she rolls out of bed and comes to school dressed in whatever she slept in, but it's not true. This ensemble was planned. The red in the pants helps accentuate the new pink streaks in her blonde hair. Bon Jovi is and always will be her favorite.

"Do you really want to talk about school, or would you rather hear about my dream last night?"

She grins and hops up and down. "Ooh, ooh—dream! I choose dream."

I knew she would choose that. She's addicted to my dreams. I am too. They're the best part of my life, even though they only happen on the full and new moon. Each time they begin at a different part—like walking in on a movie already playing. Last night I saw it from start to finish for the first time.

I try to play it cool while following the masses to the cafeteria. "They danced last night."

"Shut up! You finally saw that?"

"Yep." Saw it and felt it… Even though I had been home in my bed, my legs feel as if *I* danced for hours in high heels last night.

"What else?" she squeals as we enter the crowded cafeteria.

I nod and wave to my younger sister, Hannah, sitting at a table with some other tenth graders then say, "They almost kissed, but she turned away at the last second."

Kelli gasps.

"What show are you talking about?" an underclassman ahead of us asks.

We stop talking.

Kelli scowls.

I know she'd rather hear what happened now, but there are too many people around, and she's always respected my need to keep the dreams a secret. She's the only person I've ever told about them.

We grab our lunches and head for the lobby. It's packed with seniors and juniors huddled together in groups on the floor. With the threat of rain, almost everyone is playing it safe and eating inside. It's silly. The sky has been the same charcoal gray for two weeks now, and it hasn't rained yet. But Mankato's weather is more unpredictable than any other city's in Minnesota.

"Who's that?" Kelli blurts. I stop, catching my tray before my salad becomes part of her outfit.

I follow Kelli's bewildered gaze to our group of friends sitting at our spot by the door. Kayla, Maggie, and Jake—aka the triplets—Shawn, Luke, and Luke's brother, Mason, are all gawking at a guy standing in front of them. In fact, the whole lobby is enamored with him.

His back is to me so I take a moment to check him out. Inky black hair comes to a stop just shy of his leather jacket collar. He's wearing dark jeans and black riding boots, giving him a bad-boy edge. I could easily picture him on a motorcycle or playing in a rock band. I bite my lip while Kelli makes a moan she usually reserves for hotties.

One of his hands rests on the wall while the other helps describe what he's talking about. The confidence oozing from him reminds me of someone. Someone I'm desperate to forget.

I shiver, feeling as if someone's running an ice cube down my spine, and suddenly I remember I haven't responded to Kelli's original question. "I have no idea who that is."

As the words leave my mouth, he stops talking and turns. My mouth drops open as all breath and sense of reasoning leave me. No matter how many times I blink, the image stays the same.

He found me.

Before I can look away, I'm drowning in the dark depths of Justin's gaze. I know other people are here; I just can't find them anymore. It's only him and me, and that doesn't frighten me, though it should.

His eyes skate over me, and I release my breath, grateful to be free of his weighted stare. But before I can regain my senses, his eyes hold mine again.

My insides become a tight, jumbled knot; my pulse quickens; and my throat constricts. I'm hot all over. He had this effect on me the night we met too.

I saw him the second I entered the house that night. He stood in the kitchen doorway with several girls grinding on him, but he acted as if they weren't even there. As I watched on, he reached down, grabbed a red-haired girl, then sucked her face. His eyes stayed open, locked with mine. I couldn't turn away. I'd never been kissed like that, and for some reason, I wanted to be. Worse, I wanted *him* to be the one doing it, even though I came there with my boyfriend, Ben.

Someone bumped into me, and I lost my focus. When I looked back at the doorway, he was gone.

Panic gripped me, and I had to leave. The music was too loud, it was too crowded, and I could barely breathe. I tried to find Ben, but I got caught up in the hallway. People danced behind me, pushing me forward while the crowd thinned ahead of me.

That's when I saw him again. He had his arms crossed as he leaned on the wall. He was all dark and chiseled, and for the tiniest second, I allowed myself to fantasize that he was waiting for me—and I liked it.

He smiled and shoved off the wall, moving toward me in a way that matched the hypnotic beat of the music. He stopped just shy of touching me and said, "Leaving a party without speaking to the host is rude. Especially when I went to all this effort to impress … someone worth more effort than normal. You've offended me, but I know how you can make amends."

I shouldn't have cared about his feelings one way or the other, but for some stupid reason, I did. I looked into his eyes, expecting to find anger or at the very least disappointment. But what I found instead shocked me so much, I lost all train of thought. The look in his eyes was one I'd only seen in movies. It was lust. It was desire. And it was for me. I heard myself ask him, "What would you like me to do?"

His smile widened, and he replied, "Sleep with me."

I was so stunned, I burst out laughing. I couldn't believe he said that—or that he thought a pathetic line and wounded attitude would work. I couldn't stop laughing, even though it wasn't funny.

He didn't like my reaction. At least that's the message I took from him putting his fist through a wall right next to my head. I didn't stick around long enough to double-check.

Since that night, I've had nightmares. I was glad the Dream Girl visited me last night. Tonight the nightmares will return. Seeing him again, I'm sure of it. In them, I don't get out. No matter what I do, I end up in Justin's bedroom and do whatever it takes to please him.

"Mads! There you are," Justin says. He smiles, and his eyes shine as if he were looking at a long-lost friend.

Why is he here? Why is he so happy to see me? The answers terrify me. Instead, I focus all my attention on his new nickname for me. "My name is Maddy."

His smile widens, and I cringe, knowing I just did what he wanted—I reacted to him.

I tear my gaze away from him and search for some indication that this isn't really happening. I find none. My only comfort is that we're not alone. We're at school, surrounded by my peers. But they're not much help. Their heads lean to one side, their mouths hang open like fish, while their eyes focus exclusively on him. It's as if they're in a trance.

"What are you doing here?" I ask as casually as possible, thankful for the distance between us. It's maybe fifteen feet, but I'm grateful for every blessed inch of it.

"I came to talk to you." He frowns, as if it should be obvious.

"You *know* him?" Kelli gasps.

"We've met, unfortunately," I reply through my locked jaw.

Hushed murmurs flutter across the room as Justin chuckles. He turns his soulless gaze on Kelli. "I'm a friend of Ben's."

She fans herself as if she were about to combust. "Oh." Her voice is breathy with excitement and awe. She takes a step toward him. "Did he send you here to talk to her?"

A light turns on in the back of my mind. Ben must have told him I go to school here.

"And why would he do that?" Justin's deep voice takes on an almost animal-like purr. He's such a sleaze.

I nudge Kelli in the arm and give her the *shut-your-mouth* look. He's the last person I want knowing my business.

She bats her eyelashes and smiles coyly, oblivious to me. "Because they broke up last ni—"

"Kelli!" Last night, after Ben and I broke up, I Skyped with all my girlfriends. They call me every time they break up with a guy, so it's expected. Not that my breakups with Ben are a big deal. This was our eighth one since he moved to Florida five months ago. I just didn't want *him* to know about it.

Kelli blinks and looks at me. "What?" she asks sheepishly. "You did."

Justin smirks. "What did he do this time?"

"None of your business!" I glare at him, hoping my hatred will make him leave.

"Maddy's birthday is on Halloween, and there's a dance here that Ben won't take her to, so she dumped him," Kelli says in a rush before I can stop her.

My jaw drops. How could she tell him all that as if it were nothing?

Justin shakes his head, then rewards Kelli with a huge smile.

She flushes scarlet.

"What do you want, Justin?" I snap before their disgusting display makes me vomit.

His gaze returns to me, and he takes a long, deliberate look at all five feet five inches of me. With the way he's staring, it's as if I were dressed in something out of a Victoria's Secret catalog instead of my jeans and shirt.

"I'll tell you outside in private," he says huskily, then licks his lips.

At the change of his voice and darkening of his gaze, I resist the strong urge to back away. I know that would show how much he intimidates me. It would give him the upper hand, and I can't let that happen.

"Here's good." My hands curl tighter around my tray to keep from shaking.

His smile drops, and he advances on me.

With each step, my fear grows. My mouth drics as I breathe in quick pants.

He stops a few inches from my tray and glowers at me.

I gulp.

His mouth is set in a tight scowl. "I came here as a peace offering, Mads. If you won't speak with me for five minutes, then I'll keep asking your friends the questions I want answered. They are being quite attentive."

I don't want to talk to him. But leaving him here to keep getting spoon-fed my secrets is much worse.

"Fine." I hand Kelli my tray—her jaw is practically on the floor. I head outside ... alone ... with my worst nightmare.

CHAPTER 4

Maddy

I TAKE A DEEP BREATH, AND MY CHEST FEELS LIGHTER. I'M no longer anxious, and I kind of feel excited. Back inside, I felt like a toy winding down as it uses the last of its battery life, and now I feel recharged. Whole. Complete. My entire body hums with this new surge of energy. I want to run or jump or do anything but stand still. Mostly, I want Justin to try something so I have an excuse to attack him.

I'm not sure where this desire is coming from, but I want it more than I've wanted anything in a while. I shouldn't. I know being alone with him is dangerous, but this overanxious, jumpy sensation is better than feeling scared.

I turn around, square my shoulders, and stare into Justin's vacant black eyes. "Why are you really here?"

His eyes widen while he sucks in a breath.

If I didn't know him, I'd believe he were capable of thinking of someone other than himself. But he isn't. He thinks all women want him simply because he has a pretty face. Often the things in life with the prettiest packages tend to be the most deadly. Like poisonous flowers and venomous snakes. That's what Justin is— a deadly snake.

Standing here, closer than I ever wanted to be again to him, I notice something I didn't at his hazy party. I thought he wore contacts, but now I can't see the telltale ring of them in the whites of his eyes. Black eyes aren't natural. But as alien as they are, it's not the first time I've seen them. The Dark Prince's eyes are that way too. But he only exists in my dreams, so how can Justin's eyes be that color?

He composes himself, slipping into that mask of control he had that night. "I'll tell you why I'm here in a moment. First, I have a few questions of my own. Why do you hate me?"

"Are you serious?" I shake my head, resisting the urge to laugh, seeing it went over so well the last time.

"Everyone flocks to me. But you … you're different. Why?"

"Um … do your actions at the party ring any bells?"

"I was drunk."

"Hardly." I hadn't smelled it on him in that crammed hallway. A fact I pointed out over and over again while fighting with Ben about it. No matter how upset I said I was, he kept brushing it off and making excuses for Justin. Apparently being drunk means you can do whatever you want.

In both my nightmares and real-life thinking, I keep replaying meeting Justin in the hallway. He was so sure I would sleep with him. It wasn't an *I'm-so-hot-you-can't-resist-me* kind of way. It was something … else. As if the sheer weight of his words and the look in his eyes should have been enough to make me do as he said. No hesitation allowed.

"You're sure that's the only reason why you're antagonistic toward me?" Justin asks, raising a brow and giving me that same stupid grin he gave Kelli.

"Does there really need to be more?" Whatever made me bold in the beginning is fading. I feel as if my very anger, determination, and confidence are being sucked down through my flip-flops into the concrete sidewalk. I need to get away from him. I need to get back inside.

Thunder rumbles, and we look at the dimming sky. The crisp scent of rain clings to the air. As refreshing as it is, I don't want it to rain now.

Just in case I don't get my way, I seek shelter under the awning.

He sighs and follows me. He leans on the limestone building, crosses his arms against his chest, and smirks as if he were enjoying a private joke. "Fine. Next question. What are your plans for the weekend?"

"Did you take stupid pills for breakfast? You honestly think—"

"Careful, Mads. You remember my temper."

My eyes flash to his hands as I take a step back.

"I'm on my way to Florida to see Ben," he explains, "and I wanted to extend an invitation. Before you object, I already know your parents are in Wisconsin for your father's band and your sister, Hannah, is staying with a friend. So you can either make up with your boyfriend—and me—and have the time of your life, or you can waste your weekend doing absolutely nothing fun. It's up to you."

"How do you know all of that?"

"You'd be surprised by what I can coax out of girls your age by flashing a smile."

My mind wanders back to Kelli. She didn't even think before blabbing everything as if it were no big deal.

"What did you talk about with my other friends?"

"You. Bit by bit, I'm learning more. But so far, I can't connect any of the pieces."

I hadn't expected this straight answer from him. Good luck, Justin. My own family doesn't know everything about me. Still, I can't ignore the fact that he's here and trying to learn my whole life story. "What do you want to know?" Remarkably, I'm able to keep the rising fear from showing in my voice.

His eyes widen as he tilts his head. He gazes at me for a moment as if he were studying me. I put on my best poker face, but it must not be good enough. He shakes his head, then pushes himself off the wall. He slowly circles me, and I mimic his movements. There's no way I'm turning my back to him.

"What happened to you three years ago?"

I suck in a deep breath, shocked by his question. "Nothing." It was nothing, but it was also everything at the same time. How did he find out?

"Oh, come on. Don't be shy. Everyone in your school believes different rumors. But it's unanimous that your uncle was involved. What happened to you that summer? What made you go from a rising starlet to"—he pauses and gestures to me—"this?"

I've heard all the rumors, and it's been hard not to react to them. But letting them think whatever they wanted, however ridiculous or unkind, was better than the truth.

Ever since I was a toddler, I've spent two weeks every summer camping with Uncle Duane. At least that's the cover story. In reality, it's more like a survivalist-type TV show. Thanks to Duane and his FBI training, I know about one hundred ways to kill someone, though I'd never do it. I hate violence, even on TV. I only go along with it because it gives him peace of mind—for some reason.

But that summer something *did* happen, and it changed everything...

The blazing August heat in the vast woods of northern Minnesota seeped through my khakis and camisole. The wind did nothing more than blow strands of hair free from my braid, causing them to stick to the sweat dripping down my neck and face.

"Concentrate," Duane said sternly as I stared at the bull's-eye, ready to throw my third knife in that day's lesson.

I ground my teeth, hating that he snapped at me again. Training was never easy, but he had been riding my butt all week, and I had the bruises and sore muscles to prove it. He was right. I was distracted, and he was making me pay for it. I kept trying to clear my head and focus, but nothing worked. Not meditation. Counting to ten. *Nothing*. As much as I didn't like the idea, the only thing that could spare me from an even more grueling day tomorrow would be to suck it up and finally speak my mind.

I took a deep breath, lowered my arm, then turned to face him. "Why am I different than Hannah?"

He tensed. It was subtle, but I caught it. "You're not twins, Maddy. You're supposed to be different."

I shook my head. "It's not just her, though. I'm different from *everyone*. Every day I see people showing affection and I see the joy it brings the other person, but when someone does that for me ... I don't know. I just don't feel what I think everyone else does."

"Maddy, you can't presume to know—"

"It's other things too. Like sports. Hannah is ecstatic when she wins her heat. When my team wins a game or I get another trophy ... all I can think is, *Oh great, where am I supposed to put this one?* Same thing with the awards from my piano recitals, dance competitions, and those stupid report cards Mom stuck all over the fridge. They gush over them, and it's all meaningless junk to me. Why?"

"You've always been very hard on yourself," Uncle Duane said. "Perhaps that's my fault. Maybe I push you too hard."

"No. You're the only one who does challenge me. Everything else is like a black hole, sucking all the goodness from my life. Am I broken? Was I dropped on my head as a baby? Why am I like this?"

He opened his mouth, and for a moment, I thought he was going to give me another lame excuse. But then he closed it and sighed. "Maddy, you're adopted."

I stood there, expecting him to smile or wink or do anything to suggest that it was a joke. But the more I waited, the faster my heart raced and the harder I panted. In my mind's eye, I could see the outline of a man and woman, and even though it was just their shadows, somehow I knew with everything in me, they were my real parents. It was true.

laurie wetzel   29

My hand gripped harder on the knife as I willed myself not to cry. As tears threatened to burst out, I turned and threw the knife so it landed beside its brothers in the small red center circle.

"When?" I asked, refusing to look at him.

"What do you mean?"

"When was I adopted?"

"When your parents lived in Georgia. Your aunt Deb and I were visiting their new home. We'd just finished supper when we heard a knock at the door. On the front step lay this tiny little baby wrapped up in a blanket that had 'Madison Rose' stitched into the border. There was no note and no one on the street either. The hospital ran tests and determined you were three days old and perfectly healthy."

My vision blurred as tears welled up again.

No note.

No good-bye.

Just abandoned and forgotten.

When I returned home from that camping trip, all I could think was, *This isn't my life.* As long as I continued to be "Maddy Page," I'd never figure out who I really was and whom I should have been.

I quit all extracurricular activities and let my grades slip. I planned to eliminate all traces of my false life, but I couldn't bring myself to completely cut out the people. Instead, I kept my adoptive family—Dean, Marie, and Hannah—at arm's length, feeling angry at the years of lies. My friends were harder. They were innocent in this lie, so even though I wanted to walk away from them too, I couldn't. I settled for seeing them in school and only once in a while outside of it.

Three years later, and I'm still stuck in the same predicament. I have to pick between the lie that's familiar and the truth that's unknown. I want to choose the truth, but I can't, and I don't know why.

Justin's smooth voice interrupts my reminiscing. "Don't keep me in suspense. There has to be something more to the 'What-Is-Mads' game."

"The what?"

He continues his slow circles, but his smile drops. His brows furrow, and he meets my gaze. "Before that summer, you were enchanting."

I gasp.

"You still are, but you used to be driven. People admired you and wanted you to notice them."

I shake my head, trying to come to grips with how drastically our conversation has changed. Enchanted? Admired? "Okay, clearly whoever fed you that line of BS needs to get their head examined."

"I'll tell Amber you said so."

"Amber? As in the head cheerleader, girlfriend of the quarterback, and the hag responsible for all the gossip about me?"

"That'd be the one."

The rest of my friends ignore her, but I can't. I've been compared to her most of my life. It has nothing to do with our rank on the high school food chain, which couldn't be more opposite, and everything to do with our looks. We look so much alike, we've unofficially adhered to separate dress codes. I usually wear my sandy-brown hair down and stick to plain shirts, skinny jeans, and flip-flops—unless there's snow. Amber dresses as if she were auditioning to dance on a hoochie pole. There isn't a world where she would think I'm better than her.

"Why do you care about any of this?" I ask.

He tosses his head back and laughs. It's a rich, deep sound, and if more people were out here, I'm sure several would start laughing too, even though they didn't know the reason behind it. It's *that* kind of laugh. One that cheers you up the instant you hear it. Even though I don't like him, I can't help but acknowledge that Justin isn't always a jerk.

"Oh, don't kid yourself. I'm bored. Meddling in your meaningless, pathetic life is somewhat entertaining."

This whole fiasco today is because he's bored? No. I've been bored, and I didn't go around acting like a stalker. "I don't get you. You show up after two weeks and offer to take me to Ben? Why? It doesn't make sense."

He pushes up his jacket sleeve to reveal a black watch. His jaw tightens as he glances at it. Then he fixes his sleeve. "My offer is merely an excuse to get you out of town. But before you jump to any more conclusions, it has nothing to do with me. I'm trying to help you. Call it my first good deed."

"I don't understand. What are you talking about?"

"Be a good girl and listen to me for once—say you'll come with me."

"No."

He runs his fingers through his hair and groans. "Fine. You've left me no other choice."

He closes the gap between us and towers over me. His eyes burn into mine just as they did at the party. A dizzying fog spreads through my mind. I can't breathe. I can't blink. I can't move. What's happening? What have I done?

"Madison, you are going to Florida with me. This is not a request. Now, get into my car and don't say another word unless I tell you to." He blinks, ending our staring contest, and the fog lifts.

"I'm not going anywhere with you. Forget it!" I shout over a barrage of thunder.

He gazes at the sky for a moment. Then his narrowing eyes meet mine once more. His nostrils flare. "You're really starting to irritate me, Mads. I'm trying to do the right thing and warn you, but you refuse to listen. You have it in your head that I'm the *bad guy*. But good and bad are subjective. There are others out there—others you have been taught are good—but they still pose a threat, okay?"

Something about these words makes me freeze. What "others" have I been taught about? And why would someone "good" be a threat to me?

"I'm about having fun, partying, and playing mind games," he says. "The others are about the rules and strictly enforcing them." He pauses, glances over his shoulder for a second, then returns his attention to me and leans in closer. "I'm breaking one of them by even telling you this. But you don't play by the rules, Mads. If you don't listen, it will cost you. One of the others is on his way to Mankato as we speak. There's no doubt that he will find you. We don't have much time."

I lean back and gaze at him. "Are you even listening to yourself? Seriously, whatever drugs you're on ... you need to stop."

Justin covers his face in his hands and groans again while they slide down. Once his hands are back at his side, he grins. But it's nothing like his earlier ones. It's shifty. Twisted. It reminds me of the Grinch. "Why did I expect this to be easy with you? Do you want to die? Is that it?"

"What? No." My heart beats so hard, I can almost feel it hitting my ribcage. I take a few steps back while trying to regain control of myself and the situation.

His eyes soften as harsh lines on his face relax. "If you stay here, Mads, I won't be responsible for what happens to you."

I stare up at him, studying his expression for cracks in his *I-suddenly-care-what-happens-to-you* façade. The longer I look into his endless black eyes, they tighter the knots inside me get. "You're not lying."

He lowers his gaze and shakes his head.

I should be terrified. I can feel the urge to crumble, but I push it back by focusing on him. "You're getting out of town to avoid this 'other' guy. You're afraid?" If he's going to another part of the country to hide from whoever's coming, maybe I should go. But Florida is so far away from Minnesota. It takes Ben nearly two days to get here every time he drives up. I can't be in a car with Justin that long. And flying … my parents would have a cow.

He laughs. Hearing the low, deep rumble again causes the muscles all over my body to tighten. "I'm not afraid, Mads. He used to be fun—before he turned into the poster boy for righteousness. Now I find him irritating and his timing inconvenient. Still, he's not a threat … to me anyhow. But he will destroy you the minute he lays eyes on you. That's why you must come with me."

No. It's not possible. It's a lie. Another one of his tricks. "I don't believe you."

"Fine," he snaps, straightening himself. "Have it your way. But when you find yourself in trouble this weekend, remember it could have been prevented if you would have listened to me. *Sweet dreams*, Mads."

He takes a long, hard look at me. For some inexplicable reason, I feel as if he's attempting to memorize me. As if he honestly expects to never see me again. I should be happy about that, but it only adds to my rising panic. Once he's satisfied, he turns, then rushes down the stone steps, whistling a familiar tune I can't place. It sounds ominous, and it makes me cringe. He slides into a black sports car parked in the fire lane and drives away.

I SPENT THE REST OF THE SCHOOL DAY WITH MY IMAGINA-tion in morbid overdrive, picturing me dying at the hands of some cloaked *others*. I needed the day to end so I could run. Running *always* clears my head.

After changing clothes at home, I do a quick stretch in the driveway and jog to the park across the street. With the chilly October weather, it's mostly empty. I hate when it's busy.

As I get closer to the start of the path that borders the pond, I notice a guy sitting on a bench. A light breeze rustles his finger-length brown hair, giving him that *I-just-woke-up* style. I'd guess he's somewhere around seventeen to twenty years old, but I'm not sure. I wish I could get a better look at him, but he's bending over, tying his red running shoes.

As his fingers twist and tighten the laces, my stomach clenches. Muscles bulge in his arms. My hands curl into fists, fighting the urge to feel those muscles just to ensure they're real. They're not too big, though—just to the point where it's obvious he works out. And he doesn't have a bulky frame either. He's … perfect.

I've never been boy crazy. Hannah and my friends think I'm nuts because of it. But the closer I get to him, this strange spark of heat builds inside me.

I let out a slow exhale, hoping to remove all thoughts of him so I can concentrate on my run.

It didn't work.

Instead I speed up. If nothing else, I can put him behind me, and eventually I will come back to my senses.

CHAPTER 5

MJ

I DROP MY FOOT BACK TO THE GROUND ONCE SHE PASSES me. I should have just approached her as I've done with all my other Charges, but I couldn't. The instant I saw her, my head emptied, all sound faded, things on my periphery blurred, and even the leaves dancing in the wind stilled. It lasted only a moment, but long enough for her emerald-green eyes to pierce straight through me.

I hadn't expected to meet her until Monday, but I can't wait until then. A strange sensation is building the farther away she gets. I'm not sure what it is, but it's as if everything inside me is trying to leap out and follow her. Having never experienced anything like this before, I summon a portal to the Veil of Shadows. A silver crack of light appears, and I step inside to watch her without her knowledge.

Once the portal closes, sounds become distorted like hearing a conversation being held in another room. But colors are brighter in the portal. Time is variable, specific to my needs. Right now, I want it to stay at the pace it was on her side so I can watch things progress as they happen.

I follow behind her, trying to decipher why I had such an abnormal reaction to her. Perhaps it's not her, but the town itself—it's smack-dab in the center of a Trifecta. I've never been to one this strong before, but to my knowledge, no other towns have limestone, water, and a tragedy of this magnitude grouped so close together.

On the outskirts of town is a limestone quarry. The majority of the buildings here are made with the rock. A river cuts through the center of town, and not even a mile away is the park with four small ponds—two are used for swimming. Add to that, in 1862 they hanged thirty-eight Native Americans, marking this site as the largest mass hanging in US history.

This town should be a veritable melting pot for spirits. The elements and tragedy emit an electromagnetic energy field that supernatural beings feed off. Most just want help crossing over. But it's the dangerous ones that concern me. The ones that want to live again by plaguing the living.

I came to the park to clear out some of the spirits that could pose a threat to my assignment. I figured I would find a demon of some sort, or at the very least a lost soul, but there has been nothing. Only my Charge and a few other mortals.

Places with a Trifecta are listed inside every building in Immortal City to ensure we are well prepared for any and all types of paranormal beings when we are in those areas. But this town wasn't. Something isn't right here, and I'll have to investigate it before finishing the assignment. It would be very bad for a rookie to come here unprepared.

Perhaps I'll call Alexander down since he's yet to experience one. He should be done with his exorcism shortly. It will be good training for him.

The girl runs faster. I expected to be bombarded with thoughts and images of me being superior to her favorite male celebrity, her calling all her girlfriends to inform them of me, her trying to take a picture when she thinks I won't notice to confirm my existence to said friends, and other useless teenage notions. They've done it all, and then some. Instead she's quiet. It's refreshing, actually. Still, to ensure she's okay, I move past her to the woods so I can get a better view of her and the trail. Sometime in the near future, a demon is coming to kill her, and I can't get caught up in this town or her. When he comes ... I'll be ready.

CHAPTER 6

Maddy

MY PATH BECOMES A TUNNEL BORDERED BY TALL reeds on one side and a mass of trees on the other as I reach the backside of the pond. It's supposed to make park-goers appreciate nature more. Hide the city and the noise. That's why I came here, I remind myself.

My favorite song comes on my iPod: Delibes's "Flower Duet." In this area of the park, it's as if I've stepped out of reality and into the opera to join Mallika and Lakmé on their walk down to the water to gather flowers. I watched it on TV once with subtitles. I'd like to see it live. There's just something so inspiring about running with an orchestra cheering you on. If I pretend hard enough, I can usually picture them playing next to me, matching their pace to mine.

It's not working today, though. My head still pounds and my skin still crawls from my conversation with Justin. Making matters worse, my back is itching for me to turn around, as if someone is there.

I glance behind me, hoping to see the guy from the bench, but there's no one.

Suddenly a gust of wind swirls around me, and my music cuts out. *"Run, Maddy—just run,"* a female voice urges. Then the gust of wind dissipates, and the song resumes playing.

I turn, searching behind me for whomever the voice belongs to. I'm completely alone. I shake my head at the glitch in my iPod, and in effort to dislodge the somehow-familiar voice from my mind, I crank up my music and run faster.

A few feet later, my left side tingles.

I glance over at the woods. My attention is immediately drawn to one tree. There's nothing wrong with it that I can see, but something just feels … off. My breathing accelerates, this uneasy feeling builds in my stomach, and I feel hot. So hot. That tree is freaking me out. Almost as if a shadow is hiding behind it, watching me.

A thick silence bears down on me from all sides, causing me to stop in my tracks. Most of the trees have lost their leaves for the season, and their barren branches reach out for me like pale, frail fingers. I've been on this path thousands of times over the years, but now I can't see the clearing at the end.

Maybe this was a bad idea. Maybe I should have stayed home until my mind settled.

A massive thunderbolt erupts in the clouds. What's left of the red and amber leaves falls from the trees to collide with the dirt on the ground.

Together they swirl around me, encasing me in a fire-colored tornado. Instead of howls, the sounds of the wind are words, repeating over and over in the same female voice from earlier. *"You aren't safe here. Run, Maddy. Run."*

Her words sink in as I spin around. I expect to find her in the red and amber cyclone with me, but I'm alone. She sounds so close and familiar. I swear I know her voice.

"Who are you? What do you want?" I shout.

The hundreds of leaves fall to the ground, spelling R-U-N at my feet. A light breeze picks up, then the leaves fly innocently away.

The pounding sound of drums threatens to burst my ears.

Oh. That's me. It's my heart. My eyes blink in sync with my heart's fast rhythm as I try to push back the pooling tears.

I take a deep breath, trying to calm myself. The air smells damp, as if rain could fall at any moment. My left side twitches again, begging me to turn and focus on the woods, but I can't. Other than breathing and blinking, all other brain activity is trying to determine if what just happened really did just happen.

A twig snaps.

I'm running before I even register the thought. The trees thin out as I round the curve. I keep going, passing the second small pond on the right, all the way across the street to the other half of my route.

My footsteps change from a series of soft thuds to loud thumps as I dash onto the old wooden bridge. The opposite end of Hiniker Bridge leads to an empty parking lot and Hiniker Pond, but I'm not going there.

At the center of the bridge, I stop and lean on the railing while gasping for breath. That wasn't real. I imagined it. I'm not crazy.

I should go home, but I can't. Home is empty. This place is my safe haven. It's where I come to think or camp out in the summer with a book and my sleeping bag. If it weren't so chilly, I'd consider staying here until Mom and Dad come back.

But that was ... *insane*. I pinch myself to make sure I'm not dreaming. My arm stings, and a red welt appears when I remove my fingers. I'm awake.

To distract myself and calm down, I lift my gaze to the serene water and scenery around me. Huge maple and white birch trees line the shore. They create a barrier, blocking the pond and me from the outside world.

Already, my panic is lessening as the solitude of this place soothes my trembling soul. It's wonderful. I close my eyes and focus on my breathing. With each exhale I imagine my stress over Justin, the crazy voice in the wind, and whatever that was with the leaves exiting my body and sinking underneath the water and down into the clay below.

My eyes reopen to bright yellow ripples reflecting off the water. I gaze upward and smile. The oppressing clouds have left, and the sun has returned. I hope it stays. I hope it means all the gloom from the past two weeks is over and I can get on with my life.

Wanting to soak up as much of the sun's positive rays as I can, I slide down and rest against the back railing, stretching my legs out across the bridge. This feels great. I can almost feel the sunlight seeping into me and obliterating all traces of darkness.

The longer I stay here, basking in the light, the more the events of the park seem unrealistic. As if I imagined it somehow. I'd like that to be the case. Then I could blame it all on Justin. His message must have snapped something deep inside of me and caused me to have hallucinations. That would explain everything in the park. Normal people can hallucinate under extreme circumstances. And being forced to talk to him is definitely an extreme circumstance.

Light vibrations in the wood beneath me pull me back to reality. I glance up to my right and see a guy walking onto the bridge.

CHAPTER 7

MJ

S HE'S *here*?

After watching her disappear behind the tornado, I left the park and chased after the spirit that created it. I lost it. I'll find it, though. It interfered with my assignment, and I won't allow that.

When I returned to town, I couldn't find my Charge. I should have been able to track her with her soul's essence—each one is unique to the individual, just like a fingerprint—but there was nothing. Even when she ran past me and I followed her, I didn't sense hers. Instead, I went to every place her file said she enjoyed. The mall, movie theater, and her friends' houses. There was no sign of her anywhere. And yet here she sits, unscathed and relaxed on a bridge.

I could feel the essences of other people I encountered today, so why can't I feel hers? Is it the Trifecta? Or is it something different about her?

Not sensing her is going to make this assignment much more difficult.

Now I won't be able to ever let her out of my sight. Otherwise the demon could find her and I wouldn't get there in time. And this case is already hard enough, seeing we don't know exactly what type of demon is coming for her or when it will come.

At least I will get a heads up, thanks in part to her being the last name on the demon's hit list. At the rate he's going, he won't come after her for several months. If the Protectors watching over the other targets can't stop him, I will.

I let out a sigh, and I feel a sense of relief from it. As if the weight of boulders has been removed from my shoulders. I blink once, twice, three times as realization dawns.

After years of nothing—just a hollowed-out, empty shell, surviving off one simple goal of not failing *her*—I *felt* something. I cannot, will not, fail with this girl.

CHAPTER 8

Maddy

THE STRANGER STEPS TOWARD ME, AND I MUSTER UP A polite-looking smile, hoping he nods and keeps walking. I don't feel like chitchatting.

The light from the setting sun casts odd shadows on him. I hadn't realized I'd been here that long. He's tall. A few inches taller than Lucas and Mason, and they're over six feet. He has a medium build, but even from this far away, I can see he's all muscle.

His head tilts, and he smiles while his eyes sweep over me.

My insides tighten and twist in an unfamiliar, uncomfortable, but strangely good way. Even though there's a cool breeze, I suddenly feel hot all over. I swallow, trying to soothe my dry throat, as I continue to gape at him as Kelli gaped at Justin.

He straightens, becoming even taller, and continues toward me. His smile is more polite than friendly, but his eyes are intense. As if they're scrutinizing me. As if without even speaking to me, he thinks there is something wrong with me. *Broken.* I'm accustomed to that look. I see it every time I look in the mirror.

My jaw clenches, pissed at his reaction, and I dissect what I can see of him. His finger-length brown hair glistens in what's left of the sunlight, taking on reddish hues. Bright hazel eyes gleam as if they hold a thousand secrets. The corners of his mouth turn up slightly so they're in line with the Cupid's bow of his top lip.

A six-pack beckons my eyes from underneath his sweat-covered dark gray shirt. I don't linger on his blue shorts, but I can feel my cheeks heating at the thought. My inspection halts on his red running shoes. They're familiar, but where have I seen them?

Oh my God. It's the hot guy from the bench.

Butterflies turn my stomach into a quivering mess, and I look back at the water as my cheeks darken further.

"Hello." His smooth yet gritty voice causes the butterflies to climb higher.

Thank you. Thank you for all the craziness today that led me here. To this spot. To him.

He stops next to me and leans on my railing.

I look up, analyzing his face to decide which feature comes in second to his hazel eyes. Lips. It's got to be his lips. His cheeks lift as a cocky but playful smile appears. He arches an eyebrow. "Mind if I join you?"

He's staring, waiting for a reply. I'm not usually tongue-tied. Between him and the stress of the day, my brain is fried. I want to talk to him. I don't want him thinking I'm socially inept.

I can do this. I can talk to him. Breathe. Say something smart ... and funny ... and positive. "Sure. Why not?" Not exactly what I wanted to say, but it's a start.

He slides down and relaxes next to me. The breeze picks up his scent and blows it in my direction. A heady concoction of fresh-cut grass, fragrant flowers, dirt, and sweat wash over me. But not a gross, weight-room sweat; no, his sweat reminds me of rain.

"Did you enjoy your run?" I ask, desperate to hear his voice again and pleased with myself for uttering more than three words this time.

He snorts. "I found it very educational. Did you enjoy yours?"

Educational? At least that sounds positive. Way less crazy than mine—if I believe my hallucinations, that is. "It was ... more adventurous than normal."

He nods, as if my reply somehow made sense to him. If that's true, I wish he'd explain it to me because I'm still clueless.

"Are you all right?" he asks.

I turn, and the instant our eyes meet, muscles all over my body relax and I breathe a sigh of relief. "No," I say, surprising myself at how easily that slipped out. "I'm sorry. I've just had a really bad day."

Hey! Shut up! Hot Guy does not need to know how close my life is to becoming one of Mom's bad soap operas. All I'm missing is a friend with amnesia, or I'd be set.

"I'm all ears."

"Thanks, but I prefer to handle my problems myself."

He's quiet for a moment as his brows narrow. I think he's upset. Am I the reason, or is he having a bad day too? "You know, I didn't offer to help fix your problems," he finally says. "You just look like you have a lot on your mind."

"Trust me—you don't want to know. Plus, I don't know you."

"I've heard that's a good thing. It's easier to tell your troubles to a stranger. So if you don't know me and I don't know you, there's safety in anonymity."

"So … I can say nothing too personal? Just the high-lights?" I half-smile. I kind of like that; it's similar to the first meeting of my dream couple. They didn't swap life stories or even introduce themselves, but they still formed this intense connection.

His eyes shine with excitement. "Be as vague or as specific as you want. It's your story. You make the rules."

I never talk about my day, ever. If I opened up and let someone in, it'd only hurt that much more when they walked away.

There's something about his offer, though, that's drawing me in. I can't tell if it's the sincerity in his voice, his friendly expression, or that he reminds me of the Dark Prince more than anyone else ever has. I want to talk to him. I want to tell him all about my strange day.

"You can either keep it inside and let it consume you, or you can get whatever it is off your chest. Your choice."

He's right. Maybe by talking about them, my problems will leave. Just keep it vague, and afterward, we can go our separate ways. "I woke up late, it threw my routine off, and the day kind of spiraled downhill from there," I start.

"Routines are a safety net. My day was also affected when I veered away from mine."

"Yeah, but that's not all. At lunch, a guy I hate with a passion said some things to purposely get under my skin, and it worked. I've been a nervous wreck since he left. I've allowed him to ruin my weekend, and I guess I'm mad at myself for falling into his trap."

"It's only Friday. It's a little early to count the weekend as a loss."

"I know. I'm trying to move past it all." I take a deep breath, and I'm caught off guard by how effortless it felt. "You know, you're pretty easy to talk to."

"Thanks." He smiles again, then it disappears as he takes another look at me. "Just looking at you, I wouldn't have realized you had such a disastrous day. I'm sorry."

He's sorry? Why? He didn't have anything to do with it. But with the pain in his eyes, it's clear he's honestly bothered by this. It's so different from the *broken* assessment he had when he first approached me. Maybe I was wrong about him. "It's not your fault. But thank you," I say. He nods but doesn't reply. Even though he's the one who initiated our conversation, I'm not ready for it to be done yet. I want to keep talking to him—learn more about him. "So are you new here?"

"As a matter of fact, I arrived this morning."

"Oh ... welcome." Stupid Maddy. Just stupid. "Where are you from?" Judging from the lack of a tan, I'm guessing northern Minnesota. Maybe from a farm, seeing as he has all that upper body strength. Visions of him shirtless, driving a big tractor on a hot summer day, flood my mind and cause me to blush deeper than I've ever blushed before. I blink, trying to erase the images. "Sorry. We said nothing too personal."

"You did. I didn't. Besides, locations in our past don't make us who we are. With that in mind, I'm from all over. But I was born in Norway." His brows furrow, creating lines on his forehead.

Norway? I was way off. "I've never met anyone from another country before. Why don't you talk with an accent?" As if the scales need to be tipped in his favor any more.

He turns away and gazes over the water. "I travel a lot. I must have lost it somewhere along the way."

The abrupt change in his posture is like a big red flag. He doesn't want to talk about it, and I don't blame him. But even though I should stop, I can't. I want to know more.

"So ... are you an army brat or something?"

He shrugs. "I guess you could say that. So how do you like living in Mankato?"

"Normally, it's boring, but I don't remember any of the other places I lived, so I can't really compare it to anything."

He shifts his body toward me. "You haven't always lived here?"

If I tell him, then I'd be revealing something personal. Something I've never even told my friends. But as he said, our pasts don't make us who we are. I like that. I just wish I could make myself believe it. "No, I was born in Georgia," I reply, even though I'm not sure if it's true.

He leans closer. "And then you came here?"

"No." My heart flutters. Part of me wants to change the subject. Take the focus off me. That or leave. That's what I always do. But this other part of me wants to stay. I want to keep talking to him. He's nice, and he makes me feel better. Plus, once we stop talking, I'll have to go home to an empty house. "After Georgia, we lived in Arkansas, Oklahoma, Louisiana, Texas, Colorado, Illinois, Wisconsin, and Nebraska before we came here." I check them off on my fingers as I go, making sure I didn't miss one.

He arches a brow. "That's quite a list. Is that the order you lived there?"

"Yeah, but like I said, I don't really remember any of those places. I was two when we came here." That wasn't so bad. There might actually be something to this whole "talking to a stranger" thing. Or it could be specifically related to who the stranger is…

"Hmm, I didn't know that about you," he mutters.

"How could you?" I laugh. "We just met."

He looks at me again—amused, I think—and smiles. He has a great smile. I don't think I've ever made someone smile as much as I've made him tonight. And for reasons I can't quite explain, I like that I'm the reason behind his happiness.

"You're right," he says. He looks away for a moment, then turns back to me. This time his smile is gone, and there is this strange, almost hopeful look in his eyes. "Do you mind if I stay and watch the sunset with you?"

I bite my lip and frown. I hadn't planned on watching.

I shift my attention away from him and back up to the sky, now alight with vibrant colors of red and orange, glorious ocean blue and green, and soft shades of pink and fuchsia. "I've never really watched a sunset before."

"Never? Surely, you're joking."

"No. I mean, I've seen them, but I haven't just sat and *watched* one. It's beautiful."

He stays with me, silently observing the end of the strangest day of my life. As the last speck of light fades and twilight takes over, I know I would repeat this day in its entirety just so I could relive this moment here with him.

CHAPTER 9

MJ

I'VE SEEN THE SUN RISE AND SET SO MANY TIMES, I'VE lost count. I've forgotten how spectacular such a simple, ordinary thing as the world rotating on its axis can be.

I've forgotten a lot over the years. Like when she asked where I was from. I hadn't thought of my home in so long. But when she did, I thought of my mother, father, and my little sister, Kenna.

If I were to transfer and be reborn, my memory would be erased. I would lose them. Can I give up the only parts I have left of my family? I don't know anymore.

She gasps, and I follow her gaze to the sky. The sun is moments away from disappearing from our view. Was her response in reaction to this moment coming to an end? The many colors that have painted the sky? Or something else entirely?

I want to know what she's thinking. I try to use Cerebrallink for the hundredth time to listen to her thoughts. There's nothing. I don't understand.

The instant I became a Protector, I could hear the things people say privately in their heads. The hidden words are always the most truthful. Having access to them means people can't lie to me, as she did earlier regarding the previous places she lived. Her file says she was born in Minnesota, and our files are never wrong.

It was curious, though, that the states she mentioned just happen to be part of this case. The demon's other targets—deceased and still living—reside not only in all those states, but also in the order she listed. The only state she didn't list is Washington, where the first two victims were killed. What made her say those states in that order if her file says she's lived in Minnesota her whole life?

Even more curious, I can't sense her emotions. There's nothing to tell me what the ever-changing expressions on her face mean. I'm completely out of my element here.

It's as if I'm alive next to her.

The last of the sunlight fades in the reflection of her awed eyes. A rosy glow matching the pink of the heavens rests upon her cheekbones. The colors blend harmoniously like the smoothness of her skin. Everything is soft, muted, delicate. She's beautiful.

The thought unnerves me. I've never cared or taken notice of their physical appearances beyond what I had to in order to protect them. Why am I making note of hers?

In the half hour I've sat here with this mortal girl, I've connected to her more than the countless number of Charges I've saved. Even more so than my fellow Protectors. Is it because she's the last Charge? Is it simply *her*? Or is it because my time is coming to an end?

CHAPTER 10

Maddy

I WATCHED A SUNSET, AND IT WASN'T HORRIBLE. IT WAS breathtaking. It was like watching a work of art right before my very eyes. I will never take them for granted again, and I owe it all to my stranger from Norway.

I turn away and my eyes land on the space between us. There couldn't be more than a quarter inch separating my hand from his. My fingers twitch, aching to touch him. I want to feel the smooth skin on the back of his hand. I want to touch the ridges in his muscles and run my fingers through his hair. I want to stay here with him all night. He's peaceful. Calming. Safe.

"Are you always this quiet?" he asks.

My cheeks heat again, thankful he's unaware of my wayward thoughts. "Yeah. My dad is the same way. It bugs my mom too." Why did I say that? And why do I feel so comfortable talking to him? As if it's as natural as blinking. I need to change the subject before I say something else stupid. "So … " I draw out, "what else have you done on your first day here?"

His lips tighten and he squints. "*You* want to know about *my* day?"

I nod, unsure of why that should come as such a shock to him.

Dimples form in his cheeks as his smile widens. If it's possible, I think this might be my favorite smile of his. "My day hasn't gone at all according to plan, but unlike you, I've found the changes have been remarkably pleasant."

Remarkably pleasant ... as in, he finds *me* remarkably pleasant? I bite my lip to keep from grinning like an idiot. Oh yes, I would definitely redo this day if it meant seeing him again. I've never felt this way before. Why do I feel such a connection to him?

"Please don't take this the wrong way," he begins, "but you're not how I expected you to be."

Given the unflattering look he had when he first walked up to me, I'm not sure if that's good or bad. "So what were you expecting?"

"Like most cheerleaders—overly chipper, shallow, and obnoxiously chatty."

"*Wow.*" Did I imagine everything between us? Of course I did. I wanted him to be this great guy, so I let my mind believe he was. I'm an idiot.

He sighs and shrugs. "Sorry. That sort of slipped out."

"Please, by all means, don't hold back. Tell me what you really think of me." Jerk. In fact, he might be a bigger jerk than Justin. At least with Justin, I know what I'm in for up front.

"Forgive me. In my experience, that's what you cheerleaders are like. Clearly, you're different."

Again he calls me a cheerleader? Why does he think *I'm* one of them? I haven't been that obnoxious, have I? Can this day get any worse? "You know, next time you get the urge to tell someone your first impression of them, do yourself a favor and lie."

He chuckles again. "How about I tell the truth instead of assumptions based on stereotypes?"

"You can't fail any worse than you already have."

He shifts, and our gazes meet. The mild breeze vanishes. The bridge, trees, water, and darkening sky all fall away. The hallucinations from the park and Justin and his threats are all gone too. Even my frustrations with *him* are starting to disappear. Knots untangle all over my body, and for the first time in several weeks, I feel no fear. It's incredibly freeing. I had no idea how much that all was bogging me down. So, frustrating or not, I'm grateful to him for taking it all away.

His eyes narrow as if he isn't finding what he wants, and I glare back.

Being with him is confusing. He's toying with my emotions, but maybe it's not intentional. I've never been a cheerleader, but they're in great shape. Maybe that's all he meant? But he said chipper, shallow, and obnoxiously chatty. That describes Amber and her followers perfectly. Not me. He's wrong about me, and for whatever reason, I don't want him thinking I'm like that.

"First, I hate cheerleaders. Second, I'm not shallow. And third, I don't feel the need to fill every second with mindless conversation. But you walked up to me, and for a split second I believed your BS about 'talking to a stranger.' Then you flipped a switch or something and became a jerk. Thank you for being the lowest point in my disastrous day."

"A *jerk*?" Dozens of emotions flash across his arrogant face. It's hard to keep up, let alone identify all of them, but I catch a few. Anger and shock. Then he chuckles. Within seconds, it's matured to full-on laughter. It's deep and exuberant and makes his hazel eyes shine. I can't help it—my heart swells just listening to it. I would join him, except he's laughing at me.

This day keeps getting better and better. You know what? Screw him.

I stand and run away, this time for the solitude of home.

When I make it back to the path, I can't hear his laughter anymore. I risk a peek over my shoulder to make sure he isn't following, then I slam—hard—into another jogger.

I fall on my backside into the grass.

Perfect. Just … perfect. Can anything else go wrong today?

Harsh expletives stem from the direction of the newest victim in today's tragedies, but the ringing in my ears drowns him out. I must have hit him really hard. My whole body tingled with this rush of energy—or something—for a moment before I fell. It felt good, actually.

Other than a slight pain in my butt and a bruised ego, I think I'm okay. He sounds pissed, and I don't blame him. Time to beg forgiveness from another stranger caught in the crossfire of my disastrous life.

Cautiously, I get up, and the ringing lessens. I turn toward his dark, hunched-over form. This is so humiliating. "I'm really sorry. Are you o—"

I freeze while he rises and dusts himself off.

"But I ... you ... on the bridge ... what?" It doesn't make sense. I left him on the bridge. He couldn't have passed me and gotten in front of me like that. I would have noticed. There's no other path he could have taken. It's not possible. "How did you do that?"

His brows furrow as he stalks toward me. "Why did you leave? I wasn't finished talking to you yet."

"So, because you weren't *finished* with me ... you somehow left the bridge and popped down on the trail in front of me?" Is that right? As bizarre as it is—yes, that's what happened.

"Popped?" he says, mulling over the word. "I guess that will work for now."

So it's true. But how can it be? My body shakes as I slowly back away from him. All the years spent training with Duane, we never covered this. I'm in way over my head. I'm in trouble.

Trouble.

Justin had said, "When you find yourself in trouble ... " What if this is the "other"? The one Justin skipped town to avoid. Justin said this "other" would find me and destroy me as soon as he saw me. Is that what he's going to do now?

I know I should run. I'm working on it. I just ... "Tell me how you did that!" I shout as thunder rumbles from above. Please, rain, stay away.

He rubs his huge hands behind his neck while staring up into the black sky. After a few agonizing beats, he turns his attention to me. "I'll explain that. But first, I'm sorry for scaring you. I didn't come here with that intention."

I know I shouldn't anger him, especially if he's bad enough to send Justin running for cover, but I can't let it go. "What's wrong with you? How could you have sat there for that long pretending to be a nice guy? Was it all a lie? Was it a trick to get me to trust you?"

Time stretches on while I wait for his answer. His eyes hold mine, but there's no emotion behind them. It's as if he's lost. My eyes, I'm sure, reveal just how much he's hurt me.

"I wasn't trying to trick you or lie to you. I deviated from my plan—and with how badly I've screwed this up, I never will again."

"What are you even talking about? What plan? What are you going to do to me?"

"I had planned on meeting you Monday, but when I saw you running earlier today," he shrugs, "I followed you."

"You did?" That should scare me, but my brain won't send out the appropriate signals. I think I'm in shock. "But I didn't see you."

"I hid in the trees before you turned around."

"You were watching me?" He followed me. He watched me. My feelings *were* right—I wasn't just being paranoid.

"What else?" I ask. Please let it be a mistake. Please don't say the events in the park were all real. I felt so much better believing it was all in my head.

"I lost sight of you when that windstorm appeared."

I hadn't hallucinated. All that craziness really did happen. I'm at a loss for words. The world shifts out of focus, and he reaches to steady me, but I back away before he can touch me. "Just … tell me why. I deserve that much."

I stare up at him, and this time he has the decency to appear sincere. "There is never an easy way to say this ... someone is coming to kill you."

It *is* him. His confession shoots through me like a bullet, shattering through the numbness. "Why? I've never done anything to you. I'm nobody. I promise. Please don't destroy me!"

As I finish pleading to my angel of death, his eyes widen. But then he's quick to reapply a mask of indifference. "Calm down. Take a deep breath. It's not *me*. I'm here to help you." The words roll off his tongue with ease. It's as if he's said them before. Many times.

I didn't believe Justin, but hours later I find out he was right. I can't let myself make the same mistake with this guy. "Prove it. Prove I can trust you. Tell me the truth. If it's not you, tell me who it is. Tell me why he's after me. And tell me when he's coming."

He takes a few steps back and leans against a tree. The distance makes it easier to breathe, but I can't help notice he's blocking the only route home. "I'm afraid I don't have all the details myself yet. What I do know is that I've been assigned to be your Protector. He won't come for a while, though, so you're safe for now, and you can live your life as close to normal as possible."

All the air leaves my body, my legs turn to Jell-O, and I collapse on the ground. I can't think. I can't breathe. I can't move.

Suddenly he's standing in front of me, half of him glowing in the ominous light from the lamppost, and the other half hidden in shadow.

Considering the massive amount of information thrown at me today, I should have a plethora of thoughts racing through my brain. Instead I'm stuck on just one. Him. When we met, he had this light that reached down deep inside me and introduced me to a part of myself I never knew existed. He was good then. He might still be good now, but he's also dark. He's able to do something I can't possibly fathom, and he carries with him a message of despair—one he says he's here to help me with.

Good ... bad ... right ... wrong. It's all blending together. The lines of black and white used to be so concrete, and now there's all this gray. Once again my thoughts drift back to Justin as he said, "Good and bad are subjective." Nothing is making sense anymore. I don't know who to believe.

He bends down to meet me at eye level, holding his hand out for me. "I'm going to do everything in my power to save you. I won't fail you."

My life has been mostly good—other than my birth parents abandoning me. Today, two different people tell me I'm going to be killed. If I accept his hand, it means I accept his help—and that Justin was not only telling the truth, but trying to save me too. That alone is ridiculous. This can't be true.

I push myself off the ground, ignoring his offer to help. "No. You're lying. Tell me who put you up to this." Could it have been Justin? No. Justin prefers to mess with people himself. It has to be Amber. This is more her style. "Where is *she*?" I demand, now convinced. "And the cheerleaders? Are they recording this?"

"You have deeper trust issues than I anticipated," he says, looking at me as if I'm a project he needs to fix.

I glare at him but say nothing. I'm done sharing my thoughts with him. Instead, I turn away and focus on finding my nemesis.

My face and arms sting as branches scratch my flesh while I search for Amber, her minions, and her camera in the bushes. They would get a kick out of this. I'm surprised they've stayed hidden this long with his spectacular performance. I almost believed him. Where did she find him anyway?

He stands there, watching on as I search for his accomplice. "You continue to baffle me," he says. "First when I saw you running and later when I saw you on the bridge."

What—he wants to keep the charade going? Fine. I can multitask. That way, when I find the hag, I can make him eat his words. "You did seem surprised to see me on the bridge. Why?"

He hides a laugh by fake coughing. "It's Friday night. You're supposed to be cheering at the game."

"Oh, for crying out loud! You might be freakishly tall, but I'm flexible and will kick you where you'll feel it most!" It would make me feel so much better.

Wait. If they're cheering at the game ... how can they be here doing this whole prank? Did they ditch for me? Yeah, Amber's hated me since kindergarten, but she wouldn't skip a football game to mess with me.

"Cheerleading talk is off limits," he says. "Got it. You know, I've never met anyone like you before. I'm enjoying my time with you. You keep surprising me, and that's very rare. Are you always this entertaining, Amber?"

My search comes to a screeching halt, and I grab a near-by tree for support. Out of millions of girl names ... he calls me *that* one.

After fourteen years, I should be used to people mixing us up, but I'm not. It's not funny. Especially this time. Dread fills me as I turn to face him. "Why did you just call me that?"

"What? Amber? Do you prefer a nickname? Your file didn't list one."

"What file?"

"Your file. I have it right here if you wish to see it." He raises his hand just above his shoulder, and out of the darkness, a shimmering pink folder appears.

My jaw drops.

"I know," he says. "It's in your favorite color." He holds it out for me, but I'm too stunned to move.

How the hell did he *do* that? And why does he think it's my favorite color? I like purple, not pink.

"Well, if you ever want to look at it, just let me know." He lifts the folder up again, and it disappears into the inky blackness.

Am I dreaming? There's no way someone can do all the things he's done in the last five minutes. I pinch myself again. It's hard to do, seeing as my body's trembling, but I feel it. Somehow ... this is real.

"I'm sure you have many questions for me, most of which I can easily answer for you. My name is MJ, and I'm your as-signed Protector until you're safe. Rest assured, nothing bad will happen to you. I have a practically perfect record."

"P-practically?"

"There's only one being I've ever come across that I can't defeat, but thankfully for you, he isn't involved here."

My head nods as if his absurd story makes sense.

His shoulders drop and a small, caring smile forms. "So why did you skip the game? You've never missed one before."

I close my eyes and take a deep breath as I dig for the nerve to tell him the truth. When I reopen my eyes, I'm immediately drawn to his. They're less intense. Softer. It looks as if he genuinely cares about my answer. But he doesn't. He cares about *her* answer.

I swallow a lump in my throat and say the line I've said thousands of times before. "I'm not Amber."

CHAPTER 11

MJ

I STAND IN THE GRASS, FIVE FEET FROM HER, LISTENING TO the words "I'm not Amber" echo inside me. I dissect them, listening to her tone while comparing it to her facial expression and posture. No matter how many times I do this, the answer remains the same: she's telling the truth.

Faster than a mortal's heartbeat, I'm standing over her. She cowers back into a tree.

Lightning flashes and thunder roars as I examine her. I start with the information given to me in the file.

Her hair is sandy-brown. It isn't dyed; the roots match, and I don't smell the harsh chemicals. Her emerald-green eyes have no rim from contacts in the sclera; that is her natural eye color.

I scan down her body, analyzing every curve and muscle in her slim figure. She has the legs of a dancer and arms similar to a cheerleader. If I tell her that, I'm sure it would anger her again. She matches the description in Amber's file and has the build one would expect from the activities Amber participates in. How is she not Amber?

The file lists a scar on her right forearm from a dog bite that occurred when she was a toddler. It should be one inch above her wrist.

No matter how hard I stare at her arm, I cannot find a scar.

Somehow, I made a mistake. I am wrong. That has never happened before. Like it or not, I know what I must do.

I've never done this without first attaching myself to the person's spiritual essence, but I gaze deeply into her eyes, willing her to open her mind to me. The first image I should see is a reflection of me as she sees me, but there is nothing. Everything is dark.

The darkness must mean, for whatever reason, I'm not attaching the way I've attached every other time I've done this. It should still work the same, though. It's never *not* worked.

"When you think back on your run today," I say in the soothing voice used for compulsion, "you will remember it being normal. You never saw me. You never felt like you were followed or watched. You were never involved in a windstorm. And we never had this conversation. If we ever cross paths again, I will be a stranger to you."

A dull ache twists in my stomach, and I stop for a moment. What was that?

She blinks and her eyes widen. "Why would you say that? I won't forget you. Ever."

"Yes, you will. That's how this works. But I won't forget you."

She stares at me, and with each passing second, her expression shifts. Her thin brows scrunch closer, her eyes narrow, and she frowns. "Please don't do this," she begs.

Believe me, beautiful, if there were any other choice, I would take it. There isn't, though. After tonight, she won't remember me, and I can never see her again. I have never met anyone like her. Because of my foolishness and a Guardian's inaccurate record keeping, I will never get the chance to truly know her.

The thought of never again being in her life is unimaginable. We're not supposed to do this, but I don't care. I need a small part of our time together to stay with her, even if she doesn't remember it. "You stopped running on the bridge to enjoy the view. It calmed you. All your troubles melted away. You felt free and happy. You stayed there, watching your first-ever sunset, and it was so beautiful that you made a promise to yourself to keep watching sunsets all the rest of your days. When it finished, you decided to go home. That's what you're going to do now. Run home and don't stop for anything."

All I have to do is look away, and it will be complete. I will be erased from her memory. It's what needs to happen, but why can't I finish it? What is happening to me?

Pull yourself together, MJ. She's just a mortal. There are billions of them. Even as I think it, though, I know it's a lie. There may be billions of them, but there is only one of her. As greatly as I want to stay with her, I need to leave.

Her expression continues to change—becoming more determined than before. Again, I wish I could tell what she's thinking. She seems clever. Is she reliving our time together?

Is she putting the pieces together of who I am? I've given her more than enough reason to believe I can erase her mind. I need to hurry.

I step back and steal one last glimpse while her mind becomes her own. I then step into the Great Divide, bound for Immortal City, determined to figure out who she is.

My head throbs as I slap the file shut and toss it on the glass desk. It lands next to the thousands of other multicolored files I searched in the Records of Humanity room inside the Recordum.

I rest back on the glass swivel chair and rub my temples in a circular motion to soothe the pounding in my skull. I half laugh. I have a headache. I can still feel. It hurts, but it's a good hurt. It lets me know *she* really happened.

I still can't believe I was wrong. I've never been wrong about a Charge before. Although, technically, it was Amber's Guardian's fault. A Guardian has one job: watch over a mortal and document his or her life. That's it. The Guardian didn't make a note of this other girl who fits Amber's description. And I told her so much about us. *Keep our existence a secret*: that's our number one rule, and I broke it.

One look from her blazing emerald eyes beneath those long eyelashes, and I forgot all rhyme and reason and said whatever came to mind. Not just about what I am, but whom I used to be. I've never talked about my old life with anyone, but I *wanted* her to know. Just as I wanted to know every microscopic detail of her life. Her likes, dislikes, what she does for fun, what music she listens to, who upset her during lunch. But most importantly, I want to know her name. Stupidly, I forgot to ask. I've never had to before. How do you even do it? Do you say, "What's your name?" That sounds so strange, formal. I'd forgotten how complicated it is to be human. Knowing her name would have made my search much easier.

A man clears his throat beside me. I open my eyes, and Alexander is gazing at me. I suppose I'm an unusual sight seeing as Protectors rarely use this room, and I have made a mess.

"Problem with your case?" Alexander asks.

Part of me doesn't want to tell him about her, but I'm out of ideas. I searched through all of the records for females ages fifteen to twenty in all towns in Minnesota, Georgia, and every other state she said she lived in. While many match her description, none of them are her. "I met someone today, and I don't know who she is."

"Search her mind and find out."

"That's the problem. I can't."

"I don't understand."

My shoulders drop under the pressure of the unknown. Wanting to be rid of it, I tell him everything that happened between me and my mystery girl.

Afterward, Alexander leans on the desk, blinking several times. "So you can *feel* right now?"

After everything I said … *that's* what he focuses on? "Yes, though I fail to see—"

Alexander's fist slams into my right eye socket. The force knocks me out of my chair. Sharp, blinding agony comes from my swelling eye as my head pounds harder. "Jesus Christ!" I shout. "What did you do that for?"

"You took the Lord's name in vain," he says, shocked.

"Sorry," I mutter to the air around me. "But still, that hurt."

"Wow."

"*Wow*? You hit me, and all you can say is 'wow'?"

"I had to see if it was true." He shrugs. "I guess you can feel."

"You could have pinched me or done something less painful."

"Heal it and get over it, wuss."

With the overwhelming sensations of pain that my nerves haven't felt since my death, I'd forgotten I self-heal. I take a deep breath, even though I don't require it to exist, and focus on my eye, imagining it to be exactly how it was before a fist greeted my pupil. Slowly, my eye reopens and the pain lessens.

"Still feel it?"

"It's not as bad, but yes."

"Wow."

"Would you quit saying that?" I snap.

"Just think about it, though: not only did you stumble upon someone who is untraceable, unreadable, and unemotional—"

"She's not unemotional," I interrupt. "Her emotions switched so fast, and without access to her thoughts, I had no idea why." A wave of guilt washes over me as I think back to the frightened look in her eyes when I told her why I was there and then her desperation when she begged me not to erase her memories. I felt like, as she so eloquently put it, a jerk.

"That's not what I meant. I was referring to the fact that you couldn't *sense* her emotions."

I shake my head. "You have no idea how frustrating that was."

"Maybe the spirit that created the windstorm had something to do with it?"

My fists clench, still angry the spirit got away. "It's possible. Whoever she was, she didn't want me getting near the girl."

"I don't understand why the spirit willingly interfered for some mortal girl. Everyone knows the penalty for getting in a Protector's way."

"This girl is not just some average mortal," I say. "Not only does she possess abilities no mortal should, she knew things about my case too. She listed ten of the twelve victims' states in the exact order they appeared on the demon's list. Explain *that* to me."

He tilts his head, and I know he's trying to read my thoughts. I block him, wanting to protect her.

"She's really gotten under your skin, hasn't she?"

I turn away, unwilling to admit the truth.

"This is bad, MJ."

"Why bad?"

"Well, since meeting her, how much have you thought about the Charge you're supposed to be protecting?"

I shrug, not having an answer for him.

"I think this is why we're not meant to feel. Now you're attached to a girl you don't even know. And because you erased her memory, according to the rules, you're not allowed to see her again in case some deep, recessed part of her brain recognizes you. It would tear through the false memory you planted and either make her mentally unstable or remind her of the truth. Even the other side follows that rule."

The bitter reminder causes the dull ache in my stomach to resurface. It feels as if it were twisting in on itself. I pick up my chair from where it landed during Alexander's unprovoked attack, then I slump back into it in defeat. "I know."

He sighs and places a hand on my shoulder. My skin tingles as the area his palm touches begins to warm. Physical contact is such a mundane thing, but with that simple gesture, I feel like I'm not alone in this.

"There is something I need to say to you," Alexander begins, "and you're not going to like it: I know the reason you can't find her file."

I stare up into his brown eyes, wishing to see some sympathy or hint of what he's going to say next, but there's nothing. Is this what I looked like to all my Charges? Unattached? Uncaring? Is this what I looked like to her? "You do?"

"Yes. Her file isn't in here any longer. It's in the room across the hall."

A strange tightness builds underneath my ribcage. If it's possible, it hurts worse than his punch. That room covers the length of the building. It's the Record of Souls.

"She won't be in there," I whisper.

"The Trifecta could potentially create a spirit as strong as the one you described. It could explain why the first spirit tried to keep you away from her. It could be their territory."

"What about the fact that I can feel?"

"I don't know. But we're not going to figure it out in here."

Without another word, I leave this room with Alexander to search through the files of the dead. Please don't let her be in there.

CHAPTER 12

Maddy

I POUND THE LUMPS IN MY PILLOW—PRETENDING THEY'RE MJ's face—as I try again to find a comfortable position. What *is* he? How did he manage to disappear and reappear? I have to admit, that was pretty incredible. Same with the file. But I can't believe he tried to erase my mind. Thankfully, it didn't work.

With everything he did, I have to believe he was telling the truth about someone wanting to kill Amber. But I still can't help wondering if *MJ's* really the killer. Especially after Justin's warning. If MJ were the killer, though, he wouldn't have wasted time trying to wipe my memories. He would have killed me too. Wouldn't he have? I just don't know. It's crazy in a this-sort-of-thing-only-happens-in-Hollywood way. Even with my suspicions, I'd take him over Justin any day. Unfortunately, though, I don't get a choice at night. Any moment now, I will drift off and nightmares of Justin's house will most likely resume. It isn't fair. Not after the day I've had. If there is any way I could be spared from seeing him, just for tonight, I would be forever grateful.

My room becomes a blur and I give myself over to my dreams.

The darkness fades to reveal a party more elegant than last night's.

I shouldn't be here. The Dream Girl visits me only on the full moon and new moon. The full moon was last night, but I'm glad to skip Justin's nightmare for this extra dream. I've had the same dreams nearly my whole life, and I don't know if they're creations of my imagination or if they're *real*. If they are real—if I've been somehow glimpsing the Dream Girl's actual life—then it all had to have taken place at least seventeen years ago, before I was born. Based on the cars and clothes I've seen in the dreams, I'd say it happened no more than twenty-five years ago. If it happened at all.

This is the second dream I see of her: a summer costume party at her parents' mansion. This time, the party tent is filled with thousands of tiny twinkling lights draped in gossamer and red rose petals.

The Dream Girl is near the entrance to the tent—frozen like everyone else. She's dressed in a white gown fit for a princess bride. Intricate beading frames her midsection and continues down the front of the bell-shaped gown and the short train in the back. Her blonde hair is curled and pinned back with a few tendrils framing her heart-shaped face. Her glossy pink lips are pressed so tightly together, they're barely visible. Her emerald-green eyes glare out into the darkness beyond the tent. She's furious, and I think she was in the process of leaving.

Behind her, stuck in an endless moment like all the others, is a bleached-blond guy in a black tux. He's reaching for her as if he's trying to stop her. I gasp with recognition. It's her ex, William. No wonder she isn't happy.

This is new. I'm not sure my head can handle anything else right now, but at least I'm safe from Justin and MJ. After a deep breath, I float into her body, suppress my thoughts, and let the Dream Girl take over.

CONFUSED MURMURS AND SHOCKED WHISPERS FOLLOW ME outside as I march onto the pathway away from the wedding tent, determined to be anywhere else right now. How could they do this to me? Their only daughter ...

I've been home from that hellhole of a boarding school for only one day. I was excited for a party. Especially because it was supposed to be a "reverse" engagement party for my parents' friends: the newly engaged couple wears regular clothes while everyone else comes dressed as a bride or groom. It's not the first time they've thrown a party like this, and they've always been a hit.

But my party mood evaporated when I saw William standing at an altar. My father grabbed me by the elbow, and the tune of "Here Comes the Bride" began. This isn't an engagement party for friends. It's a real wedding—*mine*.

William followed me as I took off down the pathway. I wanted him to. We need privacy, somewhere out of sight so I'm no longer tonight's entertainment. A light on top of the terrace went out earlier tonight, which created a black spot beside the staircase. It will be perfect.

I step into the shadows. The crunch behind me announces William's presence. I turn, and in the dark I can barely see him, just his outline.

"Why the hell does everyone think we're getting married?" I hiss.

"Because we are. I thought you'd be happy. This is what you wanted, isn't it?"

I throw my hands up in exasperation. "Are you kidding me? I've told you, I'm not going to marry you!"

"It's him, isn't it? That guy you danced with on Halloween? He's why you changed from my little bunny."

This is what I get for not answering my parents' calls the eight months I was away. But I didn't want to talk to them. They refused to explain what I did to upset them so much. The only thing that kept me company was dreaming of the Dark Prince. I held on to our dance and conversations as if they were my most prized possessions. My favorite, the one I replay in my mind most often, is the Dark Prince's "possibilities and hope" toast.

I hoped there was a possibility he had feelings for me too. But are they strong enough for him to ever come looking for me again? I hope so …

My skin flushes. Thankfully, in the dark, William can't see it. "It's not about him. I'm just not in love with you, William. It's over between us."

He sighs and runs his fingers through his hair. "Maybe if you knew the truth about him, then you'd be more reasonable."

The truth …

What truth does he know about the Dark Prince?

"That guy, the one you're so hung up on, is a crook."

"What?" My heart squeezes as if it were in a vise.

"Your father invested with him and lost everything. He's broke."

"Broke?" Never in my wildest dreams did I ever expect that answer. Father has always been so savvy in his business deals. This can't be happening.

"There's a chance your father won't go bankrupt, though," William continues.

I perk up.

"My father's company could save him. He's stepping down in the fall, so I'll be in charge. I'm willing to let your father have 49 percent of the company."

"William, that's ... really nice of you."

"It's a business deal, baby. Both parties need to gain from it."

"What does that mean? What are you getting out of the deal?" A warm rush of air brushes my back. "Me. You get me."

"I hear congratulations are in order," says a deep, accented voice.

The words coat over me. Instantly, my shoulders relax and knots loosen in my stomach. I turn to the right. A tall silhouette leans on the back terrace wall. I can't be sure who it is, but I hope it's the Dark Prince.

"Thanks," William says, his voice brimming with pride. "Not to be rude, but I'm in the middle of a private discussion with my fiancée."

"Don't call me that," I bark, glaring at William.

"So should I tell your father to find a Realtor?" William asks, letting my family's situation hang like a ten-ton weight between us. I can stop it. The cost is my future and my hopes of marrying someone I love. I doubt I'm the first girl in history to be put in this position.

"Sounds more like extortion," the stranger accuses.

"Extortion?" William huffs. "Just who the hell do you think you are?"

The unknown man pulls himself off the wall. As he stands, I notice he's maybe two or three inches taller than me. My heart rate slows; its thumping rhythm leaves my ears. The Dark Prince was that tall, the perfect height for gazing up into his dark, sensual eyes. I wish it weren't so dark here. I want to be sure if it's him.

A buzz sounds above us as the broken light from the terrace turns back on. I'm not sure how, though. My father had an electrician look at it prior to the party and was told the wiring was bad.

As my eyes blink to adjust to the light, a black-suited stranger walks toward me.

I suck in a breath, and a thick, familiar scent of wood-burning smoke seeps into my system. I imagine myself sitting next to a stone fireplace, watching the dance of the orange and amber flames. A blanket of warmth and safety curls around me. It's him. It's definitely the Dark Prince.

All those months at the boarding school, I dreamed about seeing him again. Sometimes they were memories of when we met on Halloween, and instead of rejecting his kiss and my parents ruining it, we danced all night. It was perfect. But other times they were different. I would have these dreams where he visited me in my dorm room—and they felt *so real*. We'd stay up all night chatting on my bed while my roommate slept. He'd ask about my day. He'd ask how I was handling being here. And when I told him I missed him, he told me we'd see each other again soon.

There were times in the halls or around the town when I would feel heat brushing against my skin with no explanation. I would smell his campfire scent and not find anything to explain it. At other times, I thought I saw him, but when I took a second look, he would disappear. I thought I was going crazy, but at the same time, it comforted me. It felt as if he were my Guardian Angel. I'm having a difficult time not reaching out for him to confirm he's truly here and not another figment of my imagination.

His finger-length, sandy-brown hair is disheveled, as if he's been aggressively running his hands through it. He's frowning, and there's so much anger in his eyes. But underneath, there's something else I can't place. Nervousness, maybe?

"You!" William whispers. There's an undercurrent to his voice. It's obvious he knows him.

I tear my gaze away from the Dark Prince to look at William. He cautiously backs away, and once his feet hit the stone pathway, he turns and scrambles toward the tent.

I don't understand. It's as if William's afraid of him. William's afraid, yet he leaves me here by myself with the Dark Prince? Fine husband he would make.

Husband …

I shudder at the thought.

I shouldn't have to deal with this. I shouldn't have been trapped in that hellhole of a school either. Thankfully, I graduated and it's over. Now my parents want to marry me off to fix my father's mistake. A mistake he made with the Dark Prince.

I turn, and his deep black eyes are watching me. The anger is gone, and new emotions have filled them. Worry, sadness, regret. I'm not sure which. It's so hard to tell because his irises blend into his pupils.

"How are you?" he asks.

"What deals did you make with my father?"

He arches a brow. "You wish to discuss that now after being apart for so long?"

"Your business is apparently the reason I'm in this mess."

Darkness creeps along his features as he opens his mouth, then closes it.

So he's not denying it. "Excuse me," I say as politely as I can muster. I leave the grass and head up into the house. He follows without saying a word.

This has been the worst night of my life, but because he's here, it's becoming bearable. My lips crack into a smile. Yes, he really is here.

I peek at him as we climb the staircase to the second level of the house. His face is stoic, giving nothing away. What is he thinking?

My scalp prickles as we walk into my bedroom. I didn't think about where I was going. I just ended up here. I freeze on my plush white rug and watch as he scans my room. His eyes linger on my wrought-iron canopy bed.

Muscles deep inside my abdomen tighten as he moves to stand beside my bed.

His expression halts my thoughts as he runs his fingers over my silk lilac coverlet. "It is soft, like you," he says so quietly I question if I heard him right.

I can't think about him right now. I need to focus on one problem at a time. Why did I come up here? What do I want to do?

"Do you want to marry him?"

My eyes flash to his. He's watching me. Studying me. Why? "It's complicated."

With agonizing slowness, he saunters over to me. He lifts his right hand and caresses my cheek with his knuckles. "Soft," he whispers. The heat of his touch spreads throughout my body. My skin flushes. It's as if I spent the entire day lounging by the pool, being caressed by the sun.

"*Do you want to marry him?*" His voice is rougher this time while he continues stroking my heated skin.

I don't want to marry William. But even though I'm beyond pissed at my father, I don't want him to go broke either. This is the only life I've known. This is so hard.

He lifts my chin, forcing me to stare into his strange, hypnotic eyes. For a moment, I see my wide green ones, but then I look deeper into the denseness of his pupils. I imagine them being a cavern, hidden far beneath the earth's surface. So many secrets must lie behind them. I could get lost in them forever.

A fog swirls around in my head. Even though I know we're in my bedroom, I can't see it. It's as if I were drifting through space and the only thing keeping me from floating away is him.

"Stop," he says slowly. "Stop thinking about everyone else. This is your life. Your fate. Which path do you choose?"

His words take on their own persona, as if they were physical beings capable of independent thought. Two paths play out in my head. The first, I marry William and have several children. My face is haunting, pale, thin, with dark circles under my eyes. The second path stretches beyond what I can see, a symbol of the unending opportunities available to me if I turn William down.

"No. I don't want to marry him."

His eyes open, and they're shining like polished onyx. "Good."

He's happy about it? What does that mean?

"So what do you plan to do now?" he asks.

Three hundred people downstairs think I'm getting married tonight. I don't want to see them. Will my parents accept it when I tell them the wedding is off? Or will they ship me off to another remote hole in the world again? "I don't know," I say. I wish I could leave. Get away for a few days and work this out.

"Yes, you do." His voice is smoother now, like my silk bathrobe, as his words curl around me.

"Run?" I muse out loud.

He nods.

Could I run away from all this for a few days? Where would I go? A hotel? All I have is a credit card, and they can track that. I know no one and I have nothing, no means to support myself.

I wish things between me and the Dark Prince were different. If I hadn't rejected his kiss, then maybe we would have dated and I would have been able to ask for his help.

"I recently acquired a cabin," he whispers.

"What?" Why would he say that? Is he offering me his cabin? No. I can't do that. I need to stay and talk things out with Mother and Father. They'll understand. We'll figure Father's stuff out. I can even get a job if I have to.

His eyes widen, drawing me closer to him. I feel as if his arms are surrounding me, holding me close, but his right hand is still grasping my chin and his left arm hangs by his side. I'd like to be in his arms again.

"The outside of the cabin is sturdy, but the inside requires updating, new furnishings and such. Renovate it for me. I will pay you. Stay as long as you like."

"Are you offering me a job?"

"Yes. It appears I am."

A job? A cabin? His cabin. "I don't even know you."

"Say yes and you will," he murmurs.

"Are you staying there too?"

"No."

"Why not?" I didn't expect this. But retreating to his cabin sounds so right. Like a private island far removed from bankruptcy and arranged marriage. But I'd want him with me. I don't want to be alone.

"My work tends to keep me very busy. Although I have only visited the cabin a few times, I would make a point to visit you to ensure you are well. I would supply anything you need."

Can I do this? Can I leave home?

His dark gaze softens as he caresses my cheek once again. "You do not deserve to be trapped in an arranged marriage. You should be happy, as you were when we danced together. Go to my cabin. If you have a change of heart, you can leave at any time."

I was happy dancing with him. No one had ever made me laugh as he did. It was so unexpected. I spent the last eight months wishing I could have a second chance with him. If I turn him down now … I may never see him again.

Outside my room, heavy footsteps echo down the hall as people rush up the stairs. *"You're sure she's in there with him?"* a panicked man's voice asks, sounding like my father.

The Dark Prince leans in closer, and I inhale his all too intoxicating scent. The fog inside my mind picks up, and my head becomes heavy. What are we talking about?

"Say yes," he whispers.

"Yes," I answer, not remembering the question.

The bedroom door bursts open as my father and William charge in. The Dark Prince places his hands on my bare shoulder. The stress of the day evaporates as I relish the feel of his smooth, warm hands on me again.

"No!" my father screams as he lunges at us.

Darkness swallows me whole.

CHAPTER 13

Maddy

I BOLT UPRIGHT IN MY BED, FEELING AS IF I BUNGEE-JUMPED from the Empire State Building. That's never happened before. That dream was so different from previous times too. I knew William wanted to marry her, but I didn't know he was blackmailing her into it. Or that her family was involved.

I thought her parents loved her. They gave her everything. They always bragged about her. They seemed so happy. Why did they send her away? And why would they condemn her to a loveless marriage just to keep their money? I don't understand. If they really loved her, why would they do that?

The shock of her horrible, shallow family plagues me with a sense of loneliness. The house is still empty. I miss my family. I wish they were here.

I grab my phone. An alert says I missed seven calls from Uncle Duane. I'll call him in a minute. As my finger hovers over the number two on my speed dial for Mom and Dad, I notice the time. It's seven in the morning and too early to call. Depending on how late they stayed up partying with the headlining band, they may have just gotten to bed.

I guess I'll call Duane. He should be up, assuming he's home and not out in the field on a case.

"Maddy?" he asks after the first ring, sounding surprised.

At the sound of his voice, a bit of my unease fades away.

"Hey, you called?"

"Yeah, many times. Why are you just calling me back now?"

All the events of last night run across my mind. My hand covers my mouth to silence my gasp. "I got in late. Sorry."

"Maddy, what's wrong?"

"Nothing," I say and bite my lip.

"I'm paid to tell when people are lying. Come on. Fess up."

How does he always know when something is wrong? I can't tell him about MJ. Not yet. I called for another reason—telling him about MJ is just too complicated.

What kind of name is MJ anyway? Clearly it's a nickname, but for what? Something strong to match his tall, muscular body. Maybe it's something uncommon from Norway—if that really is where he's from.

"I'm waiting," Duane says, shattering my thoughts.

"Um ... how can you tell if someone loves you?"

"What? Who is he?"

"Who's who?"

"The boy who has captured my goddaughter's heart. I need to run a background check and see if he measures up."

He probably would do that. "No. It's nothing like that. I'm not talking about falling in love. I mean the other kind of love. The one between family and close friends. How can you tell if someone loves you?"

"Well, there's no right or wrong answer here, Maddy. Love means many things to different people. Think about your parents. Think about all the ways they show you they love you."

I snort. "They don't love me."

"Madison! You know that's not true."

Did I just say that out loud? Crud. But it's the truth. Should I tell him how I feel again? I opened up to a complete stranger yesterday, and it felt good. As if a weight had lifted off my shoulders. Then MJ went nuts. Would it be better talking with Duane?

"They don't love me, and why should they?" I ask. Duane sucks in his breath, but I ignore it and continue. "I'm not theirs. I'm unlovable. Even my birth parents didn't want me."

"Madison Rose Page!" he booms. "I can't believe you would say something like this. Your parents love you. The day you arrived was one of the happiest days of their lives."

"But they leave all the time."

"So?" he scoffs. "Your father loves his music. It helps him provide for his family, and it brings joy to him and so many other people. And your mother loves to go and show her support for him. They leave you because they have faith in you and trust you to make wise decisions while they're gone. That's one of the ways they're showing their love for each other and their love for you."

I guess I never thought about it like that before. "But how can they love me when I'm so ... broken?"

"You're more than your past. You are lovable, Maddy, and so you're capable of loving."

That's the second time in two days someone has mentioned the past. MJ said the past doesn't matter. Duane says I'm more than my past. Can I move beyond it? I don't know.

"I'm glad you're talking to me about this," he continues. "You may not realize it, but this is a sign that you love me."

What? No. Sure, I trust Duane's opinion, more so than anyone. But does that mean I love him? Really?

"You had something on your mind, and instead of keeping it inside, you discussed it with me," he says. "You trust me. Love, sometimes, is just that simple. It's the little things that really matter. For instance, when you all go out as a family, your father holds the door for everyone. That's him showing that he loves you. When your mom makes your favorite dinner, that's her showing that she loves you. And when Hannah smiles every time you come into the room, that's because she loves you too."

For the second time this weekend, I can't respond. I've spent the past several years wishing I was loved, and he says I've been loved the whole time.

But those examples he mentioned—doors opened and dinners made—they didn't make me feel loved. Even before I knew the truth about being adopted, I felt disconnected. It was as if a glass divider were between me, my family, and my friends. Eventually, I just couldn't keep quiet about it, so that's when I talked to Duane on our camping trip three years ago.

"What about you, Maddy?" Duane asks, pulling me from my thoughts. "Your parents leaving so much wouldn't bother you unless you missed them. And you miss them because you love them."

Is that why it hurts when they're gone?

"When you were a baby, you had horrible nightmares. You would cry for hours, and nothing would help. One night, after Hannah was born, your crying woke her up. Your father was gone, so your mother had no choice but to calm you both. As soon as you were next to Hannah, your crying stopped. Your mother moved Hannah's crib into your room, and your nightmares went away. You love Hannah. You've loved her since day one."

"But why did they lie to me for so long?"

"That's something you'll have to ask them."

I grab my fuzzy heart-shaped pillow and chuck it across the room. I don't want to ask them. They lie and Duane doesn't.

"Think about how you would feel if you hadn't been placed on Dean and Marie's doorstep. You would have never met them. You would have never met me. I, for one, would be devastated. What about you?"

The only thing I've ever thought about is why my birth parents abandoned me. But now, thinking about never seeing my family again … it's as if I were kicked in the gut. My body's trembling. I can't deal with this. It's backward from everything I've ever wanted. It hurts so much. "That's enough." I pinch the bridge of my nose to stop my tears in their tracks. "I can't talk about this anymore."

"Okay. I understand. But just think about it. I'm here anytime you need me."

"I know." My mind races for anything to forget this painful topic. "So … what did you want yesterday?"

"This might sound strange, but I had this weird feeling about you all day. Did anything happen to you?"

"No," I lie.

"You sure?"

"Yes."

"Huh. I guess this case is getting to me."

"Yeah?" I like hearing about Duane's cases, even though he's not supposed to tell me about them. They're gruesome and put most movies to shame. It's just the distraction I need.

"He's a real sick bastard. Do me a favor and be extra cautious of strangers until he's caught, okay?"

Weird. Duane's never asked me that before with any of the other cases. "Sure."

"Good. I love you, Madison."

"Uh huh," I say and hang up before he can say anything more.

I've never lied to him before, but I couldn't tell him about MJ. Duane would lock him up, cut him open, and study him. For reasons I don't understand, the thought of never seeing MJ again creates a tightness in my chest nearly matching what I'd felt for my family.

Why can't I stop thinking about him? He was clearly crazy. And again, what if Justin was right? What if MJ is dangerous? I don't know what he has in store for Amber, but somehow, I need to keep him away from her. Why her? What did she do to make someone want to kill her? Yeah, she's a hag most of the time, but that doesn't mean she deserves to die.

He plans on meeting her on Monday. I need to warn her before then. There were so many times I wanted her to just go away, and now I'm going to try saving her from a killer. Hell must have frozen over.

Not wanting to subject myself to her torments in person, I decide to call her. As the phone rings, I sit on the edge of my bed, trying to remain calm. I need to find a way to make her understand and take me seriously. Provided she'll shut up long enough for me to get it all out.

"What?" Amber answers after the third ring.

"Hey, Amber. It's Maddy ... you know, from school." Of course she knows, stupid. We were friends once.

"What the frick do you want?"

Oh, how I wish I didn't have a conscience and I could just hang up now and let her meet her fate. But I didn't expect this to be easy. "I have something to tell you, Amber. I ran into someone yest—"

"I don't care who you ran into, unless you ran into the front of a bus. Actually no, even then I wouldn't care."

Come on, just tell her. Then you can be done. "This guy I ran into—he's ... odd. He said he's looking for you."

"What do you mean 'odd'? Odd like you and your friends—or worse?"

"Pull your pom-poms out of your ears and listen, you twit. I'm trying to warn you—"

"You are so going to pay for that on Monday." She laughs. "Lose my number, Freak Show."

"Wait, Amber! Some guy thought I was you last night, and he told me someone's coming to kill you!" I yell, then regret it. This could be the last conversation we have together, and I'm stooping to her level. Please, please let her still be on the line. I don't hear a dial tone yet. "Amber?"

"What are you talking about?" she whispers.

Something in her voice catches me off guard. Her tone is nothing like it normally sounds, all bitchy and conceited. Instead she sounds … innocent. Like the Amber I used to know.

I'm sure she'll make me regret this if she's playing me, but I tell her about MJ. I leave out his disappearing act and his attempt to erase my memory. She'd think I were nuts if I brought that up.

She doesn't interrupt, which has to be very hard for her. She just stays on the line, breathing heavier as I finish. "Amber, are you okay?"

"I'm okay," she replies in a voice that's so small, timid, and meek, I know she believes me. "I'll talk to you later," she says and hangs up.

Well, that went better than expected… At least now I know she'll keep an eye out for him.

It's stupid, but there's a part of me that wishes MJ were telling the truth about being here to protect her. I enjoyed talking to him, and my body reacted to him in a way it never has for Ben. He made me feel safe like no one outside my dreams ever has. I don't know if I'm ready to lose that. But he thought he was talking with Amber, the girl he's supposed to protect. Everything we talked about was just a way to learn more about me—going through the motions of his job. I can't trust that any of that was real. I need to forget about the way I felt around him. It will only complicate things.

I need to know what I'm up against so I can figure out how to save Amber from him. In order to find answers, I open my laptop and Google: "people who can disappear and reappear."

There are over nineteen million results. As I dig through the first few pages, I make a list in my notebook that ranges from "plausible" to "I really hope that's not right." In the plausible column, I have magician. It's still the most logical explanation. In the "I really hope that's not right" column, I have several options: government experiment, alien, and supernatural beings.

I don't think Duane would be part of a government that experimented on people, but he's only one man, and he can't know everything they do.

Sci-fi isn't really my thing, so I don't know much about aliens beyond E.T. and Marvin from *Looney Tunes*. I'm not going to wear a hat made from tinfoil any time soon, but I can't weed it out yet either.

That just leaves supernatural beings. Unfortunately, it's the biggest category. Every culture has stories of supernatural beings and creatures. Some worshiped them as gods; others feared them. Those stories were the inspiration behind many fiction books, shows, and movies. There is a story and type of being to explain away everything MJ did last night. Even down to memory manipulation—what they called his attempt to erase my mind.

I don't know what answer is right, and I won't until I see him again. Calling Amber is one thing, but confronting him is completely different. And stupid. But still, I have to stop him. School will be too crowded for him to do anything there on Monday. He'll wait until the afternoon. I'll follow her until he shows up. Then, somehow, I'll keep him from attacking her. Seeing as I'm not supposed to remember who he is, it will be interesting.

CHAPTER 14

MJ

I'VE SEARCHED FIVE BLOCKS NEAR THE PARK LOOKING FOR *her*. Next I'll search every house in town if I have to. Considering I can't find her soul's essence, I'm relying on my other heightened senses—listening for movement inside a home without an essence attached to it.

In Immortal City, my search through the Records of Souls had been fruitless too, even with Alexander's help. As an afterthought, we searched the Room of Innocence as well to ensure she wasn't being tormented by a demon. We found nothing, but that only worsened my suffering.

There is only one thing left for her to be: a demon. Angels don't have access to their files. Alexander and I argued for hours about that possibility and what I must do next. No matter what I said in her favor, he kept coming back to one point: if her abilities work on me, what is she able to do to the living?

Deep down, I knew he was right. Now I have to send her back to Hell. If there is a plus side, this means I can see her again one last time without risking her mental status.

Alexander offered to help find her, but I turned him down. I wanted to be alone with her for this. I don't want to destroy her. Demons are foul beings that should be wiped from the earth. They serve no purpose other than to destroy the lives of mortals in any way they can. But she's different. Not just because of her perplexing abilities. Mostly because she has this way of looking at everything with such complexity. It causes me to take away something new whenever I look at things I've seen more than a million times.

Like the sunset. I had no idea I could *hear* the sun setting. When the vibrant colors bled into the dark blue of night, everything around us hushed in awe. I heard her. Her soft inhales and exhales that slowly raised and lowered her chest and the thumping of her heart. But I also heard this sound—undetectable to her—that accompanied the colors. I don't know exactly what the sound was, but each color had a different tone, as if each one meant something different and only the sun and moon knew the significance. It was as if they were exchanging pleasantries.

Once I became a Protector, I stopped paying attention to nature. That changed last night because of her...

Because of all that, I will always regret what I have to do today. She just can't be allowed to remain here.

The block turns out to be another dead end, so I move on to the next one near the main entrance to the park. Inside a blue house, two down from the corner, I hear footsteps unattached to a soul. I summon a portal and enter the Veil of

Shadows. Now invisible to mortals, I stand in between two square-cut bushes outside her window. My breath catches as *she* goes past. She's frowning with her arms wrapped around herself. If it's possible, she looks even more troubled than last night. Maybe Alexander was wrong. Maybe she's alive and somehow unknown to Heaven. That shouldn't be possible, but it's more plausible than her being a demon.

If she hasn't persuaded me one way or the other by Sunday night, I'll do my duty and destroy her, sending her back to Hell. I can't have her around distracting me from Amber.

CHAPTER 15

Maddy

I CAN'T STOP THINKING ABOUT MY IMPENDING ALTERCA-
tion with MJ. It's as if I'm eager to see him, even though
he may be a killer. If I can't stop, I might grow up to be one
of those pathetic women who write love letters to inmates,
thinking *I can change him.*

As a distraction, I take advantage of the empty house and
sit at the piano in the dining room. My fingers tap the keys,
searching for a song that will fit my mood. Before I know
it, I'm playing the intro to Evanescence's "Good Enough." I
stumbled upon it at the triplets' house once, and the lyrics
stuck with me. Probably because after learning about my
past, I've never felt good enough.

Not until last night, my subconscious says, but I disregard
it immediately.

After the first few notes, I put all my emotions into the
song. I play and sing my heart out, freeing myself of everything I've kept inside lately.

The floor creaks behind me. Hannah must have come home early. I feel her presence warming me as she stands just out of my sight, but I don't care. I keep playing. It's been *so* long since I've played like this.

As I hold the last note, I look up at the photographs of my family on top of the piano. A reflection moves in the frames, revealing six MJs. I gasp and turn around, but no one's there. Not even Hannah. I was alone the whole time? But how did I see his reflection? *Did* I see it? Maybe I'm losing it. I was thinking about him the whole time I played.

I shake my head, stand, then head outside to clear my thoughts and watch the sunset. I already know it won't be as grand as last night's. Watching the sunset with MJ … I wish the night had ended there. Sitting on Hiniker Bridge with him, talking and watching the fading sunlight, was probably the best night of my life.

A chill runs over me, and I hug myself, rubbing my arms for warmth. I look up and groan; dark, massive clouds encase the sky in every direction, looking as if they might burst open at any moment and unleash their wrath. Disappointed, I go back inside to escape the potential oncoming rain.

AFTER GETTING READY FOR BED, I MAKE THE MISTAKE OF turning on Lifetime. I get sucked in, watching as the lead guy tries to win the girl with love songs on a radio held high over his head outside her window. I shake my head at his corniness, but grin just the same.

The next movie is even sappier. Her parents are gone for the weekend and to sweep her off her feet, the guy lights hundreds of candles around the pool deck, and they spend the night cuddling on a lawn chair under the stars. As they make out, I huff and turn the movie off. "Ridiculous," I mumble under my breath. Still, for a fraction of a second, I allow myself to wish some guy would do that for me.

Before I get too wrapped up in a pity party, my phone rings. The song is Fun's "We Are Young"—Ben's ringtone. Knots that had been building since yesterday begin to loosen. I answer it and say, "Ben! Hey."

"Hey, Maddy!"

Hearing Ben's excited voice and knowing he's okay casts a ray of sunshine on my gloomy weekend.

He's always been able to pull me out of my funk. The night we met, my friends had dragged me to a college hockey game. Ben was the goalie. Maggie kept bumping into me and telling me he was looking at me, but I didn't pay attention. After the game, he found me outside. He was still in some of his gear and stunk of sweat. But he asked for my number. I was speechless, so Kayla gave it to him. I'd never dated before, though I'd been asked many times.

Before I learned the truth about my past, I had been happy, but I had always felt something was missing. I knew it wasn't a boy. After Duane enlightened me, I was hollow—an empty shell trying to figure out what was supposed to be inside me. No one understood this change in me, mostly because I didn't tell anyone what Duane had said.

But even when I was on autopilot, Ben saw something in me.

He called and texted and begged me to go out with him more than thirty times before I finally caved. It was different. He was different. I think that's because he didn't expect me to snap out of it as everyone else did. To him, that's just how I was.

But then he graduated and moved back home to Florida. He left me, and we've been on the rocks ever since.

"We need to talk," he now says.

Dread fills me at the despair in his voice. "I know."

"You can't keep doing this to me, Maddy. You can't keep pushing me away every time I do or say something you don't like. It hurts."

I stand, unable to sit still through such a heavy conversation. "I didn't mean to hurt you. I just—"

"Take me back. Please? I'm lost without you. I miss you."

We've been here before. Time and time again. Do I really want to get back together with him? After everything Duane said about love, how do I even feel about Ben? He's nice. He opens doors for me like Dad. He's patient with me. He's never pushed me to go any further than kissing. He does make me happy. But do I *love* him? Does he love me? How do you really know?

And what about MJ? I felt such a strong connection to him. If Ben and I are supposed to be together, why would I feel such intense feelings for someone else?

"I don't know, Ben. I'm having an off weekend. Give me a day or two to figure some things out."

"Okay. Just promise me you'll give us some real thought. I'm not ready to lose you."

I don't want to think about this anymore. I'm still so confused from my talk with Duane. I can't handle Ben adding to it. I need to talk about something else. "So how's your weekend going?"

"Actually, it's been fun. Justin's here, and I've been showing him around town."

At the mention of Justin's name, fear grips me so hard it's difficult to breathe. I don't know if he was right about MJ or if there is still someone else coming. The only thing I do know is that Justin tried to warn me and I didn't listen. Why did he do that? What does it mean? More importantly, how did he know?

"So what have you guys been up to?" I try to sound casual, but my voice wavers.

"He'd never been to Disney World, so we spent the whole day there. I wish you were here. You would've had a lot of fun with us."

"Maybe next time," I reply, slouching back down on the couch. I can't believe Justin actually went to Disney World even though he knew I might die.

"Oh! Hang on, Maddy." His voice becomes muffled. "What? You need it right now?" he asks someone on his end. "But I'm talking to Maddy... You do? ... I don't know... Okay, if you're sure." There's a pause. "Maddy," Ben says in a clear voice again. "Justin wants to talk to you."

"No, Ben. I don't—"

Ben's voice becomes distant, as if he's holding the phone away from him while carrying on a conversation with someone else. I can't make out everything they say, but I catch Ben saying he'll be back in a little while.

"Mads!" Justin enthusiastically hollers in my ear as a door shuts in the background. "I hadn't expected to hear from you again. How's your weekend going? Anything ... unusual happen?"

As much as I don't want to talk to him, part of me is curious to find out more about Justin and his connection to MJ. If I play this right, I might get some answers to the questions swimming around my head. Maybe I can narrow down my list of what MJ is a little more before Monday. "If by unusual you mean the fact that Ben called me and somehow I'm forced to deal with you, then yes."

"Jeez. What's got your panties in a bunch?"

"You're a jerk, Justin." I can't believe I just said that out loud. It felt good, though.

Laughter flows though my receiver. "You're getting more confident each time we speak. Better watch out, I might end up doing something stupid to keep you around."

"I'm pretty sure everything you do is stupid."

"That's twice you've insulted me now, Mads. It's ... refreshing."

"Whatever. Tell me the truth: What's the point of all this?"

"All of what?" he asks, feigning innocence.

"You. Why are you hanging out with Ben? Why are you asking people about me? Why won't you leave me alone? Why did you show up at school to tell me I was in danger? Why did you leave for Florida, knowing what could happen to me? What is wrong with you?" I didn't mean it to come spilling out in a rush, but with everything that's happened recently, the ability to filter my thoughts is gone.

"Cutting straight to the point tonight, huh? Fine. You've caught me in a charitable mood, so I will play along." He draws in a breath. "I came to your school to take you to safety, not just to warn you. But you didn't listen. I left because it was the smart thing to do. Florida was supposed to distract me from thinking of you, but seeing as I made Ben call you, it didn't work. You're alive—which is unexpected—but I'm glad for it. Now I can resume my previous mission of learning everything about you. But no one truly knows you, so that's been rather time consuming." He lets out the breath. "There, I answered your questions. Now it's time for you to do the same."

"What makes you think I'll tell you anything?"

"You will. One way or another, I always get what I want."

"What do you mean?"

"You know… " From the deep tone in his voice, I can sense his smirk.

"Actually, I don't. So why don't you just tell me whatever it is I did that made you take notice of me so I can stop it."

"It's not one simple thing. It's many. Just by looking at someone, I can tell every mundane detail of his or her pathetic life. You, however, are a dark spot. It's why, out of dozens of more-than-willing girls at my party, I singled you out. But that night ended in disappointment. So tell me why you're immune to me."

"Immune to what?" I ask, sitting up straight on the couch. This is it … he's going to tell me how he and MJ are connected.

"I can make people do whatever I want them to."

I asked for the truth, and he gave me a line of BS. "Omigod, really?" I ask, imitating Amber's annoying voice. "Congratulations on saying the stupidest thing I've ever hea—"

"*Tsk, tsk*, Mads. You really need to start listening to me. I told you what you wanted to—"

"No, you didn't!" I interrupt this time. "You said you can make people do what you wa—"

Make. He said *make*.

My mind drifts back to my search on the computer—specifically the sites on supernatural beings. Whenever a site discussed a being's ability, it explained what the being could *make* other people do. The other people were powerless against it. They didn't have a choice. Can it be true? Can both Justin and MJ be some sort of supernatural beings?

Justin whistles the same chilling tune from Friday while my brain is still processing this connection.

But what about magicians? Those sites also said well-trained magicians could *make* their subjects do whatever they wanted while under hypnosis. He could be using hypnosis. I don't remember him talking to people in hushed, soothing tones as MJ did to me, but the people at the party and my friends at school seemed to be in a trance around him. So maybe he doesn't need to use the soothing voice.

As frightening as the thought of hypnosis might be, I like it a little more than the next thought: mental manipulation. He could be messing with people's heads in order to make them do whatever he wants. That's ... disturbing. I really hope that's not the right answer.

"You're awfully quiet, Mads. I'm sure your intriguing little mind is trying to figure it out. Whatever you're thinking, you're not even close."

"You're evil," I say with more courage than I feel.

"What?" he asks, his tone suddenly guarded.

I'm right. He hadn't expected that. I didn't want to be, but there is no denying it now. How long has he been like this? What all has he *made* someone do? I shudder as I remember his party and what he tried to *make* me do. Is that the worst of it? Or has he used his abilities for things so unimaginable I don't even want to think about them?

"Are you able to manipulate everyone's minds, or just some people's?"

"Beautiful *and* brilliant. Will you ever cease to amaze me? Excluding you, everyone is susceptible to me."

Just how many people's heads has he manipulated? I don't have the stomach to find out. "Well, then I feel sorry for you."

"You feel *sorry* for me?" He chuckles. "This should be entertaining. Explain."

"You've made your life a lie. You've surrounded yourself with people who only do what you want them to. How can you tell what's real anymore? How can you tell what they really think about you?"

My speaker crackles with laughter. He's mocking me. Is it what I said just now, or has he been mocking me since the day we met? How can *I* even tell what's real?

"Oh, Mads, you're so naïve. You think I care what other people think? I know the trivial nonsense that resides in people's heads. Everyone's but *yours*. So how is it you can refuse my abilities over and over again?"

Another conversation creeps back into my mind. Games. He's all about playing games. He said it at school. What proof is there that any of this is real? He was already in the lobby with my friends when Kelli and I arrived. Who's to say he didn't convince them to act like his puppets and fawn all over him and do whatever he said just as a joke? Maybe he wanted to scare me and get back at me for the party.

At the party, Justin could have drugged everyone. It would explain why he expected me to do whatever he wanted. He thought I drank his drug-laced alcohol.

And MJ ... they could be friends. Maybe they're working together. Maybe they figured MJ would scare me and send me rushing to Justin. Why didn't I think of this sooner? Now I feel like an idiot.

"It's like you said, I'm *brilliant*," I tell him. "That's why I figured it out. So you can stop now. The game is over. You got me—ha, ha. I'm hanging up now."

"Wait, Mads!" he says, his usually smooth voice now strained.

"What?" I snap.

He's silent for a second. "You didn't hang up?" he asks. "You listened to me for once?"

"Obviously—though I'm regretting it already." As much as I'm convinced I have him and his games all figured out, a part of me still needs to hear more just to be certain I'm right. I can't be wrong about Justin and MJ. Not when Amber's life depends on it.

"Good. I'm glad you're still here. I have more things planned for you, and I'd hate to do something that would end our fun. So to make things interesting, the next time you see your friend Kelli … ask her about me."

"That would involve talking about you, and that isn't going to happen."

"Have it your way," he says. "On to a brighter subject: How much have you thought about me since our last conversation?"

"I haven't," I lie, letting my irritation color my voice. This isn't why I stayed on the phone. Why did he change the subject?

"You sound like you're getting mad, Mads. Ha!" He laughs. "Mad Mads."

"Hilarious. Put Ben on the phone. I need to talk to him again."

"I've sent him on an errand. If you're tired of being alone, I could leave here." His voice deepens as he says, "I could be there sooner than you thi—"

"Hell no!" I shout. How could he even think that? Pig! No. That's a disgrace to pigs everywhere. He's scum.

"Is that really how you talk to your friend?" he asks. "It's not polite."

"*Friend*? You've got to be kidding me. There's no way you and I would ever be friends! You are like the black clouds that have hung above my head since the day we met. All you do is suck the joy and happiness out of my life. I wish I'd never met you."

"If anyone else dared talk to me like that," he growls, "I would make it so they didn't exist!" Heavy breathing comes from his end for several moments before he continues, resuming his usual tone. "But I don't want to do that to you.

I'm too addicted to your unpredictability. Let me take you to your school dance. I'll make it one hell of a party."

"Are you dense? *I don't like you.* How many different ways do I have to say it before you understand?"

"Madison, I'm getting very close to losing my patience with you. You of all people should remember what happens when my patience runs thin. I suggest you reconsider."

"And I suggest you shut up and put Ben back on the phone!"

"And what if I don't?"

"Then … then … Ben and I are through. F-for good this time!" I don't mean that, but now that it's out there, it's my best chance to get rid of Justin. But I don't know if I'm ready to be without Ben yet.

"Aw, Mads—you sound like you're crying."

My fingers slide along my wet cheeks, wiping away tears. I don't want to cry on the phone with Justin. I don't want him to know how much he bothers me. I can hold on. I can get through this. I can cry when I'm off the phone.

"Damn you!" I say, latching on to my rage to keep my tears in check. "You ruin everything! Leave Ben and me alone, or … I'll tell everyone about you."

"I don't respond well to threats. Choose your next words carefully, Mads. I can be a valuable friend or a powerful ene-my. Don't say something you—or Ben—might regret."

"Go to Hell!" I stab the "end call" button, pretending it's his eye socket, then chuck my phone across the room.

I cannot *believe* I let him get to me that much. He's such an a-hole. I meant it when I said I will give up Ben to be rid of Justin. But I won't tell anyone about him. I don't believe what he says about his crazy abilities, so there's no way anyone else would.

Ben's ringtone sounds near the rain-splattered patio door. I walk over to my phone and the music ends. Then it instantly begins again, making me cringe. I'm sure it's still Justin. I don't want to talk to him. I ignore it and put my phone on vibrate, hoping that will give him the hint.

After eight ignored phone calls and fifteen texts saying, *It's Ben, I'm sorry. Talk to me, babe,* I lose my patience and shut my phone off.

In the silence, I breathe a sigh of relief, and some of the tension eases from my shoulders. But the way Justin said, "I could be there sooner than you think" is giving me the heebie-jeebies and keeping me from fully relaxing.

I'm sure it's just a vague threat, but what if he wasn't joking? What if he does have abilities? What if ... he can somehow disappear and reappear whenever he wants, as MJ can? He *could* come here—sooner than I think. As much as I'd like to run away to someplace safe, someplace Justin wouldn't know, I can't leave because MJ is out there ... in the dark ... possibly waiting for me. Fear has made me a prisoner in my own home.

To give myself some peace of mind, I walk out to the garage and dig through the shelves of my old life. The life when I participated in anything and everything I could— with boxes filled with trophies in the attic to prove it. I grab my metal baseball bat and bring it with me as I go room to room, locking the windows and bolting the doors. Once the house is secure, I sit on my bed, gripping the bat, and wait for either morning ... or Justin.

CHAPTER 16

Maddy

I'M NOT SURE WHEN I FELL ASLEEP, BUT I'M NOW FLOATING beside the Dream Girl, in the third installment of her dreams: the Dark Prince's cabin. We're in her bedroom, and she's frozen in front of a full-length mirror.

I need to wake up and watch for Justin, but I don't know how to leave the dreams. Plus, they're changing, and I need to know why. It can't be a coincidence they've gone from following the lunar cycles to happening nightly as soon as Justin and MJ showed up. At least in here, finding answers won't be dangerous. I breathe, slide into her, and let her take over.

MY STOMACH CHURNS AGAIN, AND I PLACE MY HANDS OVER it to calm my nerves. After three months of my being here alone, the Dark Prince is here, waiting in the next room to take me out on our first date.

Surprisingly, the time has flown by because every night I dreamed of him. In the first dream, he told me his name was Damien. I don't know any Damiens, so I'm not sure where the name came from, but I like it. It suits him.

The dreams were a bit strange in the beginning. It was just us ... alone ... in the cabin. Whenever we had met in person, he had been so secure in himself and his environment. But in the dreams, his confidence was gone. He stumbled over words and even his own feet. It was ... sweet. It was as if I were seeing a whole new side of him.

Each night began the same way—with us talking, dancing, and kissing. He had this way of knowing exactly what I needed from him each night—sometimes even before I did. The more I dreamed of him, the bolder he became. He was romantic, passionate, and still just as charismatic as the night we met.

The dreams were so vivid that whenever I woke up, it took a few minutes to realize none of it had actually happened. Especially when my lips still tingled with the lingering effects of his good-bye kisses.

I play with the spaghetti straps of the black satin dress he bought, trying to decide whether I should wear them the normal way or off the shoulders. The dress is already sexy, clinging to my curves and stopping mid-thigh. It makes me look so much older than eighteen.

My body tingles as I sense him behind me. I watch in the mirror as he enters the room and stops behind me. His fingers lightly press on my arms as he slides my straps up onto their rightful places. My eyes find his in the glass as he says, "Words cannot begin to describe how beautiful you are."

My cheeks burn while his eyes move up and down my reflection.

"Shall we get going?" he asks, stepping back and looking away.

I release my breath and say, "Sure."

Even though it's darker than the deepest depths of the ocean outside, he drives the Jeep with ease and precision while handling the sharp turns of the mountain. The lack of light makes the cab seem more intimate. I'm hyperaware of his every move, every breath. It's driving me crazy not touching him. I need a distraction. Something to keep my mind from picturing what he looks like underneath his suit.

"So where are we going?"

"We are here, my lady," he says, stopping the car and then getting out.

He called me *my lady*? I grin and watch him slink around the car to open my door. It reminds me of how easily he navigated the packed dance floor the night we met. Eleven months later, and I'm still captivated by him.

I gaze around, trying to figure out where he's brought me. The buildings appear vacant with no lights shining through the windows. The few streetlamps do little to illuminate the area. "Where are we exactly?"

"Someone I know owns this restaurant. The food is said to be exceptional." He offers his arm, and I graciously accept, allowing him to lead me inside.

A stout man with a thick mustache greets us. "Good evening, sir. We've been expecting you." Beads of sweat drip down his face to his yellowing collar. He wipes at it with shaking hands, and I wonder if he has an ailment of some kind. Father had a business associate who had Parkinson's disease, and he often shook like that.

Father …

My heart aches as I think about my father and mother. I haven't spoken to them since I left. I haven't even thought about them. Do they miss me? Are they okay?

"You are frowning," the Dark Prince whispers in my ear. "First dates are meant to be happy occasions."

My mouth curves into a smile, and whatever caused me to frown is forgotten.

The sweaty man leads us into a dimly lit dining area. All the tables sit empty and barren, except for one in the back of the room adorned with a pressed black tablecloth, red linen napkins, and a dozen red roses. Next to the table is a bottle of champagne in a bucket filled with ice.

The man stays only long enough to pull my chair out for me, pour our champagne—which I am surprised he doesn't spill with how bad he trembles—and inform us our dinner will be out momentarily.

I watch him scurry back to the kitchen. Something seemed odd about him. I don't think he's ill. It's as if he's intimidated by my date, just as William was.

I shake my head at the thought of William. When he set his mind on something, nothing could stand in his way. He wanted me, badly. He almost got me too with that damn business deal—until the Dark Prince appeared from the darkness.

The Dark Prince loudly exhales and I turn to face him. He's far from intimidating. Sure, he's tall and his face looks as if it belonged on a statue in an upscale museum, but that's only the surface. He's a good, generous man. He offered me his cabin and a job when he barely knew me.

Heat flows up my left arm as he grasps my hand. I suddenly feel lighter, as if all my troubles just melted away. What troubles? I have none. I'm on a date with the Dark Prince.

"I am really pleased you are still here," he says as I absorb his deep voice. "I am sure you have many questions for me. What would you like to know?"

Hundreds of questions race through my mind, but my heart only wants to know one. "What's your name?"

"Damien."

"What?" That can't be right.

"My name is Damien." His eyes flitter, showing a hint of unease in his normally controlled persona.

There are millions of names in the world, yet somehow my subconscious mind picked the right one for my dream version of him. "This might sound strange, but somehow, I knew that. I don't know how ... but I did. Did I perhaps overhear someone else call you by that name the night we met?"

"No. I have never told anyone my first name until you."

"Really? Why is that, Damien?" I love the feel of his name as it leaves my mouth. His name echoes through every part of me, heating my body until I squirm in my seat.

He leans forward, and his dark gaze fixes on me. The eyes that normally pull me in with their vastness are now cold and distant. It's as if he suddenly shut me out. I don't know why, and I don't like it.

His luxurious voice takes on a menacing tone as he says, "Your name is your identity. Your source of power. And if someone chooses to use it against you, it can be your undo-ing. That is why you did not know my name until now."

That was so dark and unexpected "Oh," I reply, unable to think of anything better.

All the times we've been together, I've never felt this uncomfortable. His presence, his scent, his touch usually soothes me. Mostly, it is his voice and the way he talks. It's so … proper. Like a gentleman straight out of the pages of a classic novel. Any discomfort slips away, and before I can stop myself, I ask, "Are you British?"

"What? No." I catch his mouth twitch as he rests back. His eyes brighten—I think he's amused by my question.

"Then why do you talk that way?"

"What way?" Judging by his smirk, I get the feeling he knows exactly what I mean.

"Well, the night we met, I thought it was just part of your costume, but you still talk with an accent, and I can't quite place it. It almost seems … old-fashioned. I mean, don't get me wrong—I like it. It suits you. It's just … " I pause, trying to find the right way to explain this.

The smirk disappears, but he still grasps my hand. "I was unaware it came across as stiff as you suggest. I suppose I speak in such a way because of my business. I work all over the world, and I refuse to adhere to one culture's norms over another's. But mostly, I suspect it is because I refuse to change who I am just to blend in."

I look down at my free hand, fidgeting with my napkin. "I'm sorry. I didn't mean to offend you. I just—"

"Dance with me," he says.

I look up, and the intensity of his gaze causes my muscles to tighten and my breathing to increase. I'm too stunned to respond.

Soft notes of a trumpet sound as he stands and walks over to me, still holding my hand.

The time we danced at the Halloween party was by far the best I'd ever experienced. But this time feels more intimate as I stand and he moves us a few feet into a clearing between two tables. It's not just because we're in a deserted restaurant. It's a combination of the smoldering look in his eyes as he stares down at me and the slow rhythm of the music that ensures close physical contact instead of the stiff waltz from before.

He places his hand at the small of my back, pressing me into him, and I rest my free arm around his shoulders. We slowly turn as the incredible voice of Ella Fitzgerald sings, "Stars shining bright above you ... " It's "Dream a Little Dream of Me."

How appropriate that this song should be playing. "I dream of you, Damien. Every night."

His hand tightens on mine, but he maintains his perfect rhythm. "Did you know a popular theory suggests that when you dream of someone, it is because you miss them?"

"I hadn't heard that before." I did miss him. Every day. "There's something else, though. In the dreams, I called you Damien. How did I know your name?"

"Another theory suggests our dreams are a window to an alternate reality. Everyone has a path—their fate or destiny, so to speak. Occasionally, there are forks in the path: dance with a masked stranger, reject his kiss, be shipped to the other side of the country by desperate parents, turn down a marriage proposal, accept a job and lodgings from said original stranger, go on a date with him … "

I stiffen as he recounts everything that has happened in the last eleven months. A strange tightness builds inside of me as those events float through my mind, but before I can figure out what it is or what it means, it's gone.

"Now say if you had changed even one of those things, your destiny would be completely different."

I know which fork I would choose to redo if I could. It's the same one I've regretted time and time again. If I could go back, I would have never rejected his first kiss.

Damien smiles. "Say, for example, this alternate-reality dream of yours is one where we kissed the first night. Everything would have been different between us. However, it is because you rejected my kiss that I looked at you differently. It is because you were sent away that I missed you. It is because you were promised to another man that I came there that night, which ultimately led to us being together now. As much as I wished we had kissed the first night, I am glad we did not. I, for one, like this path much better."

Damien's right. He's always right. But even still … "I don't think that's the real reason why I dream of you."

Our eyes lock, and the restaurant becomes a blur. All that remains in focus is him. "Do not panic," he says. His arms hold me even tighter to his strong, heated body.

He waits for a response, but my throat has gone dry. I nod.

"I am … gifted. I can access the mind of anybody I choose. I can put thoughts inside them or show them whatever I wish. In your case, I can choose to enter your mind to interact."

"You're joking," I whisper.

No, I am not, I hear him say, but his lips don't move.

All thought processes stop as I consider that I just heard him speak inside my head. My heart tries to beat faster, my nerves want to scatter, but nothing happens except my eyes blink. I want to panic, but I can't. It's as if my body is physically unable to. Why?

Damien told me not to.

Damien's thumb rubs a small circle on my back as he says, "I know this is unnatural, and your body is trying to fight against such an idea, but it is the only way we can be together as often as I would like and as you deserve. Can you try to accept this notion?"

This is so unreal. He can get into my head? I should feel violated, but ... I don't. I like the dreams. I like how we are in them. It's the best relationship I've ever had. "So, everything we've done in those dreams really happened?" All the talking ... making out ...

"Yes."

"Oh." I had wanted him to be the Damien from my dreams, and he just said he is. I thought that was impossible. But because he is able to do this impossible thing, then it means I did not spend the last three months alone.

"Did you do this other times?" I ask.

"What do you mean?"

"Did you visit my dreams or put thoughts into my head before I came to your cabin?"

"I visited you when you were at the boarding school."

I'm relieved—I wasn't crazy. "Why?"

"Partly to ensure you were okay, but mostly so you would not feel so lonely."

Why would he do that?

He cares.

This strange, complicated man cares for me. He's shown it time and time again, he is the Damien I'm falling in love with.

"So what was the new deal?" I ask, thinking again of our last dance at Halloween. I'd asked him about this at my sham wedding too, but he avoided the question. Hopefully this time he won't.

"New deal?"

"The one you made with my father."

He shakes his head and lets out a long exhale. "It appears you are meant to know the answer, no matter how much I wish to spare you from the truth." He shifts against me and looks over my shoulder as his jaw tenses. "My organization helped your father build his company. After twenty-five years, our contract was up for renegotiation. Your father wanted to cut all ties, but that is not one of the options he originally agreed to. When I came to collect his decision, he instead offered me a new deal: he would introduce me to someone," he searches for the right words, "willing to assume the agreement. He assured me this person would be willing to pay a higher price to achieve the success only I can arrange. He threw a party on Halloween and invited every success-driven, greedy, selfish person he could think of. I walked amongst them, searching for someone I thought would make a suitable replacement."

I swallow a lump in my throat, and Damien pulls back. Black meets green, and I look away, knowing what he's about to say.

"I walked the crowd for nearly two hours, but I could not focus. My attention kept getting stolen by a vision in white, standing alone on a terrace."

I can feel his fingers on my skin, tracing the edge of my dress along my back, but I'm too numb to respond.

"At first, I tried to ignore you. You were much too young and innocent to be interested in my offer. But as I was leaving, our eyes met; I could not leave without speaking to you. You were insightful, but hurt. It bothered me—and that surprised me."

I clench my jaw as I learn Halloween night—the night I thought was perfect—had such a dark purpose. How could my father have gone along with that new deal? The guests were his friends. And me ... he let me come to the party knowing Damien would be there. But what about Damien? He supposedly helped my father become the successful man he is, but then when the deal went sour, he ruined my father's business. How could I have left everything for a man I know nothing about?

Damien places his hand on my cheek and turns my head to meet his gaze. My body loosens as fears I can no longer recall leave me.

He frowns. "I intended only to dance with you to ease your worries. You were not to be the replacement for your father. But when our hands touched on the dance floor, no words could describe the feelings that overtook me. Holding you, making you laugh ... time just melted away. Then your father showed up. I knew who you were. I knew what it meant—that he thought I had chosen you as the replacement. He was wrong, but I could not correct him. I did not want to. I enjoyed the idea of you replacing him solely because it ensured I would see you again. So I left and put the decision in his hands. It is my fault they sent you away. He thought hiding you would protect you from me, but I knew where you were the whole time. He also thought marrying you to that boy would make me lose interest, but he underestimated me. He underestimated me greatly. He will never come between us again."

I should be mad. No. I should be furious. This is insane. But … I don't hold Damien responsible. He's the best thing that's ever happened to me, even if I don't understand most of it. I am mad at my father. He could have told me. It wasn't that hard.

Damien pulls me closer and whispers into my ear, "Forget about your past. It will only make you sad. Think of me instead. My life began the night I met you. I will keep you safe. I can make you happy and give you whatever life you want. Please … I am nothing without you."

"I love you," I say to him.

He pulls back, smiles, and his eyes brighten as if it were Christmas morning. He really is handsome.

Suddenly, he tightens his grip on my hand, then sends me spinning across the floor just as he did during our first dance. Before my organs have a chance to return to their homes, he tugs lightly, and I twirl back into his warm embrace. He bends me low.

"Promise me, you will dream a little dream of me," he says.

Slowly, he leans over me, as if he's unsure of my feelings. After all this time, this is it. Yes. I want to feel his lips on mine. For real.

As our lips meet, a fire rages up inside me. The tension and awkwardness evaporate, and I relax into our kiss. It's tender, delicate, sweet.

I don't want to stop kissing, and neither does he. I've waited so long for this moment.

His kiss is so passionate, so intense, and so thick with his desire for me ... her ... it suddenly snaps me from the Dream Girl. I'm drifting beside them, watching as they make out.

This isn't fun anymore. I don't want to feel how wonderful he is. I don't want to feel their love and desire and passion. He belongs to her, and I ... belong to no one.

I want to feel this for real. I want my own wonderful experiences with an amazing guy who makes me feel I'm the most important person in the world.

I can't play pretend anymore. That dreaming phase of my life is over, and even though my life is messed up right now, it's my life and I accept it. I completely accept the good, the bad, and the uncertainty that revolves around Justin and MJ.

"I don't need this," I say out loud to the Dream Girl. "I don't want to escape my life. I need clarity. If you can't give me that, then I don't need you!"

Everything begins to fade away. Finally, I can get out of here.

CHAPTER 17

MJ

OZENS OF PROTECTORS AND GUARDIANS LOOK UP from their research as I walk down the aisle in the Immortal City Library. My stomach twists in unease with each gaze following me. Their thoughts are so loud, my head feels as if it would split in two. They want to know what caused the Original Protector to come here.

I hate that nickname. I didn't chose to be the first—it just happened. All lower angels look up to me. Even the Archangels call upon me regularly for an update of Mortal Ground. The only benefit of my name is that the mere mention of it is often enough to cause a demon to surrender. But if any of them knew the truth of why I'm here, the Devil himself might gasp.

I continue past the numerous rows of identical white books lined on glass shelves and head to the section farthest back. Thankfully, it's deserted. I glance around, making sure no one is watching, before grabbing a book from the never-used genre of romance and taking a seat at a glass table tucked off to the side.

I need to know why *she* reacted so strongly to those movies as I watched her. There was this look in her eyes, as if she would give anything just to be loved like the women on screen. I could be wrong, I suppose, but I think it was the same look I've seen many times in the past. When I've seen it on those other people, I could also hear their thoughts. They were lonely, and they didn't feel worthy of love. If Alexander's theory is correct about her being a demon, does she remember what love is like? But if the theory isn't correct, and she is alive, then why doesn't she feel loved?

My mind thinks the question, "What is love?" and the book in my hand transforms into one that can answer it.

The more I read, the more questions I have. The more questions I have, the more the book changes to answer them. My mind absorbs each book's content, making my headache worse. I have never felt more clueless than I do right now.

The book changes to one with a yellow-and-black cover. I cringe, anticipating it to have an overwhelming amount of information tucked away inside. But this book is different. It seems a little easier to understand. I push on and allow the new information to sink in.

When it's finished, I sigh. Love is a lot more complex than it used to be. When did people stop giving the parents livestock in exchange for marriage? Why aren't ladies chaperoned during courtship? Why in the world is there such a rule that people must initiate only three dates before becoming intimate? I knew waiting until marriage was no longer traditional, but someone had to create *that* kind of a rule? I can't see her acting that rash. I think she would be more traditional, but I guess I don't honestly know anymore.

Behind my book, I hear loud, obnoxious laughter. I lower the book to see Alexander, dressed in a parka and snow pants, gripping his sides and slapping his knees in an overly dramatic fashion aimed at my expense. Until I laughed for real the other day, I hadn't noticed how fake his laughter was. I guess he's forgotten what the real thing feels like. He has been with me for more than two hundred years.

He stops laughing and says, "You know, I could have answered your questions."

"You know about love and dating?"

"No. But I know you're a dummy."

I close the book and see it's titled *Dating for Dummies*. It shimmers, then returns to its original, blank condition.

"So now you want to woo the demon?" Alexander asks.

"She's not a demon … for sure, anyway. I'm just re-searching different ideas about how to get close to her so I can find out what she is."

"Ah, the *Art of War* strategy: 'So it is said that if you know your enemies and know yourself, you can win a hundred battles without a single loss. If you only know yourself, but not your opponent, you may win or you may lose. If you know neither yourself nor your enemy, you will always endanger yourself.' A good plan, though I don't think the great Sun Tzu had dating your enemy in mind when he said that."

"Go crawl back to whatever frozen hole you crawled out of."

"Alaska," he replies. "And it was fine—thanks for asking."

I ignore him and massage my temples to reduce the pounding inside my skull. This isn't just a ploy to get close enough to uncover what she is. I want to test her abilities.

She's affected nearly all my senses. But there's one sense I haven't tried yet. Taste. I now long to bite into a juicy mutton and drink a glass of ale… I might have to go to a different continent to get food like that, though. What do Americans eat now? Amber's file lists she's on a diet and mostly drinks her meals. I wonder what that would taste like.

"I could help interrogate her if you'd like," Alexander says. "I don't have an assignment at the moment."

"You've interrogated someone before?"

"Sure. You wouldn't believe how fast people talk when they're tied to the tracks as a train rolls toward them."

"This isn't the Wild West," I snap.

"It's still better than wining-and-dining a demon," he mumbles.

I sigh in exasperation and drop my hands to the chair's armrests. "As I said, it was just an idea."

"Well, here's another one for you: there's no such thing as coincidence."

"I know that."

"Do you?"

I swallow the lump in my throat, not sure why I'm suddenly nervous about where he's going with this.

"Look at the facts, MJ. A demon is hunting down brown-haired, green-eyed, sixteen-year-old girls. You were assigned to protect the last one because, well, you're the best—with me coming in at a close second." He runs a hand through his hair, smoothing it out.

I roll my eyes.

"The day you arrive," Alexander continues once he's done primping, "you meet a girl who matches that very description so well, you mistake her for your Charge. She has abilities no mortal can possess, an unknown spirit is protecting her, and you later learn she doesn't even exist. You're becoming obsessed with her. She's a distraction, and she needs to go."

I clench my hands under the table where he can't see.

"Her heart beats."

"A trick. What you heard could be electronic pulses."

"I know the difference between a human heart and a gadget."

"All right. Given everything else she can do ... I'd say it's some sort of black magic. It wouldn't be the first time demons and witches have teamed up."

I hadn't thought of witches. Still, it can't be true. Bad witches smell of decay from their souls rotting. She smells of cucumbers and melons and strawberries. Underneath her soaps and shampoo, she smells even better. She is sunshine, a summer breeze, and light spring rain. It reminds me of home. I can't tell him that, so instead I say, "No witch has the power to make a demon's heart beat."

"No human can do what she does either."

"So where does that leave us?"

Silence stretches on. My stomach twists in knots, wondering what he's thinking.

Alexander stands and paces along the opposite side of the desk. "You erased her memories, right?"

I think back to that night and images of her flood my mind. Her sitting beside me, the warmth that radiated off her smooth skin, the curl of her pink lips as she smiled, the soft sounds of her voice, and the rosy hue that often flushed over her skin and drove me crazy wondering what she was thinking. Then her panic when I went after her, the fear in her eyes when I spoke the truth, and her anger at my mistake. "That's correct," I finally say.

He snaps his fingers. "Great! Since our abilities don't work on the other side, if she's a demon, she'll remember you. Find her, interrogate her—date her if you must. Just get her to reveal she remembers you and end it today."

Human, demon. Demon, human. Back and forth I go like a pendulum swinging closer and closer toward her end. I will do as he said. If by sundown I haven't found proof of her innocence ... I will destroy her. Father have mercy on my soul if I'm wrong.

CHAPTER 18

Maddy

A S I RETURN FROM MY DREAM, I FEEL SOMEONE'S hands on my arms, shaking me. Memories of last night's phone conversation drift through the dreamlike haze.

Justin's here.

I bolt up in bed, nearly smacking Kelli in the face. "Kelli? What are you doing here?"

While my panicked heart slows, Kelli stands and paces in front of my bed. "Thank God! I've been trying to wake you up for, like, ever now! I've called and texted you a hundred times this morning, but it keeps going to voicemail, so I rode over to check on you."

"How did you get in? I locked every door."

"I used the spare key in the garage."

"Oh." The shock of her presence dissipates, and I rest back against the headboard.

"What the heck were you dreaming about?"

"Why?"

She sits back down on my bed, and I meet her blue eyes for a second before she turns away. "Um, let's see—when I first tried to wake you up, you grabbed me and tried to kiss me. Like, full on make-out kiss me. Then you kept saying, 'Damien.' Who's that? Then you were thrashing around saying, 'I don't want this' and 'I don't need you' over and over again. It's like you were possessed or something."

As she continues to rattle off what I did while stuck inside the dream, a dark, hollow feeling grows inside me. How long have I been doing that—acting out these dreams?

Not able to take anymore, I tell her, "I had one of *her* dreams. I didn't know about all the moving and talking—no one's ever seen me dreaming before. Are you okay?"

"I'm fine." She bites her lip. "How are *you* feeling?"

"Tired." As if on cue, I yawn. "Even though I fall asleep, the dreams are always so real, it's as if I actually become her. My mind isn't getting any rest."

She grabs my hand and squeezes. "I don't understand. I thought the dreams were good."

"They are—or were. They're changing now. Like this one: after having these dreams for years, I'm finally told his real name. He's Damien. I still have no idea who she is, though. She has all the control."

That's not all she changed. I didn't know the real reason why she dreams of him or the reason behind why they first danced together … the "deal" can't be true. And there were times when she would think of her family or something and feel sad, then the thoughts and feelings would just vanish somehow. Maybe all this stuff going on with Justin and MJ is warping the dreams about her. Damien is good. I know that.

Yes, it's got to be because of Justin. He's affected me so much, my subconscious is seeing darkness where it doesn't exist.

"That's seriously messed up," Kelli says. "You need to tell someone."

"No! I can't. I know the dreams are strange, but … I don't want people thinking there's something wrong with me. Plus, I've stopped them. Okay? That's why I was saying, 'I don't want this'—so she would stop sending me the dreams. Promise me you won't tell anyone."

I really hope she doesn't tell anyone. If my parents found out … they might send me to the nuthouse or just get rid of me, as my birth parents did. I can't go through that. Not again.

Kelli spins the dolphin ring on her finger while biting her lip.

After watching the ring twirl for a moment, I put my hand over hers and stop it. "Please—don't tell."

She nods and looks away. Her gaze lands on the space beside me, and she frowns. "So what's with the bat?"

I look over and notice the bat I'd grabbed last night. I've never been one to dump all my problems on people, but everything is so overbearing, I feel as if my head would explode unless I told her.

The story comes spewing out of my mouth like word vomit. I start with the incident in the park—leaving out MJ's disappearing and reappearing act, magic file, and attempt to hypnotize me. She squirms during the tense parts and occasionally gasps, but she never takes her focus off me.

I tell her about my chat with Amber, and I end with how Ben and I may or may not be broken up permanently. Even though it's stupid, I leave Justin out of it. There's something unsettling about the way he mentioned Kelli and told me to talk to her about him. Whatever it is, I don't want to find out yet. I'm not ready for more bad news.

When I finally finish, she throws her arms around me, hugs me, and tries her best to comfort me. For the most part, I want to believe in her optimism, even if it's just for one day. I'm glad she came over here; her positive outlook has a way of balancing out all the negativity.

"Thanks," I manage to say. As my head clears, I realize I don't even know why she's here in the first place. "So, why did you come over here today?"

She pulls away and frowns. "'Cuz it's Sunday. We're going shopping, remember? So come on and get ready."

"Oh, yeah!" With the craziness of the past two days, I'd forgotten about our annual Halloween costume shopping. Now I'm grateful for it. Shopping is normal and well within my control.

My excitement stays with me as I shower, dress, and get ready. While in the bathroom, my mind flits back to Duane's comments about love, and I try to figure out where Kelli fits in. We were only in kindergarten when she found me crying in the rain on the playground right after Amber told me she didn't want to be friends with me anymore.

Amber and I had been in dance together, and I was better than her at it. She didn't like that. I didn't want to make any enemies, so I quit. But it didn't matter to her. She still broke off our friendship. Amber's rejection hurt. Not because she was special to me. We were friends only because our moms are friends. It hurt because I had allowed myself to get close to her, depend on her, but then she turned her back on me.

Kelli was a light in my darkness. She was so happy and friendly. I clung to her, but I vowed to never make the mistakes I made with Amber. I wouldn't let myself feel the pain of rejection again. That's why Kelli knows very little about me. It's also why I've never dated before Ben and why I continually break up with him.

I've spent the past few years building a brick wall around my heart and blocking out everything that existed prior to learning the truth about being adopted. But did I allow Kelli and Ben to dig under that wall without realizing it? Do I love them regardless of who I am?

When I come out of the bathroom, Kelli's lying on my bed, humming along to a P!nk song playing on my iPod.

"So how has your weekend gone?" I ask.

"Not as eventful as yours. Went to the football game, found dates for us for the dance, watched—"

"You *what*?"

She rolls over and stares at the glow-in-the-dark stars on my ceiling. "I've decided we can just go together."

I hop onto the bed next to her, making her bounce. "Aw, Kelli. Are you asking me to be your date?"

She shrugs and grins. "Well, since you tried to kiss me this morning, I figured dancing with you was the next step."

I grab a pillow and whip it at her; she catches it and laughs. "Ha, ha. Very funny, Kells."

She bounces off the bed and pulls me to my feet. "Come on. Let's go!"

I laugh too and follow her, but I can't keep my skin from glowing red with embarrassment. I don't like that the dreams are changing this much or that my body acts them out while I'm stuck inside. I feel like a puppet with the Dream Girl pulling my strings. Between Justin, MJ, and now this ... it feels as if I'm losing control over my life.

AFTER BIKING TO TWO DIFFERENT THRIFT STORES AND THE fabric shop, Kelli and I are all set. My backpack is overloaded with everything I need to make my perfect costume.

A thought that had been hiding in the back of my mind pushes to the forefront, and I can't shake it. It's Justin and what he said about Kelli. I need to know if it's just another joke or if it means something more.

"Hey, Kelli," I shout while pedaling my bike to catch up to her.

"Yeah?" she replies, slowing down.

"This is going to sound weird, but ... promise me that if you ever hear from Justin again, you'll tell me immediately." I can't have him trying to get close to her. Not with how easily she told him everything Friday.

"O-kay?" she says, drawing it out. "I guess I will. But who's Justin?"

What? After being so interested in him on Friday, I figured she would remember him. Although, I did say his name only once or twice during his visit. "You know, the jerk who came to lunch on Friday."

She stops her bike and stares at me with a blank look on her face.

"You were drooling over him and telling him all about my break-up with Ben… " I pause, waiting for a hint of recognition, but continue when I find none. "I left you and went outside with him… "

"I think your dreams are messing with your head. Nothing like that happened Friday."

My pulse accelerates as a horrible suspicion settles over me. "Then what do *you* remember from lunch?"

"We sat at our spot like we always do. You were with us the whole time, and no one new showed up. What's so bad about this guy, anyway?"

No matter how long I stare in disbelief, it won't change anything. She isn't lying. She honestly doesn't remember him.

Panic squeezes my lungs, and I gasp for air, but I can't get my lungs to expand. I hop off my bike and kneel in the grass as the world closes in on me. The ground shakes from thunder as storm clouds move in, darkening another day. Justin wasn't lying. He *can* manipulate people's minds. He removed himself from Kelli's. What else did he do to her?

"Maddy, what's wrong?"

Kelli's anxious voice filters in, but I can't respond. Everything I knew about life just flew out the window. If Justin really can manipulate minds, then what if MJ's not a magician? What the hell *are* they?

Kelli kneels in front of me and places her hands on my shoulders. I can see her lips moving and the panic in her face, but I can't move. Because of me, Justin hacked away at her brain.

Behind her, a white-and-silver motorcycle slows down as it drives by. The rider's white helmet turns my way, and it feels as if our eyes connect, though I can't be sure through his visor.

I don't know anyone who rides a motorcycle, but for some reason, seeing him is like seeing a light shining through the darkness. He's righted the world. I feel warm, safe, protected. It's exactly like what I felt during the sunset with MJ—before everything changed. After what seems like an eternity, though it was only seconds, the biker turns his head and rides away.

Somehow, I have to keep my family and friends safe from Justin and MJ. I can't let them know what's going on. I don't know if they're able to resist Justin's mind control or whatever it is MJ can do, but I'm not willing to find out. I need to be strong for Kelli. For all of them.

The panic lessens, and I suck in a deep, cleansing breath. It takes every ounce of strength to stand up and compose my face into an expression that I hope calms her. "Sorry, I … swallowed a bug."

She stares at me skeptically, but after a moment, her shoulders shrug and she relaxes. "That's gross and all, but I would appreciate it if you wouldn't give me a heart attack next time."

We pedal back in silence, and at the bottom of the hill leading to her house, we go our separate ways. As glad as I am to have spent time with her today, I'm even more grateful she's headed home and away from me.

I ride toward home as fast as I can. Two blocks later, my gears slip as the chain on my bike falls off the teeth. As

badly as I want to get home, I have no choice but to stop and
fix it. Luckily, I'm by Centennial Park. It's not that bad of a
place to be stranded. The cool, misty spray coming from the
fountain is refreshing.

I walk my bike in between the wooden benches and over
to the fountain. I kneel down, grab the chain, and groan,
trying to get the stubborn, greasy chain over the teeth in the
gears. A loud grumble comes from my belly.

Hunger.

When was the last time I ate? I've been so preoccupied.
I think it was Friday at lunch? No, Justin ruined that too.
Thursday night's tacos? That's over three days without food.
That's not good. Surprisingly, I don't feel weak or dizzy,
though I probably should.

"Hello," says a smooth, familiar voice. Instantly, my hunger pains are forgotten and my stomach twists in knots.

I hope it's a mistake and he's not really here.

I follow a pair of faded blue jeans to a plain white shirt
and continue up to the most handsome, yet frightening, face
I know: MJ's.

Crud.

CHAPTER 19

Maddy

MY FINGERS CURL AROUND MY BIKE TO CONCEAL MY rising panic as he bends so we're eye level.

"Problem with your bike?"

Having no other choice, I look at him. *Really* look at him. He has a friendly, polite smile that makes his hazel eyes shine so much brighter than I remember. Everything on his face is perfectly symmetrical—even down to the dimples on his cheeks. He truly is too good to be true. But why is he happy to see me after the way our last strange conversation ended?

As I sit there frozen, gawking at the gorgeous and dangerous guy who has stolen so many of my thoughts, the words he said while attempting to hypnotize me drift through my mind. *If we ever cross paths again, I will be a stranger to you.* He thinks it worked. He thinks I don't remember him.

If I don't act as if I've forgotten him, who knows what he'll do to me.

"Uh ... yeah. The chain fell off."

His smile deepens and somehow becomes even more breathtaking. It's not fair he can look that good. Not when he has so many other unfair, unnatural advantages.

He gestures to my chain. "I can help you with that, if you'd like."

Resisting the urge to shudder, I peel my eyes away from him, slowly exhale, and snap the last piece of the chain on. "I'm good. Thanks, though."

I stand and hop on to my bike. As I push down on the pedal to ride away, my foot falls to the pavement and metal clinks against solid ground. Out of the corner of my eye, I swear I see MJ smirk. I look down, and my chain is now lying on the ground, broken.

What the hell? Dad just bought me this bike four months ago. I don't ride it *that* often.

I sigh, hop back off my bike, pick up the busted chain that's now a long metal snake, then stuff it into my backpack.

His hands slide into his front pockets, and he shrugs. "Bad luck. I could give you a lift home. My truck is just around the corner."

"No, thanks." I wash the grease off my hands in the fountain, then grab my phone. Mom and Dad won't be home for several hours yet. Even though I don't like depending on other people, I either have to walk or suck it up and call one of my friends for help.

I start dialing Luke, but the screen on my phone goes black. I repeatedly press the power button and nothing happens.

"Dead battery?"

"I don't know how. It was fully charged when I left my house this morning." I stare at my dead phone for a moment before stuffing it into my backpack next to the broken chain. Bad luck is right. Horrible luck, actually. It's almost as if all these events were created so I would be here at the exact moment he was. As if we were fated to be together again.

I snort at my ridiculous thoughts. Now I sound like Kelli. "It's just a coincidence," I say mostly to myself as I zip up my backpack.

"There's no such thing as coincidence," MJ says.

I suck in my breath as his words replay in my mind. I've heard them before—countless times. Damien said it to the Dream Girl the night they met. That's twice now he's reminded me of Damien. Why?

MJ shifts from foot to foot before saying, "My offer still stands."

If Damien and MJ are right and there is no such thing as coincidence, then we were brought together for a purpose. I wanted to find him, and here he is. I can't chicken out now.

I take a deep breath for courage and say, "I was raised to never accept rides from strangers. But ... " I trail off when disappointment flashes across his face, "maybe if we sat and talked for a bit, I could get to know you. Perhaps I'll ride with you after—provided you're not a psycho killer or anything." I watch his reaction, but he doesn't even flinch.

I'm not fond of riding with a potential killer, but to quote one of Dad's favorite movies, *The Godfather: Part II*: "Keep your friends close but your enemies closer." This is my best shot to see if he's a danger to Amber.

"After you." He motions to the benches behind him, and I move to the one on the end. That way, I can run if he tries anything.

He saunters over to the middle bench with a shy, relaxed smile on his face. "So, are you enjoying your weekend?"

I make the mistake of meeting his gaze and blurt, "No."

His handsome face falls, allowing my eyes the freedom to break away.

Why can't he be just a normal guy? Why does he have to come with so much baggage? And why did I just say that? What is it about him that makes me open up so easily?

"I'm sorry to hear that."

The devastation in his voice has me backpedaling. My weekend wasn't completely his fault. Justin cast a pretty big shadow over it too. "It's okay. The weekend's almost over."

He nods. "Yes, it is. There's still hope it could end well."

"No, there isn't. My week looks equally grim too." I grimace as I think about how I'll have to tail Amber. No matter what happens with MJ, following her around is going to suck.

"Hmm," he says. "That's unfortunate. Perhaps I can help. I've heard it's easiest to talk about your problems to a stranger."

I flinch and stare at him, trying to discern if it was a threat that he repeated the same thing he said Friday. He's smiling again, and it seems friendly. So it was on purpose then?

It doesn't make sense. Why would he try to erase my memory of him, only to approach me two days later? I don't understand him or his motives. I need to keep him talking. But if I say too much about him, I'll blow my cover. What if I talk about Justin? Stick to the nonpersonal information, like Friday. "Have you ever misjudged someone really badly, even when the truth was staring you right in the face the whole time?"

"Yes." He snorts. "Quite recently, actually."

Without thinking, I smile. He's probably referring to Friday before he went all *someone's-coming-to-kill-you-but-I'm-here-to-protect-you-with-my-totally-distracting-hot-body*.

"So ... " he draws out just long enough for me to peek over at him. He's slouching against the backrest, and his long legs are stretched out and crossed at the ankles. He looks relaxed, calm, confident, and in control. And because of that, I suspect he's not—it's a lesson I learned from Duane. Something has him nervous. Is it me? Is it the topic? Or is it something else entirely? "Is this person a male?" he finally asks.

My interest in MJ is overshadowed by thoughts of Justin. "That's one way to describe him," I scoff. "Although 'evil and manipulative snake' fits better."

He sits up, his brows furrow, his jaw tightens, and his fists clench. "What has he been doing?"

The sudden shift causes my heart to flutter and my insides to tighten. I have to stop myself from smiling. I like it. I like him getting mad about Justin. "I'm sorry, but I don't know you well enough to tell you that."

"Yes, I suppose that was a rather personal question. My apologies."

I rest back and stare up at the cloudy sky. "It's all right. It's just that this whole mess has me even less inclined to trust people than normal."

He chuckles, relaxing into the bench again, though not as much as before.

"What? I don't see how that's funny." Finding joy in people's suffering is definitely a check in the bad-guy box.

"No, that's not what I was laughing about." He pauses for a moment to straighten his face. "It's just that most people your age—I mean, our age—tend to be overly trusting. It's strange to hear you say you're not. That's all."

"Well, it didn't do me any good in dealing with him."

"I could speak with him if you like. I assure you—he would leave you alone."

I hadn't expected that. It would be nice not to worry about Justin anymore, and it would clear up whether they're working together. But Justin said only I'm immune to his mind-control ability. Who knows what he's capable of? I don't want to risk him messing with MJ's head. It's bad enough MJ can disappear. "Thanks, but I took care of it," I say.

"Oh?"

"He's a friend of my boyfriend, but I broke up with him yesterday. He has no reason to talk to me anymore."

"You ... have a boyfriend?" MJ asks in a deeper tone than he's used before.

My heart flutters again and I blush. "Had," I say, though I'm not sure why.

"I'm sorry. Did you ... love him?"

"Love?" I spit the word out as if it's poison. "I'm never going to fall in love."

I hear him take a sharp breath, but I turn my attention back to the fountain. I watch the water peacefully flow to the bottom for a few moments. But then an irrational yet well-known fear suddenly sears my heart—I don't hear him anymore. Did he vanish, like last time? Am I alone again?

Panicked, I look over. He's still sitting there, studying me. Relief washes over me. That surge of fear is gone, leaving my emotions scattered. It's been so long since this has happened. I thought I'd gotten over it.

I look back at him again. He doesn't look angry anymore. Just sad. Or sympathetic. He leans closer to me, and it takes everything in me to not reciprocate. "I promise you, it will get better. I'm sorry you had such a bad weekend."

"Thank you," I say, though I'm not sure whether it's because he cares or because he didn't leave.

I can't lie to him anymore. Even though I know I shouldn't, I feel so guilty about pretending not to know him. "That wasn't everything, though. Something else happened Friday."

At the mention of Friday, he tenses.

"I learned something terrible that night."

His jaw clenches.

I take a deep breath and continue. "Someone wants to kill a girl I know."

His entire body moves closer to me as he hangs on every word. It's empowering and incredibly frightening at the same time.

"And because she's in danger, that puts me in danger too."

"No, you're—"

"I am. I look too much like this girl. So much so that"—*please don't kill me*, I silently plead—"you mistook me for her."

Suddenly his bench empties, and he's towering over me. A loud crack of thunder erupts above us while my heart races. I meet his gaze and I can't look away. His muscles bulge and quiver as he calculates his next move.

Through my fear, a familiar feeling stirs within me. My body is on edge, waiting for him to do something just so I can fight him off. I've felt it twice before: the first was at Justin's party when I ran, and the other time was Friday at school with Justin. I'm still scared, but most of all, I'm angry. I'm angry at MJ for showing up and for being so confusing and handsome and ... so *him*.

I glare defiantly as I say, "You should know—I told Amber about you."

"Why?" he snarls, and I recoil into the bench as if he slapped me.

The wind howls and whips around us. Bolt after bolt of lightning surges through the sky, and deafening cracks of thunder roar. I want to cover my ears and look away, but I can't. I'm frozen to the bench by the weight of his deadly stare.

"Because I can't let you kill her!" I shout over nature. "She doesn't deserve to die!"

"I'm not here to kill her. I'm here to *protect* her."

I wish that were true. I don't want him to be a killer. I want him to be the guy from Hiniker Bridge, the one who made me open up as no one ever has. If I were to ever fall for someone, it would be someone like that. Someone who could make me feel happy even on my worst day.

His hand slides down the back of my bench, and right before he removes it, his fingertips touch the back of my hand.

At the point of contact, my skin tremors. In less time than a heartbeat, a rush of energy hits my muscles, nerves, and veins as it moves up my arm and spreads throughout my body. I gasp. It's similar to when I touched the static electricity demonstrator at the science museum last year.

MJ gasps too. He straightens and gazes around me.

We're now standing on Hiniker Bridge.

My eyes widen to take in more of the scene around me. Everything looks normal, except the colors are more vibrant. I feel like Dorothy walking out of that black-and-white farmhouse into the brand-new Technicolor world of Oz. The pond below the wooden bridge is a deep, dark blue. Hundreds of lily pads with fuchsia flowers float along on the surface. There's a big bullfrog on the one closest to us, and his throat is puffed up as if it's stuck mid-croak. Slowly, it deflates, and his croak lingers in the air, seeming to never end.

I look up, and lightning bugs are all around us, though they're barely moving. Every flap of their little wings is visible, moving in slow motion.

The trees that form the pond's border are bursting with green leaves slanting to the right. The longer I watch, the more I can see them move up then slowly down, as if a gentle wind blows them.

Above us is a sunset so beautiful, it rivals Friday's. Mom has a photo in her office of the sun setting over an ocean with the sky a dark blood-red just like this. Eventually it will set, but if it's as slow as everything else here, I'll get to watch it longer. Enjoy it more.

I lean on the railing, captivated by the wonder and beauty of this place. Everything is oblivious to me. If it's possible, I think this is what happens in nature when no one is around to spoil it.

MJ moves up to the railing next to me. Did he send us here? I was thinking of this place right before he touched me. If he did do it, then I'm thankful. I've never experienced anything so spectacular. But why didn't this happen Friday night?

I search through every memory of that night and find my answer: aside from slamming into each other, we never touched.

His right hand reaches out to where mine rests on the railing. He inches closer, but I doubt it's because he too has been affected by the speed of this place. I think he's afraid to touch me. I'm afraid too. His first touch brought us here; I'm sure this one would bring us back.

I should run away and not let him touch me—then I could stay here forever. But the thought of feeling that strange reaction again from his touch is just as enticing. My body pulses in anticipation.

As his fingers connect with the back of my hand, the same energetic, static-charged sensation rushes over my skin. The pond disappears.

CHAPTER 20

MJ

MY HEAD WHIRLS AND I STUMBLE BACKWARDS, HOPing not to fall into the fountain, but unsure if I could stop myself. Thankfully my momentum ceases, and I find my feet. I take a deep breath while attempting to piece together what just happened.

Somehow my essence was ripped from my body and transplanted on the bridge with her, only to return moments later. It wasn't the bridge from Friday, though. It was ... different. Another dimension, maybe?

My body feels strange. Tight and loose at the same time. Is this what a rubber band feels like? Contorted against its will, then released and expected to go on as if nothing happened?

Something feels warm against my skin. I look up, and blue sky and sunshine have replaced the dark storm clouds. I twist my arm, allowing the warmth to coat both sides. Microscopic dust particles dance in the light while the sun's rays recharge me.

It's impossible one creature can do all the things I've experienced in the past three days, yet I have witnessed them in her presence. Demon, witch—I don't know what she is. But the chances of her being human continue to decrease.

I'm torn between wanting her to be human and not. I want her to be human so I don't have to end her. But if she is human, her mental status is in jeopardy because she remembers me—and knows too much about me.

I almost wish another Protector were here, stuck in this perilous position instead of me. But the thought of someone else experiencing all these things—and singlehandedly deciding her fate—is worse.

"How did you *do* that?" she asks, awestruck. Her emerald eyes draw off the green in her shirt, making them appear brighter. It was the first thing I noticed when I approached her today, and I'm still just as transfixed by them. She should always wear this color.

"I—" I begin and stop as the excited smile on her face steals my breath. How did *I* do that? Is it possible she doesn't know *she* did that? Maybe. And if so, then perhaps she is also unaware of the other effects she instills in me too.

Quickest way to find out, however, is by asking the most important question. "How do you remember me?"

She blanches before averting her gaze. "I guess I'm not susceptible to hypnotism."

Demons are arrogant. Most would have grinned then revealed themselves, not have hidden behind false magic. She's very clever, though, so her reply could have been meant to lead me astray.

My fingers tap along my pants while I try to figure out where to go from here. "Do you mind if I sit?" I stop tapping and motion to her bench. Maybe if I'm closer to her, I can tell if her heart is really beating or if it's a mechanical device or a witch's spell.

Time stretches while I wait for her reply.

"*Okay*," she finally says.

I move to the edge of her bench, sitting as far from her as it will allow, ensuring she doesn't transport me again.

She looks at the fountain, and I listen for the sound of her heart. After a moment, I hear its steady sound accompanied by the swishing of the blood in her veins and the gentle inhale and exhale of breath as it fills her lungs. It's no gadget, but it could still be witchcraft. The sounds of her life are almost relaxing. If I slept, I could fall asleep to this.

Her body sags into the bench, and she sighs.

"Are you all right?" I ask.

"I'm fine. Just tired." Loud noises erupt from her stomach, and she presses her hands to it. "And a little hungry."

"Interesting." Could a demon, under the aid of advanced witchcraft, feel tired and hungry? This does provide me with a nice opportunity to stay with her. Actually, if I remember from my research last night, eating is one of the staples of a *date*.

It would be nice to figure out one way or the other what she is beforehand, though. Especially considering Alexander would never let me hear the end of it if I discovered, after the fact, I had dated a demon. Unfortunately, I can't think of another way to find out her identity other than taking the direct approach. "Please, don't take this the wrong way," I begin, "but what *are* you?"

"Confused. Afraid. Exhausted. Take your pick. I don't care because they all fit today. There, I told you what you wanted to know, so tell me the truth. Why are you here to protect Amber?"

"Hmm," I mumble, then sigh. I'd rather talk about her than my Charge. "I can't tell you that. You know more than you should already. What I can tell you is that I am honestly here to protect her."

"Let's say I do believe you—I don't yet, but let's pretend I do. When are you planning on meeting with her?"

"She and I will meet when we're supposed to. However, you and I are an intriguing development."

"What's that supposed to mean?"

It means you have taken everything I knew about life and tore it to pieces in your small, delicate hands. "Nothing," I lie. "May I give you a ride somewhere now?" Please say yes, I almost say out loud. I've run out of ideas on how to keep her from leaving. I thought for sure breaking the bike chain would work, but she's remarkably stubborn.

"I'm good."

"No. I'm sure you have a long way to go yet. I can take you home, if you'd like. Or someplace to eat?"

"Why?"

"To prove once and for all I'm not a threat to your friend."

"Amber is not my friend!"

Her outburst takes me by surprise. Without access to her thoughts, I can't follow her logic. "If she's not your friend," I say, "why do you care what happens to her?"

"I ... I ... It's hard to explain."

"Try me."

"Look. Just because I hate her freaking guts doesn't mean I'm okay with her getting hurt or dying. Besides, if someone you knew was in danger, wouldn't you try to stop it, regardless of how you felt about him?"

For the first time ever, I'm speechless. People say they would step in and save someone in danger. The truth is, most won't—and don't. But here she is, knowing more than she should about me and choosing to engage me for the sake of someone she doesn't even like. She'll make a great Protector one day... "You really are nothing like what I expected. And I mean that with all sincerity."

"Likewise."

I grin, and everything inside me stills at the sight of her lips curling into an answering smile. I stay locked in this state of suspended awe until she blinks. Slowly I release my breath. What do I do now? How do I uncover what she is—and if she turns out to be evil, how can I kill her? I need more time.

Her stomach rumbles again. She frowns and looks away.

"Food it is then," I say. "Wait here. I'm going to fetch my truck. But just so you don't get any funny ideas ... " I pause and grab her broken bike and toss her bag over my shoulder. "I'm taking these with me. I don't want to spend my evening wondering whether you made it home okay."

Her jaw drops, and I resist the urge to laugh while walking away.

Now there's nothing she can do or say to stop our date.

CHAPTER 21

Maddy

I MELT EVEN FARTHER INTO THE BENCH AND SIGH. I KNOW this is wrong—staying here with him. Each time we're together, I learn about another impossible ability he possesses, and for whatever stupid reason, it only makes me more drawn to him.

Whatever he did to take us to that version of Hiniker Bridge was amazing. I want to do that again. Over and over. It was so beautiful. Someone who can access a place like that can't possibly be bad, can he?

Mentally, I want to study him and figure out how he can do all these things.

Physically, I want to be near him, not just for the chance of experiencing whatever that was, but also because he stirs feelings in me no one ever has before.

Emotionally, I'm confused by him. He scares me, confounds me, angers me, and annoys me. But at other times ... he relaxes me, makes me feel safe and happy, and even gives me hope.

"Penny for your thoughts," he says, and I jump. I hadn't heard him come back.

"I was just thinking about how great it would be to be a fly on the wall when you finally meet Amber," I lie. I'm not confessing to thinking about him again.

The right side of his mouth curves up into a playful grin. "And why is that?"

All too easily, I'm lost in him again, feeling myself come alive as the outside world shifts out of focus. It doesn't matter that we're discussing Amber. We could be discussing ketch-up—as long as he smiled at me like that, it would still be enticing. "Remember all those expectations you had about cheerleaders on Friday?" I ask.

"Was I close?" he asks, arching his brows.

"Closer than you were with me."

He frowns. "Is she that bad?"

I want to laugh, but I hold it in as I reply, "Worse."

His beautiful face twists as if he's just bit into a lemon, and I can't hold it in any longer. I break out laughing, and after a beat, he joins in.

Once our laughter ends, he holds out his hand to me. "Come on, let's go eat."

As I stare at his hand, the spell is broken, and reality rears its ugly head. Even though I wanted to revisit his Hiniker Bridge, now I'm torn. If I touch him, and we go there again, that will mean it happens every time. I might get tired of that. But if it doesn't happen, then I'll be stuck wondering if that time was a fluke, never to be repeated. I'm not ready to find out which way it is. I stand and ignore his hand as I say, "I think I can manage."

Sitting beside him at the bench, I hadn't noticed his scent. Now that we're inside his truck, it surrounds me. I can detect freshly cut grass, fragrant flowers, and the crisp, clean air right after a thunderstorm. It's similar to what he smelled like Friday, but more potent.

I watch him out of the corner of my eye as we drive through town. His eyes keep shifting to different parts of me, though I don't feel self-conscious. I like him looking at me. But why? Why do I feel so comfortable around him? Why do I care about his opinion of me? I don't worry about anyone else's. Not wanting to delve into this, I stare out my window and ask, "Where are we going, anyway?" I probably should have asked that before I got into his truck.

"I'm new here, remember? Where would you suggest?"

"I don't know. What do people from Norway eat?"

"I haven't lived there for quite some time."

"But you must have had a favorite."

He falls silent again. Unsure if I'm bothering him, I rest back and listen to the Lumineers sing on his iPod linked to the dash.

"Meat," he finally says.

Meat. I roll my eyes. Well, that's helpful.

I think of every restaurant in town, trying to come up with something that would suit him. Then I smile. "I think I know a place you would like."

He follows my directions to Kodiak's. A large stuffed Kodiak bear greets us as we walk through the door. The walls are decorated with murals of men hunting and fishing. A line of skinned, whole chickens spin on a rotisserie over an open flame.

He walks up to the metal railing in front of the fire, watching more than a dozen chickens slowly pass by him. He licks his lips, gazing at them as a lion would his prey.

I shiver, recalling my own fears of him Friday night.

The hostess catches our attention and leads us to a booth on the far side. I keep my eyes on the menu as a waiter takes our order. Once the menu is gone, I have no choice but to look at him. He's staring at me, but I don't sense any animosity in his gaze. Curiosity, maybe? I stare back, wanting him to know he doesn't intimidate me.

"What?" I demand.

No matter what I may feel about him, I need to remember he's still dangerous. Justin fled town to escape him, and he may or may not be here to kill Amber.

"You don't like to talk about yourself much, do you?" he asks.

I frown. He knows more about me than most people. "The same could be said for you."

He grins. "Fair enough. So if you don't talk about you, and I can't talk about me, where does that leave us?"

"You can't—or *won't*?"

His lips purse.

I cross my arms in front of my chest. "I came here so we'd talk."

He leans into the edge of the table, and the wicked glint in his eyes steals my breath. "I doubt that's the only reason."

I ignore him and take a big gulp of Pepsi. Thankfully, the waiter arrives with our salads and a plate of fresh baked bread.

I take a bite of my salad, and it's delicious. MJ takes a bite—and stills. His eyes flash to mine for a moment, then they close as he chews and swallows the bite. When they reopen, his pupils are wide, excited, and he slowly savors his food.

I've never seen someone eat like him, like this is his first and last meal. Every single bite is fully enjoyed before he eats the next. I can't look away. Normally, he's so confident and closed off, but now I'm getting a glimpse into the real him. He's just a boy, perhaps nervous to be here, just like me.

"Don't you like your salad?" he asks when he places his empty plate on the edge of the table.

I look down and notice my fork is resting on my plate with what was supposed to have been my second bite. Embarrassed by how long I watched him, I flush and focus on eating my salad.

When our main course arrives, he eats each thing on his plate separately, enjoying it in the same strange way. And I'm lost, staring at him again. The way he appreciates each bite makes me feel as if he hasn't eaten in weeks. I can only eat half of mine; I should eat more to catch up to the many meals I missed, but I'm stuffed from my salad and bread.

He stares dejectedly at his empty plate; I offer him the rest of mine.

He eyes my steak and licks his lips. "You're sure?"

I nod. "You seem hungrier than I am anyway."

"Sorry. It's been so long since I tasted food." His eyes dim before glancing away. "Food this good, that is."

I slump back into the booth and watch him continue to savor every bite. I think he was telling the truth the first time. But how could he not *taste* food before this? A disability of some sort? Or what if he is a secret government experiment? Something like that is bound to have side effects. Maybe losing his sense of taste seemed like an okay trade for all the superhuman abilities he got in return. But then how can he suddenly taste things now?

"So who were you trying to call earlier?" At my blank stare he adds, "When your bike broke."

"Right. My friend Luke, for a ride. He has a truck too."

"Your ex?"

A sip of pop gets lodged in my throat, and I try to hold it back so I won't spit it all over him. "*Luke*? No. We're just friends."

He nods, seemingly satisfied with my response. "Why didn't you try your parents?"

"They're not home."

"Where'd they go?"

"They were in Wisconsin for the weekend. My father's band was playing there. They'll be home before it gets dark tonight."

"Do you have any siblings? Did anyone stay with you?"

His anxiousness stirs something unfamiliar inside me. My heart feels heavy with sympathy for him. I don't like being the cause of his worry. I want to do whatever I can to fix it, even if that means opening more of myself to him. "My little sister stayed at a friend's house."

"So you were alone all this time?"

"It's fine. It's like this most weekends."

He reaches across the table to where my hands rest along the table edge, but I pull them away before he can touch me. He pulls his hands back but leans into the table and says, "Yeah, but you've never run across someone like me on other weekends."

He has a point. I shudder as I remember Justin.

"I'm sorry for scaring you," he says. The sadness in his voice pulls on my heart. I glance up, and he's leaving his seat. He stops and stands next to mine. "Can I take you somewhere? Make up for everything I put you through and end our date on a positive note?"

My mouth pops open, and I'm sure the smack can be heard throughout the whole restaurant. *"Date?"*

CHAPTER 22

Maddy

M J THINKS THIS IS A DATE? WHY WOULD HE THINK that? This was just a way to have more time to interrogate him and hopefully figure him out. Plus, when he brought up eating, he didn't say anything about it being a date. I wouldn't have come then. I didn't even like going on dates with Ben. Besides, people don't go on dates with strangers. They date people they are interested in.

I blanch at the direction of my thoughts.

MJ can't *like* me. He's confusing, mysterious, and possibly dangerous. And he nearly attacked me at the park!

As he stands at the edge of my booth seat, I scan his expression, noting the small, nervous smile on his lips and almost hopeful look in his eyes. He's serious. The whole time I sat here observing him, he thought it was a date.

Oh man.

Oh man, oh man, oh man. This is not good.

"This is not a date," I tell him.

He slumps down onto my seat, and I scoot back to the wall. I'm cornered. I search around desperately for a way out, but there isn't even enough room to crawl under the table.

"Why not?" he asks. His voice takes on a sullen tone, much like Amber's when she doesn't get her way. "We went out to eat and got to know each other a little better. That makes it a date."

"You don't even know my name!" People at nearby tables look our way. I'm sure I'm verging on hysteria, but right now I don't care. I still can't get over he thought this is a date.

He stares at me as if I told him one plus one equals seven. He's just not getting it. Why doesn't he understand? It's as if we were on two different worlds.

Wait—he's from Norway. Maybe he *doesn't* know what a "date" is here.

I take a deep breath in an attempt to lower my voice. "M.J … here, dating is when two people *like* each other. They do things together—like go out to eat and then go do something fun, like a movie. It's different than this. We don't know each other. We're not together in that … way."

"Oh." He frowns and slumps back into the backrest. After a moment, he turns to me and asks, "What's your name?"

I smile. "Maddy."

"*Maddy.*" He whispers my name and visibly relaxes. It seems not knowing my name has tormented him, but I don't know why.

He stands and holds out his hand for me. "Please come with me, Maddy."

I hold back, still nervous to touch him. "Why?"

"Because tomorrow I start protecting Amber, which means today is my only chance to get to know you."

Silence grips me so hard, even my heart momentarily stills. All of the moments we've shared since Friday—both the good and the bad—float through my mind. Why do I feel so at ease with him? Why have I told him so much about me? Why does he remind me so much of Damien? And why am I now panicking at the thought of never seeing him again?

So many questions that still aren't answered. It can't be over yet. I know next to nothing about him. "What about when you're done with Amber?"

"When this case is over, I'm leaving. I put in for ... a transfer. All we have is right here. Right now."

I don't care about the damage this will do. I *have* to know him more. One day is not enough, but if it's all I've got, I'm going grab it with both hands and never look back. I nod wholeheartedly. I suspect no matter what he asks, at this point the answer will always be yes.

I follow him to the truck, lost in my thoughts. If today is my only shot to know why I react to him the way I do, then getting answers on Amber's behalf can wait until tomorrow. For the rest of the time we're together, I'm going to focus only on him and the feelings he instills in me.

He drives a few blocks before stopping. I look up at the neon sign on the building and turn back to him. "Bowling?"

"You said people eat, then do something fun. So now it's a date." He exits the truck before I can protest.

I have to fight to keep from grinning as I climb out and say, "It's not a date." He smirks, and I march into the building with him close behind.

After changing shoes, selecting our balls, and entering our names on the electronic scoreboard, MJ bowls first. He stands at the lane, watching his ball roll toward the pins, and I get the first glimpse of his tight jeans hugging his butt. I sigh. He really does seem perfect. It's not fair.

MJ gets a strike. An overwhelming sense of pride flows through me, and suddenly I'm applauding and beaming at him. "Nice shot."

He bows before taking his seat. And once again, MJ reminds me of Damien—he bows often in the dreams.

I walk up to the ball receiver, and my fingers slide into the holes of my swirled purple ball. I take a deep breath before striding down the lane and sending my ball at the spot right off the center, knocking all ten pins down.

"Great job, Maddy!" MJ calls.

I have an almost earsplitting grin on my face at the sound of *his* voice saying *my* name again. After a moment, I push down my elation and take my seat. "Thanks."

Not to be outdone, MJ gets another strike. "Top that," he challenges.

My heart flutters. "Is that a dare?"

He nods slowly.

"Game on," I say, and his grin widens.

As I'm lining up my shot, MJ says, "If I beat you, you have to admit this is a date."

The ball shakes in my hands as butterflies fill my insides. Heat flushes through my body, making my hands sweat. I can't let him win. Not because this is *not* a date, but because it has been *so* long since someone challenged me to a game of anything. I return to the ball receiver, put my ball down, and run my hands over the air vent before picking up my ball again. I hear MJ chuckle.

With a new reserve, I stride down the lane and thrust my ball with all my might.

The pins scatter.

Another strike.

MJ doesn't stand a chance.

I sashay down to him, smile innocently, and bat my lashes at him. "You're up."

"Asia."

"Huh?"

"You're up … you know, *Europe*. So I say, Asia. Get it?"

"I know your secret now," I whisper. MJ stills. I lean in closer, but not enough to touch him as we still haven't touched since by the fountain. "You like lame jokes," I say.

"It's okay. My dad tells them too. He would get a kick out of that one."

MJ lets out a long exhale, and his shoulders drop. He gazes down at me and smiles. "Just for that, you're going down."

The game goes fast as we continue to battle back and forth, both scoring strikes. As hard as I try, I can't remove the smile from my face. When he's like this—carefree, fun, normal—I almost forget the other parts of him—the disappearing, the memory erasing, and that rush of energy responsible for teleporting us—exist. They just don't seem to matter. Dating him could be fun, for a while. Until his assignment ends and he leaves me.

In his last frame, MJ bowls two strikes, then leaves a seven-ten split. I hear people groan. I look around to see a large group of spectators has gathered around us. I look up at the scoreboard. MJ finished with 298. I'm on pace to bowl 300. A perfect game ... with twenty people watching.

Whenever I've bowled in the past, I've always made sure I stayed under 200—even though I could bowl a perfect game each time. But this time, I wasn't paying attention to my score. I lose myself when I'm with him. I didn't even notice the crowd until now—until it's too late.

With my family, I should be used to being in the spotlight. They all are. Dad's on stage in front of thousands of people every weekend. Mom goes on TV to promote her books. And Hannah has been on the news several times when she breaks records in swimming. But I hate it. Knowing so many people are seeing me and thinking about me ... I don't know. It's just always made me nervous. Even before learning the truth. I'm good at all the sports and activities I've tried. Great, actually—and it comes so easily. But I'm not a showoff, and I hate being the center of attention. Maybe this aversion to attention is something I inherited from my birth parents. Maybe they were shy. I don't care. I don't want to be like them.

The happy bubble we'd been in vanishes as if someone popped it with a pin. I can't get a perfect score. But I can't let MJ win either.

The first ball rolls, knocking down all the pins. Crud.

I grab my second ball and toss it down the lane without even taking the time to line it up. But all pins scatter in another strike.

With the third ball, I take a deep breath, and this time aim off to the left. The ball knocks down all but three pins that wobble, causing a hush to fall over the audience as they watch those three stubborn pins that hold my fate.

I breathe a sigh of relief when they steady. My score is 297. Not perfect, but not enough to beat MJ.

The crowd disperses, but I can't stay here. My hands shake at my sides, and my chest is so tight I can't breathe deep enough. "Can we leave, please?" I ask.

He nods, and I change shoes, then rush outside to calm down. A harsh wind greets me. I hug myself and keep walking through the parking lot, trying to decide if I should just walk home or accept another ride from MJ.

"Stop, Maddy," MJ says, running up to me again. "Are you mad at me, or is it because you lost the game? Help me out here. I don't know what's upset you."

One day. That's all I get with a boy who is almost perfect for me.

I stare at his plain white shirt, knowing I can't look him in the eyes if I want to get through this. "Thank you for the date. It was great, really. But I need to go home now."

"Let me drive you."

"It's okay. I'll walk."

"No. We're eight miles from your … neighborhood. I still have your bike and bag. Come on."

He has my stuff, so I should ride with him, but I can't find the desire to do it. What's the point? Either way, this is the last time we can be together. "Good luck with Amber," I say, and I mean it. "It was surreal, but nice meeting you, MJ."

I turn away from his stunned, heartbroken expression and head for home.

CHAPTER 23

MJ

SHE CAN'T LEAVE ME. NOT YET. WITH HER, IT'S AS IF I were alive. I don't know why. I don't know how. Most importantly, I don't know if it's permanent. I'm not ready to find out.

I race across the parking lot, and in the time it takes for her magnificent human heart to beat, I'm standing in front of her. "Stay," I plead. "If you don't want me to drive you home then fine, I'll walk with you. Just ... don't say goodbye. Not yet." She doesn't reply. Her heart is racing and her hands shake at her sides. Something has her panicking.

Is it me?

Sure it is. I got so caught up in her, and I kept revealing my abilities. I nearly bowled a perfect game. That's not common, but somehow she kept right up with me.

I run my fingers through my hair, desperately trying to figure out what to do. If I could calm her down, maybe then she wouldn't leave.

Inspiration hits. She affected me through touch; maybe I can do the same. I have to try. Hopefully we don't go anywhere.

"This can't be the last time I see you," I say. "Please let this work." I reach out and grab her arms, absorbing the soft, silky texture of her skin. As my essence drifts into her, I picture waves washing up on the shore. After a few seconds, her heart responds and slows.

Good. That's very good.

I branch out, following the flow of her blood as it travels throughout her body. There are dark pockets—muscles and tissue clenched with worry and fear.

So much fear.

How did I not know she was this terrified? I focus on it, trying to break it up and understand why it's here, but nothing comes.

Her eyelids droop.

Oh no. She's getting too relaxed.

Before I can stop, she sways and collapses into my arms.

Hmm ... first date and I put her to sleep. I'm not off to a very good start. I shake my head, lift her, then walk to my truck. How on earth am I going to explain this when she wakes?

It's been nearly twenty minutes since I heard the last police siren. The town is buzzing with thoughts of Maddy. It's late, and they've been looking for her. My arm tightens protectively around her midsection as she slumbers against me in my truck.

I've tried to wake her. So many times. But she won't wake up, not until she's ready. Why is she so tired? I suppose it's my fault. I said it at dinner. *You've never run across someone like me on other weekends.* The whole weekend she was terrified because of me. For as often as I watched her, I knew something was up, but I had no idea. And to repay her, I nearly killed her.

I will never forgive myself for that.

I've gone many lifetimes and never come close to finding something like this. Like her. What is she? How did she bring us to the bridge? Looking back at it now, it was incredible. I could feel my body was still at the fountain, but I could also feel everything at the bridge. The bridge was so much more potent, as if it were real and the fountain were a dream.

Now she's here, in my arms. This feels so natural. As though my body was carved for the sole purpose of holding her. Even asleep, she affects me. Her heart beats so strongly against me, it feels as if my own heart were beating again.

I'm sure she's human. She has to be. But all her abilities keep me from being 100 percent positive. There is a way to know for sure—a test I've had with me all day. I just … I don't know what I'd do if I were wrong and she turned out to be a demon. I can't destroy her—not now that I've met her. I shouldn't have dragged this out for so long.

Taking care not to disturb her, I reach into my pocket and wrap my fingers around a velvet bag I picked up from the weapons shop before leaving Immortal City. I pull it out and roll it around in my hand, juggling the objects inside.

If humans were to find this, they'd think it was just a bag of gemstones. Expensive, for sure, but they are so much more than that. Segrego Stones are twelve enchanted gems that reveal demonkind. Each stone is a different color and cut, representing a specific type of demon. When a gem is near its corresponding demon, it turns black. Even witchcraft cannot shield a demon from these.

I open the bag of stones, close my eyes, and dump the contents into my palm.

Please don't let any be black.

I peek at my palm and shift the rainbowed gems around. I sigh with relief when I don't find any black stones. I pack the gems back up and place the bag in my pocket.

There. That's the final test. She's human. A remarkable, incredible, life-altering human. Alexander, or anyone else, cannot deny it now.

I need to tread carefully now. So far, she appears to be mentally stable, but without having access to her thoughts, I don't know where her limit is. One reveal too many, and she could snap. She's strong. Brave. But that doesn't make her invincible.

I sniff the air above her hair for the hundredth time since leaving the bowling alley, then sigh. Even though it's the dead of night, she still smells of a warm summer day.

Part of me wants to take her and run. That way, I can always feel this and always have her. But what she does, and what she is, goes beyond me. She must have been created for a very specific purpose. I can't be that selfish.

There is one other thing I'd like to try while she's so blissfully unaware. It will be my and the moon's secret...

CHAPTER 24

Maddy

SOMETHING RUBS AGAINST THE TOP OF MY HEAD, AND I think of home—Mom used to rub my hair like that when I was sick. I liked it. Not wanting to ruin this unexpected moment of peace, I resist the urge to fully wake up and instead allow my other senses to come back to me.

My legs are stretched out across something short, like a loveseat or a bench seat in a car. Something heavy is lying across my stomach. My back's pressed into something firm yet soft, and my head rests against something comfortable but also boney. Whatever it is … it's as if it were perfectly molded to me.

It happens again—the movement that woke me up—and my eyes flutter open in response. There's a soft green light coming from my left. I think it might be a clock, but my eyes are too fuzzy to focus on it. Where am I?

Scattered images flow through my mind. I remember my bike breaking by the fountain … MJ showing up … seeing the bridge ... riding in his truck ... dinner ... bowling ... him holding my arms ... feeling so relaxed ...

Suddenly the pieces snap together. I'm in MJ's truck. I'm sleeping by him. How did I fall asleep? I wasn't tired. What happened?

His chin moves for a third time against the top of my head as he inhales deeply, then sighs.

What do I do? Do I let him know I'm awake? Do I stay frozen? This feels strange. I don't know him and he doesn't know me. Why is he holding me like this? And why haven't I put a stop to it?

He moves again, and everything inside me stills, waiting to see what he'll do next. His chin moves farther back as he inhales my scent again, then I feel something press against the spot right above my ponytail.

He kissed me.

In a flash, I'm up against the passenger door, reeling not only from surprise, but also from the current that zapped through me. It was like the shock from dragging your feet across the carpet then touching a doorknob. I still feel it, pulsing through me.

"Why did you do that? What the hell were you thinking?"

He doesn't answer. Instead he slowly brings his fingers to his lips and lightly touches them. He pulls his hand away and stares at it as if he expects it to be different somehow.

"I'm sorry," he says. "I don't know what came over me. You were lying there, asleep, looking so peaceful, and it *felt good* holding you—" His hand falls to his lap before he stares out the windshield.

I don't want to hear more, and thankfully, he doesn't continue. I turn my attention to the outside world and notice for the first time the darkness that exists outside of the truck. "What time is it?" I cringe, hoping the dread inside me is wrong and I haven't slept through what little time I had left with MJ.

"Eleven thirty."

"*What*? How could you let me sleep that long? My parents came home hours ago. I was supposed to be there. Do you have any idea how much trouble I'll be in? Take me home now!"

I've never broken curfew before. Even in those first few months when I was über pissed after finding out I had been lied to my whole life. What will my parents do? I'll be grounded for sure. But for how long?

As I continue to think up possible punishments, the view outside my window becomes all-too familiar. MJ's driving to my house without me telling him the directions. How does he know where I live?

Before I can ask him, he turns onto my street, and all air leaves my body in a muffled cry. In front of my house sit several police cars, two FBI vehicles, all the band members' cars, and Kelli's parents' van.

Something's wrong. Something's happened to my family. Please let them be okay. Please don't make me be alone again.

I can sense MJ watching me, but I don't care. I just want to know what's wrong with my family.

He pulls into the driveway, and before he can cut the engine, the truck is surrounded. All faces but three are a blur. Mom, Dad, and Hannah are all here. Everyone is okay. So why are they staring at us with looks ranging from relieved to angered? What did we do?

My curfew ...

All this is because of me.

After everything Duane said yesterday about my family loving me, I don't want them to be mad at me. I wish MJ could just fix this. Take me away again and make it better. Maybe ... he can.

I reach for his hand, now resting on the seat between us. His jaw tenses. I'm sure he knows what I want him to do. Will he do it? Will he take me away from this and bring me back to his version of Hiniker Bridge or some other beautiful place?

As our skin connects, the hairs on my arm stand up as his enigmatic current works its way through my system. The leather of his truck seat vanishes, and instead, I'm now sitting on the bridge.

It's different than last time. The colors are just as beautiful, but it's nighttime. I rest back on the boards and stare up at millions of shining stars.

The air is filled with the sounds of humming bugs, but the noise is slower than I'm accustomed to, so I can't tell what they are.

It's warm again. It smells more fragrant too. I can pick out flowers and grass and campfires with roasted marshmallows and pizza pies. It's all around us. I think ... it's summertime here.

I look over, and MJ's resting on his side, his head is propped up on his elbow, watching me.

"Does this happen every time you touch someone?" Even as I ask him, I know the answer. We've touched five times, but this is only the second time it's happened. The first time was when I slammed into him on the path. We touched only a moment before flying apart, but I did feel a brief flash of something enter me. I thought it was just from the force of our collision. But maybe it was MJ? I've felt the current every other time we've touched, so it must have been him. The other times we've touched and didn't come here were when he held my arms before I fell asleep and when he held me in the truck. Wait—did he make me fall sleep? If so, I don't like it.

"No." He shakes his head for added emphasis. "This doesn't happen every time I touch someone."

"When does it happen, then?"

"I'm not sure. It's never happened before today."

So I'm the first … I like that, even if I still don't know what this is. I look around at this beautiful, peaceful place only MJ has access to. Come tomorrow, not only will I lose him, but I'll lose this place too. My chest tightens, and I can't help but feel disappointed. "Is this real?"

"It feels real, though we're not fully here."

"I don't understand."

"Well, do you remember Friday when I appeared in front of you on the path?"

I stifle a laugh. "Kinda hard to forget."

"Yes. I guess that's true. What I did then is like this, but slightly different. I believe a part of us is here, but not *all* of us."

"You lost me again."

"Hmm ... do you mind if I ask you a personal question, Maddy?"

My body tenses. He knows so much about me already, but this is the last day I'll get to see him. "Okay."

"Do you believe in God?"

I swallow a lump in my throat and clench my jaw. *God turned his back on me a long time ago, and I've done just fine without him. Not once have I seen a so-called sign of him or his angels, like all the religious freaks on TV talk about. God is a myth, like Santa. The Bible is just a book. And other than sitting on top of a Christmas tree or making a great Halloween costume, I doubt angels even exist.* But there's no way I can explain that to MJ. I shrug.

MJ lets out a long exhale. "All right. What about spirits or crossing over or life after death?"

"I guess." *Where is he going with this?*

"I can work with that. I believe this is an out-of-body experience. We're on a different plane, and our bodies are back in my truck."

"Seriously? You really expect me to believe *that*?"

"Do you have a better explanation?" he snaps.

Crud. I think I offended him. "No. It's just a little far-fetched, that's all."

Why is it, though? Between my dreams and MJ's and Justin's growing list of abilities, the world is so much bigger than I knew before. I'm here—I know that for certain. And I'm with MJ. Why am I wasting our time together trying to dissect this? I should just appreciate it. I wanted this.

"I don't care about what this is or how it works," I say. "I'm just glad we're here together."

"Me too," he says. Even though I don't look over, I can hear his smile in his words. "What were you thinking, the two times we've come here?"

If I tell him the truth—that I wanted to come to the bridge to be with the sane, safe, normal version of him—he might read into it. I'm not ready to explore the possibility that I *feel* something for MJ, so I don't want to vocalize it. He deserves an answer, though, so I tell him the partial truth. "I wanted to escape and go someplace I felt safe and happy."

I go back to concentrating on the stars. With ease, I pick out Ursa Major and Minor, Scorpius, Virgo, Draco, and a dozen more I have copied in this exact pattern on my ceiling. A bright light appears—a shining, pure-white beacon with a long tail. "What is that?"

He follows my gaze. As the light moves closer to Draco, he says, "Make a wish." Our eyes meet, and he adds, "It's a shooting star."

I wish he would open up and talk to me as easily as I do to him. Well, maybe it's not *totally* easy to talk to him, but it's easier with him than with anyone else. If he opened up, then there wouldn't be all this uncertainty around him and my feelings for him.

We both watch in silence as the shooting star inches its way across our sky.

"I'm sorry for scaring you back at the fountain. You ... *remembering* me was unexpected."

I don't know if he's talking because of my wish, this place, or some other reason, but I'm grateful for it. "That's the third time you've apologized for scaring me. Is scaring people a habit of yours?"

"No, but each time you've been scared and we've touched, we've come here."

I swallow a lump in my throat as I realize he's right. Why would *my* emotions cause him to bring me here, though?

"Knowing that," MJ continues, "part of me wants to try again."

My breath hitches. "In order to do that ... we'd have to see each other again."

He grins. "I'm working on it."

"But I thought tonight is all we get. I don't understand."

"I'm not sure I can handle this being the last night I spend with you."

My gaze lands on the shooting star again, and I make another wish that MJ and I will see each other after tonight. It's not about uncovering what he is or what he does; it's simply to spend more time with him.

I'm glad for the time we've had today, even though I was asleep for a huge chunk of it. I still don't understand how that happened. There is no possible way I would have gone from a panic attack to asleep so quickly. Especially not while I was with MJ. Unfortunately, I don't see any way to figure it out other than just asking him. "Did you *make* me fall asleep?"

He sighs.

I look over, and our eyes connect.

"Before I tell you anything more about me, can you promise me something?" he asks.

"What?"

"No matter what happens, don't change who you are."

"Why would I—"

"Just promise me you won't let it affect you."

As I look at him, I notice a tightness around his lips and eyes. He's honestly worried about how I'll react. I get it. It's why I haven't told my friends about my past. Whatever MJ is, he thinks telling me will change the way I think about him. He's said over and over again he's here to protect Amber. If that's true, and I now think it is, then he has to be good. "Okay. I promise."

MJ smiles and rests back to gaze at the sky. "I'm ... different."

I snort. "No kidding."

He flashes me a look, and I bite my lip. "Sorry."

He takes a deep breath and continues. "I have *abilities*. One of which I use to sense and alter people's emotional and physical needs. For some reason, though, it doesn't work with you."

I should be freaking out, but I'm too caught up in the later part of his admission. "Why not?"

"I don't know. When we touch, I can feel your needs, but I can't find the reason behind them."

"So if I was sad and I touched you ... "

"I'd feel sad too."

"Hurt?"

"Yes, I would hurt too."

"A-afraid?"

He doesn't respond instantly as for the others. I look over, and he's watching me. His eyes are dim, and he's frowning. "Why are you afraid, Maddy?"

I grind my teeth and stare down to the boards between us. It's true; he can tell what I'm feeling. I definitely don't like that. If we're able to see each other again, I'll have to monitor my emotions before touching him.

"If it's me," he begins, "you don't have to fear me. I won't scare you again."

I don't reply. I want to believe him, but the odds aren't in his favor.

"I panicked when you tried to leave." He stops, and I look back up at him. "I wanted to make you stay, but I knew my mind-altering ability wouldn't work on you. I did the only other thing I could think of. I put you into a state of deep relaxation—though I hadn't intended for you to fall asleep. Still, watching you sleep is better than watching you walk away."

"So ... you *drugged* me?"

"No. That's not what I did."

"You affected my body without asking my permission. It's close enough. And you still expect me to trust you?"

"You still don't trust me?"

I huff in response.

As much as I dislike what he did, there's a part of me that's glad he did it. I was so overwhelmed by all the attention at the bowling alley, I couldn't think straight. I had to get away, even though that meant getting away from him. He erased all that panic and calmed me. Nothing has ever stopped my panic attacks that fast. "How many abilities do you have?" I finally say.

"Hmm ... I don't know. I've never counted."

I rest back and watch the same shooting star pass over Virgo. This is crazy. Everything he's saying should have me panicking, but I'm not. I search myself, just to make sure there isn't a block on my emotions, like Damien had done to Elizabeth in my dream last night. But there isn't one. I feel ... completely comfortable with MJ here.

"Are you okay?" he asks.

"Peachy."

"Did you mean what you said in the bowling alley parking lot? About the date being great?"

I grin. "It wasn't a date."

"I won, so you have to admit that was a date. And just so you know, it was the best date I've ever had."

I've had many dates with Ben, but I've never felt as relaxed, happy, and more like myself than I did with MJ. Even with freaking out at the end. "Me too."

"So what brought us here tonight?"

Dang. I forgot we aren't actually here and that there's a huge, disappointed mob waiting for me.

I glance over at him. His eyes are filled with a look that reminds me of our first night together when he said, "*I'm going to do everything in my power to save you.*" Back then, he thought I was Amber. Now he knows different, so why is he looking at me as if he will do whatever it takes to keep me safe?

So what did bring us here? Even though I barely know him, I don't like lying. But saying nothing—my usual response in situations like this—doesn't feel right either. "Because my family is disappointed in me, and I'm afraid to find out how badly I hurt them."

"Would it put your mind at ease if I told you everyone outside my truck was relieved you're okay?"

A heaviness around my heart lifts. Does he know that, or is he guessing? Either way, I say, "It does make me feel better."

He slowly releases his breath. "Good."

I hadn't noticed this until now, but his voice sounds lighter. Less ... stressed. Has he been this worried the whole time we've been here?

"When we go back, my family is going to want answers. What should we tell them?"

"The truth tends to work best in situations like this."

"So what's the truth?"

"We talked at the fountain, and I offered you a ride when your bike broke."

"Am I supposed to know you?"

"Well, Friday was ... interesting, but if it comes up, say we ran together."

Perhaps it's the depth of his gaze or the strength of his words, but deep down, I know this is important to him.

I'll say what I must to protect him, and after that, he'll leave. "Stay with me," I blurt.

"What?"

"You said it yourself—tonight might be all we've got together. Stay, just until everyone other than my family leaves." Maybe keeping him close will give me the strength to face the consequences.

"If I promise to stay, can we head back now? I know time runs differently here, but I don't know the exact speed."

I take one last fleeting look at the sky. As the shooting star moves out of sight, I look back at him and nod.

Slowly, his hand moves to mine. I take a deep breath, and his static-energy fills me. I exhale as the scene changes. We're back in the truck, staring out at the crowd.

"Huh," he says, and I turn to him. "It's 11:36. When we left the truck, it was 11:35."

All that time, and only a minute passed here. "So what do we do now?"

"I think it's time we greet your party." He lets go, then steps out of the truck. He grabs my belongings from the truck bed and enters the frenzy I created.

Inside I'm trembling. Something makes me brave enough to exit the truck. But whether it's fear of what the police and FBI might do to him or some residual feelings from his touch, I can't be sure. All I know is that I'm not ready to be apart from him.

CHAPTER 25

Maddy

MJ AND I WATCH ON FROM THE SAFETY OF THE DINing room window as my parents thank everyone outside for helping *search* for me today. The majority of them leave, and I know what's next isn't going to be pretty, but I don't care. All that matters is that MJ's standing beside me.

The entire right side of my body is buzzing, begging me to move. Wanting to touch him to see if we stay here or leave again. This time, I want to stay. With the exception of sleeping, I've only ever felt his hand. I try to imagine what it would be like to hug him and feel his whole body. Warm. Strong. Safe. It would be like the completeness I've felt in my dreams when the Dream Girl and Damien are together, before the dreams changed.

"Your mother and sister seem close," MJ says.

Standing beside Dad, Mom has her arms wrapped around Hannah. They're both tall and thin and have brown eyes and hair, though Mom's hair is short and layered and Hannah's comes down to the middle of her shoulder blades. "Yeah.

They've always been that way. Mom wasn't supposed to be able to have kids, so it's a miracle Hannah was even born."

MJ is silent for a moment before asking, "Wouldn't you be a miracle then too?"

My hands clench into fists at my sides. "I'm *not* a miracle."

"How far apart are you and Hannah?"

"Nine months."

"That's not possible."

I turn away from my family and meet his dazzling hazel eyes. "Why not?"

"Because it takes time for a woman's body to heal after pregnancy. The closest two kids should be is ten and a half months."

My eyes widen as I finally realize what MJ might discover if we keep going on this point. He can't know about this. Not yet. "Hannah was born premature," I say.

"You're breathing faster. Are you all right?"

"Not really."

"Why?"

I can't tell him the truth. Instead, I pick a lesser reason. "I'm nervous about why some of the people are staying."

He stares at me for several moments before turning his attention to the remaining crowd. "Do you know them?"

Even though it was a ploy to change the subject, now I really *am* worried about it. "Most of them." I point with shaking fingers to the smaller group. "The spikey-haired blonde cop is Anne. She's dating the band's drummer, Pam—the short-haired brunette woman next to her." I take a deep breath and move to the two people dressed in black suits.

"You see the tall guy in the middle next to the red-haired lady on the phone?"

"I see him," he says. His voice changes for some reason. He's almost snapping. "You know him?"

"He's my uncle and godfather. I talked to him yesterday morning."

His eyes narrow as he stares at Duane. "You told him about me, right?"

"No. Why would I?"

He flashes his attention back to me. "After everything you saw me do ... it doesn't make sense that you would keep it to yourself."

I shrug. "I didn't think he would respond well if I told him I met a boy who disappeared right after attempting to erase my memory."

His lips twitch again as he fights a smile. "No. That wouldn't have gone over well."

Duane's head turns, and he glares at MJ through the window. Without thinking, I lean closer to MJ.

From the corner of my eye, I catch his hand moving toward mine. "Don't be scared," he whispers. "Don't think about anywhere else."

Trying not to think about something when someone tells you not to is like a dog trying not to eat a biscuit someone has placed on its nose. It's possible, but not without enduring mental torture. He grabs my hand, and I gasp as heated vibrations reverberate through me, causing the hairs on my arm to stand up. I'm not sure if it's because I'm more awake this time, or if it's because I'm not thinking about anything, but it feels more powerful. It's stronger, faster, deeper. I feel so … alive. I imagine it's what my phone feels like when I plug it in.

The current lessens as it flows from me and back into him. He gasps as the hairs on his arm stand up too. His eyes flash to mine. Time slowly ticks by as the current continues to flow between us.

"We stayed here," he says. "I hadn't expected that, but I'm glad. As much as I enjoy going to the bridge, I'm glad I can touch you without being uprooted—or putting you to sleep."

"Me too." I turn my gaze away from him, and I'm reminded of where I am and what is happening. "Thanks for staying, but you should leave now. I don't want them blaming you." And if there is even the smallest chance that MJ is a government experiment, a superhero, or whatever, I have to keep Duane away from him.

Movement to my right claims my attention again, and I turn to see MJ lifting his free hand cautiously to touch me. His other hand is still holding mine. Everything in me stills, waiting to see what kind of reaction multiple points of contact spur. My hand tightens around his as he inches closer. "Don't think," he says. "Don't move. Just … be here with me."

Slowly, as if savoring every second, he grabs an unruly strand of my hair and tucks it behind my ear. His knuckles slowly slide down my jawline, igniting a flame inside me.

"Everything is going to be okay, Maddy. They're just worried about you. I can see that now. If you were mine … I would be worried too."

My entire body pulses in the wake of his touch. His words *"if you were mine"* keep circling around in my head, and with each rotation, something inside me grows. He makes me feel happy and less broken. I feel I could take on the world as long as he's beside me. Whatever he is, I don't care. I've never felt anything like this, and I'll go to Hell and back to keep it. Regardless of what happens to me, I have to protect him. I have to keep him safe, always.

He grins and squeezes my hand again. My body responds with such intensity, I almost feel as if I were floating. I don't want it to ever stop. I want to stay strong. I want to be brave. I want to feel safe. He gives me all of that. I want to hold him forever, even if it's only his hand.

"Tomorrow," he says, pulling me from my thoughts. "I'll find a way to see you."

"Promise?"

His grin turns into a joyous smile. His hazel eyes brighten, making him look as if he were glowing from within. It's devastatingly beautiful.

My body flushes, but I don't want to turn away in embarrassment. I never thought I would feel this. I don't deserve it, but I want it. I want to spend time with him. Get to know him. Have him look at me as he is now—as if I'm his whole world—over and over again.

A man clears his throat behind us. MJ lets go of me and steps away. His body stiffens. I follow his gaze to Duane, my family, and Pam and Anne.

"Madison," Duane says sternly. "Go in the living room with your parents. I need to have a few moments alone with your guest."

My eyes return to MJ and I see him glaring at Duane. Whatever MJ is, he isn't a big fan of the government. Is it true then—is he some experiment? Is Duane the reason why MJ is what he is?

I move between them.

Duane's furious eyes land on me. I want to recoil. I've never made him mad, but I stand my ground. It's my fault Duane found MJ. I can't let Duane take him away. I can't let them experiment on MJ as if he were a lab rat. "No. I'm not leaving him alone with you."

"Madison," Duane growls, "get—"

"It's all right," MJ interjects. He steps forward and grabs my hand. "I'll be fine, and so will you."

"You're sure?"

He nods.

I don't want to leave, but staying will only raise suspicions. However, if Duane tries to take MJ away, I will barricade the door. I need MJ. He makes me feel safe, happy, and complete in a world that no longer makes sense.

Reluctantly, I leave his side and move to the living room.

CHAPTER 26

MJ

N O MATTER HOW MANY TIMES I THINK THINGS WITH Maddy can't get any stranger, I'm proven wrong. She's in the living room, being questioned by the woman she called Anne. And I'm sitting at her parents' dining room table with Duane the Shadowwalker—who's posing not only as a human, but also as her uncle.

To the untrained eye, he looks composed and in control, but I can see the bead of sweat falling down the side of his neck, and I can hear his fingernails scratching his pant leg under the table.

He should be nervous. He knows what Protectors do to Shadowwalkers—he stood by my side during his training as I carried out the sentence on three separate occasions.

The instant I get him away from her, I'll send him to Hell. Not only is he a disgrace to me and all Protectors, but he's using Maddy for her abilities. She doesn't belong to him.

I felt it earlier—her soul. I listened to it while she slept. There were so many emotions floating around in it, and even though she was unconscious, I couldn't understand why those emotions were there.

When I kissed her … it was like kissing a lightning bolt. Raw. Powerful. Uncompromising. I've never felt anything like it. If she hadn't pulled away, I don't know if I would have been able to pull away from her. Something entered me. It immobilized me. It wasn't bad. It was … unexpected. But the most astonishing thing is that it was only a kiss on her head. What would it be like to *really* kiss her? What would happen if I marched into the living room, pulled her against me, and kissed her? Right here. Right now. In front of everyone.

I'm sure the Shadowwalker would take issue with it, but would Maddy? She didn't seem that mad about the kiss. Just surprised.

When we touched by the window, and my essence completed a cycle through her, it came back stronger. Her essence had attached itself to me. Somehow hers is fractured. It's still more powerful than any I've ever felt, but there was this sound with it. I imagine it to be the sound of grief. But not from mourning the loss of someone else. More like her soul mourning *her*. As if a part of her is missing. It could explain why I can't sense her essence outside of her. But what caused her soul to break?

"I know why you're here," the Shadowwalker says. "And judging by what I heard outside, you noticed some … things about Maddy."

I momentarily put aside my hatred for him as I lean closer. "Do you know what she is?"

His fingers stop scratching, and he narrows his eyes. "What she is isn't your concern. She's not your Charge."

He dares to throw the rules in *my* face? He broke most of them when he walked away from his duty as a Protector and stayed down here after his first solo assignment. He was only one month into his training with me. He had potential for greatness.

If I were following the rules, I would have sent him to Hell the second I saw him. But for Maddy's sake, I'm waiting. I'm breaking a lot of rules lately. But because of that, Maddy is still alive. According to the rules, I should have sent her to Hell as well.

He has to know too that Maddy violates our rules. Maybe that's why he's so nervous. "It doesn't matter that she's not my Charge—I am *very* concerned. She's unknown to Heaven, able to resist most of my abilities, and has a Shadowwalker pretending to be family. Her very existence breaks several of our rules."

He tilts his head and leans closer. "What do you mean, she's unknown to Heaven? Did you check the Records of Humanity?"

I nod.

"What about the Room of Innocence?"

I glance back at Maddy, and she's gazing at me inquisitively. She shouldn't be focusing on me with everything going on in there. I wish I knew what she's thinking.

"A-and the Record of Souls?"

I sigh and turn back to the Shadowwalker. His eyes are wide, no doubt realizing what this means. "She is not known to us."

His eyes plead and he reaches for my hands, but I quickly move back. "She's human," he says. "I promise. I met her when she was three days old."

"What do you mean? You've known her that long?"

"Yes. I've watched her grow. She's human. She's good. She's innocent. I don't know how or why she does what she does. Believe me—I've tried to figure it out. But there's nothing. No explanation."

"When did she start having abilities?"

"As far as I can tell, at birth."

We both look out to the living room. Her mother is questioning her now. With our heightened senses, we can hear them.

Maddy is telling them about her bike breaking down and her cell phone dying. It makes me shake my head. I had to go to such lengths just to get her to talk to me. She's so guarded. Even now, after everything we've done together, she still doesn't trust me. Is the Shadowwalker why she doesn't trust people?

Maddy's mother comments that Maddy looks pale and questions when she last ate. I don't think she's pale. Maddy's perfect. Beautiful. I can't help but smile and think of our date. The food was amazing, but Maddy made it unforgettable.

Her mother presses her for what else she ate this weekend. I don't see why she's making such a fuss. Maddy seemed to handle the weekend fine on her own.

Maddy's sweet voice fills my ears as she says, "I ate Thursday night."

I suck in my breath, and Duane does the same thing. Maddy's staring at the floor, unwilling to look at anyone.

It can't be true. She couldn't have gone that long without nourishment. She hasn't eaten since Thursday night, yet she didn't even finish her food with me several days later? She wouldn't lie about it, would she? She doesn't seem like the type who seeks attention that way.

If it is true, how is it possible? She should have been weak, dizzy, but she wasn't. Either she's lying or she has more abilities than I've noticed. But I've only been around her a few days. What more does the Shadowwalker know about her?

"Does she know what you are?" I ask.

"No. I haven't touched her since she was a baby."

"With all the things she does ... how can you resist?"

"It's difficult. When she was a baby, she cried a lot. I was the only adult who could calm her, but it took a great deal of my essence to do it. She was so scared and unhappy. But even then, as a tiny baby, I couldn't figure out why she felt the way she did."

I shift closer to him, determined to learn all I can about her.

"The first time I held her, her essence flowed into me, making me actually *feel*. All those years I had stayed down here, living in the shadow of what I remembered feelings to be—I wasn't even close to the real thing. That day, she filled me with love and brought me to my knees. I vowed to protect her always, and that's what I've done."

"How do you keep her from touching you? She can feel our essence too, and that shouldn't be possible."

"Maddy has grown up thinking I have what mortals call germophobia—a fear of germs. I altered her family's memories to support it."

"I see." I take a breath. "Does it fade—the feelings she gives us?"

"Yes. If you leave her alone, you should be back to normal in a few weeks."

"You and I both know I can't do that. She's afraid of something, and I don't think it's just me."

I listen in as her mother continues questioning her. My insides tighten when she says Maddy looks exhausted and they've heard she hasn't slept all weekend. It makes sense now. That's why she was so tired. Between not eating and not sleeping, I know I'm to blame.

"You need to leave her alone," he insists. "You're here on a Charge. My guess is you mistook Maddy for Amber. It's easy to—"

"How do you know so much about my Charge?"

"I track killers with the FBI. I've been assigned the same case. I know it's a demon, so I'll keep the government from finding him. I knew Protectors would be sent, and I'm sure the demon does too. He'll be killing faster now. Once he comes here, what do you think he'd do if he saw you with Madison?"

I slump back in my chair. He'd confuse them, just as I did Friday night. All I want now is to be near her—but that could be the very thing that kills her.

"If you care for her, you'll leave this house and never see her again. If she dies and she's unknown to Heaven, that's it. This otherworldly girl will either be sentenced to Hell or cease to exist. Can you face eternity knowing you brought that fate to her?"

All the air rushes out of my body as the weight of her life once again rests on my soul. I turn back to her, memorizing as much as I can about her—the way her soft arms wrap around her torso, the color of her eyes that match the emerald gemstone still in my pocket, and soft pink lips I never got to touch.

Goodbye, my Maddy. I stand and find the strength to walk out the door and leave the best thing that has ever happened to me.

CHAPTER 27

Maddy

EVEN THOUGH THE KITCHEN STANDS BETWEEN US, I CAN still see MJ. Both his and Duane's lips are moving rapidly, but they're talking too quietly for me to hear.

Things aren't much better in the living room. Dad, Mom, Pam, and Anne are my judges, jury, and executioners. Hannah was sent to bed, though I'm sure she's at the top of the stairs listening.

I've watched enough cop shows to know what comes next. I want to get through this fast. The longer I'm separated from MJ, the bigger the risk. Not just for him with Duane, but me too. My throat burns as I hold back my fears and anxiety. I can't cry in front of MJ. If I can just detach myself from the whole situation, I think I can pull this off.

Anne's face is expressionless, but I can see in her eyes she's struggling. She still pictures me as an insecure, shy little eight-year-old secretly dancing in the corner of the garage while the band practiced.

She takes a deep breath to steady her nerves, and we begin her interrogation. "Are you okay?"

"Yes."

"Did he hurt you?"

"No!" I didn't mean to shout, but I had no idea they thought that. My eyes flash behind her to MJ. He's nodding as Duane talks, but MJ seems ... upset about something. I wish I knew what they were talking about.

"Who is he?" Anne asks.

"MJ."

"And how do you know this *MJ*?" Her eyes narrow as she says his name.

I can feel a smile forming as the memory of how we met runs through my head. It's almost comical now, but still confusing. "I met him at the park on Friday, and we went running together," I half-lie. I ran, he apparently watched.

"What have you been doing since Friday night?"

"I watched TV, did some homework, and went shopping with Kelli this morning." There's no need to go into the horrible details of Justin. Not like they would believe me, anyway.

Mom leaps up from the couch, making us all jump. "We get home from a nice weekend away, and you aren't here. There's no note saying where you are. Hannah hasn't seen you all weekend. I tried calling you. I tried texting you. What's the point of having a cell phone if you aren't going to answer it? I called all your friends—thankfully, at least Kelli saw you today."

I know I've upset Mom in the past. She wants me to be perfect like Hannah, but I'm not. I'm flawed and have been since birth. That's something she will never understand. Still, she's the only mother I've ever known, and now I've hurt her. I can't even look at her.

"I'm sorry. My bike broke on my way home. I tried to call a friend, but the battery on my phone died."

Mom sighs in exasperation, and her voice softens. "You look pale. When's the last time you ate?"

My eyes fly up to her face, and it's filled with concern— she still cares for me. "Earlier, with MJ."

"And before that?"

I cringe, knowing they will make it a big deal when I admit the truth. It's not like I was starving myself. I was just so distracted by everything. "I ate Thursday night," I confess.

Multiple sharp breaths sound all around me, even from the dining room. I can't find the nerve to look at MJ. I don't want to see his expression.

Anne tries to regain control, probably to keep me from closing up. "Okay, but where have you been since you left Kelli?"

I hold back my joy at our not-a-date date and continue my recount of today. "While I was dealing with my broken bike, MJ was driving on Belgrade, and he saw me. He offered to give me a ride. I agreed. We went to eat and hung out for a while. But then I fell asleep in his truck before I could tell him where I lived." I've never slept in a boy's arms before— not even with Ben. It was great.

"You look exhausted too," Mom says before Anne can continue her questioning. "Kelli told us you've barely slept all weekend."

Nausea and panic ripple through me, and my eyes fly to MJ. Please, Mom, stop talking. Please don't let him hear.

His posture stiffens, and his eyes met mine. They're … hurt. Does he worry he's to blame—that I haven't been eating or sleeping because of him? I don't want him to think that, but I can't tell him the truth either. My problems are not his responsibility.

Mom falls to her knees in front of me and hugs me. It's the biggest display of affection she has shown since I shut her out, but I can't react. I'm frozen, trapped by the enraged and pained expression on MJ's face.

"Why? Why didn't you tell me you haven't been sleeping, Maddy?" she asks. "It hurts me so much that I had to find out from your friend. And do you know what it was like when we couldn't find you or contact you tonight? Do you know the horrible things that ran through our heads? We thought you were lying there, injured, in a gutter somewhere."

Even from this far away, I can see MJ flinch.

She releases me only to grab hold of my hands. "We called Anne and Duane to see what we could do."

I break away from MJ's gaze to see the tears pooling in my mother's chestnut-brown eyes.

"We knew, according to Kelli, you were alive earlier today. But after shopping, your day was blank. Anne called in to the station and put out an Amber Alert. Duane called in favors with his team, and they flew up here. We tried to piece together your weekend with the little bits you told Kelli. I don't know how you're even functioning right now. I can't get over the fact you haven't slept well since Wednesday!"

Her voice becomes white noise as my eyes flash back to MJ's. There's pain and confusion in them.

Duane says something, and MJ's face falls. He looks at me, but it's different than all the other times. Suddenly, I feel so cold. An ache builds in my chest, and even though there are a half-dozen people here, I feel lonely.

I watch with a sense of numb detachment as MJ stands and walks out of my house without so much as a second glance my way.

As the door closes, my panic sets in. I have no idea where he lives, and I don't know his number. All I have is his name, and that's useless. He's the first person to make me wish the feelings that exist in my dreams were a reality. Now he's gone before we ever had a chance to begin.

My will shatters. Tears run down my cheeks. "I'm so sorry. Please don't … " I couldn't get the words "leave me" to escape my mouth. It hurts too much. As if someone put my heart in a vise and squeezed all the blood out of it. I can barely breathe. Why does this hurt so badly? I hardly know him.

My mother throws her arms around me, hugging me and saying how glad she is I'm home safe. But I can't reciprocate. All I can think about is how her hug is keeping me from running after him.

When she finally releases me, MJ's long gone.

I walk to my room in a haze. To my family, each teardrop means I understand just how much I hurt them and the seriousness of my actions.

But I'm not crying for their benefit. I know I hurt and scared them, and I should feel bad about that. I should feel *something*, but I can't. I'm numb. Hollow. Empty. It was so easy for him to leave—as if I meant nothing to him.

I just want to lay here, listening to the rain pelt my windows.

A knock on my bedroom door makes me cringe. What more could they want from me? I wipe away my tears on my sleeve. "C-come in."

Duane enters, and my lip quivers. Before tonight, I never would have done anything to upset Mom, Dad, or Duane. I managed to hurt all of them today. Part of me wants to get up and run into his arms, but Duane is a germophobe. He would hate it if I touched him, so I stay put instead.

He's quiet and hard faced for a moment, then his expression softens, and he sits on the edge of my bed. "Madison, I know what happened between you two on Friday."

I hold my tongue, resisting the urge to say, *I highly doubt that.*

"Why would you break every rule I've taught you during our camping trips for a boy you don't know?"

Duane's seen some pretty twisted things on the job, so I never balked at his rules. There's more than twenty of them. But the most important one and the one he drilled into me repeatedly is, always tell him when I meet someone. Doesn't matter if I say hi to someone at the park or if we get a new student at school—he wants to know every detail about them. But even after knowing MJ for less than a day, I couldn't stand the thought of Duane hurting him or the possibility of never seeing him again.

"I didn't want you to know about him. He's good. I *know* that."

But it's not the only time I've broken that rule lately. He doesn't know about Justin either, but that's not because I want to hide him from Duane. I just don't want Duane to be ashamed of me for making poor decisions, which led me to meet Justin. That party didn't feel right the moment I stepped through the door, but I still stayed for Ben.

"Hmm," Duane says as his light-blue eyes meet mine. "What else did MJ tell you? Do you feel strange in any way? Do you have any desires to do anything you wouldn't normally do?"

Weird. It's as if he's trying to see if MJ messed with my mind. Sure, he tried to erase it, but he sucks at it. And he wouldn't make people do things. MJ's not like that. Justin is.

My grief steps back as realization moves in: Duane knows something about MJ and Justin. Is it true, then? Did Duane have a hand in their creation?

"No, I feel fine," I answer. "Why? What do you mean?"

"Madison, you trust me, right?"

"More than I trust anyone."

"Good. I can't explain why, but you're not allowed to see MJ ever again. He's not what you think. He's a threat to you."

"What are you talking about?"

"Maddy, think about it. MJ's in town to protect someone from a killer, and he mistook you for her. The killer may know who MJ is, and he may know MJ's trying to protect this other girl. What's to stop the killer from mistaking you for her if you're with MJ? I can't have that."

"Is that what you told MJ?"

"Yes, and he agrees, so you will never see him again."

That's why he looked so devastated and guilty. He *was* leaving me.

Duane keeps talking, but I don't hear what he says. MJ left me. After today, after everything we did and he said … he just walked out.

Duane stands and pauses on his way to the door. "You're so special, Maddy. I'm not just saying that as your uncle and godfather. Get some rest. And no more of this not-eating business. You need to keep your strength up. That's an official order from the government. I'll see you soon. I love you."

As the door closes behind him, I fall back on my bed. Special? Does he mean I'm a freak? Why now? In sixteen years, no one other than Amber has ever said or done anything to make me feel like a freak. And now Duane, MJ, and Justin have in the same weekend. What's wrong with me?

I change into PJs and climb back into bed. I bury my head in my pillow and listen to the rain while silent tears fall.

CHAPTER 28

Maddy

MY BODY SHIVERS UNCONTROLLABLY, BUT IT'S NOT from crying. I'm cold ... so cold. I don't remember opening the window, but it's freezing in here.

I roll over in search of my missing blankets, but instead my skin burns as something very cold and wet sticks to it.

My eyes pop open, and everything is white. I can barely see. An arctic wind whips around me, bombarding me with little snowflakes that sear my flesh. The chill in the air steals my breath and turns it into puffs of vapor.

I examine what I can see of myself. My skin is pale, not the beautiful, sun-kissed tan that the Dream Girl has. I'm me and I'm solid. So I'm not dreaming? How did I get outside? I don't remember being told that I sleepwalk, but I'm learning a lot about my sleeping habits lately.

How far did I walk? I can't tell. It's a blizzard out here, but it's not supposed to snow for another month.

A burning sensation builds in my feet; my leg muscles cry out as if they were on fire. I have to get out of this before I get frostbite.

In the distance ahead of me, I can make out the shape of a building. I think it's a home of some kind, but I'm too far away to see for sure.

The snow crunches as I try to run toward the building. It's difficult, even without the violent shaking and overwhelming numbness creeping up my legs. The snow is up to my calves. I'm so cold. I just want to stop and rest awhile, but there isn't another soul out here.

The snow rises up past my knees as more snowflakes descend from the sky. A strong wind catches me off guard, and I fall into the snow.

I could stay here. The snowdrift is blocking the wind, and it's soft. The numbness is blocking the pain. Death would be peaceful. Like falling asleep.

My family's disappointed faces from last night drift through my mind. If I stay here, that will be the last thing they will remember about me. It would be the last thing MJ remembers about me too. I don't want that.

Slowly, I get up and trudge on. It's hard; I can barely lift my legs. They're heavy. So heavy. My insides feel as if they are beginning to crystallize. If I fell over again, would I shatter like an icicle?

Snowflakes stick to my clothes, and the unrelenting wind quickly turns them to ice. The only warmth I have left in me surrounds my heart.

The building is closer. It's a cabin, and there's smoke coming from the chimney. The thought of a fireplace gives me the strength to lift my legs up the three wooden steps of the cabin's porch, despite my upper body shaking so badly I can't control myself.

The chattering of my teeth competes with the howling of the wind. "P-p-p-please, let s-s-someone be h-h-home."

With shaking hands, I reach out for the door handle, and it swings open before I touch it. I shuffle in.

I can't tell what's in my periphery. The only light is in the room ahead of me, and it does little to illuminate this room. I know I need to move toward it, but I'm so tired. My body aches from shaking so much. The few muscles I can still feel are being poked by thousands of tiny, imaginary needles.

It is just a little farther. You can do it. You are a fighter. You can survive this. You need to survive this. So much depends on you surviving this.

It's strange—it was my voice, but those weren't my thoughts. It's as if someone else put them in there, like when Damien spoke inside the Dream Girl's mind last night. The cold must be messing with my head.

I continue through the doorway.

I can see the fireplace is the source of the light. I'm sure it's warm in here, but I can't tell. I'm still so numb.

Do you see the blanket? Go to the blanket. You can sleep once you reach the blanket. Rest now. You are going to need it.

I listen to the strange voice and search the room. In front of the fireplace is a blanket stretched out on the floor. I drag my heavy body to it.

My body collapses onto the wooden floor, and I wrap myself up like a twitching burrito. I'll rest my eyes for just a minute...

TALKING AND LAUGHTER INTERRUPT MY DREAMLESS SLEEP, but I can't make out what they're saying. It's soft, like whispering. My eyes open, and the fire is almost gone. The bottom is filled with blaze-orange embers that smell heavenly, like the maple chips Dad uses in the smoker for ribs.

I can't think of home yet. My family's pain, anger, and disappointment are more than I can bear right now.

I'm still cold, but at least I'm not shaking as much as before. My body aches in protest as I slowly sit up, flexing every joint down to my toes to ensure there's no frostbite. I sigh with relief. I'm good. I'm sore, cold, and hungry, but good.

Clinging to the fuzzy hunter-green fleece blanket, I look around at the place that saved my life. The room has wooden furniture with huge red cushions. The walls are wooden logs. Above the fireplace is a painting I recognize as a Thomas Kinkade.

I've been here before, but when?

Someone giggles in a different room, then my jaw drops as they walk toward me.

You have got to be kidding me. After this strange near-death experience fighting through the snow, I end up in the Dream Girl's cabin? But it doesn't make sense. I'm me, not her. And my body hurts so much from the cold. This can't be a dream. How is this even possible?

I thought I was done. I said I didn't want to do this. I didn't have a dream when I slept in MJ's truck.

MJ.

I can't. I can't think about him. It's too much...

The Dream Girl tugs Damien's hand, pulling him to the couch. "I didn't know you could cook," she says. "I'm stuffed—that was delicious. I'm glad we're snowed in."

"I have never had someone to cook for. I am glad you liked it," he replies.

I remember which dream this is, and I don't want to stay here. It's Halloween, the one-year anniversary of the night they met. They talk all night. And they kiss.

Seriously, what did I do to deserve this? I pull the blanket back over my head. There's no place like home. There's no place like home... Come on—if it worked for Dorothy, it can work for me.

"There are bumps on your skin," Damien says curiously.

"I'm fine, Damien," the Dream Girl replies.

"No. You are cold."

Hey, oblivious one. You see the shivering blanket in front of the fireplace? Yeah, there's a person under it who's way past cold.

"I'm fine, really. Leave the fire alone, and stay here with me. You'll just have to warm me up," she says.

I've played this scene enough to know the choreography by heart. They're on the couch, and she's trying to keep him from standing up.

"The fire is low, and you require a blanket," he says, gently pulling away from her. "I do not wish for you to become ill."

She'll let go, and he'll walk to the fire and toss a log on it. Then he'll grab the blanket and go back to her. I've seen it all before. Now send me home.

Wait!

I'm in front of the fire. He's going to come right to me. And if he doesn't notice me when he adds the firewood, he will when he takes away the blanket. I'll be saved.

The floor creaks as he walks closer. Another step, and he'll either kick me or step on me. I'm still so numb, I doubt I'd feel a thing. But just in case, I pull my legs in tight and brace for impact.

As his foot connects with me, images of bloody faces withering in agony from being burned alive surge through my mind. Their high-pitched shrieks threaten to rupture my eardrums. My hands fly up to try shutting them out. Everything evaporates.

THE SOFT SHEETS OF MY BED HAVE REPLACED THE FUZZY blanket, so I know I'm safe in my own room. But I can still hear the screams.

Oh … I'm screaming too.

I stop and listen for a moment to make sure no one heard me. All I hear is my father's snoring. Mom must have her earplugs in. Hannah and Dad could sleep through a heavy metal concert in the hallway.

My face is soaked with tears, and my body shivers, though I can't tell if it's from being cold or being terrified.

I curl up into a ball and rock back and forth on my bed. I don't know what happened in the dream. One minute I was on the floor, slowly thawing out and regaining the use of my limbs—moments away from them finding and saving me.

Then Damien stepped through me, and I saw faces—so many faces—of people being burned alive. It was the most horrific thing I have ever seen.

How did I see those horrible things? I don't understand. It didn't happen until Damien and I connected, but he couldn't have anything to do with what I saw. He's good. He's always been good. But what other explanation is there?

Have I been wrong about him, like I misjudged Justin and MJ? I formed my opinions based on information the Dream Girl showed me. But that's changing now. She's been showing me more. Between the deals he made with her father, the way he sometimes controls what she's thinking, and how he can insert himself into her dreams, I know she had been hiding dark things from me about Damien. The question is, why is she choosing now to show me the truth?

No matter how long I stay in bed, I'm not going to get any warmer. I have to shower for school anyway. Even though it's just after five in the morning, I might as well get ready. It'll probably take me a while today.

Normally my showers are scalding hot, but I know that'd be bad this morning. If my body goes from extreme cold to extreme heat, I can damage my nerves. I don't want nerve damage at sixteen, so I turn the knobs to what should be lukewarm. As soon as the water touches my skin, I still recoil as if I touched the burner on a stove.

This is crazy. I never even left my bed, but my body's reacting as if I really had been in the snow. How can a dream do this? It shouldn't be possible. At least it was just a dream, though.

I feel as if I've been given a second chance at life. I'm not going to waste it.

I will sort out my dream business. There has to be a reason why I have them and why they changed. I will figure out who—or what—Damien is. I need to know if he's somehow capable of the horrible things I saw.

I will find MJ. I will find out exactly what he and Justin are. I will find out why some of MJ's abilities work on me and why some don't. Threat or not, I still feel safer with him than I do with Justin. I'll just have to keep my feelings for him in check. After all, I thought Damien was perfect. And now he might be a truly Dark Prince.

CHAPTER 29

Maddy

I HATE BEING COLD. EVEN THOUGH IT'S SUPPOSED TO BE IN the upper sixties today, I toss on a tank-top, long-sleeve shirt, V-neck sweater, and a hooded sweatshirt instead of my standard T-shirt. My toes still feel frozen, so I make the painful decision to leave my flip-flops at home and opt for my cowgirl boots and thick socks too.

But it doesn't help much. I need something better. Something to warm me up from the inside out and replace the horrible things I saw and felt. Hot cocoa and fluffy white marshmallows may not suffice, but they'll help.

Downstairs, I make my warm chocolaty salvation. I take a sip and feel a small spark of warmth as it slides down my throat. This is what I needed.

While I'm making my second cup and eating a blueberry muffin, everyone comes down to grab breakfast. When they take in my outfit and the powdered chocolate mess on the counter, they stop and stare. I guess it's a little odd.

After everything that happened when I came home last night and then during my dream, I don't want them to be mad at me. I want them to forgive me and still love me.

Air is squeezed out of me as my entire family hugs me. Before I have a chance to relax into this rare family moment, they pull away as if I stung them.

"You're so cold," Mom says as they all exchange worried glances. She places her wrist against my forehead and checks me for a temperature.

Great. As if I need another reason for them to worry about me. "Relax," I say. "I had a dream about snow, and when I woke up, hot chocolate sounded good. I feel fine. I'm sure it's just from not sleeping lately. I just need a few decent nights to catch up." If I'm ever able to sleep without dreaming again.

"No," she says adamantly. "I'm calling Dr. Marks's office. With you not sleeping or eating, and now how cold you are, I'm worried there could be something wrong."

"Mom, I feel fine, and I'm going to school. I have a test and a speech today I can't miss." It's true, but I don't care about them. All I want to do is follow Amber to find MJ.

"Maddy, you need—"

"I promise, if I don't feel well, I'll call you."

She taps her toes for a moment then stops and throws her arms around me. "Oh, Madison. I died a thousand times yesterday thinking something happened to you. I love you. You know that, right?"

No. But I'm starting to. "Um—sure, Mom."

She lets go and fans herself as if she's trying not to cry. "Okay, but I want to know right away if you feel like coming home. You've been through so much. I don't want you over-doing it today just because of a test and a speech. You need sleep too. A few hours in a truck and a little last night isn't enough."

The truck. Why did she have to go there? My arms wrap around me in an effort to keep from falling apart as the memory of MJ leaving comes barreling back. Somehow, I need to move past this. If I'm going to see him face to face, I need to stay strong.

"Oh, another thing," Mom says, and I resist the urge to groan, wondering what else she wants. "Were you in the office this weekend?"

"No. Why?"

"Duane wants to take you to Canada next summer, so you'll need a passport. He wanted me to grab some of your documents so he could take them with him last night, but I couldn't find your birth certificate or Social Security card."

Canada? I suppose we have stayed at most of the national parks in the state. I shrug. "I haven't seen 'em."

The first time I saw my birth certificate was after Duane told me the truth. I thought it would give me a clue about who I am, but it was a dead end. Dean and Marie are listed as my birth parents. Other than Duane, no one in the government even knows I was adopted.

"Okay ... well, we're going to be late if we don't get going," Hannah says, motioning for me to follow her to the door. Her chestnut eyes are bright, full of promise for the day. She's such a morning person.

Thank you, I mouth to Hannah, and she smiles back conspiratorially.

"Maddy," Dad says, "why don't you ride with me today? I'd like to have a word with you."

This is the first thing Dad's said to me since Thursday. I know I disappointed him last night. It hurts me more than anything. Even a tiny bit more than MJ.

"I'll take you to school, Hannah," Mom says.

Hannah gives me a look of sympathy. This is weird. Why do we all need to ride separately? Hannah and I always walk or ride our bikes together when she doesn't have swim practice, unless there's snow.

Dad must want to talk to me *alone*.

I do want to apologize to him, so I grab my backpack, follow him to the garage, and get into his white Buick Skylark.

"Duane told us what you talked about when you called him this weekend," he says as we pull out of the driveway. "About love."

"Oh." Well, now I know what was up with the uncharacteristic displays of affection in the kitchen.

"He was right. I do love you, Madison. We all do."

My heartbeat quickens when I turn to look at him. "Even after yesterday?"

We pull up to a stoplight, and he meets my vulnerable gaze. If he says no, I don't know what I'll do. "There is nothing you can do or say that will ever make me stop loving you. I love you unconditionally, and I always will."

"But ... but I'm not *yours*."

"I can never replace your birth parents. I thought—we thought—if we never mentioned them, you would feel you belonged with us. But I know now that was wrong. I think you need to find them, Maddy. They left a hole in your heart no amount of love from us can fill."

"I'm sorry, Dad. I'm sorry for worrying you yesterday, and I'm sorry for not talking to you about this. But I'm not going to find them. They didn't want me, and I don't need them. You're my family." They've *always* been my family.

His eyes, one blue and one green, glint with unshed tears. "I'm pleased to hear you say that, but how could you possibly think they didn't want you? Giving up a child for adoption is one of the most difficult decisions a parent can make. It's a decision you're stuck with for life. Before you write them off completely, try to put yourself in their shoes. They could have been struggling financially. One or both of them may have been ill and not able to provide for you in all the ways you deserved. There are so many possibilities, but not wanting you isn't one them. If that were the case, they wouldn't have taken the time to name you."

The light turns green. I turn and stare out my window, unable to respond.

I hate my birth parents. But that hasn't stopped my stupid heart from wishing they had never given me away and that they loved me.

"Is this what has been keeping you awake at night?"

"No." I have a strong desire to laugh. My birth parents are a piece of cake compared to boys who have a seemingly endless supply of abilities, ranging from disappearing to mind manipulation.

"Oh? Then does it have anything to do with the young man you were with last night?"

I close my eyes and bite my lip. Oh, Dad, if only I could tell you... "Some."

"Whatever it is, I can help. This old man was once in high school too, you know."

I wish it were just a normal high school boy problem, but I'm not normal and neither is MJ. Worse yet, Dad can't know about this. Justin may come back one day, and anyone who knows about him will be in danger.

I need to distract Dad. This subject isn't safe. "We don't ride dinosaurs to school anymore, so I think things have changed a little from *your time*."

"Dinosaurs! I'll show you a dinosaur." Before I can stop him, he grabs my overly ticklish spot right above my knee.

In the crammed confines of the passenger seat, I squirm and laugh uncontrollably. I hope no vehicles pass us—I'm sure I look like an idiot. "Stop! I surrender! No more old man jokes!"

"Always my ego booster. Sorry, kiddo, but I couldn't resist. I wanted to see you smile before I dropped you off."

As I look at him, I see it—his love for me. Whenever he looked at me like that in the past, it made me feel guilty. As if he were doing it only out of pity or obligation. But this time, it's different. Maybe I'm different?

I smile. I am loved. The notion fills me, spreading a little more warmth outward from my heart. If he can love me, even though I'm not his daughter by blood, then there's hope for me after all.

"So ... did you get a chance to look at my bike?" I ask.

"Yeah. I'll get a replacement chain later today. New chains don't normally break like that. It must have been defective."

"Yeah. Maybe." It was good MJ was there, though. Walking home with a broken bike would have taken forever.

But what if … MJ *is* the reason my bike broke? I mean, what are the odds he would show up right when I was stranded? Not to mention the fact that my phone stopped working then too. It sounds crazy, but maybe it's true. I don't know what he can do. I don't know what any of them can do or how they're connected.

Everywhere I turn, I'm surrounded by danger. Damien claims my night. MJ and the killer claim my day. Justin claims my future. It's closing in. But how can I prepare for it when I don't even know what I'm facing? MJ is my best hope of solving this. Somehow, I need to find him and get him to talk. He can be my daytime mission. At night, I'll work on Damien.

I need to know if Damien is *real* or just a realistic figment of my overactive imagination. If he is real, then maybe he killed all those people I saw when we touched. I don't like thinking that, but with all the changes in the dreams and the anger and violence I sensed in him last night, I can't ignore it. I hope I'm wrong. If there's even the smallest chance he's a killer, learning as much as I can about him could help save not only future victims, but the Dream Girl as well. She can't die. I have to protect her from him. I just hope I don't die in the process.

That would definitely suck.

Dad pulls into the school parking lot.

We say our good-byes, and I head into school with my head held high. In spite of Justin, MJ, my dreams, and my past, my dad loves me unconditionally.

CHAPTER 30

MJ

I T'S BEEN EIGHT HOURS SINCE I LAST SAW MADDY. EIGHT long, agonizing hours. Decades have passed faster than this. To distract myself, I'm doing what I've been assigned to do: protect my Charge.

I haven't introduced myself to Amber yet, but I've been with her in the Veil of Shadows for the last twenty minutes while she chats with her friends before school. All I've managed to do is count the ways she differs from Maddy. Each time I look at her is a painful reminder of what I can't have.

To make matters worse, everyone here is talking about Maddy's disappearance last night. Apparently she's a student here. I hadn't planned on that. Thankfully, there are more than three hundred students in their grade alone, so the chances of me running into her are slim. A brief glimpse in the hallway from time to time. It would be torture, but it would be far worse if they shared a class together.

The mere thought of seeing her again has my stomach twisting in on itself. The only thing that could save me from months of torment would be for the killer to break his pattern and come for Amber now. I'd send him to Hell, easily, and then I could go back to Heaven and be reborn.

Thinking about it now, I know I can't do that. The pain of knowing her and never seeing her again is excruciating, but it would be worse to forget her.

I will send word to the Council to cancel my transfer once Amber's first class begins.

The laughter and conversations of Amber, her friends, and every other student stop as all heads turn to the door.

I follow their gaze, and there stands Maddy.

CHAPTER 31

Maddy

I DON'T KNOW WHAT WAS HAPPENING BEFORE I WALKED into school, but I can't shake the feeling they were all talking about me. I hang my head and walk to my locker. My heart races every time someone whispers as I walk past them.

Is this some kind of joke? I showered. I'm not sick. Why are people treating me like a pariah? My fingers ball into fists, and my leg muscles twitch as I fight the urge to run away. I should've stayed home.

At my locker, all my friends are there. They've decorated it with a big balloon that says "Welcome back."

Being that I never actually *went* anywhere, the balloon is a bit like pouring salt on my wounds. My friends didn't mean it like that, though.

The wind is knocked out of me again as Kelli, Kayla, and Maggie all hug me.

"Oh my God, Maddy, we were so—"

"Worried about you," Kayla and Maggie say, one beginning and one ending the sentence. Their brother, Jake, nods his agreement from behind them. The girls let go, and Shawn, Luke, and Mason wave as they move closer to me.

Jeez, this is more hugs than I've had all year. "I know. I'm sorry, guys." A small smile tugs at the corners of my mouth. "Thanks for the balloon. I like it."

The balloon floating high above everyone's heads, above all the negativity that exists outside my small circle, is a helium-filled sign that I too can rise above it all.

My friends glance at each other, wordlessly asking each other whether any one of them gave me the balloon. They shrug when it appears it didn't come from any of them. I brush it off and open my locker. A mass of flowers tumble out like an avalanche. There must be hundreds of them scattered at my feet. They're all lavender roses. "Wow! You guys, this is … too much."

"Um, Maddy … " Kelli says nervously.

I look up at her, now beaming with how deeply they all care for me.

"We didn't do this," she says. My other friends all nod as I turn to them for confirmation.

"So, if you didn't do it, then who did?"

"Well," Shawn says, "it's quite simple, really. You have an admirer."

Immediately, I think of MJ. My insides grow warmer, fighting against the coldness left over from the morning. "Why do you say that?"

"Because he sent you lavender roses," he replies matter-of-factly.

I narrow my eyes in confusion, and Mason asks, "What the heck does that have to do with anything?"

Shawn rolls his eyes through his Harry Potter–style glasses. "Every flower has meaning. Not just type, but color too. Purple, or lavender, roses are used to signify love at first sight."

I gasp. MJ is declaring his feelings through flowers? And he feels so strongly already?

"There's a card!" Kelli squeals. Maggie, Kayla, and Kelli huddle together, clasping hands and trying to conceal their glee.

I look again at MJ's affections sprawled out at my feet. Near my locker is a red envelope. It's thick and heavy. It must be one of those cards that plays a song or recorded message. I glance around, and now there's a large crowd gathered near me and my friends. At the center is Amber, glaring at me and my flowers.

I wish they weren't here. That way I could hear MJ's message in private. But I can't wait—I want to know what it is. I rip the envelope open.

There's a picture of a chess piece, the black queen, on the front but no words. Flipping the card open, a song begins, and I see the inside is blank. On the third note, the card falls from my fingers as I recognize the song. Marilyn Manson's version of "Sweet Dreams."

It's the song Justin whistled when he left the school Friday.

The balloons and flowers are from him.

I back up into the row of lockers. "Get rid of them! All of them," I say, stunned.

"Jeez, Freak Show." Amber laughs. "You didn't get enough attention last night?"

It only takes a moment to realize Amber is the reason everyone other than my friends is whispering about me. Her aunt is our neighbor, and she gossips almost as much as Amber.

I look up at her, and she's holding out her phone, recording this. I scan over the rest of the crowd, and they're all amused, watching my horror. The only ones straight-faced are my friends, but their eyes betray them. They're shocked and worried by my reaction.

I take a deep breath and step aside. "You like them so much, you can have them."

"Fine," Amber huffs. "I'll take them. Whatever idiot sent them is obviously too good for you anyway."

Students rush at the flowers and card, eagerly snatching away Justin's taunting message. Once all the flowers are gone, the crowd breaks up with several guys whistling the eerie tune.

I shiver and wrap my arms around me, trying to keep myself together.

Most of my friends say their good-byes and head off to class. The only one still left with me is Kelli.

"So what's with the outfit?" Kelli asks, curiously looking me over.

"It's nothing. I'm fine." I stab a pen into the balloon, successfully deflating it.

"You really expect me to believe you after whatever just happened?" she asks, pointing at the broken stems, petals, and leaves left at our feet.

I shrug and toss the balloon in the garbage.

"You're not even going to attempt to explain?"

"Nope." She doesn't remember Justin, so there's really no point. I slam my locker shut and walk the mostly empty halls toward chemistry with Kelli by my side.

"Whatever. Even without the strange flower giveaway and the defenseless balloon mauling, I can tell you're not *fine*. You want to know why? 'Cuz you're wearing socks. You hate socks. You wear flip-flops until there's measureable amounts of snow on the ground. Is this because of Norway?"

"Norway?"

"Do you know more than one person from there?"

"No."

"Good. Then that's what we're going to call him. Now answer me."

I hold myself even tighter as MJ's face comes barreling back. I take my seat at our black lab table. She gazes at me, still dissecting my out-of-character attire, awaiting my reply. She's not going to let this drop, so I consider my options.

I could tell her the truth. She's the only person who knows about my dreams and witnessed their craziness first-hand. But if she knew what happened in last night's dream, she would insist on telling my parents. They would make me see a doctor, and I would most likely be locked up. Even I know that dream was so far beyond crazy, it scares the crud out of me.

I can tell her the partial truth, admit this is a product of a dream. She doesn't need to know it was one of the Dream Girl's.

And lying full-out to her is not something I can do. She knows me too well.

"I had a dream about snow last night. I was stranded somewhere, but I found a cabin and warmed myself up in front of the fireplace. I guess thinking about snow for that long made me cold. If my system wasn't so out of whack from this weekend, I'm sure I would be all right by now."

"Huh. Weird. But at least it wasn't one of *her* dreams. No offense, but you looked like poo yesterday. Today you seem better—other than being cold and rejecting some poor fool's attempt to win your heart."

"What?"

"Well, it's obvious Norway didn't do that. He's not the Manson type. Who else are you hanging out with outside of school?"

"How do you know it isn't someone from here?"

"Please. No one here is that romant—"

"He is *not* romantic! He's a jerk. Plain and simple."

"A mighty fine jerk," she mumbles under her breath.

"What? Did you *see* him set that all up?" Please tell me she didn't. He's still in Florida. He has to be. He just used his mental abilities to *make* someone else do this.

"I didn't see him, but I wish I would have. I have to settle for imagining him." Kelli's eyes drift off as she says, "Your admirer has smooth black hair that hangs just shy of his eyes, which are piercing black. He always has a smile 'cuz he likes to joke around and be the life of the party. He wears all black too, giving him this dangerous, edgy look. But no matter how hard you fight it, something about him draws you in. Eventually, you will go to him. You can deny it all you want, but a guy like that isn't going to walk away from you. Just give up now and go to him. It will save you a lot of heartache."

I blink repeatedly, holding back my fears, at her precise description of Justin. Yesterday her memories of him were gone. Is his ability wearing thin—is she remembering him again? Or has he done this new trick to her? Is she another one of his messages?

"I'm not going to him. Ever."

"If you say so." Kelli turns the page in her chemistry book and reads about the lab we're doing tomorrow. She whistles "Sweet Dreams," and I cringe, knowing there is no denying it: Justin made her do this. He found her and turned her into a pawn in this sick, twisted game he's playing with me.

I'll fix it. Somehow I will make him leave my friends alone.

As Kelli and I make our way to choir, many eyes are still on me. Even though I avoid looking at them, they take turns whistling Justin's song as I pass by them. Even though he's thousands of miles away, he's made it feel as if he were right next to me. It's as if he wants me to know there's no place I can hide from him.

"So," Kelli says. My insides twist in knots, hoping she's not going to bring up Justin again. "If you won't talk about your swoon-worthy admirer, what did you and Norway do yesterday?"

When I think back to my time with him, it makes some of the dread of the day melt away, enabling me to take a deep breath. Even though MJ's not here, just thinking of him makes me feel safe. "We sort of had a date."

"What!" she fumes. She grabs my arm and yanks me to a stop. She narrows her eyes and glares at me.

I get why she's mad. If I were half the friend she is, I would have called or texted her during my date, as she has done on hers—from the bathroom or during some moment the guy wasn't looking. But MJ consumed my every thought when we were together.

He claims a lot of them when we're apart too.

"Sorry," I mutter a weak apology. I'm not sorry I didn't tell her; I'm sorry I hurt her feelings.

"I spent hours yesterday panicking, searching for you, thinking you'd been destroyed. And you were on a *date? With him!*" Kelli's pupils dilate. Blackness spreads over her calming blue eyes as her body shakes.

On reflex, I step back from my friend. "Why did you say *destroyed?*" And how did her eyes change? What did Justin do to her? What did he tell her?

After a moment, she sighs and runs her fingers through her hair. Then her body stops shaking and her eyes return to normal.

"I'm sorry," she says. "I just hadn't expected that. But I should have after seeing your faces last night."

"What do you mean?"

"It's obvious you've fallen off the deep end for him. I've never seen you look at someone like you looked at him. It was like the old Maddy was back. If things keep going like that, I'm sure you'll end up married someday."

I ignore her remark about the old me and instead focus on me being married to MJ. I've never really thought about marriage before. What would it be like to spend the rest of my life with him? My heart starts to flutter. I like the idea much more than I should. He deserves someone better than me. I wouldn't even know how to love him. I don't even know how to date properly.

"What makes you so sure? You didn't see his face when he walked out last night."

She lets go of me and smiles a bright, genuine Kelli smile, and I know she's come back to me at least for the moment. "I didn't need to. I saw his face in the truck when he brought you home. I'd rate it somewhere between Romeo and Edward."

"What?"

She rolls her eyes. "He had this look. It's like he would do anything for you. Romeo killed himself when he thought the love of his life died, then she killed herself because she couldn't be without him either. Edward denied his feelings as long as he could to protect his love from himself, but when they finally got together, she died to stay with him."

"So you're comparing MJ and me to couples that died? That's not very reassuring."

"It's romantic. Both couples couldn't envision life without the other."

"No. It's stupid. Pretty sure they got along just fine until they met the other person."

"Yeah, okay. But when you meet the one you're supposed to spend the rest of your life with, something like sacrificing your feelings—or even yourself—to stay with that person won't sound stupid. It will make sense," Kelli insists.

"If that's what true love is all about, you can keep it."

A future like the one she's talking about would end with me getting hurt. Regardless of my foolish heart, I need to remain neutral. I can't get caught up in feelings and false hope. Not when there are so many terrible truths waiting to be discovered. I need to put aside my feelings and find answers. And the best way to do that is through Amber.

"Come on," I say. "Let's get this day over with."

The stares, gossiping whispers, and whistles to Justin's song continue all through choir and math, making it impossible to concentrate. I try to block them out in Spanish, but my concentration snaps when a note appears on my desk. Not normally a big deal sitting by Kelli, but this isn't her handwriting.

> *Are you ok? My aunt said you were with some guy who isn't from around here. Is he the guy you were talking about Saturday morning?*
> *—Amber*
> *PS: If you tell anyone about this, I will deny all of it and say you're crazy. And because everyone already thinks you are, everyone will believe me.*
> *PPS: You look stupid.*

I look across the room to where Amber sits.

Why the heck would she care if I'm okay? Other than our phone conversation Saturday, we've barely talked since we stopped being friends ten years ago. She wouldn't have cared what I did all weekend if I hadn't called her and told her about MJ possibly being a killer.

That's it, isn't it? She thought something happened to me. She isn't the heartless witch everyone thinks she is. She was actually worried about me. *Wow.* Inside that fake Barbie doll exterior is a heart. Who knew? I write a note back to her.

> *I'm ok. Yes, I was with him. It's complicated. And don't worry. I don't want people thinking I talk to you either.*
> *—Maddy*
> *PS: No matter what you wear, you will still be a hag.*

I sound less than thrilled as I ask people to pass the note back, hoping they'll assume it's full of insults instead of concern. Kelli narrows her eyes at Amber. It worked.

After class, Kelli's almost jumping out of her skin as she bounces along next to me while we walk to our lockers. "Okay, I can't take it anymore. Tell me what the hag said."

I smile, glad to see she's still herself. "Promise you won't tell?"

She rolls her eyes. "Like I want people knowing we associate with her."

"Point taken. All right, brace yourself. It's pretty messed up. She asked if I was okay. And she wanted to know if I was with ... Norway."

"Holy cow!" she yells as we stop at our lockers. Most of the heads in the overcrowded hallway glance our way. Thankfully, once they see it's us, they go back to whatever they were doing.

"*Sh!*"

"Sorry, I just didn't think *it* had emotions. Learn something new every day."

"Apparently."

Kelli and I grab lunch, then head for our spot in the lobby. Our friends are already there, immersed in conversation, but they stop as we sit down. A smile forms on their faces as they greet me. I resist rolling my eyes and briefly smile back.

"How's your morning, Maddy?" Shawn asks.

"It's been fine," Kelli answers for me.

My friends glance between Kelli and me as our circle fills with uncomfortable silence. I turn away and bite my lip, wishing things could go back to normal.

"Hey," Kelli says as she puts her hand on my knee. "You okay?"

Before I can answer, my phone buzzes. "Hang on." I pull it from my pocket and dread fills me when I see Ben's name on the screen. I don't want to deal with this, but I need to. I need to know how he is, and I need to make sure Justin hasn't changed him as he changed Kelli.

I sigh. "Just a sec, I'll be right back."

CHAPTER 32

MJ

I'VE SPENT THE LAST FOUR HOURS IN THE VEIL OF SHADows watching Amber. I'm now convinced the Fates are mocking me. I'm trying to stay away, but Maddy is in every one of Amber's classes. I've had to endure the sight of her sinking deeper and deeper into her hooded sweatshirt. Even the air surrounding her is cold. It worsens every time someone hums or whistles that song.

My new emotions are affecting my grasp on Cerebrallink. The other students' thoughts and images keep appearing as clearly as if they were my own. The sad, disconnected look in her eyes today reminds them of the first day of their freshman year. Then they think back to the Maddy they all used to know and secretly admired.

The first time I saw that image they remember of her so happy and innocent and driven, it took my breath away. What I wouldn't give to somehow have her smile at me now as she did back then.

But that girl vanished. I searched through all their memories, especially her close friends, trying to figure out what happened to her. Whatever it is, it involves her uncle, the Shadowwalker.

It's unanimous he did something to her. Amber's theory is the most popular—that he violated her. My body shakes as I hold back my rage. He said last night he hasn't touched her since she was a baby. He must have lied. And to think, I showed him mercy on Maddy's behalf last night. There will be no mercy next time. He will pay for what he's done to her, then I can help her find herself again. After I deal with her current situation, that is.

I was right in my suspicions that more is going on with her than what happened between us this weekend. Something about the roses and card frightened her. I tried to find out who sent them, but the card was blank. Whoever it is, she thankfully doesn't seem to mirror his feelings for her.

I know I should stay away. It would be safer for her. But I can't. Not until I know she's okay. I'm going to find out what is going on, starting with listening in on her phone call.

CHAPTER 33

Maddy

"Hey," I say into my phone as I walk outside for some privacy.

"Dang it, Maddy," Ben says. "I've been freaking out ever since your mom called, and all I get is hey?"

Great. Thanks, Mom, for creating an unnecessary problem. "I didn't know she called you. I would've called you, but my phone needed to charge."

"Your phone was dead—that's the story you want to tell me? Whatever. I guess it doesn't matter. Anyway, I'll be there by the time you're done with school."

Several students walk out the door, whistling Justin's song. I shiver and move farther down the sidewalk. "Why are you coming here?"

"Hmm, let me think. I get a frantic call from your mother saying you disappeared. So I got in my car to come help find you. I'm almost through Iowa now."

"Thanks, but I'm fine. You can turn around."

"Seriously? What did I do? Is this because of Justin?"

"Actually, yeah. I hate him. You need to stay away from him."

"Really? Because I think he's great. Do you know he was so worried about you, he changed his flight and went home early just so he could look for you?"

My heart leaves my chest and squeezes into my head, pounding out a rhythm so loudly, my body twitches along to the beat. I've managed to hold back my fear about Justin only because of the distance I thought was between us. Knowing he's back in town has me petrified.

"He was searching for you all night," Ben continues. "Even though he knows you hate him."

My legs wobble, and my breathing accelerates. I close my eyes and fight against my fears.

"To me," he begins, "that says way more about who he is than the mistake he made at a party. I know you're still in high school, Maddy, but sometimes people are idiots when they're drunk. You're hot, okay? He hit on you. That's it. He says he won't do it again. He truly wants to be your friend."

Justin can't be here. He's afraid of MJ. It's too soon. I don't know what he can do or how to protect anyone from him. "I d-don't know, Ben," I say. "A lot has happened over the last few days, and I need more time to figure things out."

"Well, I'm less than two hours away. Please let me pick you up so we can talk. Just … say yes, even if it's only for an hour or two."

Branches rustle in the bushes behind me. Muscles in my back spasm, and I feel as though someone's watching me. I hold myself even tighter and walk closer to the door, ready to either run into school or down the steps in case Justin is here.

I need to keep Ben away from him. Protect him. "All right. You can pick me up, but I'm grounded, so we can't go anywhere."

"That's better. I'll see you soon. Bye."

"Bye."

As I head back inside, I toss my lunch in the trash and head off to sixth period English, not bothering to go back to my friends and explain. I can't sit with them and pretend everything is fine. Not now that my nightmare is back in town.

"GOOD AFTERNOON CLASS," MS. BELKER SAYS AS THE BELL finishes ringing. "Today we're continuing with our creative writing pieces from last week. Madison, we left off with you. Please come up to the front and read your poem."

Ms. Belker is wound tighter than the gray-haired bun on top of her head. She's the only teacher who calls me by my full name. It's annoying. Dean and Marie didn't choose that name for me.

At the front of the class, I ignore the snickering and whistling of Justin's song and seek out my only allies. Luke and Shawn are smiling and encouraging me to start. I can do this. I read:

Him

When will I meet him?
Where will it be?
Will it be by chance?
Or an act of destiny?

I've never been good with patience.
And I'm stubborn as can be.
Surely you can send him early.
Do it just this once, for me?

Rules were meant to be broken.
I will even ask you please.
Send me my true love.
So he can set me free.

"I'm here," says a male voice from the doorway.

CHAPTER 34

Maddy

HEAT POOLS UNDER MY CHEEKS, TURNING MY SKIN crimson, as the hysterical laughter begins. I expected them to laugh at my poem. But I didn't expect to hear that voice so soon. Especially not at school.

The voice belongs to MJ.

"Settle down," Ms. Belker says. I hope she doesn't think I asked him to do that. I don't need detention right now. "And who might you be?"

"I'm MJ, but I think I'll go by *him*." He smirks and winks at me.

The room erupts in laughter again.

I can feel tears building, but I'm not sure if they're because he's making fun of me or because I'm seeing him again. Either way, I don't want anyone, especially him, to see them.

With as much dignity as I can muster, I head back to my seat, sink down in my chair, and pull my hoodie up to hide from everyone. Of all the times for him to show up, it had to be after *that* poem.

Oh God. I really hope he was joking and he doesn't actually think it's about him—I wrote it long before I even knew *him*.

"Is there a reason you disrupted my class?" Ms. Belker asks. Her tone stops the laughter.

"I just finished filling out enrollment papers in the office. I'm now in your class." He hands a piece of paper to her, and I swear under my breath.

MJ grins, and for a brief moment I wonder if he heard me. But then I shake it off, knowing that's impossible.

Ms. Belker glances at the paper and back at MJ. "If you plan on remaining in my class, you'd be wise not to cause any more disruptions. The only open seat is in the back next to Madison. Because you took such a shine to her, you may sit there for the remainder of the semester."

I groan. I wanted to see him. I have so many questions. But I'm not ready. I have no idea what to say to him.

Shawn and Luke glare at him with hostility. The rest of the class looks at him with sympathy. I focus on not looking at him at all.

"Hello, Maddy," he says quietly as Ms. Belker calls the next student to recite a poem and all attention turns up front. "I wasn't expecting to see you today, but I'm glad for it."

"So … does this mean you aren't going to follow what Duane said?"

His smile drops.

Good. He can't just show up and be happy. Not after leaving me like that.

"He told you?"

I nod.

"Unfortunately, he's right. I do have to stay away from you."

What little hope had been building from the moment he walked in vanishes. "Then why are you here?" My voice sounds hollow, matching the emptiness I feel inside.

"It's Monday."

I wait for him to say more, but he doesn't. Instead his gaze flickers toward the front row. Oh ... Amber. He's on his protection detail. He isn't here to see me.

Fine. If he's going to act as if yesterday meant nothing, then I will too. "Just leave me alone, MJ." As his name leaves my lips, I feel a twinge of pain deep down inside. It showed on my face, and he saw it.

Embarrassed, I turn away, fold my arms on my desk, and rest my head on top of them.

I can't do this—I can't be around MJ, even just to learn more about him. It hurts too much. I just have to forget him and figure everything out with Justin and Damien instead.

I half-listen to the other poems of the day. Tom's is about football. Big surprise. Amber's is interesting, though. It's about her fears of love. She's also adopted, but she doesn't hide it as I do. She always seems so strong. I never thought it bothered her. Maybe, underneath all her bitchiness, she really does have a heart. A heart that's broken, like mine.

WHILE GATHERING MY STUFF FOR NEXT PERIOD, MJ BLOCKS my exit. "Are you okay?"

I glare up at his antagonizing, confusing, heart-stopping-ly beautiful face, and a bit of my irritation melts away. It's become my favorite freaking face in the whole world. Seeing him again under these circumstances may not have been ideal, but he's here. And aside from when he was mocking me, he doesn't appear mad at me.

"I'm as okay as I'm going to be." I shrug in defeat. It's too much work to be upset with him.

He runs his fingers through his short brown hair and sighs. "Your poem was unexpected."

"I didn't know you were a poetry critic."

"Well, I do believe you told me yesterday that you would never fall in love, yet today you recite a poem about doing that very thing."

"Yeah, well … when I write, I lead with my heart."

"Your heart?" he asks in surprise.

Have I really come off that cruel to him? My mind races through our strange encounters for an example of why the thought of me having a heart should be so shocking to him, and I come up with nothing.

I push that aside and ask a question that's been in the back of my mind. "Why did you kiss me while I was asleep?"

He blushes and stares at the ground. "It … was an experiment."

Now *I'm* an experiment? Some seventh-period students start to trickle into class as we're still standing there. Great. If I don't hurry, I'm going to be late to another class.

"Move," I say.

MJ steps aside, but to my simultaneous horror and relief, he continues walking alongside me.

"Experiment ... " I mutter to myself.

"If it helps ... " He pauses long enough to make me glance at him. "I enjoyed it."

Warmth pools around my heart as hope blossoms inside me. Maybe he doesn't hate me. Maybe, if I tell him a little bit about how I feel, he'll keep talking. "I'm sorry about last night."

He stops and stiffens, then catches back up to my fast pace. "Any parts specifically?"

Everything. But the only thing I'm willing to admit is, "My uncle."

"Hmm. We'll discuss that later."

Does he mean after school later or just later in general? If it means he plans on talking to me again, does it really matter when? No, it doesn't.

Still, I'm not ready to let him entirely off the hook. "That was rude, by the way—leaving last night without saying good-bye. Where did you go?"

He smirks. "Home."

Duh, Maddy.

"I'm grounded for a week," I say. "Were your parents as upset as mine when you got there?"

He stiffens again. "No."

"Lucky."

His face contorts in pain.

Does he feel responsible for me being grounded? It was his fault, but I don't care. Spending the day with him, being in his arms ... I wouldn't trade those memories for anything.

"It's okay. Don't feel bad. I don't have much of a social life anyway," I add, trying to make him feel better.

"No. It's not that. It's … um … my parents are dead, Maddy."

I freeze in the hallway outside my next class. How? When? Why? Who is he staying with? Is he alone? "I'm so sorry," is all I manage to say.

His eyes drift as if he's lost in a memory, then he peers down at me. "I don't know why I told you that. It happened so long ago." His fingers slide up my arm, though I don't think he's aware of it.

My skin quivers while the all-too familiar current of energy connects us. I glance behind him to ensure we're still at school. A student runs behind us with his arms overloaded with books. We didn't go anywhere.

When the current reaches MJ, he slowly comes back from wherever his mind went. His fingers stop sliding along my skin once he reaches my cheek. "I always say too much around you."

"No, you don't. If anything, you do the exact opposite. You start to tell me something, then you stop and leave me hanging." Like right now. His parents' deaths may have happened a while ago, but the pain in his eyes says he's still grieving. Whatever happened to them, it couldn't have been good.

The bell rings. I'm late. "This is my class." I nod to the doorway behind me.

"Mine too." He smiles and tugs me into geography.

MJ sits on the opposite side of the room. Occasionally, I glance his way, and I catch him looking at me, but he turns away every time. I try my best to ignore him and focus, but it's so hard after the way our conversation ended. Plus, Tom keeps whistling Justin's song whenever the room is quiet.

At the end of the hour, Tom and some other brainless jock start talking with MJ about sports stuff, so I rush off without him. I need time to think.

MJ's revelation has left me reeling. I'm at a loss for how incredibly sad I feel for him. More than anything, I want to know when and how. Did it happen when he was still in Norway? Did his parents die together, or did he suffer two different times, for each one's death? Was he forced to be on his own, or did he have to go into foster care? Is he adopted? Do we have that in common?

Does his parents' death have to do with what he is? Does he blame himself? Is that why he's trying to save Amber—to make up for not saving them? I bet that's it. I need to find out more. More about them. More about him. Just ... more.

CHAPTER 35
Maddy

IN GYM, WE'RE PLAYING BASKETBALL, AND MJ AND I ARE on opposing teams. For whatever reason, he's guarding me. He keeps brushing against me as he twists around on the floor. Each time, I feel that strange, enigmatic pulse of energy, and I momentarily panic, fearing our minds will wander again.

I'm fairly certain now it occurs only if I'm the one thinking about going somewhere else. Maybe that's why he keeps touching me; he's checking for himself too. I wish he'd stop. It's distracting. I'm having enough trouble concentrating as it is.

Sweat glistens off MJ's body, making his outdoorsy scent more potent. It curls around me, and I'm lost in him, repeatedly drifting through every moment we've had together and wishing there were more.

I shake my head and refocus on the game.

My team's down by two points, and there's enough time for one last shot. Shawn is my team captain. With how great he is, he should be able to tie it up.

Shawn shifts around, trying to slip past his guard and find an open shot.

Suddenly he launches the ball in my direction. I snatch it and dribble in front of MJ. Why the hell did Shawn pass me the ball?

Dang it.

I'm outside the three-point line. I glance around the court. From the excited faces on my team and forlorn faces on MJ's team, everyone expects me to make the shot.

MJ's brow is raised as he watches me. Can he sense their expectations? Everyone remembers I used to play basketball. I played almost every sport at least once, and I was naturally great at them, but I played basketball the longest. I wish they would just forget it.

But this is such an easy shot, even with MJ towering over me. I've got him used to blocking me from the left. All I'd have to do is fake left, make the shot, then we'd win the game.

My team begins chanting, "Page! Page! Page!"

I cringe, hating that nickname. I just want this stupid game over with.

I fake left, and MJ falls for it. At the last second, I adjust my stance. Silence fills the gym as the ball hits the rim and bounces off. I turn away so no one sees my smirk. If I had made it, just as if I had gotten a perfect score yesterday, people would be reminded of the girl I used to be. But I'm not her and I never will be again.

MJ's team celebrates while my team hangs their heads in defeat.

Coach Anderson blows the whistle, and everyone heads for the locker rooms. Tom slams into me, nearly knocking me over. He mutters a lame apology, then whistles Justin's song again before running into the locker room.

I wrap my arms around myself, dreading the after-school hours. If Justin did all this inside the school, what awaits me outside it?

MJ comes running up to me. "So you used to play basketball?"

"It was a long time ago."

"How long?"

"Middle school." I don't want him asking around about this. If he did, everyone would tell him I was supposed to play on the varsity team freshman year. I couldn't—not after learning the truth. I'd always thought my knack for sports, music, academics, and dance came from Dean and Marie. They're talented, driven, successful people. And Hannah is top of her class and the best swimmer in the state for her event. It made sense. But that notion was shattered.

"Why did everyone expect you to make that shot?" he asks, bringing me back from the past.

I shrug. "The game was on the line. No matter who had the ball, my team would've hoped they made it."

"Yeah, but my team expected you to make it too."

"I don't know," I reply, exasperated, and head into the locker room.

Maybe I do need to stay away from MJ. I say too much around him, and all it will do is get me hurt. I need to focus on Damien and Justin. MJ needs to focus on protecting Amber. Preferably without touching her …

IN THE PARKING LOT, SOMEONE CALLS MY NAME. I SEARCH the crowd and see a hand waving in my direction. The crowd parts enough so I can see whom the arm belongs to. Ben leans against the hood of his maroon Civic. With his sandals, khaki shorts, and polo shirt, he looks as though he belongs on the beach with a surfboard, not in Minnesota right before winter.

"What are you doing here?" I ask.

He frowns and his body slumps. "You forgot I was coming?"

I stare blankly at him for a moment, then remember our phone conversation at lunch. I smile weakly. "Sorry. I had a really crummy afternoon." My right foot kicks some loose gravel while I wait to see if I'm forgiven.

"Want to talk about it?"

"Not really."

After seeing how Kelli had acted because of Justin today, I don't know what I expected from Ben. I thought Ben would be different too. Justin must not have done anything to his head yet.

He reaches out and grabs my left hand. Other than the temperature difference between my hand and his, his contact sparks no other sensations. It never has, but for reasons I don't want to think about, I miss the static-charged rush and the possibilities of leaving wherever I currently am and heading to someplace better.

"Let's go," I say. "Mom will be home in a few hours. I'm not supposed to have visitors, so you need to be gone by then."

"Okay." He lets go of my hand, and we get into his Civic. Inside, the speakers rattle, and I cringe as Marilyn Manson sings "Sweet Dreams." I shut the radio off.

"That's a good song," Ben says.

"The Eurythmics's version is better."

He chuckles as we leave the parking lot to drive to my home.

"WANT A POP?" I ASK, OPENING THE FRIDGE.

"Sure."

I grab a can of Ben's favorite diet cherry cola and pour myself a glass of water. Knowing I like my space, he sits at one end of the couch and I sit on the other. He pops the top and takes a long drink while I rub my finger along the condensation forming on the outside of my glass. It's so uncomfortable, not knowing where we stand, even the water is sweating.

"How's your job?" I ask.

"I finally got the bugs worked out on the new software we're developing. We're pitching it next week."

"Good luck." He's only twenty-one, and he's built this great future for himself. His confidence truly amazes me sometimes.

Ben moves his hand slowly toward me. With each inch, nervous pressure builds inside as my mind wanders back to holding MJ's hand last night and all the amazing things that occurred with such a simple, everyday thing. And yet, that won't happen with Ben. Everything will be the same as it ever was. After a moment, I reach out and place my hand in his. His hand is warmer than normal. Sweaty.

"Are you okay?" I ask. His hands haven't sweated this bad since we first started dating.

He puts his pop on the coffee table and moves closer to me. "There was this fleeting moment Sunday when I thought you were gone. It's just ... weird seeing you sitting there in one piece."

"I'm sorry. I didn't mean to make you, or anyone else, worry about me."

He releases my hand and touches my cheek. I flinch, and he frowns. His pensive eyes met mine. "The whole way here, I thought I lost you. I think ... I think I'm in love with you."

Love? I *like* him. He's nice and all. But love? We've only been together for seven months. "Ben, I—"

"*Shh,*" he says, placing a finger over my lips. I freeze, unsure of what he'll say or do next. "I think I know what you're about to say, and I'm not ready to hear it yet." He removes his hands from my face and grabs my other hand.

I don't want to break his heart. But I just don't want to stay together when I know he deserves more than I can give him.

His thumb rubs the back of my hand. "You have really soft skin, but ... cold." The sense of wonder in his voice causes me to lift my gaze back to him. He's fixated on the top of my hand, where he's tracing the blue veins. "You're not normally so cold."

I shift in my seat. I don't know if he's acting this way because of me or because of Justin. "It's been a weird couple days."

"Are you nervous?"

I look up from our hands and meet his brown eyes. "Why?"

He grins. "I can feel your heart beating through your hand. It's increasing."

My throat dries, and I take a sip of water. After I place my glass down on the side table, I turn around, and Ben leans in so there's only an inch or so between us.

My breathing continues to rise as his hand softly caresses my cheek.

His pupils enlarge, and he licks his lips. "I thought you died this weekend. I thought he found you and that I lost you forever."

"Ben, it's okay. He wouldn't—wait. You thought *who* found me?" I lean back into the armrest to put some space between us, but only gain an inch.

His forehead creases. "I know why he was drawn to you."

"Who, Ben? What are you talking about?"

"I shouldn't have let you stay here. I should have made you come to Florida. I'm here now, though. Everything is going to be fine. I can keep you safe. You're so unique, Mads. I need to know what you are. I have to feel you close to me."

Mads? Before I can respond, his hand slides behind my neck, and he leans forward so his lips press against mine.

It's slow, delicate, cautious—as if he's trying to make up for everything that happened this weekend.

Part of me wants everything to go back to the way it was. Ben's normal. He doesn't have any crazy abilities. I don't have anything to be afraid of when we're together. He doesn't have a dark side. He's safe. He's comfortable. And no matter what I do, no matter what I say, he keeps coming back to me. He will never truly leave me.

But I can't do this. I have to be fair with him. I can't keep stringing him along when I know my feelings don't match his. "Ben, stop," I say and pull away from him.

He rests his head against my forehead, and our rapid breaths mingle. "You have no idea how incredible that felt," he says.

I sigh and stand, turning away. Looking at the glass patio doors, I catch his reflection. He's feeling his lips, just as MJ did the other night. Even after kissing Ben, I immediately think of MJ.

I cross my arms and turn to look at him. "We can't keep doing this. We need to end it ... for good this time."

He stands, and his mouth sets into a hard line. "Why?"

My heart rate climbs as I watch all traces of brown vanish from his eyes. Oh Ben, what did Justin do to you? "B-because ... I'm not ready for the kind of relationship you want and deserve."

"You know what I think, *Mads*?" he says, sauntering toward me.

"Please don't call me that."

He tilts his head to the side, just as Justin and MJ do. "Why?"

"Justin calls me that, and I hate it almost as much as I hate him."

His mouth twitches into an odd smile. Like the Joker's from the Batman movies. He's never smiled like that before. "Why is that?" he asks.

He really wants to talk about Justin now? What if Justin is somehow making him ask this? Maybe he turned Ben into his little errand boy.

"Because Justin's using you for his own selfish needs," I tell him. "You can't trust him. He's an evil, deceitful liar."

He chuckles. "Enough, Mads. Talking is overrated."

Quicker than I can blink, he moves from the couch to me, and I freeze in shock. MJ and Justin are the only two people I've ever seen do that. Ben is not like them. He can't be.

One of his arms slides around my back while his other hand grabs my head just below my ponytail. He presses me into his hard body and kisses me again. His kiss is faster, hungrier, and more aggressive as his tongue invades my mouth.

This can't be happening. This isn't him. He's always respected me and never pressured me before. I've always been able to trust Ben, but seeing him with eyes as black as Justin's and acting so much like him … I don't know what he'll do.

I move my hands to his chest and shove him away. "I wanted to talk to you—not do this. We're over, Ben. Leave. Now!"

"No," he growls and backs me into the glass patio door. His hand grabs my waist and squeezes until it hurts. "This is about me, not you! For everything you've put me through, all the waiting you've made me do, you can behave for once and give me what I deserve. I can't believe you went on a date with *him*. Did you kiss *him*? Did you let *him* touch you?"

"What are you talking about?"

"Oh, Mads, don't play coy with me." Ben runs his nose along my neck. "I know all about your date with the *Protector*."

My skin tingles as that familiar rush of adrenaline fills me. It's faster and stronger than normal as it seeks out my fear and turns it into anger. My rage is so palpable it's consuming me. I can't calm down, and I don't want to. It feels … good. So much better than being scared. Instead of holding back, I give in and let my emotions control me.

The thought swirling around in my head is Justin is responsible for this. He's ruining everything, and for that, he's going to pay.

Suddenly I kick Ben in the crotch. He doubles over. Then I punch him in the face, hitting both his cheek and nose.

I didn't think about doing that. I just … did it. Immediately, my tingles and rage vanish. "Ben, I'm so sorry. I didn't even realize I did that. I'll go get you some ice." I'll need something to get the blood out of the carpet too. I don't need to explain this to Mom and Dad.

I turn to leave the living room. As I walk pass Ben, he grabs my ankle. I tumble to the ground. Panic ripples through me as he climbs onto my back. "That wasn't very nice, Mads. You're going to pay for that."

Ben wouldn't do this. This is a dream. A really bad dream.

Hot air blows against my neck right before he sniffs my hair. I grunt and try to buck him off. "You smell so good," he croons. "So sweet."

I close my eyes and think of the bridge ... of MJ ... of my happy place.

My phone buzzes in my backpack, distracting Ben long enough for me to throw him off and rush out the door.

CHAPTER 36

MJ

THIS IS WRONG. I SHOULD BE WITH AMBER, BUT NO. I'M ignoring my assignment again for Maddy. I don't know who that was who picked her up. But right before he got into his car, he stared directly at me—somehow picked me out of a crowd of more than two hundred students—and grinned.

Now I'm here, pacing in the park near her house like a moron, trying to come up with a more substantial reason to go to her house than a grin.

Thunder rumbles, and I look up to find nearly black clouds that weren't there a few minutes ago. What is with this town and the weather?

I could call her. That way, if she's fine, then I'll know right away. But if she sounds troubled or doesn't answer, I can be there in less than a second.

I take out my phone and dial the number I found in the files I borrowed from her house last night.

The phone rings, but her voicemail picks up.

Rain bursts from the clouds, instantly soaking everything. In the distance, I hear the sound of a drum. It's pounding so fast. Accompanying it is the sound of two things smacking wet pavement. I turn toward the park entrance, and my breath catches as Maddy rounds the corner.

Tears mixed with rain fall down her face. Her eyes are wide and filled with fear. An overwhelming need to grab her and whisk her away to safety consumes me. Right before she touches me, the boy she left school with appears. His eyes are black.

Oh, Heaven help me, she's been found!

CHAPTER 37

Maddy

MY ARMS AND LEGS PUMP FASTER, DESPERATE TO GET away from Ben. I'm almost to the park. I'm almost safe. It's the middle of the afternoon—someone has to be there.

The bushes end, and the first row of parking stalls comes into view. My panic lessens as I find relief. Someone's there. My already-racing heart trembles when I realize it's MJ. He shouldn't be here, but I don't care. I wanted him to be the one to save me.

Somehow I find the strength to run faster—eager to get to him and have him wrap his arms around me and do whatever he does to disappear and take me far away from Ben.

But right before I can launch myself into him, his body shakes, his eyes darken, and he vanishes.

Even though I need to keep running, I stop and stare at the empty space that once held MJ.

It was all my imagination. He was never really here. He's off protecting Amber somewhere. I just wanted him to be here because he's the only person who truly makes me feel safe.

Any second now, Ben is going to catch up to me and finish whatever horrible thing Justin told him to do.

"Get the hell off me!" Ben shouts from behind me.

I turn, and Ben is on his stomach ten feet away. The bottom half of his face is covered in blood. His eyes and forehead are scrunched up as he fights to get MJ off his back.

MJ *really* is here? I blink a few times, and he's still there.

Rain pelts them from every angle as a fierce wind blows, though I don't feel any of it. I think I'm still in shock.

"This has nothing to do with you," Ben shouts. "She isn't marked. She's fair game!"

"Consider this me claiming her," MJ growls.

He came for me. He saved me. He really is a hero. My hero.

Aside from looking furious, MJ seems to be in control as Ben unsuccessfully struggles to break free. Every move Ben makes to dig himself out, MJ anticipates it. Within a few seconds, one of MJ's hands has secured both of Ben's arms behind Ben's back, and the other hand holds Ben down. Ben is strong—I didn't realize how strong until a few minutes ago. But if MJ can restrain him with minimal effort, how strong is MJ?

MJ looks up at me. As I stare into his eyes, I notice it's stopped raining. Downpours of that magnitude don't vanish so quickly.

"Are you hurt?" MJ asks.

"Yeah, you're hurting me!" Ben shouts. "And that bit—"

"Not you," MJ snarls into the back of Ben's skull. "You deserve to suffer!" He looks back up at me. "Madison, *did he hurt you?*"

"I-I don't think so," I whisper. I can't tell. Other than relief that MJ was here and awed gratitude that he saved me, I feel nothing.

His attention returns to Ben. "I'm not allowed to do anything to you ... yet. But if you ever come near Madison again, I'll break the rules, hunt you down, and give you exactly what you deserve. Even if I have to switch sides to do it."

MJ's hazel eyes blaze with a ring of red. It sends shivers down my spine. Thunder rumbles as lightning strikes the ground all around us.

That's the third time today that someone's eye color has changed. Eyes don't suddenly change color. So how did Kelli, Ben, and MJ do it? Between Damien and Justin, I've gotten used to the black. I didn't like seeing it on Kelli or Ben, but it wasn't nearly as terrifying as the dark crimson next to MJ's pale features. What is he? What are they?

"Madison," MJ snaps, and I jump.

I refocus on MJ, not understanding why he's angry with me.

He takes a breath and says, "Didn't you hear me? I just told you to back up. I'm going to let Ben go."

My body clenches with fear again. I don't want MJ to let him loose. Not after everything Ben tried to do. But MJ can't hold him forever. I nod and take a few steps back.

He lets Ben up. MJ backs up toward me with his arms outstretched in a defensive position. Ben stands and walks in a slow half-circle near MJ, with his eyes fixed on me. The blood on his face and clothes makes him look like a hungry carnivore and I'm his next meal. MJ moves in front of me, blocking my view of Ben.

"Leave," MJ demands. "I'm not going to let you come near her again. Go to your car while you still can, and go back to Florida." Never turning his back on Ben, he pushes against me, forcing me backward toward the park.

Florida? I never told him Ben lives in Florida. How did he know that?

I peek around MJ. Ben's narrowed eyes focus on me. "You won't be here forever, Protector," he hisses. "One day your assignment will end, and you'll leave. When you do, I'll return. I'm not known for my patience, but I'm willing to make an exception for her. She's worth it and you know it. See you soon, Mads." He winks at me and saunters up the road, whistling that damn song.

As he moves out of sight, MJ lowers his arms and turns to face me. The redness has left his eyes, making him less frightening. Before, he looked on the verge of killing Ben and the only thing that seemed to stop him was me being a witness. It's not a comforting thought.

"I know you're scared," he says. "But don't think about being anywhere else right now. Okay?"

I nod once; it's the best I can do.

His hands slowly come up and wipe away a wet trail of rain and tears from my cheeks. With his intimate touch, soothing energy flows into me. I take a shaky breath as my anxiety eases. He's here, standing right in front of me. I want to reach out and touch him so badly, but I can't. I don't know anything about him.

"I don't know about you," he says, "but I'm pretty pissed and need to blow off some steam."

Pissed doesn't even scratch the surface of what I'm feeling.

Even though MJ frightens me, I don't want to be away from him. Not until my nerves calm down. "What do you have in mind?"

"This." MJ turns me around, and in the spot where he first stood when I came into the park now sits a motorcycle. I *know* that wasn't there before, so how is it here now? At the moment, I don't really care. I add it to my *what-the-hell-are-they?* pile, then focus on his motorcycle.

White curves cover the body while chrome decorates the handlebars and pipes. Thunder rumbles, though it's not as loud as before. The thought of riding this sends fear rippling through me, but for reasons I can't explain, I feel drawn to it. It looks familiar to me.

"I've never been on a motorcycle before," I say.

He sighs, and his warm breath coats the skin on the back of my neck. "Do you want to go for a ride?"

"Okay," I reply numbly.

He reaches around me for something, but I'm too caught up in the massive polished engine to see what he grabs.

"Here. Put this on." He places a white helmet with silver decals of what look like angel wings in my hands. Huh. He didn't strike me as the religious type. But then again, he did mention God yesterday.

I stare at my wide green eyes in the reflective visor. They're darker than they used to be.

"On second thought, I'll do it." MJ takes the helmet back. "I want to make sure it's on right."

He lifts the visor, positions the helmet on my head, and tightens a strap under my chin. He tilts my head, and I meet his eyes. "I'll get on first to hold the bike steady. Watch how I do it, and climb on behind me. Close the visor by pressing down on it. You'll hear a click when it's done. Next you'll have to wrap your arms tightly around me. When you're ready, tap my chest twice. Okay?"

I nod, and the heavy helmet wobbles a little in the free space between my head and the loose foam.

"Good." His knuckles slide down my neck, sending his familiar current flowing through me.

Even though I'm scared of what he's capable of, and I know I shouldn't fully trust him, my body betrays my mind. My heart beats faster, my nerves become a jumbled mess, and my skin tingles. When his hand leaves my skin, my body screams for it back.

He grabs the handlebars, and his left leg swings up and over to the other side. He lets go, slides all the way back to the passenger seat, then slides forward again.

That's weird. Why didn't he just sit in his own seat? It looked as though he was wiping something off my seat.

Oh. The rain. He was drying my seat.

Great.

I'm full of conflicting emotions over him right now, and he goes and soaks his butt drying my seat. What kind of guy does that?

A guy that likes you, my subconscious sings.

Not wanting to linger on any more thoughts of MJ or his butt, I climb onto the white deathtrap, shut my visor, and wrap my arms around him.

As I grab hold of him, sharp, shooting pains sear through my left wrist and up my arm. MJ shivers, and I let go, pulling my hand back. The memory of punching Ben comes back. I roll my joints and flinch a little. My wrist isn't broken, but it hurts. My side and my knees hurt too.

If all of this pain is because of Justin screwing with Ben's mind, I need to figure out exactly what Justin is and what he's capable of.

MJ looks over his shoulder. "You okay?"

"Yeah," I shout and place my arms back around him, more carefully this time. His energy flows into me, and I concentrate on the moment, trying not to think about anywhere else right now. I wouldn't want to accidently uproot us.

I tap him twice with my uninjured hand. He nods, then the bike roars to life. I can feel the power running under my seat. It's strangely comforting. Almost safe. Is it the bike? Is it MJ? Or is it both?

"The road is still slick with rain, so we're not going to go very fast," he shouts over the massive engine. "This is going to be cold, but at least the rain stopped." His hand moves on the handlebars, and the bike jolts forward. His body moves in sync with the bike, used to the pull of the wind and force of the engine. I cling to him, even though it hurts, and smile at how effortless it is to be with him right now.

CHAPTER 38

MJ

I WILL NOT THINK OF THE PAIN. I WILL NOT THINK OF THE pain. Over and over, I repeat that mantra as my left wrist throbs, making it difficult to grip the handlebars.

The first time I felt it, when she grabbed me, I nearly blacked out. But then Maddy pulled her hand back, and the feeling vanished. That's how I knew it was her. Her wrist hurts that badly, but if it wasn't for her touch, I would have no clue. She seems mostly unaffected by the pain. Is it because she's in shock, or does she somehow tolerate pain better than any of the millions of humans I've protected over the years?

For everything that's happened today, I'm amazed she hasn't transported us to the bridge. In hindsight, riding a motorcycle with her probably wasn't the best idea, but I needed something to distract me from killing her ex.

I saw what happened at Maddy's house through Ben's thoughts. It wasn't Ben's fault he acted that way—he's possessed, though I couldn't tell who the demon was. Still, his essence felt familiar. I've probably sent him to Hell before. I hated letting him go this time. He's still a threat to Maddy. But I couldn't exactly perform an exorcism in front of her. I'll be in enough trouble as it is once a Protector arrives to exorcise Ben. One look in Ben's memory, and the Protector will see me protecting Maddy—who is not mine to protect. This is bad. Whoever that Protector is, he or she will question it, which will bring unnecessary attention to Maddy. She's already got too much as it is.

When I peeked into Ben's memory to see when the demon possessed him, I saw the demon wasn't attached to Ben. He's just the vessel to get to Maddy—controlling his thoughts but not fully attached to his body. Almost as if he were a passenger inside Ben's body. How did this demon find out about her? How long has he known her? What does he know about her?

I'm sure the Protector assigned to Ben should be arriving soon, and Ben's memory will be erased. He'll be back to himself.

Will Maddy take him back then? Does she love him? Muscles all over my body clench at the thought of her in the arms of someone else. As painful as it is, he must have made her happy at one point, though, and her happiness is all I want.

If I hadn't been at the park, I could have lost her. Where the hell is her Guardian? He or she is supposed to be watching her from the Veil of Shadows so things like me, Ben, and his demon don't happen. I haven't sensed a Guardian any time I've been near her.

That's not right. A Guardian is supposed to have been watching over her since the day she was born, keeping record of every important detail in her file. A file that doesn't exist.

Maddy not having a Guardian could explain why she doesn't have a file, but that doesn't explain why she doesn't have a Guardian. Yet she has a Shadowwalker posing as her uncle. Every day I spend with her, all I do is wind up with more questions.

I turn the bike back around and head for her house, determined to finally get some answers.

CHAPTER 39
Maddy

MJ STOPS THE BIKE OUTSIDE MY HOUSE AND CUTS THE engine. I lean back to catch my breath while he hops off. Butterflies flutter in my stomach as his knuckles graze my jaw while he undoes the strap on my helmet. He gently takes it off and smiles before smoothing out my hair.

"I'm glad we stayed on the bike," he says. "As great as my reflexes are, I don't think I could operate a motorcycle while not being mentally present." His eyes lighten as his shoulders relax.

I bite my lip and try to block out the events that took place before our ride. Remarkably, it's easy, and I know it's only because of MJ. "I'm glad we stayed put too," I say.

His fingers slide down my neck, shoulders, and arms, igniting a fire everywhere they go, and come to a stop at my waist. I expect him to just help me off the bike, but instead he lifts me up, pulls me against him, and wraps his arms around me.

Being pressed up against his whole body ... it's like nothing I've ever felt before. It's the same intense feelings I felt last night when we touched in front of the window, but because it's all of him, it's even better. I want him to hold me tighter. I want this exhilarating energy to never leave me. It moves through me at a slower pace than usual. It's as though it's exploring me from the inside out, memorizing every molecule of my genetic makeup.

As it reaches my heart, I gasp. The hole I've always felt there, suddenly feels patched. I don't know why or how. The only other times I've come close to feeling like this was when I joined with the Dream Girl—or, for some reason, when I've had that rush of adrenaline when I've felt threatened by Justin, MJ, and Ben.

No.

I will not allow myself to have these feelings for a boy I hardly know.

"Let me go." I shove against him and sharp pains return to my wrist.

For a moment, he looks confused, but then obliges. My body sags as the incomplete feeling reclaims its hole in the soft tissue of my heart. I turn and head into the house. He follows.

Once inside, I go right to the cupboard under the sink and grab carpet cleaner and a scrub brush, then I walk into the living room. There are several drops of blood on the carpet and a small circle where Ben fell. I sigh, then get to work erasing the evidence before Mom and Dad get home.

MJ bends down and scrubs the largest spot with a brush he must have grabbed on his own. "You'll probably have to change your clothes before your parents get home."

I pause my vicious scrubbing and sit back on my knees. "Why?"

"You have blood on your back."

I shrug out of my hoodie and stare, dejectedly, at the bloody handprints and red streak that stretch from the bottom all the way up to my shoulder.

"I can take them to get cleaned, if you'd like."

I turn away and hold back my urge to shudder. "No. I'd only be reminded of what happened every time I wore them."

He doesn't reply, so I clean in silence. Once finished, I sprint up to my room, wash my hands, remove the rest of my bloodstained clothes, then throw them away. After changing, I grab the garbage bag and go back downstairs.

MJ leans against a wall in the kitchen near the table. His arms are crossed and one leg is bent, propped on the wall behind him. Seeing him now, it's as though the earlier events hadn't happened. He looks completely relaxed and in control. How is that possible?

"What are you?" I drop the garbage bag and take a step closer to him.

He frowns. "What do you mean?"

"You know exactly what I mean." I glare at him. The time for games is over. I will never be put in that kind of situation again because of MJ and Justin. "Whatever you can do, it isn't normal. I know you're not a magician. So, you're either a secret government project, like a superhero, or you're something I don't know about."

"And what makes you think that?"

Now or never. I can do this. "Your strange talents. Your obsession with saving people. The way you and Ben talked. I've thought about this all weekend, and I can't stand not knowing the truth anymore. Tell me what you are."

He pushes away from the wall, then grabs a bowl of grapes from the counter nearest him. He shoves the bowl at me. "You watch too many movies. Eat."

"Why."

"Because we just did something fun—went for a motorcycle ride—and now if you eat, we can call this another date."

I shake my head. Of all the ridiculous things he could say, calling this disastrous day a date is about the craziest. "It's not a date! You don't like me. And I have no idea who or what you are."

He slams his hands down on the table. His breathing accelerates as he scowls. "You think I don't like you? Maddy, with all the abilities you've seen me use, do you really think I have to enroll in *high school* to watch over Amber?"

My jaw drops, but no words come out.

"No. I don't," he says. "I did that for you."

My heart slams into my chest. "Why?"

He searches my eyes for something unknown to me. With each tick from the kitchen clock, his harsh expression softens until his eyes look so desolate, I have to hold myself back to keep from hugging him.

"After what your ... uncle said, that me being with you puts you at risk, I tried to keep my distance. I told myself I'd concentrate on Amber, my assignment. I was with her all morning, but everywhere I went, you were there. Every hour, your suffering grew. I wanted so badly to comfort you. After your phone call at lunch, I couldn't stand it anymore. I decided I had to pose as a student. I had to talk to you. I had to make sure you were okay."

"You saw all that?"

He nods.

He spied on me. Again. But I'm glad he was with me all day. Otherwise I'm sure Justin would have shown up again. MJ kept me safe, even though neither of us knew it.

His knuckles graze my cheek, and I lean into his comforting touch. His energy flows into me, filling me with a sense of peace, safety, and hope. It moves to my heart and pools there, weaving its magic into the hole, trying again to fix the damage created by my birth parents.

Knowing the hole will come back as soon as we break contact, I move closer to him, desperate not only to feel his arms around me again, but also wanting to escape the pain of their rejection.

He leans down, pressing his forehead to mine. "What more do I have to do to show you how I feel?" Sadness coats his voice, and I'm reminded of his admission last night—that he can feel my emotions and my pain when we touch.

I break away, ending his healing current, and I cringe as my heart aches for my birth parents, for me, and for MJ.

I push the pain away and focus on MJ. He's here, even though Duane told him to stay away and even though he's supposed to be protecting Amber. He saved me from Ben.

It must be true. He really does like me. If I were more like my friends, that realization would be enough for me to admit my feelings for him, and then we'd be a couple. But I'm not them, so it doesn't matter that my stomach goes crazy with butterflies whenever he's around. And it doesn't matter that he makes me happy and I want to spend time with him and miss him when I can't. The fact that I like him is meaningless when compared to everything else.

My heart flutters. I really do like MJ. I blush and pop a few grapes into my mouth. As ecstatic as that makes me feel, I still don't know, fully, if I can trust him—not until I know what he is. "So … you still haven't answered my original question. Government experiment, superhero, or something else. Which is it?"

He sighs, shaking his head. "I wasn't created in a lab somewhere."

"What about an alien?"

"No."

"Mutant?"

"No."

"Warlock?"

"Wouldn't that fall under the category of magician?"

"Magicians are usually fake. Warlocks and witches could be real. So are you one?"

"No."

Stumped, I rest my chin on my hand and huff in exasperation.

"Give up?" he asks.

"No. But I've made some good progress on my list."

"You have a *list*?"

"Uh huh." I toss a few more grapes into my mouth.

"Of what you think I might be?"

I nod.

"I don't suppose you could just let it go?"

I narrow my eyes at him. "If I did a bunch of crazy things that you couldn't explain, would you let it go?"

He smirks and shakes his head. "You win. So, now it's my turn to ask questions. How's your wrist?"

I shift and hide my hand behind my back. "What are you talking about?"

He sighs. "I know you're in pain. I feel it when I touch you, remember? So please, don't lie to me."

Before I can say anything else, he grabs my arm and pulls my hand forward. Warmth and buzzing goodness flow through me as his energy enters my body once more. But instead of immediately flowing back into MJ, it pools in my injured wrist for a moment, then reconnects with him. He cringes as if it hurt him. Then he turns my hand from side to side, carefully flexing my wrist joints to inspect the damage.

"Has Ben always treated you like that, or did he seem … different?"

I pause. I'm not ready to tell MJ about Justin. Justin made it seem as though he knew MJ. Whatever that means, I don't have the strength to hear it today. I reveal as little as I can. "Ben's never acted that way. I guess it doesn't matter now. We're officially over, and he's headed back to Florida."

I'm not mad at Ben because I know Justin made him do it. It's the only thing that makes sense. With Ben on his way home, Justin can't trick me like that ever again. Ben's safe from Justin, so that just leaves ... everyone else. My shoulders sag as the weight of the unknown hits me.

"I'm sorry that happened to you," MJ says. "Are you going to be all right?"

He continues inspecting my hand, while I do my best to think about his question. His touch is distracting. The current hums through me again, exploring more of the dark places I don't want him to know about. But my fear, grief, pain, and abandonment are momentarily replaced by a heat spreading throughout my body. Why do I still react to him like this?

By the time he's finished checking my hand, I feel as if I were on fire. But I want more. I lick my dry lips. It's so hard not to lean forward. My free hand grips the table to ensure I don't do something stupid ... like kiss him.

"I'm not going to be all right until you tell me what you are," I finally answer.

He groans and turns away. He mutters to himself as he opens the freezer and grabs an ice pack. He comes back and places the ice pack on my hand, cooling the flames inside me. When his eyes lock on mine, they ignite the fire again. "I can't tell you what I am. So please, don't ask me that again."

"Are you a cop? Are you working with the government? Duane?"

His eyes narrow, and his mouth tightens. It's subtle, but still enough to make me pause. "Am I right? Is Duane why you can't tell me?" It explains the odd behavior between him and Duane last night.

"I'm not a cop, FBI, CIA, or any other organization referred to by its initials."

"Why were you even at the park? I thought you had to be by Amber all the time now."

"I do. But I couldn't help myself. I came to the park because I was worried about you—I wanted to be nearby."

At his admission, something stirs inside me. Joy, surprise—I don't know. But I like him caring enough about me to be worried.

"I called you, but you didn't answer. I was on my way to your house when I saw you running through the park."

The happiness I felt just a moment ago disappears as I recall the park and the events that followed. "What did Ben mean about me being fair game and not marked?"

Both hands run through his hair as he looks up at the ceiling and sighs. "Most of the things that happened today I can't explain to you. If you were anyone else, I could."

"Why would that matter?"

"Everyone else is preprogrammed to ignore the things I do, but you notice everything. When people do notice my abilities, the only defense I have is to alter their memories, but that doesn't work with you. You've seen me for who I am, yet you're still here." He grabs my chin, forcing me to meet his gaze as his energy resumes its place inside me. It's pulsing again, matching the quickened pace of my heart. Once more, the pain that always resides there is gone. "I'm in awe of your strength and courage."

I gulp as he stares down at me with a look of trepidation. No one has ever spoken to me like this before. I don't handle compliments well. But coming from him … it just means more. Being with him, I don't feel so heartbroken. If it's possible, I feel worthy of him, his attention, his praise, his … love?

I've only known him for four days. Four terrifying yet perfect days. "But you don't even know me. And you refuse to tell me anything about you."

"I *can't* tell you."

"Why?" I beg as my lips tremble.

"Sometimes people get hurt around me." The same distant, pained look from school claims his eyes, and somehow I know he's talking about his family. I was right. Something happened to them because of what he is. "I don't want that for you," he continues. "I need to protect you and keep you safe. I shouldn't be around you, but I've never felt anything like the way I feel when I'm with you. It's like … everything before you was just … vacant."

"Vacant," I repeat in breathless wonder.

"I can't even go a day without seeing you," he admits quietly, like some forbidden secret.

My breath hitches at the thought, but then I shake my head. "But you didn't see me Saturday."

"I spent the whole damn day thinking of you. It drove me crazy. That evening, I couldn't stand it anymore. I tried to find what house was yours, knowing you had to live somewhere near the park. I heard you—playing the piano. I watched you from … outside the window."

So he *was* watching me! Nice to know I'm not crazy.

"Sunday I was determined to talk to you. I followed you around on my motorcycle while you shopped with Kelli."

"That was *you*?" That's why his motorcycle seemed familiar. I had seen it before.

He smiles again, confirming my suspicion.

If he did all that to see me, maybe he *did* plan for my bike to break near the fountain too. Can he break bike chains and drain phone batteries?

Even though I know it's ridiculous, I smile. No one has ever gone through that much work just to talk to me. I'm not worth the trouble. And still he stayed near me, even though I told him several times today to leave me alone. I'm glad he didn't listen. "Thank you—for being there today."

He frowns. "There will be consequences for what I've done, but I couldn't let him hurt you."

"What consequences? You saved me. Why would you be punished for that?"

His pained eyes stare down at me. "You're not mine to save. But I couldn't sit by and let that happen to you."

"Who was supposed to save me? No one else was there." A shudder runs through me as I think of what would've happened if MJ hadn't been there.

"You're right, no one else was there." His body shakes, and he clamps his eyes shut. "If anything would have happened to you—"

"I'm fine," I say, touching his smooth cheek to calm him.

His eyes reopen, and a new, unfamiliar look claims them. "Every time we touch ... " He places his hand over mine and closes the gap between us.

My heart lodges itself firmly in my throat as our bodies connect.

"You just ... you contradict everything I know. My life was neat, organized, and simple. With you, it's mayhem. It's a bloody mess. But the joke is, I don't think I can live without it now—without you."

Even though I know there are reasons why I shouldn't be hanging on his every word, I can't think about them. Every part of me is silent, waiting for MJ to speak again.

"Please tell me how you feel," he says. His cool breath falls on my lips as his hazel eyes burn into me, pleading for me to tell him everything in my heart.

Everything he said, I feel it too. He makes me feel things I never thought I would. He makes me feel special and safe, and he makes me forget everything bad. With him, my past and the horrible things in my present don't matter. I need to touch him and be held by him. I need to kiss his magnificent lips and give in to all these strange desires coming over me.

My heartbeat is in sync with the pulsating sensation across my skin, urging me to reach forward just a little bit. He's so handsome. So strong. He's everything I want and everything I thought I didn't deserve.

But there are reasons why we shouldn't be together, and as long as he's this close to me, I can't concentrate on them. I need him to move. I need to think. I need to breathe.

"I need air."

CHAPTER 40

Maddy

THE CRISP OCTOBER AIR HITS ME AS I RUSH OUTSIDE ON the deck. My skin stops tingling, the butterflies in my stomach settle down, and pain resumes its place in my heart and wrist. I breathe deeply and let the cold air extinguish the fire within me. All that remains tense is my stubborn heart.

I like him.

I like him more than I have ever liked anyone. I can't keep ignoring my feelings—it's impossible now. It's not just the mystery surrounding him, the way he makes every horrible thing disappear, or even that I feel closer to him than anyone I have ever met. It's that when I'm with him, I feel … whole.

My back tingles as I sense MJ behind me. My body begs me to turn around. Now that I know what his touch can do, I crave it as my lungs crave oxygen. But I have to resist. I need to know who he is and why I feel so strongly about someone I barely know.

"So, let's say I tell you how I feel," I say, my back still to him. "Then what? How are we going to spend enough time together to figure out where this can go ... when you're busy protecting Amber?"

"We can spend time together once Amber is safe and my assignment is done."

"So when will that be?" I whirl around to face him. I don't care about the ramifications; I need to see his expression.

His gaze drops to the deck.

"How long before the killer is caught?"

He opens and closes his mouth several times before saying, "I don't know."

I close my eyes, trying to block out the truth: I'm falling for a guy who's responsible for keeping Amber alive. I want to be with him, but every minute I spend with him puts her in jeopardy. If the roles were reversed and it was my life on the line, she wouldn't care. But I do. I'm so torn. MJ is perfect for me. It's just ... my happiness isn't worth her life, no matter how cruel she is.

"It doesn't have to be between you and her. We'll see each other all day at school. And I don't always have to be with Amber. We can take it slow."

"But you said you'll be in trouble after what happened today. Won't continuing to see me make it worse?"

"I don't care."

My mouth drops. Those three words resonate inside me. Each time, it grows louder, challenging my negative thoughts. I suddenly feel as though anything is possible, as long as I'm with him. I can move beyond my past. I can face Justin. I can be loved and love someone else.

"But what about your transfer?" I ask, remembering the biggest reason why we will never work: he will eventually leave me. My chest tightens at the thought of being without him. As crippling as it is to fathom now, I know it would only be more painful if we spent more time together.

"I cancelled it today."

My insides swell with such joy that, for a moment, I can't breathe. There was this impending finality to our time together, and now that's gone. But as happy as I am, I can't allow him to do that for me—I'm not worth it. I have no idea what that transfer is for, but he wanted it before he met me. Whatever it is, I can't let him give that up because of me.

"Why?" I ask. "It doesn't ... it doesn't make sense."

"The transfer I requested isn't the kind you're used to. When we transfer ... it's a fresh start. Our minds are wiped clean of everything." He pauses and his eyes soften. "No matter what happens between us, I don't want to lose the memory of meeting you."

My eyes close, allowing his words to wrap around me. The coldness I first felt when I came out here is gone as warmth and happiness fill me from the inside out. I don't want it to ever go away. I open my eyes again and feel as though my face is shining with joy.

MJ inhales sharply before taking a step toward me. "If you'd like, when this is all over, I could quit my job and stay here."

I stand immobile, staring at a boy so complex I'm lost. At first, his many abilities terrified me, but now ... everything about him touches me in a way no one ever has. Now that I know him, I'm no longer afraid. His abilities are a comfort to me. I *wanted* him to use them today to keep me safe.

"You would stay for me?"

He takes a step closer. "I have no ties anywhere else."

My silly heart beats faster with every word. My hands tremble. Half of me wants to go to him, to ignore my reservations and allow myself to explore these feelings for him. But my logical half is fighting back.

The Dream Girl has Damien, and he might be evil. She knew nothing about him, and she left with him...

I back away from him. My chest hollows as every confident, happy feeling he instilled inside me abandons me. MJ refuses to tell me about himself, even though I've asked many times. He's connected to all of it, to Justin and Damien. I can't fall for a guy I barely know, I can't be like the Dream Girl, even if it means breaking my own heart in the process.

"You can't do that. You can't stay." I surprise even myself by sounding firm. I take another deep breath and continue. "You're good at your job. You saved me. You're trying to save Amber, and all I've done is get you into trouble. I'm sorry, but I'm not good enough for you. I'm messed up more than you could ever know. You deserve better."

The joy in his eyes and wide smile is gone in less than a second, leaving him stone-faced. "I know more about you than you think."

"You don't know anything," I snap.

He closes the distance between us, but I'm too stunned to move. He grabs my chin and forces me to look into his beautiful hazel eyes. The healing energy I crave rushes to my heart, filling the hole again and giving me a glimpse at how easy life would be with him.

"I know you carry your pain everywhere you go. It's why you've put barbed wire around your heart. What I don't know is why. Tell me, please. What did he do to you to cause you to go through life like this?"

"Who?"

"Your uncle."

I pull away from him, hating how he can make me go from feeling complete to broken in an instant. "*Duane*? He didn't *do* anything!"

He flinches and clamps his eyes shut. When they reopen, they're narrowed. Through gritted teeth, he snarls, "He did though, that summer. Tell me what he did, and I will make him pay for it."

He's been with me four days, and already he's caught on to what everyone else has missed. But how did he find out about that summer? I've been cautious with what I say—not wanting a guy who is so new and mysterious to know every-thing about me. Is he just that observant? Or does he some-how care for me more than anyone else?

"You're wrong," I say. "He *helped* me."

"It doesn't look that way."

"He told me the truth—which is more than I can say for *you*."

"I know for certain he doesn't tell you everything," he states matter-of-factly.

"So now you're an expert on me and my life?"

"I could spend a thousand years studying you, and it wouldn't be enough."

His confession demolishes my anger like a stick of dynamite. The rapid change has left me confused, vulnerable, weak. "A thousand? Am I really that complicated?"

"No." He smirks. "A thousand years used to seem like a long time. Then I met you." He pauses and his smirk disappears. His eyes widen. "If I were with you ... I have a feeling infinity wouldn't be long enough."

"Stop." I place my hand on his chest. His energy flows into me, and I close my eyes to fight against the exhilarating feelings, the completeness, and the desire to run away with him. "Just ... stop talking."

His thumb brushes my cheek, making it even harder to fight him off. My body hums along to the tantalizing rhythm the energy creates as it races through me and connects back to him.

His eyes dim. His brows pull together. "You truly have no idea what you are, do you?"

I pull back from his touch and glare at him, yet again frustrated at how easily and frequently he toys with my emotions. I feel like a yo-yo, bouncing high and low from my perch on his finger. "What *I* am?" I ask. "I'm not the one with all the abilities. You can talk all you want about how you might *feel* about me. But at the end of the day, it doesn't matter if I can't trust you."

In a few seconds, tears will spill out. I need to get away. I need to appear strong, even though I'm crumbling inside. As calmly as I can manage, I leave him and head for the door.

The clouds open up and rain lightly falls. Tears slide down my face as my heart breaks. My defenses are so weak that if he comes after me, I'll give in. We'd be so happy. I'd be safe. Justin wouldn't come after me. He could help me figure out Damien, and together we'd save Amber.

"I'm sorry, Maddy."

My body trembles with the pain of my decision to reject him. I know I shouldn't, but in a stupid moment of weakness, I look back at him.

The deck is empty.

So that's it? After everything he said ... he just left? I didn't hear him leave.

I never expected to find someone like him. Now I've let him walk away. Twice.

I WANT TO SEEK SOLITUDE IN MY ROOM, BUT STOP IN THE kitchen. The bag of my bloody clothes is gone; he must have taken it. I shake my head at his complexity and walk up to my room.

My room offers little comfort, but I don't really want to be comforted. I did a stupid thing today. Well, many stupid things recently. And I need time to deal with them. I need to grieve, accept it, and move on.

I hurt him again, and he was already hurting. Whatever happened with his parents, he blames himself. And it's clear his nightmare isn't over. Who else got hurt around him? Who did this to him?

I collapse on my bed. My eyes burn, but I have no more tears left. The only thing that helps is keeping them closed.

In the darkness, the red, screaming faces from last night's dream reappear. Damien was the one guy I thought I could always depend on. No matter what, he was always a gentleman, so charismatic and tender. I never wasted time thinking about the perfect guy because I already had him.

I'm not ready to have him fall off the pedestal I put him on, but I don't have a choice. The faces I saw, the things he thought ... there's darkness in him. I don't know how or why he connects to MJ and Justin, but I need to figure it out.

If the Dream Girl sends me back, I have to pay attention. I'll stalk Damien and figure out as much as I can about him.

I underestimated Justin; I won't do it again. I failed with MJ.

At least I can still figure out if I'm dreaming about a killer.

CHAPTER 41

Maddy

A T SOME POINT BETWEEN BLINKS, MY BEDROOM morphs into the Dream Girl's cabin. I don't feel as if I'm floating, so I must have connected to her right away. I turn around, and Damien stands a few feet away. He's in a dark gray suit, and he's smiling that same dazzling smile he always does when he sees me—her, the Dream Girl.

But while his smile is contagious, I don't feel giddy as I normally do when she sees him. I feel empty. Did something happen? Are they fighting too?

"I have missed you," he says in his familiar, accented voice.

His words curl around me like a velvet blanket. He means it; I know he does. In his handsome features I can see the toll their separation has taken. Maybe the vision I saw when he passed through me wasn't real. Maybe the cold caused me to hallucinate. Someone who looks like that couldn't possibly do the unspeakably horrible things I saw.

He opens his arms, ready to engulf me in one of his amazing hugs. After the day I've had, I could use a hug like that. Even if it isn't meant for me.

I throw my arms around him and wait for all the lovey-dovey emotions she feels for him—and I feel for MJ.

Instead, strange flames surge through me the moment his skin touches mine. It's hot, but it doesn't hurt. Every spot the flames touch feels energized and alive. My muscles twitch, anxious to move.

I need to find MJ. I'll demand he tell me what he is. No more changing the subject or distracting me with his touch. Then it's Ben's turn. I don't care that Justin *made* him do it. He needs to pay for what he did today. I was so weak and naïve to walk right into his trap. Ben took advantage of me. And MJ just let him walk away!

But Justin … he's the one who really deserves to be punished. He's going to undo what he did to my friends. Then I'm going to kill him.

I need to wake up. I need out of this dream so I can stop him before he hurts anyone else.

I break away from Damien's embrace and head for the door. But in one step, the lust for vengeance leaves me.

I don't understand. I wanted Justin to pay. I wanted to hurt him.

"Damien, I don't—" The words stall on my tongue when I turn back to him and see he's hugging and kissing the Dream Girl. He had walked right through me to get to her.

I wasn't inside her? *I* was somehow hugging him? So everything I felt—the energy, power, and rage—is all attached to him?

Crud. They're leaving. I need to stay close to him—observe him. Find out as much as I can about him so I can help her. She's not safe with him.

Snow blankets the outside just as it did the other night. There are no other houses in sight, so wherever this is, it's remote. I remember from previous dreams that the cabin is in the mountains, but I don't know where.

While Damien holds the passenger door for the Dream Girl, I run on the shoveled snow path to the back of the Jeep to look at the license plate.

Nothing. No license plate. Okay . . What about his car? Damien bought the Jeep for the Dream Girl to use, so it stays here. Damien must have driven himself in another car.

But there's no other vehicle here. Not even tire tracks from someone dropping him off. The only footsteps in the snow are the ones we just made leaving the cabin.

How did he get here? Come to think of it … I've never noticed another vehicle when I've been here.

At the sound of her door shutting, I race for his. He beats me. One moment he was at her door, then he just appeared in front of me and opened his door.

It has to be a product of the dream. He can't really move that fast. These are her dreams, so maybe I'm only shown what she sees.

I sneak into the back of the Jeep just before he closes the door.

As we drive into town, the scene of him suddenly appearing beside his door plays over and over in the back of my mind. I can't focus on that right now, though, so I push it away. I need to pay close attention to him.

I watch them through dinner. Every second he's a gentleman. He opens doors, pulls her chair out at the table, stands up when she leaves to go to the ladies room, and stands again when she comes back.

After dinner, they go to a movie. While waiting to buy snacks, a guy cuts in front of them to refill his drink. Damien's eyes change from black to familiar scarlet. Pure hatred emanates as he moves toward the man, intent on grabbing him.

What do I do? Can I even stop him? I can't just let him attack this guy.

I step in front of Damien, determined to stop him.

He reaches for the man's shoulder. I try to shove his hand away, but my hand goes through him. Scorching heat burns inside me as if my blood turned into lava. I cringe in pain and pull away. The burning disappears the instant we break contact.

Whatever he intends to do to the guy, it's going to be bad and I can't stop him.

Right before Damien touches the stranger—he stops, drops his hand, and looks to his right. The Dream Girl rests her head against his arm, and her fingers lace with his. She's concentrating on the snack choices listed behind the counter. She has no idea what almost happened.

He blinks, and his eyes change back to black. He smiles and kisses the top of her head.

I don't get it. He looked ready to kill that man. But as soon as she touched him, it vanished. She's the only reason he didn't do something terrible.

I claim the open seat next to him for the movie, anxiously waiting for the next clue that will help me figure him out, but he behaves as normal. He holds her hand the whole time.

I know what I saw and I know what I felt. He's powerful. He's evil. He has to be. He has difficulty controlling his anger, and somehow he can appear out of thin air. He can probably disappear too. His eyes turn scarlet when he's angry.

Just like ... MJ.

CHAPTER 42

MJ

THIS IS RIDICULOUS. I SHOULD BE WITH AMBER. INSTEAD I had to come back here. I couldn't concentrate. Not even enough to summon the Veil of Shadows to hide me while I'm here. I kept picturing the demon returning for Maddy. I'd never forgive myself if something happened to her while I wasn't around to protect her.

She's asleep. I've watched many Charges sleep before, and I don't recall any of them moving or talking as much as she does. She didn't do this in the truck.

Being with her again, it's impossible not to reflect on today. What was I thinking, saying all of that? What did I expect? *Hey, I know your ex-boyfriend just attacked you, and you saw me use even more of my abilities, and they frightened you, but date me. Be with me. Forever or just a day. It doesn't matter, as long as I get to hold you and comfort you and make you smile as you did for a brief moment on the deck.*

When she smiled, she shined with a light so bright from within, her eyes glowed as if they were gemstones held underneath the brightest light. In that moment, I felt a flutter inside me. Then five back-to-back, strong, and steady thumps reverberated through me. It shook my entire body. I realized what it was … my heart was beating.

Those next moments were a blur. I didn't realize what I was saying until I'd said it. It's true, though. I would walk away from all that I am. I'd become what I detest more than a demon: a Shadowwalker. For her. Only for her.

My heart stopped again, and clarity returned when the light faded from her.

I thought she shared my feelings, but she wants the one thing I can't give her: the truth.

If I tell her what I am, it's signing her death sentence. Mortals can know the truth of our existence only when they are under our protection. Then once the case ends, their memories are erased, and our secret is safe once again. But I can't erase Maddy's memory. If I told her what I am and she accidentally said something to anyone about it, Heaven would find out. They would have no choice but to follow the rules I'm not following—they'd kill her. I can't allow that to happen. I can't lose her like that.

I'm selfish. She's still in jeopardy of losing her mind whenever I'm near, but I can't stay away. She's my life support. Being away from her would be like pulling the plug. It could take minutes or it could take weeks, but eventually I'd go back to empty nothingness.

She's strong, though. If she were going to lose her mind, it would have happened by now. Maybe her mind is somehow protected from a breakdown, in the same way it seems to be protected from my mind-accessing abilities. Maybe there is no danger.

Regardless of what transpired between us today, I had to make sure she was safe. Even though I compelled Ben to leave, the demon controlling him fought against me harder than any had ever done before. Once the demon leaves his body, it can come after her again. It's not just him that worries me, either.

He was right. She isn't marked.

Because she's my Charge, Amber's soul is now marked with the silver seal of the Protectors. It is a sign visible to demons and other spirits, warning them the mortal is off limits. Any demon choosing to ignore the mark will receive a swift ticket back to Hell.

Maddy is not my Charge—or anyone's, for that matter. But if I had access to her file, I could mark her soul too. It wouldn't make her invincible to demons, but it would at least warn them to stay away. Without that file and without a mark, she's free game. What happened today is proof of that.

Her heart races, and before I even think it through, I'm standing over her. Beads of moisture form across her forehead. Her eyelids are fluttering. Is she having a nightmare? Should I wake her?

"Evil," she mumbles.

I stop breathing.

"Scarlet ... disappear ... MJ."

She's having a nightmare about me? She thinks I'm evil?

"No!" she shouts.

I leap back into the corner a second before she bolts up in bed.

CHAPTER 43
Maddy

I WAKE TO THUNDER SHAKING THE HOUSE AND LIGHTNING flashing through my window.

I sit up and hug my knees, curling as small as I can while tremors ripple through me. I don't want MJ to be the same as Damien. I feel safe and happy and complete with him. If he's evil too, I'll never recover.

Something moves in the corner, and I freeze. Someone's there. I can see his tall outline as lightning continues to flash, acting like a strobe light. My heart beats so hard I feel each rapid thump in every inch of me. I know if I blink, I risk giving the shadow a chance to flee.

He knows if he moves again, there would be no denying his existence.

My eyes burn, and I want to shut them so badly, but then I'll lose my only chance to find out who it is.

A loud bang sounds to my left, and on instinct my head follows it. Throwing open my door, Mom rushes in and turns on the light.

My attention flies back to the corner, but it's too late. He's gone. Her distraction let him escape.

"Madison, what's wrong?" she asks. She follows my frightened gaze to the corner and breathes a sigh of relief when she sees it's empty.

"I ... I ... I had a bad dream." I take a deep, slow breath and wipe my eyes before turning to face her.

She climbs onto my bed, and after a moment of hesitation, she rests her hand on my arm. "You sounded so terrified, I thought someone was in here."

Someone was in here, and she let him get away. But if I tell her that, she'll probably think I'm nuts. "Sorry, Mom. I'm sorry about everything. I don't know what happened."

"*Shh.* It's okay. You are okay, aren't you?"

Maybe it's the feelings I'm beginning to reexplore for my family, or maybe it's the sheer weight of all my problems. Whatever it is, I open my mouth to say I'm fine, but instead I answer, "No."

"Oh!" Mom says, as surprised by my answer as I am. "Okay. Well, I was on my way downstairs when I heard you scream. I couldn't sleep, so I was going to work on your Halloween costume. You can help if you aren't too tired."

If I go down there, I'm sure we'll talk about all the stuff going on lately. I don't know if I can deal with that right now, but there's no way I'm staying up here. "That'd be great," I say.

She heads downstairs, and I head into the bathroom. I splash cold water on my face. I look horrible. My complexion is dull, my eyes are bloodshot, and I have dark circles forming under them. I don't know how many more nights I can keep this up.

I peel off my sweat-covered clothes, but stop when the movement causes the muscles on my right side to ache. There's an odd bruise forming there, a big blob with five long lines reaching around to my back.

Ben's hand.

Shaking, I turn in front of the mirror to inspect the rest of the horrible reminders of what almost happened today.

Both my knees and my right hip are bruised too. Those bruises are a different color than the one on my side. They look older. I hit my knees when he tripped me, but I don't remember hitting my hip today. The only time I hit both my hip and knees was during the dream the other night when I fell on the blanket.

No.

It shouldn't be possible. My body was still here in my bed. Dreams can't do that. But the evidence is all over my body. If falling in a dream can bruise me, what would've happened if I never made it to their cabin?

As much as I don't want to admit it, I don't think these are dreams. They're something abnormal. Something like MJ, Damien, and Justin.

A gasp sounds from the doorway.

Oh crap—Mom!

I spin around, but no one is there.

Did I imagine it? Am I on the verge of a mental break-down?

Not wanting to linger on thoughts of my mental instabil-ity, I cover the bruises under new clothes and make my way downstairs. There's no way I can tell her about this, but just being near her will help me.

I find her in the downstairs office sitting on the floor with fabric scattered all around her. She motions to the desk, and there's a cup of hot chocolate and a bowl of popcorn waiting for me.

Duane's voice echoes through me: *It's the little things ...*

I smile at her caring gesture and sit at the desk. After several bites of popcorn, I take a break for some hot chocolate. Steam curls up around me, and I inhale the sweet smell of cocoa. I blow on it a few times, then take a sip. It's extra chocolaty, just how I like it. She did this for me. She loves me.

A file on the edge of the desk catches my eye, and I open it. It's my missing documents Mom couldn't find this morning. "You found them?"

"Yes. They were in the filing cabinet the whole time. I swear I looked there, though. Oh well. I set them out so I would remember to send them to Duane."

Camping in Canada ... that should be fun. But why does he need them so early? We don't go camping until August. That's ten months away. It can't take *that* long to get a passport.

Bits of paper crinkle, and I tear my focus away from the folder to see her smoothing out fabric with brown paper pinned to it. "What do you think? I made a pattern and pinned it to the fabric already."

I look skeptically at the odd shapes of brown paper over fabric. Somehow Mom will turn that into a dress? "Cool. That looks great."

"Perfect. You can help me cut it out."

I hate this part, but it's my costume, so I grab a pair of scissors and get to work. The cutting hurts my wrist, but I push through it. She can't know what happened. Not just because I'm grounded and Ben shouldn't have been over anyway, but because she'd tell Dad, and he'd probably kill Ben. As angry as I am, I don't want him dead.

Justin, maybe.

"Since you had a bad dream, that means you must have slept a little tonight, right?"

"A little," I lie.

"Maddy, I wish you would talk to me."

I glance up in time to see her brush away a tear.

"You've always been so closed off. Even as a baby. You would cry to be held, and I would pick you up, but then you would cry harder. I know it's ridiculous, but I thought you were crying because *I* was holding you and not someone else."

"Mom ... no. I'm sure that's not—"

"It's like you knew I wasn't your real mother. I tried to love you the same as I do Hannah, but you're so independent. Then when Duane told you about your real parents, you shut down. I didn't know what to do. So I fought my maternal instincts and let you be alone like you wanted. I do love you, though. Regardless of whether you love me back."

All this time I've watched her grow closer to Hannah while growing more distant with me—and I caused it. I kept her at arm's length as I do with Kelli and Ben. I was so focused on how much Mom and Dad hurt me, I didn't even think about how much I was hurting everyone in return.

I rush over, fall to my knees, then throw my arms around her. "I'm sorry, Mom. I didn't mean it."

"*Shh, shh.*" She strokes my hair as she used to when I was young. Tears fall down my cheeks and onto her fuzzy gray robe.

I kept wishing my birth mother loved me, but in the process, I turned my back on the one mother who does. Marie has always been there for me. No matter what sport, recital, or performance it was, she was in the front row with the video camera. And when I quit them all, she never pushed me for a reason. I can't believe I've been so blind.

"I'm so sorry. I'm glad you're my mom."

She leans back to look at me, tears streaming as she smiles. "I love you, Maddy."

"I do too." I sniffle. I know she wants me to say *I love you too*, but I've rejected those words for so long, they just won't come.

She sighs, and her smile drops a little. "I'm not trying to hurt your feelings, but you look exhausted, sweetie."

"I know. It's been a crazy couple of days, but it's getting better."

"Would Ben have something to do with that?"

"Nope." I stand and walk back to my piece of fabric so she can't see the guilt in my eyes.

"Do you know what happened to his face? It was swollen and discolored when I saw him. I think his nose is broken."

Yeah- -my fist happened.

Wait.

"When did you see Ben?" I ask, trying to sound calmer than I feel.

"He and a friend stopped by to talk to you while you were asleep. You didn't tell me Ben was in town."

He didn't leave town. He came back here. With a *friend*? Was Ben the one in my room?

"His visit was … unexpected," I manage to say through my closing throat. My hands shake, and my heart thumps so loudly, I swear she can hear it. "W-who was the friend?"

"He said his name was Justin," she says over a crack of thunder. "He's quite the charmer. I've never heard you mention Justin before. Why?"

I should've known Ben would go running to Justin and be talked into staying in town. "Justin's a liar, Mom. He's a self-centered, egotistical Neanderthal, and I can't stand him."

She looks at me. I sink into my chair, knowing a lecture is coming. "That's not a very nice thing to say about a friend who cares for you as deeply as Justin does. He was very insistent he talk to you. I tried to wake you, but I couldn't. You should call him—put the poor boy out of his misery."

Oh, I'd like to put him out of his misery, all right. I can't *believe* he came here and talked to my mother. I couldn't stand it if Justin did something to her.

"Actually," I say, "do you mind if I go talk to Ben now … on the phone?"

She smiles. "I think that's a lovely idea. In fact, you're no longer grounded, so you're welcome to go to Justin's house. I know he's eager to see you. He said if you don't want to go to him, he could come back over here. It's your choice, sweetie."

The grandfather clock in the dining room chimes once, signaling it's one in the morning. Mom wouldn't normally let me go over to a friend's house at this time of night, especially not a boy's house.

She picks up her scissors and continues cutting my costume while humming.

Thunder rumbles and lightning flashes through the window, momentarily turning the room white. As soon as the light fades, dread fills me, squeezing all the good feelings I had found here with her. I shiver.

She's humming Justin's song.

Justin altered my mother's mind.

I back out of the office with a shaking hand covering my mouth. That settles it. I have to go to Justin now.

Even though I don't want MJ involved, I wish he were here. He would know what to do. He would give me strength and courage.

I return to my room and grab my phone. I text Ben, knowing Justin will see the message: *U win*.

CHAPTER 44

Maddy

STORM CLOUDS BLOCK MOST OF THE MOON AS I WALK down the dark streets toward Justin's house. The bit of the moon that is visible reminds me of Justin's sideways grin. I'm sure he's overjoyed, waiting for my arrival. Well, he can wait a little longer. I'm taking my time.

I'm determined to go over there and command that a-hole to restore my mother's, Kelli's, Ben's, and everyone else's minds to their original states. But I just need time to figure out what to say to him.

By the second block, goose bumps cover my arms underneath my shirt. Seeing as I've survived much colder weather, I'm not going to let a little chill stop me. I have to do this. Yes, it's stupid. I know that. But I don't have any other choice. I rub my arms and keep going.

"A little late for a stroll," says a voice in the darkness beside me.

I jump, and the sky erupts with booming thunder and brilliant flashes of light that illuminate my companion. It's

MJ. Once my heart leaves my throat, I ask, "Where'd you come from?"

"I was ... in the neighborhood."

He's full of it. Amber's house is nowhere near here. But I don't want to push it. I don't want to find hope where I know there isn't any.

A light rumble sounds again, and I stare up at the sky. It's been storming so much lately. Way more than normal. And it all started when Justin came to town. It's as if even nature were as upset as I am by his presence.

"So why are you out here?"

I consider refusing to answer his question, but one fight a day is enough. "Couldn't sleep."

"Want to talk about it?"

"Nope."

He reaches for my hand, but I back away. I can't let him touch me. There are too many emotions flowing through me, and he'd be able to sense them all. I can't give him another reason to be suspicious of me.

He shakes his head. "I don't want to fight with you, Maddy."

A cool wind blows, causing me to shiver. I hug myself, fighting against the cold and the pain I'm causing MJ.

Justin can wait a little longer. This may be the last chance I have to talk with MJ. I need to set some things right between us.

"You left."

"What?"

"You didn't even bother to say good-bye. You just ... " I take a deep breath and start again. "You're rude. That's the third time you've left without saying good-bye, and I don't appreciate it."

MJ stares at me for what feels like an eternity. He's not going to answer. I guess I deserve that for rejecting him.

I want to keep walking, but my body won't move. My willpower is drifting farther away the longer I stay with him. How can he make me feel so weak and so strong at the same time?

"Maddy, has anyone you've known ever died?"

"What? No?"

"Were you left alone as a child?"

"No. Why are you asking me that?"

He runs his fingers through his hair and sighs. "Just checking. I thought I had figured something out about you, but I was wrong."

"*Okay* ... well, now you have to tell me."

"It's silly, but for a moment, I thought you had autophobia."

He thinks I'm nuts enough to have a disorder? "I'm not afraid of cars."

"No, Maddy." He smiles. "Autophobia is the fear of abandonment."

My chest constricts, and my side throbs as I breathe in quick pants. He can't know the truth. Not yet. Not while there are so many things I don't know about him.

"You've displayed several of the symptoms for it, but there's no reason for you to have it. Usually it develops when loved ones die or the individual is left alone frequently as a child. Forget I brought it up."

"Do you have autophobia? From your parents' death, I mean?" I ask, trying to shift the focus away from me.

"No." He looks away with pained eyes.

Over and over again, I hurt him even when I'm not trying. "I'm sorry."

He looks back at me. His eyes are brighter, shining in the glow of the little moonlight. There's a hint of a smile on his lips. "Can I show you something? I know you've seen me do a lot of strange things, and I'm sorry I haven't been as open about them as I'd like to be. But I would really like a chance to show you I'm ... the good guy."

Now, of all times, he chooses to start opening up to me. What other wish of mine is going to come true right as my world hangs in the balance?

"Any other time I would say yes, but I'm busy tonight."

"Please," he begs. "It's important to me. You're important to me."

My heart flutters as those last four words echo inside me. The eagerness shining from his eyes reminds me of our not-a-date date on Sunday. For those few hours, Amber, the killer, and Justin didn't exist. It was just us. We were happy. But we were under pressure, having only limited time together. MJ's responsibilities sealed us to only that one day. Tonight, it's my turn to be the responsible one.

I want to feel the way we felt on Sunday, even though it will be short-lived. "Okay. But once I see it, I really have to go."

His smile widens, and he holds out his hand for me. I take a deep breath to bury my thoughts about Damien, Mom, and Justin, then I entwine my fingers with his.

As anticipated, his energy rushes into me. Part of it stays in my heart, repatching the hole as if it were pavement in the street. The rest swirls all over me, and I suddenly feel warm. I snort. He's a walking space heater. Earlier, that might have freaked me out. Now it's comforting. Is that because of my fears of Justin? Or am I so far gone that the strange and unusual no longer affect me?

He turns us around, heading away from Justin's house and my house. We keep walking, neither one of us speaking. It allows me a chance to embrace the fact that—for the moment—we're together.

He takes me to the path where we first met—my safe haven. When we round the curve to Hiniker Bridge, I gasp in shock.

Hundreds of candles float on the water and sit on the bridge.

"You did this for me?" I ask breathlessly, unable to look away.

"Yes."

"Why?"

"Because this place is special to you, and you talk more freely here."

"That's not what I meant."

He's silent for a moment. The buzzing warmth inside me picks up, attaching itself to my feelings of inferiority already resurfacing. He squeezes my hand. "Because you're worth it."

Tears prick my eyes as I gaze at what he's done for me. Honestly, I don't know how to react to this. It's too grand, too romantic, and I don't deserve this kind of gesture. I can't reciprocate.

But even as I think about how unworthy I am, I know it isn't true. Is that because of MJ? Is his calming energy still flowing inside me, keeping me warm, guarding me against my past, allowing me to see beyond the voices that have always shouted out how broken I am? When I'm with him, a new voice can be heard. One that says, *Why not me? Why can't I have a guy like him? Even if it's just for the night.*

I want to believe that voice.

"Thank you," I say.

An overjoyed smile lights up his face. "You're welcome."

Hand in hand, we walk to the center of the bridge and sit. I still can't believe he did all this for me after I rejected him. I really don't deserve him.

"Don't," he says.

I look over at him. "Hmm?"

"Whatever you're thinking, don't think like that."

"I thought you couldn't read my thoughts."

"I can't. But I can sense your emotions and feel your heartbeat, both of which just dropped considerably."

"But it's true—what I was thinking. I don't deserve you."

"Your perception of yourself is absurd. Regardless of what we are, I'm determined to show you your worth."

Not wanting to sour the night further, I simply say, "Good luck."

He smiles, then it falls. "How long can you stay?"

I rest my head on his shoulder in an effort to be closer to him while also hiding my expression. I don't want to leave. "Not long."

His thumb rubs circles on the back of my hand.

"Shouldn't you be with Amber?" I ask.

"She's fine."

I peek at him. The fire reflecting in his eyes causes my stomach to flutter. He's so beautiful—and incredibly, he's here with me. But he shouldn't be. I push back the feelings overtaking me.

"MJ … as grateful as I am you did this for me, you have to stop. Amber is your priority. She's your job. Someone is coming to kill her, and you're the only person who can stop that. I would never forgive myself if something happened to Amber because you were with me."

He takes a deep breath and calmly says, "Nothing is going to happen to Amber."

I shift on the wooden boards, sitting on my knees so I can fully face him. "Unless you can see the future, you don't know that."

"I don't need to see the future. The killer has a pattern. He's going through a list of victims. Many victims sit between Amber and the killer. They all have … someone like me watching over them and trying to stop the killer. If those victims die and the killer isn't stopped, then I will worry about Amber. And you as well. Until then, she's fine."

I don't know if he's serious or if he's downplaying the situation for me, himself, or both of us. "Killers break their patterns all the time. Especially if they know the authorities are close to catching them. You can't put her life at risk like this, MJ. It's not fair to her—or me."

His energy picks up inside me. His thumb stops rubbing the peaceful circles on my skin. His jaw tenses. "You don't know what I do. People just like Amber face danger every day, and it falls on me to stop it. Sometimes … sometimes bad things happen, and I can't always prevent it. The world moves on. I move on. I save someone else. It's a vicious, never-ending cycle."

I can't imagine carrying the pressure of strangers' lives on my shoulders. It must be an incredible burden. And if they are anything like Amber, I doubt they make his job easy. Do any of them thank him?

"The faces I saved and most of the ones I've lost are a blur." He squeezes my hand. "But you are the first good thing that's happened to me since I started doing this. To be honest, since even before then. There will always be another Amber. There will *never* be another you. Forget her for tonight. Stay with me as long as you can. I need you."

I know this will anger Justin. I'm sure he'll be furious that I don't show tonight, and he may even exact his revenge on someone other than me, like the coward he is. But for now, I don't want to deal with that. Maybe that makes me selfish and a coward too. But I need MJ. More than he could possibly know.

I sit back, pull my knees to my chest, hug them with my free arm, and rest my chin on my left kneecap. "My plans can wait. I'd rather stay with you."

His body relaxes into the railing and his expression lifts as the seriousness of our conversation ends. "When do you need to go home?"

I close my eyes to help fight against the thoughts of Justin. "My mom thinks I'm at a friend's house, so I don't have to leave til probably morning."

Even though I don't look at him, I sense the smile in his voice as he asks, "Promise me something?"

I peek at him. "What?"

"Don't go anywhere. I'm going to get you a blanket."

"Okay."

He vanishes, taking his warmth and energy with him, only to return a second later carrying a sleeping bag and pillows.

"You're not going to tell me how you did that, are you?" I wrap my other arm around my legs. Though the candles' heat helps keep most of the cold at bay, they're not as warm as MJ.

Instead of answering me, he spreads out the double-sized sleeping bag and pillows.

I shake my head. "This inability for us to talk is what's driving a wedge between us." He stiffens. "There has to be some give-and-take, otherwise we'll always be stuck repeating this same argument. I don't want that."

He stares up at the sky and sighs. "You're right. Okay—tonight we will each share a small secret."

"Seriously?" Excitement spreads through me at the thought of solving some of MJ's mysteries.

"Seriously. Now let's get in." He motions to the sleeping bag.

I scramble into it. If he were any other guy, I would have said no. Regardless of what MJ is, I trust him not to try anything. Plus, I miss his warmth.

MJ crawls in and zips it up. There isn't much room in here, but I try to stick to my side of an imaginary line in the bag. Still, our bodies touch at our knees and hands. The multiple points of contact create a circuit, allowing his energy to flow continuously between us.

I smile, letting myself rejoice in the completeness I feel when we're together.

"So," he says, "you want to know how I retrieved the sleeping bag so quickly. I'll tell you—if you tell me where you were going tonight."

My smile falls, and I drop my gaze to the red plaid pattern lining the bag. "What you're asking me is not a 'small' secret."

"You think me revealing one of my abilities isn't a big deal too?"

"No. I ... " What do I want? I told him I wouldn't be with him unless he told me what he is. At least he's trying. I'm not.

My thoughts scatter as my phone buzzes in my pocket.

"Do you need to answer that?" MJ asks.

I grab it. Ben's name is displayed on the screen.

I take a deep breath, preparing for what I'm about to do—open up to MJ. I turn my phone off. It's time to start telling MJ the truth. It won't be everything—I can't be that exposed. But telling him about Justin is easier than talking about myself.

"I was on my way to see a guy named Justin."

MJ's brows pull together. "At this time of night?"

"It was sort of a snap decision. He's been an ongoing problem for several weeks now, and I'm tired of it. I'm tired of him."

"Is this the boy you mentioned Friday and Sunday?"

"Yes."

MJ falls silent. His eyes search mine as his jaw tightens. "Is he dangerous?"

I keep my breath steady and block all thoughts of Justin. "Not to me," I lie, hoping Duane's lesson on beating a polygraph will work against MJ's ability to feel my emotions.

MJ nods, buying it.

I wish I didn't have to keep Justin from him, but I can't risk Justin hurting MJ. Not just because of how deeply I care for him, but also for Amber's sake. Who's going to protect her if MJ's gone?

"Is he the one who sent you the flowers this morning?"

I cringe, wishing MJ didn't know about that. "Yes."

He grabs my hand. I close my eyes and absorb his tender embrace. "My offer still stands. I could talk to him for you. He would leave you alone."

"No. Justin's manipulative. He has a way of twisting things around and making people see things his way. I need you to stay on my side. You give me strength and courage."

"You're sure?"

"Positive."

"All right. But if you change your mind, all you have to do is ask."

"Thanks."

"Anytime. Now it's my turn to talk."

I rest my head on my arm, grateful my turn has finished.

"Last night, when we were on the bridge, I told you we were on a plane separate from the one our bodies were on. What I do to disappear is similar to that, except I stay in one piece."

I do my best to stay calm and not react, knowing he would sense it. "Where do you go?"

"There is a place that exists between the world of the living and the world of the dead. It has many names: the Beyond, Limbo, the Veil of Shadows, the Curtain, the Third Dimension ... the list goes on. It works similarly to what you and I have experienced. Time moves differently, allowing me to disappear for great lengths of time, while only a second or two passes here."

"I see." I try—really hard—not to think about how *unnatural* and insane his explanation is, but it's just too absurd. He walks between the living and the dead? What the hell does that mean? My chest tightens, and my breathing hitches. His warm, soothing energy pools where my fear is building, and he frowns.

I reach out and stroke his smooth jaw line. "It's okay," I say, reassuring us both. "It's just a little jarring to learn that such a thing exists. That's all."

He nods. "I understand."

"So how can you do that?"

He pauses before saying, "In order to tell you that, I'd have to tell you what I am."

"And you won't do that?"

"*Can't* do that."

I huff and turn to face the sky. All the storm clouds are gone. There aren't as many stars as last night, but I'm actually here with him, so that makes tonight even better.

Without warning, I yawn. I've slept out here hundreds of times before, though it's never been quite like this.

The golden glow around us dims as hundreds of candles extinguish.

"Did you do that?" I ask.

"You should rest. I'll wake you at sunrise."

I'll take his nonanswer as a yes.

Maybe I should have stuck to my original plan tonight, but who knows what I would have walked into at Justin's house. What's the harm of getting a few hours of sleep before dealing with Justin? If anything, I'll be better suited to handle him.

Here I'm safe. It's a feeling that's becoming rare, and I doubt it will exist in the future.

I roll back over to face MJ. "Good night, MJ."

"Sleep well, Maddy."

CHAPTER 45

Maddy

THE CHIRPING OF BIRDS PULLS ME FROM THE MOST REST-ful night of sleep I've ever had. Even my body temperature is in a state of perfection. And I know it's all because of MJ. On nights I don't dream, I toss and turn all night, battling with my blankets to find a balance between too hot or too cold. MJ's energy stayed with me all night, alternating between warming and cooling me. I doubt I would have even needed the blanket with him at my side.

My eyes flutter open to MJ's bare chest. When did he take his shirt off?

My head rests in the nook of his shoulder, my left arm lies on his firmly toned pecks, and my left leg is draped over his jeans. His arms are wrapped around me, holding me to him.

So much for staying on my own side.

In the space between my face and hand sits a two-inch scar across his chest. It's horizontal, so I don't think it's from a surgery, though it's right near his heart. Without thinking, my index finger moves to trace the line, but MJ's hand scoops down to stop me.

Blood rushes to my cheeks, reddening them. I am not only embarrassed because I tried to touch his scar, but also because I spent the night with him. It was beyond anything I could have ever imagined sleeping with a guy would be— and we didn't even do … that.

"Hey," I say, then bite my lip.

"Morning," he says in a smooth, uplifted voice.

Butterflies spring to life inside me.

"I was just about to wake you," he says. "The sun is going to rise in a minute. Because we've already watched a day end together, I thought you'd like to watch one start together."

My lip slides out from my teeth's grasp and shifts into a shy smile. "Sure."

We both gaze at the trees bordering the east end of the pond. The birds fall silent and the air around us stills, as if nature were holding its breath in anticipation of the dawn.

The deep dead of night gives way, and a light pink-and-orange glow streaks across the sky, signifying the sun is close behind. The colors brighten as a vibrant speck of yellow peeks over the treetops.

"Breathe, Maddy," MJ whispers.

I inhale as the sun stretches its way across the horizon, bringing with it muted shades of cyan, dusty rose, and fuchsia. The barren branches in the trees wave their hellos, and the birds sing their sweet morning songs.

MJ's arms tighten around me for a moment, then he slowly loosens his grip. "I suppose I should take you home now."

I bury my head in his soft skin to hide my disappointment. His fingers play with my ponytail while I'm faced with the shocking revelation of how *right* and *easy* it feels to be with him.

Am I making a huge mistake? Should I just toss all my inhibitions aside and indulge in him for the short time he's in town? I doubt I'll ever come across anyone like him again. He's already done more for me than anyone before. Isn't this what your "other half" is supposed to do—make you strive to be a better person? With him … it's effortless.

MJ ESCORTS ME HOME. AT THE DOOR, HE SURPRISES ME BY kissing my hand.

Everything in me stills as a force so powerful, so magnanimous, enters me at the exact spot his lips meet my skin. If it were possible, I'd think I was suddenly made of something indestructible like a tank or a bulletproof vest. Or … a diamond. Nothing—my past, Justin, Damien, and even the questions still surrounding MJ—could break me.

He lets go, and the sensation lingers, attaching itself to my muscle fibers, bones, and soft tissue, strengthening me to face what's still to come.

"I'll pick you up in an hour for school," MJ promises.

"Can't wait."

MJ chuckles and strides down the driveway.

I shake my head and smile, knowing full well I must be three shades of red.

I shower and take more time than usual to get ready, ensuring my hair is perfectly straight and my makeup is flawless. Unlike last night, nothing hurts. Even the bruises from Ben and my dreams have vanished from my skin. I'm not sure how, seeing as they were pretty dark, but I take it as a good sign that today is going to be great.

I check my phone messages. There are eight missed calls from Ben and one text. I open the message, and it reads: *You brought this on yourself.*

Even Justin's veiled threat isn't enough to dampen this day. I close the message and stick my phone in my pocket.

In the kitchen, my parents are having breakfast. Hannah must have left for swim practice. I bounce up to them and plant a kiss on their cheeks. "Good morning. Beautiful day, isn't it?" I pour a glass of OJ and take a huge gulp.

"Well, someone sure woke up on the right side of the bed this morning," Mom says, smiling into her tea.

Right side of the bridge with the right guy, I think to myself. A sheepish grin slides across my face. I turn and grab an apple to hide my delight.

"Well, whatever it is," Dad says, "I'm all for it."

"Does he like lasagna?" Mom asks. "I was thinking of making it for dinner tonight."

"I'm not sure," I reply, smiling at the thought of having dinner with MJ. He'd probably think it was a date again.

Crud.

"Who are you talking about, Mom?" I say, trying to play innocent. But it's too late. This means I've been caught red-handed. They know I stayed out all night with a boy.

They must have seen MJ walk me home. I'll be lucky if they only ground me to graduation next year.

"Why, Justin, silly," she replies.

I drop my apple. It rolls across the tile floor. Mom picks it up and places it on the countertop.

She's still being manipulated by Justin. Strangely, I'm not *afraid*—just caught off guard. The residual effects of MJ's kiss pick up inside me, keeping me from panicking.

"Yes, things must have gone well last night—you came in after the sun came up," Dad adds with a strange smile—almost as if he's proud.

He's happy about it? Dad would never be okay with that. He told me he would shoot the first guy who slept with me. Rubber bullets if I was over eighteen; real ones if I wasn't.

Justin messed with my dad too?

This ends now.

"I didn't go to Justin's." I smile as their faces fall, knowing one way or another Justin will hear this. "I bumped into MJ along the way and spent the night with him." A car horn sounds from outside. "That's him now. I'll see you later." I wave to my stunned parents and leave before they can say anything.

On the way to MJ's truck, I stop when I see not only is he not alone, but Amber is in the passenger seat. Why is she sitting in the front seat? And why is he okay with that? Wouldn't he want to sit by me?

Get a grip Maddy, I scold myself. I sound like a stupid, jealous, insecure brat. I snort. I sound like Amber. I guess this just means MJ has officially begun his assignment with her. That's good, right? That means she'll be safe. I wonder if it's anything like when Duane has to protect someone. Does MJ have to be by her all the time? Does he have a partner? Is he staying at her house? I know so little about him, but what I do know has me falling for him—hard.

Shaking my head, I climb in the back behind her. Actually, this allows me a golden opportunity to check out MJ as we drive.

"Freak," Amber says in her usual greeting.

"Hag," I reply back, though there's no malevolence in my voice.

"You're looking well, Maddy," MJ says.

Butterflies soar up to my throat, making it impossible to respond for a moment. Once they've calmed, I reply, "I slept well."

A smile breaks across his profile. "Me too."

I lean back into the leather seats and use the short drive to study MJ, taking in everything from the exact angle of his hairline to the vein in his neck that sticks out every time Amber talks. And after the third time of seeing his cheek move to accommodate his grin, I know he's just looked at me in the rearview mirror.

At school, he opens both Amber's and my door, then takes my hand. I still feel the lasting effect from his kiss earlier, but now it's even stronger. I can feel his energy working its way through my many layers to strengthen me once more.

Hand in hand, we walk through the school doors. This is the first time I've ever held a guy's hand here, though I don't think people will notice—thanks to the smile that nearly reaches my ears.

The lobby is packed with people catching up with each other before class, but in unison, all conversations stop. Everyone turns and stares at us.

"That's right, everyone," Amber says, pushing ahead of us. "Your queen has arrived."

Nothing.

I can't even hear any distant noise from the hallways or classrooms.

My skin prickles, and an uneasy feeling builds inside me. This is the second day in a row I've been met with silence upon entering the doors. I can't go through another day like that. My smile falls, and I grip tighter to MJ's hand.

"Great!" Amber snaps at me. "He forces me to show up here with *you*, and in just five short minutes, I've caught your *loserness*."

"Bite me," I reply, but there's no emotion behind it. I'm too preoccupied watching the silent crowd stare with vacant expressions. I feel as though I walked in on a herd of zombies and at any moment they're going to charge and eat me alive.

Distant sounds of thunder rumble through the corridor. I shiver.

"Are you all right?" MJ asks.

I turn and meet his gaze.

"Your pulse just skyrocketed, as did your breathing," he says.

I look down at our hands held together. This simple act so many people do is responsible for betraying my emotions. I release my breath and say, "Just getting a bad sense of déjà vu."

"Yesterday?"

I nod.

He smiles reassuringly and tucks a strand of my hair behind my ear. "It's not the same. You *know* I'm by your side today."

He's right. Just a little bit ago, I was full of excitement for the day and ready to face anything that came my way. Yet after a few signs of something bad, I falter. I can do this. MJ is with me today. As long as I have him, everything is going to be just fine.

Our peers silently move off to the side as we make our way down the hallway. Their eyes are on me, but they're looking through me. As if I were invisible. A shadow. A ghost. As if I never really existed.

"Okay. This is just creepy," Amber says, walking close enough to MJ that their arms touch.

"I agree," he says, though his voice is detached. He's not listening. He's preoccupied, looking around with a frown. I haven't heard him talk like that since the night we met.

He stops, and I follow his gaze to my friends standing by my locker. They're smiling. A tightness in my chest eases. At least they're normal.

Then my small spark of relief is snuffed as I see a new balloon floating above their heads. Butterflies and smiley faces line the outer edges. It used to say "Get Well Soon," but two words are crossed out. One word remains.

Soon.

This is Justin. All of it. He didn't just mess with my parents' minds as punishment. He messed with everyone's.

"What's wrong, Maddy?" MJ asks. The tension in his voice only makes my friends smile wider.

"I brought this on myself," I say, repeating Justin's text message. I let go of MJ and open my locker. Hundreds of roses fall to my feet—again. But they've all been painted black.

"Black roses," Shawn says, "signify death."

"Maybe you should have done what he asked," Luke says.

"Good-bye, Maddy," Kelli says, and all my friends leave.

A tremor runs through me, but I fight the urge to panic. I can't let MJ see just how scared I am. After a moment, I start picking up the roses and throwing them in a trash can.

"I think ... " MJ says, pausing long enough that I look up at him, "we should go, Maddy. This doesn't feel right."

"This is a game, MJ. If I run home, I'll be doing what he wants. This is my school. Those are my friends. I'm not going to let him win."

"You said he wasn't dangerous."

"It's a balloon and some flowers. It's fine."

"A message about death is *not* fine."

"This is his sick version of a joke. He's pissed because I blew him off last night. That's all."

"What about your friends? The rest of the school? I know you can tell they're acting strangely."

"I told you—he twists people around. One flash of his stupid smile, and people do whatever he wants."

"Not you?"

I shake my head.

He runs both hands through his hair, yanking on it as he groans. Then he drops his hands and says, "There's nothing I can say to make you leave, is there."

"No."

He's silent for a moment, then he helps remove the blatant signs of Justin from the halls. The mute zombie students, however, remain. Amber was right—they are creepy.

Right before I walk into chemistry, my phone buzzes with a text message. I open up what I'm sure is going to be another threatening message from Justin, only to find it says: 7.

What the hell is *that* supposed to mean? Is it his IQ? Highest grade he completed before dropping out? I sigh and put my phone away, then sit at my desk.

We're doing a lab. Kelli won't let me do anything. She keeps shoving me out of the way and taking from my hands the chemicals we're supposed to be mixing.

"Seriously. What is going on with you?" I demand.

She stops and turns, glaring at me. "You would know if you kept your word."

"What?"

"I was at a party last night. The guest of honor never showed. Apparently she ditched us all to sleep with some guy. But she's rude like that—lying to her friends and family and never appreciating the things we do for her."

"Kelli, I—" I stop, lost for words. How does she know?

"Why are we even friends?" I stare at her in disbelief, so she continues, "You know what I mean. Come on—you're brilliant, gifted, gorgeous. And if all that isn't enough, you're a medium too."

"*A medium?*" I spit the words out. They leave a foul taste in my mouth. "What the hell, Kelli?"

"At least, that's what Justin said when I told him about your dreams."

I grip the countertop as the room spins. "You told *him*?" She promised she would never tell a soul that secret, then she spills it to my worst nightmare.

"He and I have been together since the night you disappeared. He honestly cares for you, so I thought maybe he knows what your dreams mean. And he does."

My body is frozen with fear. I never once thought the dreams held any real meaning to them. I don't want to find out the significance from *him*.

"He says Damien murdered the Dream Girl."

No.

She's not dead. She can't be. She's just a dream. She's not real. And Damien loves her. He wouldn't hurt her.

"She's been trying to get you to help her for years," Kelli continues in my stunned silence. "Therefore, you're a psychic medium."

Glass breaks at the table behind us.

Usually, broken glass creates a commotion. But Mr. Simmons stays at his desk, silent, as he has been most of the morning. He shouldn't just sit there, knowing a student could be hurt. The other students stay focused on their work too, acting as if nothing happened.

What did Justin do to everyone?

The sound came from the direction of MJ's lab table. It can't be a coincidence that it happened right after what Kelli said. She wasn't talking that loudly, but I've suspected MJ has heard things I—or others—have said at times when he shouldn't have. Given all his other abilities, he could have heightened sense, such as hearing. As much as I don't want to see his expression, I have to look. I have to see he's okay. Slowly, I turn around.

There's glass all over his table and blood dripping from his hand.

The phrase "if looks could kill" was clearly created for the look he's giving me.

I deserve it. I've kept so many things from him when he's been risking his life for me. I keep screwing up over and over again.

I have to get out of here.

I bolt from the room, racing toward the bathroom. I need a few minutes to calm down.

But halfway to the bathroom, MJ appears, blocking me.

His angry and hurt eyes burn into me. "*You're psychic?* Just when were you planning on telling me this? Never, right? You have so many secrets. I don't get you. You're so closed off. Not just with me, but with everyone. And the most confusing part is, there is no reason for it! You have a great family who loves you. You have friends who worship you. And all you do is push them away. You've done it to me several times now. It's like you're ripping my heart out and stomping all over it. I can't deal with this, Madison. I don't know how."

"I know," I whisper.

He's right—he shouldn't be dealing with me. He should be focusing on Amber. He came here to protect her, and I keep getting in the way. But he's even more right about me and everything I am. I shut myself off from the world to avoid being hurt, and in return, I hurt everyone who's given me a chance. A chance I didn't deserve in the first place.

"Do you know?" he accuses.

My numb heart aches with the betrayal I feel from him. If I owe him anything, it's the truth. Even if it means he won't care about me anymore.

I throw my hands in the air in defeat. "What was I supposed to say? I have these weird dreams where I'm other people, and they're so realistic, I don't actually sleep. Do you know how crazy that sounds? Kelli is the only person I've told, and that's because I thought she wouldn't judge me. She loved the dreams, and so do I. Or I did." I point with my hands as if Kelli were standing there next to me. "And look what just happened. Kelli told—even though she promised she wouldn't. And now I hear I'm suddenly a psychic! That's total BS! Justin's wrong. He has to be. Please don't think I'm crazy, MJ. I couldn't stand it if you thought that."

He takes a few deep breaths. I brace myself for him to come unglued, to tell me how nuts I am—and how nuts he is for falling for someone like me.

"You're not crazy," he says. "You're … unique, but I've known that about you all along."

I stare up at him, searching for any signs that he's lying, but there's nothing. "You have?"

He reaches out to touch me, but stops right before we connect. His eyes search mine, and I know he's checking to make sure I won't send us anywhere. I nod, so he grabs my hand. His energy flows into me, getting caught in the emptiness growing inside my chest.

"I don't know what I have to do or say for you to open up to me, but trust and respect go both ways. So I can't be with you if you're going to hide so many things from me."

My heart constricts, and I gasp for air. He's still leaving? Even after I opened up to him?

He's leaving *because* I opened up to him. I knew it. He does think I'm crazy.

"I understand," I finally say.

A fresh batch of tears threatens to fall. I can't break down in front of him again.

"Can I have a few minutes alone?" I ask. "I need to calm down before going back in there. And you should probably have the nurse look at your hand."

"My hand's fine," he says softly.

My eyes flash to his hand. The blood's gone. There isn't even a scratch. "But I saw the glass, the blood. How?"

"Self-healing is another one of my abilities. I was planning on telling you about it this weekend—perhaps on a date. I guess not anymore." He shrugs. "I'll give you a few minutes of privacy."

MJ releases my hand and leaves me much as he did the first night we met—completely and utterly confused. Except this time he took my heart with him.

I HIDE OUT IN THE BATHROOM FOR THE REMAINDER OF class. Justin made my biggest fear a reality: I'm hopelessly alone, abandoned by everyone. Somehow he's managed to accomplish this in a building full of twelve hundred people.

But I can't blame it all on him. MJ was my fault.

By the time I make it to third-period math, I get a third text message from Justin: 5.

Thunder and lightning rattle the windows from the storm brewing outside. I shiver as I sit down, now understanding the meaning behind Justin's texts. I was thinking the same thing just a moment ago. Five more hours to go.

He's counting down until I'm done with school.

CHAPTER 46

MJ

I'VE NEVER SEEN A PLACE THIS AFFECTED BY A DEMON. Does that mean this *Justin* is a demon? How does he connect to Maddy?

There's a block in the students' and teachers' minds, like a brick wall concealing the demon from me. Their minds are being controlled by him, forcing them to do whatever he wants. That's the work of an Influencer; however, I've never known one that can alter so many minds at once. Usually an Influencer can control one, maybe two minds at a time. This one has controlled twelve hundred.

Being that Influencers can't possess people, I don't think it's the same demon that caused Ben to attack Maddy. But with how strong this demon's powers are, I can't be sure. In order to have this kind of power, someone must be helping him.

As much as I despise asking for help, especially from someone who isn't a Protector, I have to. Only one person in this entire school can help me figure this out—Ms. Morgan, the substitute math teacher. I'm certain there's a reason why she's unaffected by the mind control.

I walk up to her desk while every student but Maddy works on the pop quiz in, as Amber says, *creepy* unison. Even Amber in the front row, not under the demon's control thanks to my marking her, seems as engrossed in the quiz as the rest.

In the back of the class, Maddy's doing what she's done most of the morning—staring out the window, undoubtedly to avoid looking at me. I know I went too far earlier. I just … I had no clue about her dreams or the possibility of her being psychic. My emotions are clouding my judgments. I got too close to her too quickly, and in the process I missed so much.

As much as I despise this too, I have to keep my distance from her today. Just until I uncover what's going on here. I'm sure she thinks I've been ignoring her since our fight, but I can't deal with that now. I take a deep breath and focus on keeping her safe.

A stack of folders is scattered on Ms. Morgan's desktop. She grabs a lavender one and sticks it in a drawer. "MJ," she whispers.

"Shadowwalker," I reply, cutting to the chase.

With the town having a Trifecta, I figured I would eventually run into other beings. Shadowwalkers can be hard to find. I recognize a few, such as Duane, but I don't know them all. Living down here as humans, they're cautious, and they assume average lives. If it weren't for Ms. Morgan's immunity to the demon's compulsion, I would have never noticed her.

I should send her to Hell, especially to keep her away from Maddy. But I have a feeling that—just as with Duane—

there's more to Ms. Morgan than I currently suspect. I'm remembering now that she conveniently became a sub here on Friday, the day we Protectors became aware of the demon killing girls such as Amber.

"I'm not a Shadowwalker," she says, "though I won't tell you what I am. Not until I have to. You've seen many things in the past five days, MJ. Majority of that exists outside of Heaven. I'm one of them." She glances in Maddy's direction. "I *can* tell you we have a mutual interest. And I suspect she's the reason behind all this *Children of the Corn* behavior."

I follow her gaze. So she does know Maddy. How and for how long? And if she's not a Shadowwalker, what is she? Maybe Maddy's life can still surprise me after all.

"Something tells me you've been in her life longer than Friday," I say, my eyes not wanting to move from Maddy.

Her voice lifts. "I've been with her since she was a baby."

I look back at Ms. Morgan, and she's smiling. "But she doesn't know you?"

"No."

A knowing look in Ms. Morgan's eyes speaks volumes. She's affected by Maddy, just as I am. I'm betting the Influencer is too. So Maddy can affect all sides?

Keeping her safe just became an impossible task.

Angels and demons have fought on Mortal Ground many times over relics and pride. If word spreads that a mortal can make the dead *feel*, there would be nowhere to hide her. I need to contain this.

But first I need to focus on the present problem. "Does the name Justin mean anything to you?"

Her smile falls, and she meets my gaze. "I've overheard her talking about him. Do you think he's involved here?"

"Yes. Can you gain access to the school's security cameras? If we could get a visual of him, I could find out for sure what we're dealing with."

"I'll work on it."

"You know where to find me when you do."

CHAPTER 47

Maddy

I HESITATE IN THE LOBBY, TRYING TO DECIDE IF I SHOULD eat with my friends. I don't really want to sit with them, but at the same time, I don't want to *not* sit with them.

Sick of feeling alone, I join them. They continue their conversations as if I weren't here.

"And the shag carpet is so vintage," Kayla says.

"I loved the gold couch," Maggie says.

"Not to mention the rabbit ear TV," Jake adds. "I think it's a collector's item now."

My lips quirk up into my first smile since school began. Listening to the triplets talk makes this day seem almost normal. Maybe they're not under Justin's control right now. "Did you guys go to your grandparents' house or something?" I ask, trying to sound interested.

"You would know if you had come last night," Luke snaps.

And I fall deeper into my pit of despair as I realize they're talking about Justin's house. Thinking back to the party, I remember how the place didn't really seem his style. It was old-fashioned. I had mentioned it to Ben, and he said the furniture had come with the house; Justin hadn't had a chance to buy new stuff. The night of that party was his first day in town, and that was almost three weeks ago. I'm a little surprised he hasn't changed it yet.

"So you never answered my question," Kelli says.

I take a bite of my salad as she glares at me. I swallow. "Sorry. I didn't know you were actually speaking to me again."

"Yeah, well, we all want to know why you're friends with us." The others nod their heads in the creepy unison that now causes my skin to crawl.

I'd like to think they wouldn't really question this outside of Justin's influence. But after learning how much I take for granted, maybe they don't honestly know.

"I'm friends with you all because I like you. You're good, honest, funny, smart, caring, adventurous people, and together we're stronger. We bring out the best in each other. You bring out the best in me."

"If that was true," Kelli says, venom coating her words, "you would hang out with us more, and you sure as hell wouldn't ditch us the minute *he* rolled into town."

I follow her gaze to MJ. He and Amber are heading out the front doors. I'm sure they're going to have lunch together somewhere off campus.

He'll probably think it's a date.

Just then, Amber touches his arm flirtatiously. He doesn't shrug it off.

A muffled cry escapes my lips as betrayal, jealousy, and loneliness shred apart the last remaining ounces of strength I have left in me.

Everything has to be connected. If that's true, then Justin has manipulated even MJ's mind, turned him against me, and made him fall for Amber. He took my source of strength and power. The roses were fitting; a part of me died here today.

My school day started with that damn word looming over my locker, and now it ends with it glowing on my phone. I'm not scared or nervous anymore. Justin's been toying with me for so long, I just want it to be over. Not soon. Now.

Something unexpected is at my locker again: MJ and Amber. I gather my things and ignore them as they've ignored me since everything that happened in chemistry.

"Maddy," MJ says after a moment. My heart flutters. "I was wondering if you'd like to join us for dinner and a movie tonight."

I trample the butterflies awakening in my stomach. I try to regain control over my stupid love-struck heart, refusing to let him have this much sway over me.

"I don't feel like being a third wheel. Have a good time, MJ." My voice rings with emotions I'm trying to quiet, but I do mean it. Even though Amber is all kinds of wrong for him, I want him to be happy. Once he's free of Justin's mind control, I hope MJ finds someone who will give him that—even if it does end up being Amber.

She brushes up against him, and I flinch before turning back to my locker. Not knowing when—or if—I'll come back to school, I pack everything.

"See, I told you she was busy," she says sweetly to MJ. "Come on."

"What are you doing?" he snaps.

The frost in his tone makes me do a one-eighty to make sure it isn't meant for me.

It isn't. Somehow he seems even taller as he stares down at Amber, glaring into her eyes, both of them unblinking. I may have been joking about not wanting to be a third wheel before, but now I feel as if I'm intruding on a very intense moment between them. Yet I can't bring myself to look away.

"I'm flirting with you," Amber replies in an unusually, unnaturally flat voice. I would have expected her to deny it or play coy—not come right out and admit she's being a harlot. But MJ does have a way of getting people to open up and reveal things they wouldn't normally do.

"Why would you do that?" MJ asks. "You know the rules. I am here to protect you. Nothing more. During school hours you are to act normal. Tom is your boyfriend. You shouldn't flirt with other guys. It's wrong. And you know how I feel toward Maddy."

"I'm doing it because it upsets Maddy," she replies, still flat. "I want to make her think you and I are dating now."

MJ breaks away and stands in front of me, his eyes pleading with some raw emotion I've never seen in them before. "I'm so sorry, Maddy. I'm sorry if she"—he glares again at Amber—"gave you the wrong idea."

I grind my teeth, trying to chew everything that just happened, break it up into manageable pieces. "You're not ... together?"

"No." MJ shivers as if the idea repulses him. "It's you, Maddy," he explains. "Only you."

"Hey!" Amber whines, her voice back to normal—unfortunately. We both ignore her.

"So, she was just playing you against me," I say, more for my own clarification than as a statement to MJ. It's just Amber playing some stupid mind tricks—not Justin. MJ isn't under his control ... yet. I breathe a small sigh of relief. And I roll my eyes at Amber.

"So now that you know the truth, would you be up for spending the evening with us ... me?"

The quickened beats of my heart echo throughout my hollowed, empty shell of a body, causing me to almost shake from its intensity. I can't just forget the pain that fast.

"What about this morning?" I ask.

He sighs, and his shoulders drop. "I was angry, and I said some unkind things in the heat of the moment. I'm sorry. We both have secrets, so it was unfair to react the way I did. The only way to trust each other enough to share those secrets is to spend more time together."

I hug myself as my stomach twists and turns, a victim caught between dead space and a spark of hope—both of which MJ created.

He's built me up so much over the past few days, strengthened me in ways I never knew were possible, and made me feel whole. Then he took all of that from me when he walked away. I became a ghost in his absence. How did I unknowingly put so much faith and trust and power in him in such a short period of time? I knew better. I can't put myself through that again; I'd never survive.

I'm sick of feeling broken because someone else let me down. I need to learn how to build myself, strengthen myself, and make myself whole. Me. No one else. I can look to MJ for support, but I'm ultimately responsible for myself.

I don't want to hurt him, but he needs to know what he did to me. I grab his hand. I feel tension and disarray as his pulsing energy scatters, confused by all the emotional scars inside me. It spreads through me, like a spider web, reaching into each vacant space. It takes almost a minute before it returns to MJ.

He gasps, nearly crumbling before me. His arms are around me before I even notice him move.

"I'm sorry." His breath blows along the part in my hair as he continues to apologize. His energy picks up, already retracing its steps to rebuild the damage.

But all the pain inside me isn't just from him. Justin had his turn too. He's reached deep inside and scooped everything out of me as if I were a pumpkin, priming me to be carved and decorated to his liking. But what Justin doesn't realize is that MJ is like a forever-burning candle, warming me from the inside out and guarding me from darkness.

I've played the pawn too long in Justin's game. I am the queen of my fate. Starting now, I'm playing by *my* rules.

"Dinner and a movie sound great," I reply as I cling to MJ's chest, breathing in his natural, outdoorsy scent. Amber huffs out her disappointment, but I continue ignoring her. "I just have to send a quick text."

His lips brush against my forehead. Just as I was this morning, I'm overcome with such a forceful current of his energy, it encases me like an invisible, unbreakable shield. On the inside, I'm still fragile and learning how to be stronger, but at least on the outside, I feel as if I can take on the world.

I smile up at him before grabbing my phone and texting back to Justin: *Soon doesn't work for me anymore. I'm done playing your games. Have a nice life.*

I know he'll be pissed. And I'm sure he'll think of something even crueler tomorrow.

All that's left for him to take away is MJ. And if I had been in my right mind earlier when I feared MJ was under his control, I would've remembered that Justin doesn't like MJ. He's afraid of him. MJ is safe. Justin has no more plays left that can hurt me.

"Ready?" MJ asks.

"No," Amber scoffs before I can reply.

MJ turns back to her and glares. "Enough. You can keep up the routine of being a brat while we are at school, but after hours, you will be respectful and courteous to Maddy. There is no other option. Do you understand?"

"Yes," she whispers, then pouts.

My jaw drops. I've *never* seen anyone put her in her place before. Way to go, MJ.

He turns to me, smirking. "Are *you* ready?"

I tuck my phone away and nod, ready and waiting for anything he has in mind.

He takes my hand again. I close my eyes, allowing myself to focus solely on the buzzing warmth spreading through my system, following my veins and muscles to the core of me, my heart.

Yet it doesn't make me feel whole as it has every other time it's pooled there. Perhaps today was more damaging than even I wanted to realize. I have some work to do to make myself whole, but I know I can do it.

Right before the three of us leave, Ms. Morgan, the substitute for math, comes running up to us. She's pretty and young—I think we're her first job out of college—but weird. She's spent most of the three days she's been here staring at me.

"MJ," she says, breathlessly. Her eyes flash to me and back to MJ so fast, I can't be sure I really saw it. "I need you to come with me to the office. I have the … information we discussed earlier."

MJ's body tenses against me. "You found it?"

"I believe so, but I'm waiting for you to be sure."

"Understood. We'll be there in a minute."

She backs away, turns, and rushes up the stairs, presumably to the office on the second floor.

"Maddy, I need to speak with Ms. Morgan for a moment. I'd like you and Amber to wait for me in the office lobby."

I blink more than usual as I stare up at the rigid determination on his face. I know I'm paranoid because of Justin. But even without that, this is about as normal as liver-flavored ice cream.

IN THE OFFICE, AMBER AND I STAND OUTSIDE THE CONFER-
ence room. She inspects her nails while I pace and glare at
the closed door every time I walk past it. What are they
talking about? Why does she need him?

To distract myself, I make a snap decision to talk to Amber about something drifting in the back of my mind since
yesterday.

"So … I liked your poem."

Her manicure inspection stops, and she arches her brow.

Okay, she's not ignoring me. Should I dig deeper, or
shouldn't I? "Have you ever tried looking for your birth
parents?" I ask.

She snorts. "It was just a stupid assignment. Don't try to
read anything into it and think you know me or something."

"No. That's not what I meant. It's just—"

"Look, I don't want to hear some BS that you know how
it feels or whatever. You. Don't. Know." She pokes my chest
to punctuate each word—one of her most annoying habits.

I smack her hand off me, already regretting bringing
this up.

She scowls at me. "And just so you know, I did look into
them, but it was a dead end." She turns away.

"What do you mean? What did you find?"

She sighs, and her shoulders slump. "They're *dead*. They
both died the day I was born."

Dead. I never thought of that. I can't … I can't think
about the possibility of mine being dead too. It's too painful.

I swallow a lump in my throat. Against my better judgment, I put my hand on her shoulder. "Amber, I'm so sorry."

She turns, and her eyes are watery. I've never seen her cry—ever. She's always so mean and nasty. Maybe that's just a front, her way of not letting people get too close. Perhaps we aren't that different after all.

Even as she dries her eyes, a smirk forms and she nods at the door. "They're talking about you."

I forget Amber's brief array of emotions and stare dejectedly at the door. "Yeah, but why?"

"It's obvious, isn't it? They're trying to figure out what happened here today."

"What?"

"Ms. Morgan is the only person in this whole school outside of us who hasn't had her lobotomy card stamped."

I think back on today—she may be right.

"They know you're connected to it."

"How do *you* know this?" I give her a look, then squint at the door, expecting it to suddenly be made of glass so I could see what they're doing.

"Because I was sitting close enough to overhear their discussion this morning in math. I only caught some of it. But I know they're looking at the security camera footage near your locker. They're trying to find out who Justin is."

"*No!*" I fall to my knees. Lightning flashes through the room, blinding me. The floor under me shakes with aftershocks from the mind-numbing thunder. As it fades, I hear a thud.

Amber is lying face-down on the carpet.

"Amb—"

A soft rag presses over my mouth and nose. An arm wraps around me from behind.

I scratch and kick, trying to pry them off me and alert MJ. But the thunder returns, drowning out my sounds of struggle.

A sweet smell enters my nose. Darkness looms on the edges of my vision. The odor fills me. Chokes me from the inside out. My hands stop scratching. My legs stop kicking. Darkness calls.

I have no choice but to answer.

CHAPTER 48

MJ

"**C**AN YOU GET A BETTER LOOK AT HIS FACE?" I ASK.

"This is the best angle we've seen," Ms. Morgan replies.

The screen on the laptop shows a man with brown hair filling Maddy's locker with the black roses. I think it's Ben. No matter how many different video files we look at, his face is hidden.

He reaches behind him, and someone offscreen passes him the balloon.

"Someone's with him! Find recordings of them walking into school and out. This has to be our guy."

"Already on it."

The screen changes, showing all twenty views from cameras on the first floor and outside of the building.

Suddenly, lightning flashes through the outside windows and thunder shakes the room. We both look at the door behind us.

"You've figured it out, haven't you?" she asks.

I've been questioning the town's strange weather since my arrival. But now, after Ms. Morgan looked to the door too, I realize Maddy's emotions affect the weather.

The few times I've seen the sunshine, we were together and she was happy. Thunder and lightning seem to appear when she's scared or mad. The rain hurts the most. That's when she's crying. I made her cry yesterday.

With thunder and lightning like that, I'm torn between wanting to rush out there to see if she needs help and wanting to stay in here to give her some space.

I reach out to listen to Amber's thoughts using Cerebrallink: Amber told Maddy we're looking for Justin! Is Maddy afraid because this means I've learned another thing she tried to hide from me? Is she afraid of my reaction, seeing as I blew up then just walked away this morning when I learned one of her secrets?

Thunder rumbles again, louder than I've ever heard it. I stand to check on Maddy.

"Hold on—I found it!" Ms. Morgan exclaims.

I stare at the door for a moment, but the thunder quiets, so I turn my attention back to the screen. I see two men walk out of the school. One is clearly Ben. He shouldn't still be in town. The other has black hair.

"Zoom in," I say. I focus on the one thing that interests me: his eyes. They're black. He's a demon.

A glare of sunlight suddenly shines on the screen, blocking out the image. "Close the shades. I need to get a better look at who we're dealing with."

She reaches to shut the mini blinds.

"Wait," I say, more to myself than her.

Her hand stills.

Sunlight. Maddy.

"Maddy can't be happy," I say. "She's with *Amber*. It must mean—"

We both run to the door. Across the aisle, lying on the floor in front of the desk, is Amber. I can hear her heart from here; she's unconscious but alive.

I look left, right, everywhere, but Maddy is gone. Wherever she is, I know she's unconscious too.

I failed her.

"Help me find her!" I plead, my breaths coming faster than they ever have before.

Ms. Morgan looks up with tears in her eyes. "I can't interfere."

With those words, I turn all my panic and rage at the blonde-haired, blue-eyed woman responsible for all of Maddy's troubles: her Guardian. My hands clench at my sides, and my muscles twitch, wanting so badly to destroy her for all the pain and suffering she's caused Maddy.

Where was she when Ben attacked her? Or the three days I spent following her, watching her, and debating to *kill* her? And Justin—Maddy said he's been an issue in her life for weeks now. And if all that isn't enough, she allowed Duane to be in Maddy's life, and he somehow hurt her three years ago. None of this would have happened if Ms. Morgan had done her damn job and watched over Maddy.

"How?" I snarl.

She shakes her head and turns off the glamour spell. Large white-feather wings appear behind her. She stretches them out, revealing the signature Guardian bronze coating the tips of each feather. My own wings itch to be released from their spell. Then Ms. Morgan disappears.

I stare at the now-vacant spot, disbelieving what I'd just witnessed. Guardians can't physically appear down here. It should be impossible. They once had the power to appear on Mortal Ground, but then a group went rogue, and the Council stripped all Guardians of that ability. So how did she do it?

If I have any chance of finding Maddy, I need to first bring Ms. Morgan back. As Maddy's Guardian, she has to know more than she said. Hopefully she'll know wherc Justin took her. To get Maddy back, I'm going to need some help.

CHAPTER 49
Maddy

I OPEN MY EYES TO A PERFECT, CLEAR BLUE SKY. MY HEART pounds. The hand with the rag is gone. I think that was chloroform. Duane has warned me about it before. I mentally explore my body to make sure I'm not hurt.

When everything checks out okay, I spring up, desperate to run to safety and find MJ. But I fall back down. I'm not dizzy; the ground is unstable. It's like walking in one of those bouncy castles at carnivals. The ground is white as far as I can see, but it's not cold like snow. The air isn't cold either. It feels like a warm spring day.

My fingers run over the ground, trying to figure out what it is. It's layered. About a half inch down is the squishy, pliable, bouncy surface. But on the surface, it's a dry mist. I fan it, and a little puff of white rises up, then breaks away.

It's a cloud.

My heart sinks.

I'm dead.

I close my eyes and say a silent prayer. *God, I know I've ignored you and blamed you for … everything, but if you could just make it so I'm not really here, I'd stop hating you.*

After a deep breath, I open my eyes. Nothing has changed.

"At least I didn't feel any p-pain." My voice cracks as I hold back my tears.

In the distance, a small figure appears. Her long blonde hair and white dress dance in the wind as she runs toward me. She must be an angel. They really do exist.

She's frowning, and worry radiates from her emerald-green eyes. Still, she's pretty, and it means I'm no longer alone, so I lose some of my panic.

As she gets closer, I realize it's the Dream Girl. Kelli and Justin were right: she's dead.

She's dead. A strange pain surges through me, momentarily stopping my heart. I've known her my entire life. She's always been a constant. I could always count on her. I can't envision my life without her.

Still running, she slams into me and wraps her arms around me. A warm rush of energy enters me, but I'm too shocked to concentrate on it.

She's touching me … and I didn't get pulled into her body as I do in my dreams.

I throw my arms around her, hugging her back. She's real. I'm not crazy.

The hug doesn't feel awkward—like ones between strangers. I feel as if I know her better than I know myself. I've been a passenger inside her body. I've felt her joy, pain, grief, heartache, loneliness, and love. I've listened to her thoughts. I've seen the world through her eyes.

I never thought I would ever meet her. This *is* a dream come true—even though I don't understand how it's possible.

"Oh, thank heavens you're okay," she says.

"Okay? But I'm"—I pause to find the strength to say the word out loud—"dead. How is that okay?"

She pulls back. Tears well up in her eyes. She places her hand on my cheek, keeping her pulsing sensations flowing through me. On instinct, I lean into her comforting gesture.

"You're not dead. You're just unconscious."

"What? I'm not … I don't understand."

A small, reassuring smile forms on her dusty-rose lips, and she nods. "I know. It's okay. Take a deep breath, and I'll share with you what I can."

I do as she asks. She takes her hand off me and motions for me to sit. Without her touch, emptiness consumes me, exhausting all my strength and thought processes. I didn't want to feel like this again, especially not so soon. Her touch reminds me a bit of MJ's. I've got to learn how to not rely so much on that energy. But it's hard to think about anything when it seems Justin was right—Damien murdered her. And I missed it.

I sit, unsure of what else to do.

"First things first, I think it's about time I introduce myself, don't you?"

I nod as words fail me.

"I'm Elizabeth."

I close my eyes and grasp her name as if it were my lifesaver.

"Breathe, Maddy."

I suck in as much air as my lungs can hold.

"Good. Unfortunately, I need to tell you some things that will be difficult to hear. You mustn't panic. We don't have the time. Nod if you understand."

I do.

"Now then. You are here because I brought you. This is not Heaven. You are not dead. For the moment, you're safe."

I breathe a little easier hearing that.

"Damien created this place for me. It's a replica of Heaven."

I blink repeatedly and gaze around the pristine but empty space. She's here all alone? Finally, I find courage to speak. "Why was your name hidden from me in the dreams?"

She chuckles and pats my knee. "You talk in your sleep. Damien and I are well-known among our kinds, so I couldn't risk someone overhearing our names. They can't know we're helping you. Not even MJ. Not yet."

"I can't do that. I can't keep hiding things from him."

She sighs. "After what you've seen in the dreams, you have to suspect Damien and MJ are alike. Unfortunately, there is too much history and bad blood between them for MJ to understand Damien's willingness to help you."

"What history?"

"Someday, I'm sure MJ will tell you everything. And when that time comes, I hope you can remember the good, kind Damien you've gotten to know through your dreams."

I resist the urge to scoff now that I know the truth of Damien. I wish she would just tell me now, get all the bad stuff over with. But because it's not her story to tell, I can understand not sharing it.

"Why do I dream of you, Elizabeth?"

"I've been sending you my memories ever since … I met you. I hoped if you grew up knowing Damien and me, it would help you trust us."

"When did you meet me?"

She tilts her head up to the sky and takes a deep breath. "I met you the day I died."

I inhale sharply. Kelli warned me, and I knew it the moment I saw her, but it's still hard to hear her say it.

She continues, "I was standing in front of my light, waiting to cross over into Heaven. It's more glorious than people say it is. But I felt something pulling me away. I had to follow it. When my light faded, I found you. You'd just been born, and you were crying and alone. That wasn't right. I brought Damien to you, and he could tell right away you were different. He didn't think we would ever be able to keep you safe and hidden from others like us, but I offered Damien something I knew he couldn't refuse."

"What did Damien want?"

She takes a deep breath. "My forgiveness."

"He killed you, didn't he?"

"He had a hand in it," she says. "But I've made peace with his actions. If it hadn't happened, I wouldn't have been able to watch over you and protect you for the last seventeen years."

She may have made peace with it, but I sure as hell haven't. I will never trust him. Ever.

"Why have you been protecting me? I don't get it. What am I?"

"We're protecting you because you're *unique*. You exist with one foot in the mortal world and one foot in the immortal."

"I don't understand."

She frowns. "I can't tell you what you are, Maddy. You have to discover it for yourself. You need to open your eyes and start recognizing who you are and what you can do. If you do that, more than one life will be saved today."

The gravity of my situation hits me, and I fall silent again.

"I know you don't realize this, but you've been training for this moment your whole life."

I stare up at her hopeful expression, wishing it would do something to untangle the thick net of secrets, lies, and mysteries that have joined forces to trap me and hold me prisoner.

"Come on." She stands and holds her hand out for me. "There's something I'd like to show you."

Like a frightened child, I take her hand. A peaceful feeling grows inside me as her energy works its way into my system, chipping away at the darkness. "What *is* that?" I ask, looking at our hands.

She turns to look at me, then follows my gaze. Her energy cycles through my blackened soul and reconnects with her. She sighs. Her energy flows back into me again, but this time it's slower, heavier—almost as if it doesn't want to feel this much misery.

"What you feel is my spiritual essence. Through it, we can sense someone's thoughts, feelings, desires, hopes, dreams, and their own essences. We can also use it to heal, as you saw MJ do to his hand this morning. Or alter their memories when necessary. It's also how we travel between worlds."

"I don't understand."

"Everyone, both alive and dead, has spiritual energy. It's their essence. Their soul. Just as with fingerprints, no two are alike. Now, MJ and Justin can do all those things I mentioned previously just by being near someone. If they know the person well enough, they could be on a different continent and still link with the person. But with you, it's different. They have to touch you in order for their essence to work, and even then, not all of it does."

I think back to my limited time with MJ and Justin, trying to figure out what I've seen and experienced. Of course, MJ's touch affects me. He can tell how I feel, just not the reasons behind it, so that must mean my head is private. There have been a few times when MJ's essence has pooled in specific areas of me—damaged areas. Was that him trying to heal me? Maybe. Justin has never touched me, so I don't know what effect he would have. But the mind-altering ability doesn't work on me for either of them, and for that, I'm truly grateful.

"I think I understand now," I finally say.

"Good. Though I must warn you: when they touch you, they can either heal you or harm you. You must be careful."

"What do you mean?"

"I'm sorry—I can't elaborate further."

Without another word, she leads me through the clouds to no place in particular. It's all the same; just an endless view of clouds and sky in every direction. It's a beautiful, empty cage.

"You're not alone," she says, swinging our still-joined hands. "I've been with you always, even though you haven't fully realized it."

My lips crack into a smile.

"I speak to you sometimes in the wind. I like to imagine that's why you feel so comfortable outdoors."

I *do* feel more at peace outside. And a voice on the wind … "Was it you, Friday, speaking to me at the park?"

"Yes. I was trying to get you away from MJ, but I was too late. He'd already taken notice of you. Seventeen years without a hint of danger, and you manage to get found by members of both sides in the same month."

"Both sides?"

"MJ and Justin are like two sides of the same coin. They can't exist without the other. They balance each other, though they are very different and loathe one another."

"Oh."

Up ahead, something rises up from the misty ground. It's a fountain. It's big—at least fifteen feet around. The stones surrounding it are pearl white. The center is made of three cascading tiers. The crystal-clear water flows down them so seamlessly, it's almost hypnotic. At first glance, it looks as if the water is no more than a foot or two deep. But when I gaze down into the clear water, the fountain doesn't appear to have a bottom. Weird.

"What is this?" I ask.

She smiles, and her eyes drift off, lost in another time. "Damien gave me this so I could watch over you."

I look between her and the fountain while I struggle to keep up with our conversation. "This … is how you knew about MJ?"

"Yes. I also use it to send you my memories."

Her memories. "You mean the dreams? You send them to me?"

"Yes."

"So … I'm not psychic?"

She laughs. "No."

I breathe a sigh of relief. I knew it. Justin is full of BS—I'm not psychic.

I look at the fountain and think of the dreams—her memories—that I've had my whole life. They mean so much more now. I've grown up experiencing key moments in her life while she's been up here watching on as I live mine. I want them back now, the way they were before she and I separated.

"Why are the dreams broken?" I ask.

She turns and grabs my forearms. "Broken? What do you mean?"

"Well … " I pause while I try to figure out how to explain. "I didn't know what the dreams were or why they changed recently. I tried to stop them. Now I'm separated from you in them, and I almost died on Sunday night trying to reach the cabin."

She gasps, dropping her hands. "No. That wasn't supposed to happen. I'll fix it. I'll find a way to turn them off. I promise."

"What do you mean? I thought you controlled them." If she doesn't, then who does? Who else hijacks my head?

"I do, but I had it set so that if we suspected you were in danger, the dreams would play out continuously until you learned everything you needed to know about Damien and me. That way, we could make the necessary preparations to either relocate you or bring you here. There aren't many memories left that I wanted to share with you."

My mind is churning through everything she just said, picking it all apart to choose which shocking thing to freak out about first. If I were *found*? *Relocate* me? Bring me *here*? Do I even get a choice about any of this?

"But if you aren't linked to them anymore," she continues, "that means your mind is open to any one of us who knows about you. Someone else could use it to show you things, as I have. They can use it to make you do things or to find you."

If I was in shock from what she said before, this news is even more horrifying. It means I'm the one thing I hate being: vulnerable.

She places a hand on my cheek, and tears pool in her emerald-green eyes. "You need to go back to your life—even though you are in much danger there. And I need to stop the dream sequences."

I place my hand over hers, not just to feel more connected to her, but also to borrow more of her essence. It can keep me strong enough to get through this. "Who else knows about me?" I ask.

"I don't know, but everything's going to be okay." Her head bobs in agreement, though I don't know if it's for my reassurance or her own.

She whirls around and drags me to the fountain ledge without saying another word. On the surface of the water is a picture of a teenaged boy and girl. They're dressed in what seems to be strange Renaissance-festival type clothing. My heart flutters as I look at the boy's face.

It's MJ.

He looks the same age as now. But his eyes are different. Less ... serious?

The girl in the fountain sort of resembles Elizabeth. Younger, though it's hard to tell with all the dirt smeared on her face. Her hair is just as blonde, and she has similar green eyes. "Is that you?" I ask.

"No."

"Then why does she look like you?"

Elizabeth grabs me by the arms again and the desperation in her eyes snaps me back into concentration. "I will explain everything to you later, but right now you need to listen and pay attention. I can show you MJ's truth. The things you will see are terrible, but you have to bury that pain." She pauses before adding, "Justin is on the other side, so I can't show you his truth."

MJ's truth ... Justin's truth ... what is she talking about? And why is MJ's terrible? What happened to him?

"When you wake," she says, "you will be at Justin's house. You need to focus and think back to your training. Trust nature and yourself. And do whatever is necessary to get out of that house. Justin wants to know what you are. You must keep your true identity a secret. Everything will be lost if they discover who you truly are. It's crucial you stay hidden."

My heart races. *Justin's house.* He took me? Suddenly I feel so foolish for egging him on and hiding him from MJ. Justin can erase peoples' minds and do who knows what else, and I continually challenged him. For that, he's going to make me suffer.

"Please," I beg as my body trembles. "Can't I just stay here with you?"

She stares at me for a moment. I can see the turmoil in her eyes. Then she shakes her head. "No. I'm so sorry. But if things don't go the way I hope, I will do what I can to bring you back here. For your sake, I hope that doesn't happen. Stay strong, Madison. I love you." She pulls me into her and wraps her arms around me.

Before I can reciprocate, she lets go, then pushes me into the fountain.

CHAPTER 50

Maddy

I WAIT TO FACE-PLANT INTO THE WATER, BUT IT DOESN'T happen. Instead, I fall deeper and deeper into the deceiving fountain. But it doesn't feel as though I were plummeting to my doom. It's gentle; I'm like a leaf in a light breeze.

After what feels like hours, a light shines under me. I wince—preparing for the pain—as I finally hit something solid.

All at once, blood-curdling screams rip through my eardrums.

They won't stop.

I try to cover my ears, but I can't move. I can't even open my eyes, though I don't want to. I've heard screams like this before—when I was inside Damien.

These are the screams of people being tortured.

The air is thick. It's hard to breathe. It stinks of manure and something god-awful. I don't know what it is, but it's the worst thing I have ever smelled. It's like when Dad burned himself with the soldering iron, but a million times worse.

"Are you injured? Can you stand?" asks a heavenly voice next to me.

I would recognize that voice anywhere.

MJ.

My eyes finally flutter open, and my head turns toward him in a motion far slower than I'd like. MJ stands over me, holding out his hand. He's dressed in the same weird Renaissance clothing from the picture in the fountain.

Behind him, the sky is a dark gray. Low clouds of black smoke rise up and threaten to block out the sun. The smoke is thickest in the place from where the screams emanate.

I want to throw myself into MJ's arms and get the hell out of here. But instead, my arms move along the dirty, uneven ground. I'm dressed in the same itchy brown outfit as the girl next to him in that picture.

I've become that girl.

Elizabeth sent me here for a reason. She said she'd show me MJ's truth. I'm not getting out until I see what it is. As I do every night Elizabeth visits me, I relax my mind and let this Village Girl take over.

I TURN AWAY FROM HIM TO SEE WHAT TRIPPED ME. MY heart stills—it is a large bone. A leg, perhaps; though at this angle, I do not know if it belongs to a beast or a man.

"Are you injured? Can you stand?" he asks again, much louder this time as the screams grow nearer.

I take a deep breath of the tainted air and look at the warrior, the one Mother dreamed about. If his blood is spilt, the kingdom will fall. Sigurdsson, leader of the Birkebeiner faction and destroyer of my future, will be victorious in his plot to overthrow the king. If I can get the warrior to safety, the kingdom might have a chance. I have to keep him safe.

I nod in reply to him, not wanting to give away our position.

He offers his hand and looks around the rubble of mud, stone, and smoldering hay that once housed the bladesmith, his wife, and their three daughters. The girls are safe, but I fear their parents met the same fate as mine.

A tear springs to my eye, but I brush it away. Today is not the day for grief.

The thick laughter of several men can be heard near the hut still standing to our left. Before I can think, the warrior pulls me to my feet. We run north toward the fields and forests to safety. Beyond them lie the castle walls.

The screams from the center of the village do not lessen in volume the farther we run. My stomach clenches when I think of all the lives lost—beaten, stabbed, then burned alive—in the name of my betrothed.

The warrior suddenly halts, and I ram into the back of him. His shoulders drop. I shift around to see what causes him such despair. The field, our only means of escape, burns beneath golden flames that stretch up to the heavens. We are trapped.

I bite my lip so he will not see it shake. His palms are heated, becoming moist with the sweat of his fears, but his face is set like stone. He looks around, then points to the round hut that once belonged to my aunt and uncle. The hay on the roof is intact, and the clay and stone walls look undamaged.

Even though hope is lost, I allow him to pull me into their home. The walls reduce the sound of the devastation closing in on us.

"Do not fear," he says as he barricades the wooden door. "I will not let any harm come to you."

My chest heaves from my rushed breath and racing heart.

The ground shakes, and the sound of thunder fills the room. We both peek through cracks in the walls to see many men on horses riding up the path we took.

He grabs my arm and pulls me to my aunt and uncle's resting area. "Go underground. The outsiders may not know about the cellar."

"Come with me," I plead. "They are not after you."

The sound of the horse hooves stop. He lifts the cowhide on the floor and pulls up a hatch within the floorboards, revealing the underground food cellar. "I am a warrior. We do not hide. Go now. Keep still. Do not reveal your location—no matter what you hear." He positions himself in front of the door with his sword drawn.

Knowing I cannot deter him, I sit on the ledge, ready to jump down. "Do not let them find me. They will kill you for aiding me."

He nods.

I slide down into the hole, then pull the boards back into place above me. After a moment, a soft thud lands on the boards as he replaces the cowhide covering.

It is dark and musty. I never liked going into our own cellar whenever Mother asked me to gather food. My aunt and uncle have no children, so their cellar is even smaller. The walls are only an arm's length away. The ceiling is low— the warrior would not have fit.

The room above me fills with heavy footsteps. I hear loud grunting, and metal clangs as swords cross.

Something heavy falls to the floor, then another. I know the warrior would not go down without a fight. I wish I could see what is happening.

More footsteps rush in, belonging to at least seven men. Metal falls to the floor, and the fighting stops.

"Where is she?" asks a stern male voice.

"I am alone," responds a voice I recognize as the warrior's. My breath comes a little easier, knowing he is still alive.

"Do you know who I am?" asks the same stern voice.

"Sverre Sigurdsson," the warrior replies.

I clamp my hand over my mouth to silence myself. He found me.

"You ... " the warrior continues, his voice growing in strength, "are the liar who claims—"

There is a loud thud above me, and a man groans.

My stomach churns, fearful the one groaning is my warrior. *No!*

I break through, separating my mind from the Village Girl's. MJ is suffering. He's hurt. I can't see him. I can't help him. I feel so powerless.

Even though I'm not in my own body, my chest tightens and my stomach churns in knots. If I were physically here, I would have vomited. I wait to hear anything that will let me know he's all right.

"That is no way to speak to your king," says the voice I think belongs to Sigurdsson. "Where is she?"

"You are not ... my king," MJ says breathlessly. "No one ... is here." His voice is weaker, strained. What are they doing to him?

He groans. There is another thud, and dust falls down on my—I mean, the Village Girl's—head. MJ must have fallen to the floor again. The floor creaks and he moans as I hear him being hit over and over again. The Village Girl's heart races, and she fixes her eyes on the hatch door, dreading the moment MJ reveals her location. He doesn't say a word.

Why did Elizabeth send me here? What the hell is this? I don't want to hear this. I don't want to listen to him suffer. I can't even help him.

The floor shakes as things fall and break. I think they're searching the room. If they move the bed, they'll find me ... her ... us.

"I know she is here. She belongs to me, and she will be found." Sigurdsson's voice carries a detached air of condescension. I don't care if he is a king; I want to kill him for hurting MJ. "If you cooperate, I might let you live. You are Magnus, son of Odin, are you not?"

Magnus? Is that what the *M* stands for?

"I should kill you," Sigurdsson continues, "but I could use your skill with the blade."

There's another muted cry from MJ.

Please make it stop. I can't take it anymore. He doesn't deserve this. He was just trying to help her.

Light suddenly floods my hiding place as the hatch opens and a man appears. I myself can't run away, and the Village Girl can only just stand there. He's three times her size. There's no way she could fight him and live.

Through my fear, the Village Girl's thoughts filter into my mind: *If I die, they will kill him. He needs to live. He risked his life to save me. I owe him a life-debt. If I can lead them away, he may live. Then I shall plan an escape from the hell that awaits me with Sigurdsson.*

The man is too tall and too fat to come down into the cellar. His barbaric hands grab the Village Girl and hoists her up to the surrounding party.

MJ is lying on the ground, covered in blood. There are three other bodies lying still around him. He must have killed them. His nose looks misshapen, his lip is cut and bleeding, his eyes are swelling, and his hands are wrapped around his torso. I want the Village Girl to look away, but she doesn't. I'm a prisoner in her body.

The man I assume is Sigurdsson starts circling me ... us. The Village Girl remains still. Having done this before with Justin, I know she's trying not to show her fears. I try to force her arms to move so I can attack Sigurdsson and hurt him for what he's done to MJ.

Sigurdsson's eyes are black, just as Ben's were. Dirt clings to every inch of his face. He spreads an evil smile, revealing many missing teeth.

"The rumors of your beauty do not do you justice." Her skin crawls as he stops and sniffs her hair. "You shall make a fine wife."

"Don't touch her," MJ says, struggling to stand.

No, MJ, I want to scream at him. Please be still. Don't let them hit you again. I couldn't bear to see it.

Sigurdsson turns back to MJ and signals two of his men to stand him up. I gasp at the sight of one of the men holding MJ. Even though he's covered head to toe in dirt and blood, I would know him anywhere...

Damien.

His eyes are black as always, though a different black than Sigurdsson's. Sigurdsson's are dull, as if the life has been sucked out of him. Damien's almost shine, matching his joyous grin. There are people on the floor, dead, and others whose lives hang in the balance, and Damien is loving every moment of it.

This is not the man who loves Elizabeth. This is a monster. This is the Dark Prince.

"Ah, yes, you," Sigurdsson says. "I have no use for liars." In a swift motion, Sigurdsson plunges his sword into MJ's chest.

I scream and thrash inside the Village Girl, trying to get to MJ as he falls to his knees. But my screams are muffled by something. As if something is pressed over my mouth. The sound is also overshadowed by distant thunder, though I feel its aftereffects rattle my bones.

He's dying.

My bruises from falling at the cabin flash in my mind's eye. That was a dream—or so I thought. Elizabeth said this is MJ's truth. What does that mean? If MJ dies here ... will he die in real life?

I try to force her to move to MJ, to help him, to stop the blood from running down the smooth, muscled chest I lay on earlier this morning. I can't compel her, but I can suddenly sense *my* arms and legs. They won't move either. They're stuck, held back by something. The confusion pulls me, trying to rip me from the Village Girl.

A brush of wind blows near my ear. *"Wake up, Maddy,"* a voice says. I recognize it as Elizabeth's.

AT THE SOUND OF HER VOICE, I STOP FIGHTING INSIDE THE Village Girl. MJ disappears. I peel open my tear-drenched eyes.

I'm immersed in darkness. Shaking and crying uncontrollably. Bound and gagged on a bed.

CHAPTER 51

MJ

THE SUN MOCKED ME FOR HOURS, SHINING BRIGHTLY ON the darkest day of my life. The sunset, once beautiful, is now a cruel reminder of what I lost.

Now I walk along the darkened sidewalks of neighborhoods that have been combed over ten times, listening for a heartbeat unattached to an essence. Again, I turn up empty.

My hope is dwindling. I can't find Maddy, and I don't know Justin, so I can't search for his essence. I knew this wouldn't be easy—things with Maddy seldom are. The only thing that has gone right was finding the Guardian, Ms. Morgan.

I SUMMONED THE VEIL OF SHADOWS AND RUSHED OUT OF the office after Ms. Morgan. Though I couldn't see her, I could sense her essence. I followed her all the way to her exit point. Once outside the Veil, I gazed around at my surroundings, trying not only to find her, but also to get my bearings.

The air was thin, suggesting I was high up—possibly on a mountain. The downward slope of a gravel driveway helped support my theory. In the distance far below me—beyond what any mortal could see plainly—I saw a city and building I recognized: the Space Needle.

Seattle.

An errant thought raced through my head: Seattle was where the demon serial killer from my case killed his first two victims. Of the states where the demon's targets have been found, Washington is the only one Maddy said she hasn't lived in. So why, out of all the places in the world, did Ms. Morgan come here?

I pushed the thought aside, vowing to return to it later. I didn't have time to focus on that. Maddy's life was at stake.

Behind me sat a small log cabin. The door was open. Ms. Morgan must have gone inside it.

I sprinted up the three wooden steps of the front porch and rushed inside. Immediately, a heavy sensation filled me, pushing on me and making me want to leave the cabin. I ignored it.

To the right was a kitchen with clean but outdated appliances. To the left was the eating area. Ahead of me was a living room with wooden couches and red cushions. The place appeared well kept, but something felt off. Not only did the house feel empty, as if no one had lived there for years, but the pressure sensation still gnawed on me and made me feel as if the place was somehow forbidden too. As if it was protected by some sort of spell.

Ms. Morgan's voice called out from farther in the house. "Thank Father you're here!" Her footsteps quickly echoed down a hallway. "She's been taken by the Influencer. I need your help to find—"

As Ms. Morgan entered the kitchen, her face fell. "*You?*"

I couldn't even muster a smirk. "I'll go out on a limb here and guess I'm not who you expected to see. So who are you meeting? Who else knows about Maddy?"

She shook her head and stepped back. "You can't be here. You need to leave. You're supposed to be looking for Maddy."

"I will. But to do that, I first need you to answer my questions. How can you be her Guardian? Why have you allowed so many bad things to happen to her? Where is her file? Why didn't you request a Protector to keep her safe from Justin when he first discovered her? And how are you walking on Mortal Ground?"

Her eyes shifted to the doorway. I glanced behind me, half expecting someone to be there. There was no one.

"Talk," I demanded. "The more time you waste, the longer Maddy is with that demon."

"All right," she said as her body sagged. "I'll tell you what I can." She took a deep breath. "By now, I'm sure you realized something happened to Maddy's soul."

"What—"

"I don't know. It happened before I found her."

"Found her? What do you mean?"

"As you know, when children are born, we Guardians follow their essences and guard them from inside the Veil of Shadows. But before I could get to Maddy, her essence disappeared. Like you, I can't sense it. I thought it meant she died. I completed the necessary paperwork and returned to Heaven to wait for her, but she didn't come. A day later, I left Heaven to search for Maddy. With Heaven thinking she died, I was technically a Guardian without a soul to guard. That's never happened before. It made me exempt from the restrictions placed on Guardians centuries ago. My abilities returned to full strength, allowing me to walk on Mortal Ground again."

I shrugged. "Yeah, well, you still haven't said how you found her."

She gave me a tight smile. "As I was saying, I went looking for her. When I finally found her—weeks after she was born—I quickly discovered three other beings had found her first. They were hiding her. Thankfully, they wanted to help protect her from those who would do her harm."

"You all have done a *great* job, recently," I said, not hiding my sarcasm.

"So quick to pass judgment," she said, her blue eyes icy. "You've barely scratched the surface of who Maddy is and what she can do. You don't know the lengths we've gone to keep her safe. You don't know the danger she is in every minute of her life. Nor will you know if you continue to speak in such a way about things you do not understand."

I frowned and took my verbal lashing. I could have argued, but she was right—I don't know all there is to know about Maddy. I need to find her so I can.

"So, who were the ones hiding her?" I tried to keep my tone even.

"I can't tell you that."

"Why?" I snarled.

"Given who you are, do I really need to explain?"

I glared at her, not understanding what she meant. Then it hit me—I'm the Original Protector. I've sent more beings to Hell than all the other Protectors combined. In the minor battles of the Holy War, I was Heaven's sword. Obeying the laws is my creed. Demons and other spirits have pleaded with me to spare them, but I haven't. Not once.

I don't win every time—such as with the demon that killed me, my family, Lifa, and her descendants. But I've won often enough that my reputation precedes me. It wasn't until Maddy that I paused to weigh the consequences of destroying her. I am so glad I did.

I thought back to the day I met Maddy and the spirit that tried to hide her from me in the park. "The others helping her aren't angels, are they?"

"No, but that doesn't mean they won't fight to keep her safe. They were the ones who convinced me to keep her file from Heaven."

"Why? If I had it, I could protect her."

"If you had it, all of Heaven would know about her."

"How is that a bad thing?" But even as I asked the question, I knew the answer. What she does goes against Heaven. Others would come to kill her. That must be why she didn't request a Protector when the Influencer appeared.

"Surely by now you've realized the line between good and evil is an illusion," she said. "And when it comes to Maddy and what she can do, all bets are off."

She was right. As much as I hated to admit it. But none of the information so far could help find Maddy. "Who is helping the Influencer?"

She shook her head. "No one—that I know of, at least. His powers have been strengthened, though I don't know how or why. He's able to utilize abilities outside of his demonic rank."

"He certainly has stronger mind-control abilities than all other Influencers," I agreed.

"Yes. And he was the one possessing Ben."

"How do you know this?"

"The others informed me of it."

"So … if you knew who he was already, why did you do all that with the security footage today?"

"To help you. I wanted to tell you what was happening, but since I can't interfere, I couldn't. Instead I guided you to the truth." She smiled. "I have faith in you, MJ. I believe your conviction to save Maddy. I also believe you really do love her. You're good for her. She's becoming the strong woman she needs to be to survive in a world where millions will be after her. Go now. Please save her."

MY MIND IS STILL TEEMING WITH EVERYTHING THE GUARDian told me. I'm fairly confident the Shadowwalker and the spirit from the park belong to that group. The fourth member has yet to reveal him or herself to me. Where the hell are they? Why aren't they helping find her? When this is done, and I get her back, they will tell me everything. From the beginning. That way I can do what they have failed to do— keep her safe. But none of that will matter if I don't find her.

Knowing the Influencer has a home in Mankato, I'm focusing the search efforts there. I called in some help: Alexander and two other Protectors. Thankfully, none of them were currently on an assignment. Alexander is paired with me, searching for her. When the time comes, he's prepared to get Maddy to safety while I fight the demon. The others are protecting Amber and watching Maddy's house.

If Maddy weren't so complex, I would have the other two Protectors with me also, but they're too new to the situation. In comparison, Alexander has known about Maddy and her abilities for several days. I don't know how the other two will react to her. I can't deal with that today. They're risking a lot to help me, and I trust them. But just not where she's concerned.

Returning from his search in the park, Alexander places his hand on my shoulder. "I'm sorry, but we've scoured this town for six hours and turned up nothing. She's gone. The demon left with her."

"No!" I break away from him. "I'm not giving up. I'll find her—no matter how long it takes."

Thunder and lightning rumble as the once-clear sky disappears behind dark storm clouds. Instantly, I'm running toward Maddy's school, where the clouds are thickest. I can't risk using the Veil of Shadows to get there. I need to watch every second of the sky in hopes she'll show me where she is.

"What is it?" Alexander asks as he runs alongside me, looking up at the sky.

"Maddy's awake."

CHAPTER 52

Maddy

LIGHTNING FLASHES BEHIND A CURTAINED WINDOW, revealing things unfamiliar to me. Wilted plants sit on a dresser. Framed photographs of a stranger's family hang on a wall. A patchwork quilt covers the full-size bed I'm lying on.

Thunder booms and echoes inside my head. I want to cover my ears, but my hands and feet are bound. The restraints bite into my skin each time I move. It's useless, but I scream for help behind the tape covering my mouth.

I take deep breaths to think of something to calm me. MJ's face. But it morphs into how I saw him last—dying—bringing me back to my current despair.

He can't be dead. Whatever Elizabeth showed me, it wasn't his truth—whatever that means. It's just a coincidence he has a scar on his chest right where Sigurdsson's sword entered him.

I need to find him, make sure he's okay.

I have to get out of here.

I'm not a victim, I'm not a victim, I tell myself over and over again.

I think back to my camping trips with Uncle Duane. He's taught me how to get out of almost any situation. Elizabeth told me I've been training for this my whole life. Was she referring to my time with Duane?

I think of the speech he gives every time.

It doesn't matter how big your opponent is or how strong he or she is, Duane would begin. *It doesn't matter what weapon he or she is using or the location he or she has taken you to. All of that is a variable. The one thing that is and always will be constant in any situation is* you. *You are the key to your survival. Your own fears are your actual enemy. Give into them, and you will fail every time. Master your fears, and you will master your fate.*

I close my eyes and concentrate on calming myself—inhaling and exhaling through my nose, trying to find a happy medium between my terror, grief, and desire to live.

After several moments, my body stops shaking and my eyes stop watering. If I want half a chance of surviving, the first thing I need to do is get myself free.

I wiggle my wrists against the restraints, wincing as they again dig into my flesh. I recognize the pain. I'm tied up with a zip tie. Thankfully, Duane showed me how to get out of one last summer.

I roll over onto my stomach. I take a deep breath, preparing for the agony I'm going to inflict on my back. Pulling my wrists as far apart as I can to stretch the zip tie, I lift my arms as high as I can behind my back, then slam them down on my lower back. The zip tie snaps under pressure, and my wrists burst free.

My hands and fingers tingle as blood rushes back to them. My spine aches from the hit, but I don't have time to focus on that. I turn over and get to work on removing the zip tie from my ankles. I insert my pinky nail into the locking mechanism, freeing the teeth so the end slides right out. Blood rushes to my now-freed feet as well.

I will never roll my eyes during one of Duane's survival talks again.

Saving the worst for last, I feel the tape on my mouth. The thickness and grooves reveal it's duct tape. I peel back a corner, pull my skin taut in the other direction, then brace myself for the inevitable burn of ripping layers of flesh. I rip it off fast like a Band-Aid. I bite my lips and resist the urge to scream. The storm outside picks up again, and thunder mutes my muffled cry.

I pat my sensitive mouth to numb some of the pain, then move on to my next task: figuring out where I am. I crawl along the bed, feeling my way to an edge. I freeze as I see a dim light on the floor. It's maybe four feet away, glowing under a closed doorway. Quietly as I can, I tiptoe to the door and listen.

Nothing.

No sounds, but a strong scent attacks my nose. Is it … pickles?

My heart leaps to my throat as I turn the knob, thankful the door doesn't squeak. As the door widens, I see candles lining the edges of a linoleum floor. The walls are peach.

More candles line a seashell-decorated countertop and reflect in the mirror. It's just a bathroom.

I flick the light switch, but nothing happens. The power must be cut.

I turn to leave, but freeze when I see the bathtub.

Short silver hair rests on the tub ledge. A head is bowed down. The water is a slimy brown-and-green mixture. A kneecap sticks out above the water, the skin tan and leathery as it sags from the bones.

On impulse, I kneel down to see the face.

An elderly woman—jaw hanging open. Cheeks hollow. Vacant, hazy eyes sunken in.

My hand flies to my mouth to cover my scream as I race from the room. Thunder and lightning shake the house as I slide down the wall outside the bathroom.

I pull my knees to my chest and rock back and forth, sobbing for her, MJ, and me.

Justin killed her. I just know it. There's no denying the horror she faced as she took her final breaths. She's been here so long.

My friends' conversation at lunch about vintage furniture runs through my mind. This is her house. That poor woman. She's somebody's mother, grandmother, and maybe great-grandmother. That bastard left her to rot in a bathtub, covering the smell with candles and pickles. Wait. *Formaldehyde*. Duane took me on a tour of a morgue once, and I remember the formaldehyde smelled like pickles.

Coolness suddenly touches my hands. My head snaps up, expecting to see someone, but no one is there.

The sensation moves, as if my hands are being rubbed. Even though I don't feel her essence, I know it's Elizabeth. She's trying to comfort me.

I dry my eyes on the back of my hands and slowly stand, leaning against the wall for support.

"*Madison ...* " a voice sings outside my room.

My lip trembles. I hold back another wave of panic as Justin's voice reverberates through me.

"Come out and *play*," Justin says in the same teasing tone.

Lightning flashes through the curtain, showing me a different door—out of this room and into whatever fresh hell he's created for me.

This is still just a game to him. But it's so much more than altering people's minds and turning them against me. I thought facing him meant throwing some snide remarks in his face and maybe doing a few defensive moves if he got physical. But now I understand. He *killed* someone.

I have to get out of here. But that may mean fighting for my life. Maybe even killing him.

I can't go out there empty-handed. I need a weapon.

Lightning flashes again, illuminating what looks like a closet this time.

Elizabeth told me to trust nature and myself. If I take that message literally, then she wants me to ... trust *nature*. Lightning has been bending a sliver of light through the curtain, showing me different things in the room. Is she doing that? If so, then she wants me to see something in the closet.

The doors slide along their track, making noise. My heart stops, but I don't hear anything coming from outside my room.

Everything in the closet is veiled in darkness. Then several lightning bolts flash through the room, illuminating a basket of yarn on the floor. The elderly woman knits.

I bend over and dig through the yarn. I find a foot-long metal knitting needle. I rub the tip. It's pointy. It's not great, but it will do. I tuck it up my sleeve, gripping the end in my armpit and hoping it won't fall out.

I think back to drills with Duane's stuffed target dummy. Where would this needle do the most damage to Justin, should I need to use it? His eyes, ears, and neck, in that order.

I take a deep breath. Justin is a real person … not a dummy. I don't want to kill him, but I may not have any other choice.

I head for the door.

"Stay with me," I whisper to Elizabeth.

The hallway is just as dark. My eyes still haven't adjusted to it. I stick my arms out to feel my way through the narrow hallway. I keep them low to avoid pictures and any other decor.

On the left side, I feel a doorway. I stand there for a moment, trying to remember the layout of the house. I think this is the hallway where he tried to seduce me. If I'm right, the doorway is to another bedroom. There should be a bathroom on the right, the living room ahead.

As I walk past the doorway, a rush of heated breath blows against my cheek, moving my hair.

I throw myself against the adjacent wall. I stare at the doorway. Lightning flashes through the bedroom windows, revealing the doorway to be empty.

I let out my trembling breath. I hope it was just Elizabeth. But I know it most likely wasn't.

I keep moving. After passing the bathroom, I stand in the entrance to the living room. The bay windows are barely visible. It's dark outside. I have no idea how long I was unconscious. Maybe it's day and the storm clouds are sealing off the sunlight. Or maybe it's night and the streetlights aren't working. Maybe it's a mixture of both.

The room is unnaturally quiet. Even the rain has stopped pelting the glass. To the right of the window I see the door. Justin's not here. If I'm fast enough ... maybe I can make it out.

I can do this. *I can do this*, I repeat once more.

I push off the wall and dash for the door. Right before I grab for the knob, the lights turn on and blind me. I hear a girl's muffled scream.

A light breath blows by my ear. *"More than one life ... "* Elizabeth whispers.

Justin has taken someone else.

My chest heaves in anger. I turn to see which one of my friends he took. I know it's either Amber or Kelli.

Her arms and legs are tied with rope to a dining room chair. A mass of wavy brown hair shields her face as she cries. But I still know who it is.

Hannah. *My sister.*

I rush to the chair and kneel in front of her. I search the room for any sign of Justin, but we seem to be alone. I place my hands on her face, forcing her to look me in the eyes. "I'm going to get you out of here," I say.

She sniffles and nods.

"This is going to hurt—I'm sorry." I grab a corner of the duct tape over her mouth, then rip it off. I muffle her cry as thunder rumbles again.

"B-B-Ben and s-s-some guy named—"

"*Shh*. I know. You're going to be fine," I reassure her as my heart breaks. Ben helped him. I can't leave him here—not with a killer. He's under Justin's power and can't save himself.

"Once you're free," I tell Hannah, "run. Don't look back. Don't stop until you get home. Bolt the door, call Uncle Duane."

"Wh-what about you?"

"I need to get Ben out of here—wherever he is. This is my fault."

I examine the rope and knots around her ankles and wrists. It's a square knot and it's tight. But Duane has shown me this knot before.

As I work to free her, something doesn't feel right. Why would Justin turn on the lights to show me my sister, then leave me alone to set her free?

This is a setup. All of it. The poor woman in the bathtub, the breath in the hallway, and now Hannah—he scripted it all. I'm doing everything he wants. What other choice do I have, though?

My pulse climbs as I try to ignore thoughts of what may be coming next. Instead, I focus on my sister. No matter what, I have to get her and Ben to safety.

Finally, she's free. Her arms are around me before I can react.

"I'm so scared, Maddy."

"It's okay, Hannah. I'm not going to let him hurt you. I love you so m-much." My voice falters at the end as I realize the truth: I *do* love her. I'm just so sorry it took until now to admit it to both her and myself.

She holds me tighter and sobs harder. "I love you too."

Slow, overly dramatic clapping echoes behind Hannah. Even though she's taller than me and less than a year younger, I shove her behind me. I take a deep, steadying breath.

I face Justin.

Dressed casually in dark boot-cut jeans and a black shirt, Justin leans against the kitchen doorjamb, watching me pour my heart out and enjoying every minute. The gold couch has been shoved against the wall, the wooden coffee table is broken in half, the rabbit-ear TV has a hole in the screen the size of someone's foot, and red plastic cups are scattered everywhere. I'm not sure if this redecorating took place at the party last night or if Justin took out his anger at me on the house.

"Such a touching display," he says and stops clapping. "Well done, Mads. I didn't think you cared."

Hatred rises in my throat, but stalls on my tongue.

He straightens and takes a few steps into the room. I push Hannah backward as MJ did to me on Monday in the park.

"It was so much fun turning everyone against you," he says. "How did it feel knowing you couldn't hide from me?"

Horrible. But there's no way I'm telling him that. I grit my teeth. "Not everyone. You missed one." I never would have gotten through today if it weren't for MJ.

He huffs. "I couldn't very well announce my presence to *him*. You do realize you could have ruined all my fun if you would have just told him the truth about me days ago, right? But you're so untrusting, you just kept quiet while I continued tormenting you."

No. He's wrong. I kept quiet to protect MJ—mostly. "H-he can't withstand your abilities like I can."

Justin's head flies back as he laughs. "Oh, Mads. Don't you get it? He and I are the same. We can't affect each other. The only thing we can do is send the other back to … well, where beings like us come from. We come back, though, and do it all over again. It's so *boring*. That's why we play with you all. It's fun for *us*, and it pisses *them* off." He smirks. "So you see, it could have all been over Friday night. I wouldn't have been able to mess with your friends, family, or the school if you would have just told him the truth."

"What *are* you?"

"There's a time and place for everything, Mads. There are too many witnesses right now. And unlike *him*, I don't waste my time altering memories unless I want to. Right now … I'm not feeling that charitable. I have a better solution to that problem."

The poor woman's face in the bathroom runs through my mind. Fear squeezes my heart and lungs. Because of me, Ben and Hannah might share her fate.

A light breeze picks up and swirls around me. I can sense Hannah looking around for the source, but I know the windows and doors are closed. Justin's eyes stay locked on me as he arches a brow.

"Don't think like that, Maddy," Elizabeth whispers in my ear. *"Don't let your fears defeat you."* Then the wind disappears.

She's right. This is what Justin wants: to upset me. He's distracting me, and I'm letting him.

I swirl around and shove Hannah toward the door. "Run!"

After a second of hesitation, she runs to the door. I immediately turn back to face Justin.

"Tsk, tsk, tsk," he says, shaking his head. "So predictable."

Hannah screams behind me. I spin back around to see Ben holding her.

He grins, his face appearing over Hannah's struggling body. "Hey, Mads."

"Let her go." I don't care if he's under Justin's control or not. I will kill him if he hurts my sister.

"Why would I have him do that?" Justin moves between me and my sister.

My shoulders sag as a heaviness fills me. People I care about—no, *love*—have had their lives turned upside down because of him.

"Why am I so important to you?" I ask.

He tilts his head to the side and gives me a cursory glance-over. "You aren't important—only what you do."

My eyes shift between him and Ben and Hannah. She's still trying in vain to escape Ben's grip, but failing.

Justin sighs, following my gaze. "You're not going to concentrate as long as she's here, are you?"

I freeze on Hannah's panicked face as I think about what that could possibly mean. "No! Don't hurt her."

"Let her go," Justin commands, to my surprise.

Like a good dog obeying his master, Ben lets his arms fall, freeing my sister. Hannah stares at me for a moment. Then she does exactly what I told her to—run.

CHAPTER 53

Maddy

With Hannah safely out of Justin's house, I let out a trembling sigh of relief. At least one of them is safe.

"What about Ben?" I ask. I glance at him still standing beside the door. He has the same blank stare the zombie-like students had. He's waiting for his next order.

"He's my added insurance to make sure you stay put. Once we make our deal, I'll release him."

Everything in me clenches at the familiarity of his words. I turn back to him, staring into his black eyes, and suddenly I think of Damien. Not the Damien I'd once thought of as perfect. But the new, manipulative, controlling monster unaffected by suffering and death. His and Elizabeth's relationship began with a "deal" and ended with her death. Now I might share her fate.

"What deal?" I ask.

"We'll get to that in a moment." Justin strolls to a bar in the corner and grabs a glass and a bottle of brown-colored alcohol.

"Bring her."

A second later, Ben grabs my arm and shoves me into the chair that previously held my sister. He turns it around so I'm facing Justin.

For a moment, I consider grabbing my concealed knitting needle, stabbing Ben in a nonfatal area, and running for the door. But then I remember Justin and Ben's speed. I know I wouldn't escape. Plus, it would just give away my only defense.

Justin pours a drink before sauntering toward me. "Bourbon?"

I shake my head.

"Suit yourself," he says, then guzzles it down. "It tastes better than I remember. All thanks to you."

"Why would I make it taste better?"

He closes his eyes and takes a deep breath. His body shivers, and when his eyes reopen, they're darker. His pupils and irises blend together and enlarge until the whites of his eyes disappear.

"Do you smell it, Mads? Taste it?" His tongue runs across his lips. "Everything *you* feel, you manifest into the environment around you. The air is so thick with your pain, fear, and anger, I can almost taste your tears. It's intoxicating."

"W-what are you talking about? You're crazy."

He shakes his head. "Mads, you're so naïve. It was supposed to be a mild October, yet it's been cloudy and raining off and on since the night you met me. Your fears have blocked out the sun."

I turn away. I can't affect the weather. That's not possible. He's a lunatic.

"Do you know your town has the worst weather accuracy in the world and it's been that way for fifteen years? What happened here fifteen years ago? Hmm?" He pauses, waiting for my reply.

I reluctantly shrug.

"*You* moved here."

Lightning flashes against the front window as thunder booms again.

He smiles at the display raging outside. "You do that when you're scared. Thunder and lightning have been helping you since you woke up."

He thinks I'm doing that? I smile, thinking about how Elizabeth seemed to be guiding me with the lightning tonight. "That wasn't me."

His brows narrow in confusion, then his smile widens. "You are in such denial, it's almost pathetic. You know what normally accompanies the thunder and lightning?" He gestures to the window. "Rain. You know why it's not raining now?"

He squats down in front of my chair, resting his elbows on his knees and stroking his chin. Ben's hands grab my shoulders, holding me down and preventing me from attacking Justin.

I shake my head, both at Ben's devotion to his master and in reply to Justin's question.

"It isn't raining because you're not crying."

My gaze flies to the window. Lightning streaks across the sky, illuminating raindrops left over on the glass from the last downpour—the one that occurred while I cried in the old woman's bedroom.

My mind races through nearly seventeen years of memories. Sunshine when I'm happy. Downpours and storms when I'm not. I always thought it was just a coincidence. Could he be right? Did I, not Elizabeth, create the lightning that guided me in the bedroom?

Justin has known me for two and half weeks, and he figured this out ... why didn't I?

"What *am* I?" I ask breathlessly.

"You're strong, there's no denying that. I can't find your essence. I can't read your thoughts or influence you. You block all of my God-given powers."

God-given powers? I've heard this kind of psychobabble before from cult leaders and killers Duane has caught. Each one of them claimed he was doing *the Lord's work*. For years, people like that only strengthened my belief that God didn't exist. That he wouldn't allow people to be so cruel.

But after seeing Elizabeth ... I know he's real. He has to be. So does that mean it's all real—angels and demons and the Devil? Maybe.

One thing is for certain, whatever allows Justin to control people—Heaven has nothing to do with it.

"You arrogant, manipulative psychopath! You honestly believe *God* gave you the power to manipulate people?"

He flashes me a wicked grin and stands. "Of course he did. What I don't know is how you managed to acquire the ability to manipulate people too."

"*Me*?" I fume, and Ben's hands tighten on my shoulders. "How dare you. I'm nothing like you."

Justin snorts. "No? Look at your life. Your close little circle of friends. You pushed them all away three years ago, yet they don't give up on you. They stay, eager for whatever scraps of attention you'll give them."

"You don't know anything about my friends," I say. But I grind my teeth, hating that he might be right. I know I hurt them. I made a mistake. And if I ever get out of here, I'll fix it. I'll make it up to them.

"Then there's Ben." He points at Ben, who just continues to hold me down. "A successful, handsome twenty-one-year-old college graduate dating a high school junior. You two don't make sense. He follows you around like a lovesick puppy. It's pathetic. Why him?"

"Why not him?" I ask in exasperation. "He's everything you said and more. He's a good person. He accepts me just the way I am. He's never tried to change me, like everyone else has."

"You hear that, Ben," he says, smirking. "You're a *good person*. Unfortunately for you, none of that sounded like love to me."

Ben's hands tighten on my shoulders, though I don't think he's trying to hurt me. If anything, it's from me hurting him.

"Leave him alone," I say to Justin.

Justin sighs. "Fine. We'll move on to my favorite topic: me. Your emotions are so powerful, you reach into me—into places that have been dark for so long. You stir emotions I thought were gone. Now I feel guilt and remorse and sympathy and pain," he says, counting them out with his fingers. "The one benefit my kind has is that we don't have to deal with all that. Then you brought it all back for me." He pauses and glares at me.

My heart quickens, but I keep my fear from showing on the outside.

He smirks. "But there is an upside to your abilities too. I also feel joy and pleasure and excitement and desire and hundreds of other emotions I'm only just beginning to understand. Food has taste again. Scents consume me. But the one I'm most grateful for is touch. I missed that one more than I had realized. We're going to have a lot of fun together, Mads. I owe it all to you." He stands, grabs the bottle of bourbon, raises it as a toast to me, then takes a long swig.

All those websites about supernatural beings and government experiments … none of them mentioned any "powers" like this. If what Justin says is true, then I'm a bigger freak than anything I read about.

My vision sways like a branch in the wind, and I lean back into the chair.

The bourbon swishes in the bottle as he taps it against his leg. "*He* must feel all this too." The disgusted look on his face makes it clear who he's referring to.

My first date with MJ enters my mind. The way he savored every bite and how he said, "*It's been so long since I tasted food.*" And then there's the way he reacts to my touch...

Justin takes another swig from the bottle. "It's why he's addicted to you like a fat human is to food."

It takes a moment for his word choice to sink in, but a tremor eventually runs through me. "Why did you say … *human*?"

Justin's lips twitch. "See, that's another piece to this enticing 'What-Is-Mads?' game. If you were a boring waste of space like Ben here, that little word would have gone in one ear and out the other. Revelations like this are what's kept me from cheating and ending our game prematurely."

I've been holding out for any logical explanation about Justin and MJ, refusing to waste any thoughts on them being something … *other*. But the evidence keeps piling up. I feel as if I were Alice, falling down the rabbit hole into a world of nonsense and make-believe. Her story ended with it all being a dream. I don't think I'll get that lucky.

"You want proof of how dimwitted and feeble your brains are?" he continues. "Your own nose is actually in your field of vision, but your brain ignores it. It doesn't see what's literally right in front of your face. So when one of us comes along, your brains ignore our abilities and things we say that might … alert you to our superiority."

I can believe the part about my mind choosing to not focus on my nose, but the rest of it … There is no way anyone could ignore the things he's done—not just me.

"Stop lying," I shout. "You're not superior! You're a head case. And even that doesn't make you special. There are mental hospitals full of murdering psychos just like you."

He shakes his head, amused. "The things that come out of your pretty little mouth, Mads … You're living in a fantasy world, even though the truth is also right in front of your face."

"I doubt you've told anyone the truth in a very long time."

Justin places his drink back on the bar and lets out a sigh. "This is getting us nowhere. It's time to make a deal." He waves his right hand in the air. Out of nowhere, a long golden piece of paper and a black feather pen appear in his hand. MJ did that the first night we met with Amber's folder.

Something bangs in the kitchen entryway. I look over, and all breath escapes me. The kitchen table hovers in the air, trying to come into the room.

As it backs up and bangs again, something inside me snaps. All thoughts stop. There is nothing to explain what I'm watching. My emotions, confidence, and hope abandon me. Why did I think I could do this—go up against a killer? And not just any killer. One who can manipulate minds, manifest objects out of thin air, and make tables levitate.

He can do all this, yet the cruelest thing he's done was let me fool myself into thinking I could handle him. Why didn't he just reveal himself that first night instead of dragging this out for weeks? A sense of numbness builds. I latch on to it— it's better than being terrified.

Justin turns his empty hand, and the table mimics his movement, turning on its side to fit through the doorway. Once through, it returns to its upright position, hovers over, then drops down in front of me. Ben scoots my chair so the edge of the table jams into my ribs. The chair's armrests block an escape out the sides.

Justin slams the paper down in front of me. It appears to be a scroll—its top and bottom slightly curl. The edges are charred, as if it sat too close to flames. It's long too—about four and a half sheets' worth of paper—but I don't see any seams. The entire length is filled with iridescent black ink. Under different circumstances, I would have admired the calligraphy. Closer to the bottom, the print gets so small, I can't read it without a magnifying glass.

In the boldest and biggest lines at the top, is my name. I read on:

> *Madison Rose Page will hereby and forthwith consent to whatever her master, Justin Nathaniel Adams , wishes, for the extent of eternity, covering both this life and the afterlife, or until he releases her.*

It keeps going, but I don't have the stomach to read anymore. My *master*? *Both this life and the afterlife*?

"What is this?" I ask in a weak voice.

"It's a Binding Agreement, binding your soul to me for as long as I wish." He leans in real close. "And given everything you do, I have no plans of ever releasing you."

I swallow a lump in my throat. "What does it mean to bind my … my soul to you?" I can't believe I actually said those words. I have a soul. I should have figured it was included in the believing-in-God-and-Heaven package, but it didn't dawn on me until now. It's mine. *My* soul. Not even a minute after learning of it, I have to sign it over to Justin? I can't believe this is happening.

He sniffs my hair before whispering in my ear. "It means you'll be my pet. You will be at my beck and call. You will do what I ask without hesitation, or the contract will be void."

"Wh-what would happen then?"

"I'd exact my revenge on your family, friends, and anyone else who has ever had the unfortunate pleasure of meeting you."

The many faces of my family and friends play out in my mind: My friends happy and laughing at one of Jake's jokes. My dad smiling right after he said he loved me yesterday morning in the school parking lot. My mom falling to her knees and hugging me Sunday night when I came home late. And Hannah, earlier, when we embraced and I said—out loud—that I loved her. I love them all.

The happy images morph into the rotting corpse of the old woman. That is how Justin would exact his revenge.

I take a deep breath, trying to sound strong as I say, "If I sign this ... everyone will be safe from you?"

"*Yes.*" Excitement rolls off his tongue.

"Forever?"

"*Yes.*"

There is no way out. *This* is what I must do to keep everyone safe. I just can't believe it came to this. A single tear rolls down my cheek and falls onto the contract. It sizzles, and a puff of smoke rises.

When that paper burned my tear, it also destroyed my last hope. This *is* real. I don't know how, but it is. My life is over.

I doubt Justin would let me stay with my family and friends until I finished high school. There was so much I wanted to do. Not just to fix the pain I'd caused everyone, but also for me. After what Amber said in the office, I wanted to find my birth parents. I wanted to know who I am—especially after everything Justin claims I can do.

But none of that matters now. Not really. Not now that Justin has threatened my loved ones. Their fate rests on me signing my life away, indefinitely, on some enchanted, evil paper.

I take my last breath of free air before whispering, "W-where do I sign?"

Justin grins.

In one swift motion, Ben grabs my right arm and slams it down on the table.

"What are you doing?" I yell. My left hand scratches at his fingers to loosen his grip. The room flashes from continuous bolts of lightning like strobe lights. Fixtures and pictures shake as deafening thunder roars.

"In order for this to be valid," Justin explains, "it has to be signed in your blood."

Ben slides my sleeve up to my elbow, and something silver catches my eye. The knitting needle. It's now or never.

I grab the needle, raise it, and thrust it down to stab Ben's hand. But right before it can pierce his skin, the needle disappears from my hand.

I look up in shock, only to find Justin holding it. "Naughty girl … " He feigns disappointment before tossing it across the room. "Now where were we?"

Ben's hands tighten on my arm. Justin jams the feather pen into my arm between Ben's vise-like grip. I scream and struggle, but they ignore me. The long black feathers slowly turn red as the pen absorbs my blood.

I keep waiting for that familiar rush of adrenaline to fill me as it has every other time I've been in danger. But I don't feel it. If there was ever a time when I needed that extra boost, it's now.

By the time the top feathers are red, my head is spinning, dizzy from the blood loss.

"There," Justin says. "It's full. Now all you have to do is sign."

Suddenly, a rush of wind bursts through the room, scooping up the contract and carrying it out to the kitchen.

"NO! GUARDIANS CAN'T INTERFERE!" he booms. He grabs the table as if it weighs nothing. He hurls it against the wall, smashing it into the already-broken TV, destroying both of them.

"Hold her!" he shouts to Ben as he races to the kitchen. Ben grabs my wrists and twists them around behind the chair. Warm liquid drips down my right arm from my wound.

I slouch back into the chair. *Thank you, Elizabeth.* I thought my life was over. She saved me. I can't see her, but I know she's here in some form.

Things crash and bang as Justin rips apart the kitchen. What if she's really there, in the kitchen, with him? I turn my head toward the doorway, trying to see, but I can't. Is she facing a killer for me? How can she fight him?

He didn't seem surprised by her presence—just angry. And what did he mean by Guardian?

Does that … did he mean *Guardian Angel*?

She could be an angel. I thought it when I first saw her today. She does watch over me. She's here helping me now. And it's not the first time. She's been with me my whole life. I need her. I can't lose her. Somehow I have to help her.

In a moment of clarity, I'm reminded of what Justin first said. He doesn't affect MJ. MJ could help me keep everyone safe.

I need to get out of here. I have to find MJ. But I don't want to leave Ben—not with how angry Justin is.

I sit up straight and struggle against Ben. "Ben, please let me go. This isn't you. You wouldn't hurt me like this. I know … people who can help us. They can keep Justin away. They can help you. Please, Ben."

His breath blows on the top of my head. "Quiet."

"No. We have to get out of here. Justin is a killer, Ben. Don't you get that? Do you understand what he wants to do to me? I know you care for me. You need to help me, please. We need to run."

"Your life is with Justin now."

My head hangs down. He doesn't care. "Then I've lost you to him. There's nothing left of the guy I fell for."

The grip on my arms loosens. "Did you … love me?"

I close my eyes as a small spark of hope ignites in my chest. I think I might be getting through to him. If I keep this up, I can get him out of here. "I wouldn't still be here, trying to save you, if I didn't love you … at least a little."

"A little?"

"I'm not *in* love with you, but that doesn't mean I don't love you, Ben."

His fingers dig into my wrists as he squeezes them, slamming me back in my chair. My arms feel as if they were one pull away from being ripped from their sockets.

"I chased after you, begged you over and over to go out with me, dated you for seven incredible months. And then you just ditch me for one of *them*."

"No, I didn't."

"Liar!"

I whimper as he pulls tighter on my arms.

"I saw you with him last night!"

"You *what*! Were you following me?"

He's silent for a moment, then he proudly admits, "I've been following you all week because *he* never left your side long enough for Justin to get you."

Today wasn't the first time Justin tried to get me? And each time he couldn't, it was because of MJ. I knew MJ protected me at school, but the rest of the time …

"What are you talking about? Other than school and when you forced yourself on me, I've barely seen MJ."

"Right—you've barely *seen* him. Last night, what were you doing before you *slept* with MJ?"

I flinch from the snarl in his tone. "Nothing happened, Ben."

"Answer my question!"

I whip my head back, trying to see him behind me. "I was on my way here."

"Exactly! And he just happens to show up and stop you. A little too convenient, don't you think? You think Justin's the bad guy? At least he's up front about his intentions. *MJ's* the one sneaking around in your house and watching you when you sleep."

I shake my head, refusing to fall for his tricks. "He wouldn't do that."

"You think he really loves you?" he sneers. "You make him *feel*, just as you do Justin. That's the only reason MJ wants to be with you."

My heart falters. MJ is the first person I've ever connected with. Every moment spent with him—even the bad ones—has made me want more. I feel so strong and happy and beautiful with him. He makes me feel whole. I like him. More than like. And I know he has feelings for me. He admitted them yesterday. He wouldn't trick me as Justin does. MJ's good.

"No," I say. For the first time since this morning, my voice is clear and free of fear. I take a deep breath and continue, "It's not true. I know how he feels."

"You are nothing to him!" He pulls tighter, and I cringe and fight the urge to cry out in agony.

"Enough," Justin says, walking back into the room. "Let her go."

Ben immediately complies. I bring my arms forward and rub my wrists. I still see indentations and cuts from the zip ties. Blood is still dripping from the pen wound, but it's slowed. Scars from everything I've gone through tonight.

Everything I've *survived* tonight.

Justin picks up the bottle of bourbon and chugs it, nearly empting it. "I have to agree—*him* being in your bedroom the other night pissed me off the most."

"Why?" I ask on reflex. I'm still preoccupied with my wounds. A moment later, I drop my arms. MJ was in my bedroom?

"Because of all the times I watch you, that is *my* favorite."

I blanch. Not only has MJ been in my room, but Justin too. Was it Justin I saw last night? "When were you my bedroom?" I demand.

"I went over there the night we met here at my party—to finish where we left off. Then while you were asleep," he pauses and smiles, "you said my name. It was out of terror, but it still stopped me. Thousands of women have said my name before in similar settings, but this was different. Your sweet voice, filled with the panic you associated with me, resonated deep in my core. It was like hearing my name for the very first time. After that, I went back every night, hoping to hear it again."

"Shut up," I say, stunned. "You're drunk."

"This?" He shakes the nearly empty bottle. "As great as it tastes, it would take a whole hell of a lot more to affect me. I only indulge in it for sentimental reasons. But you wouldn't understand that. You're just an insignificant little insect, only here for my amusement. Yet … I can't stop thinking about you. Thursday night, I had resolved to kill you—"

I shiver.

"But your dream was so different that night."

Thursday night I had Elizabeth's Halloween dream. I spent the night in bliss—while he stood over me, intending to kill me. But it also means he knew about my dreams before talking to Kelli.

"You looked"—he stops and glances at me—"happy. You moved and talked incessantly as you slept. I was mesmerized. As dawn approached, I knew you would be getting up to run, so I turned your alarm off. You woke before I could kill you."

All morning I was mad about being late for school, when really I should feel lucky I even woke up at all.

Between MJ, Hannah, Ben, and now this … my brain, my heart, and everything else is wearing thin. My arms wrap around me, trying to hold it together.

"I couldn't understand it. Seeing you like that made me feel things I hadn't felt in so long. I had to get away from you. I was several states away when I got the tip about the *Protector* coming, so I tried to warn you—"

"Why warn me when you nearly killed me?" I snap.

He chucks the bottle against the wall behind me. I flinch as it smashes, causing lightning to flash and thunder to rumble.

"Don't interrupt!" he barks. He runs his fingers through his black hair and exhales—instantly losing his anger. "It's rude. Anyway, I knew he would be drawn to you too. And because of everything you do, I knew he could mistake you for my kind and destroy you."

While I can't fathom being mistaken for one of Justin's "kind," my mind drifts back to MJ towering over me at the fountain, nearly attacking me when I revealed I still remembered him.

"As much as *I* wanted to kill you," Justin continues, "I couldn't let someone *else* do it. So I came back for you. I tried to take you away from here before *he* arrived. But you refused to listen."

Now more than ever I'm glad I said no that day. Not only did it result in me meeting MJ, but it saved me from just disappearing. If I had gone to Florida, no one would have known what happened to me. It could have been me lying in a bath as well.

Or maybe it just delayed the inevitable. "D-do you still want to kill me?"

"Come on, Mads." He shakes his head. "You're my golden ticket to feeling alive again. I have no idea how you do what you do. I don't know if it stays with you in the afterlife."

"Wh-what do you mean feeling alive … again?"

He smirks as the words hang in the air. "Everyone seems to be breaking the rules for you, Mads. You have what seems to be a Guardian interfering. A Protector abandoning his Charge for you. Then there's me … negotiating a deal to keep you, a human, by my side forever."

He drops the contract in my lap. "Time to sign before anyone else shows up."

My jaw drops as I stare down at the parchment that seals my fate, the one Elizabeth stole to stop me from signing. "How did you get this? What did you do to her?"

Justin narrows his eyes. "You know who that was?"

I glare at the monstrous murderer. I don't know if he harmed Elizabeth. But this does provide me with something I haven't had yet. Leverage—he wants to know about her. This takes some of his power over me away. This is my chance.

"I'm not saying another word until you let Ben go."

Justin smiles and turns to Ben. "Ben, I release you."

Ben nods, then walks into the kitchen.

"Who is she?" Justin asks.

"*Did you hurt her?*" I spit out through my locked jaw.

"I sent her away."

"Where?"

He holds out the dark-red feather pen. Half of it is back to black as my blood drips out of the tip. "You'll find out once you sign the contract. Better hurry before we need to refill it."

Once again the power shifts back to him—Justin has what I want. Elizabeth is gone, and I don't know what he did to her. Ben is now free. I can only hope Hannah is safe. I should have told her to find MJ.

I'm on my own. I'm running out of options. I grab the pen.

Justin points to a blank line at the bottom. "Sign it," he demands.

My hand hovers over it. This is it. My life must end so everyone else can be safe. "D-do I need to write my full name, like how it is at the top?"

"It doesn't matter."

I look back up at him, not understanding.

"You could draw a picture of a unicorn for all I care. All that matters is that your blood touches the contract while the pen is in your hand.

My eyes widen, and I look at the pen in a new light. A fat drop of blood clings to the end.

Suddenly, Ben reappears, slowly creeping up behind Justin. He's holding a huge knife. Tears spring to my eyes. I haven't lost Ben after all—he must be free from the mind control. He's going to stab Justin.

Justin doesn't take his eyes off the pen in my now-trembling hand. I hold my breath and wait. Ben raises the knife with both arms over his head.

He impales the knife deep into his own chest.

"*No!*" I scream. The contract and pen fall to the floor as I rush to him. "*What did you do*!" I scream at both him and Justin.

Ben falls to his knees. I put my arm behind him to lay him down. I strip off my shirt, leaving me in a tank top. I place my shirt around the knife, trying to stop the bleeding. There's so much blood...

His eyes, brown again, stare up at me, but the light is already fading in them. My shaking fingers stroke his shaggy brown hair while my tears fall on his pale cheek.

"You're going to be fine," I say through my trembling jaw. "You're a fighter. You don't give up. Ever." I hold back a sob.

I figured I would be mad at him for a while. I figured we would work it out. I figured we'd stay friends. But now ...

"Don't just stand there," I yell at Justin. "Help me! Please!"

Justin moves to Ben's other side, bends down, grabs the knife, then pulls it out. Blood gushes out over my hands as I scramble to stop the flood.

Ben's body twitches as he chokes on his blood.

"No, no, no!" I say, shaking my head. "Please don't leave me, Ben." I lean in and place a kiss on his lips, tasting the metallic bitterness.

He gasps as if he's trying to say something. I lean my ear over his mouth.

With a staggered breath barely above a whisper, he asks, "Forgive me ... "

"*Yes.*"

Then there's nothing. No more breath against my skin. He's gone.

CHAPTER 54

MJ

I WATCH THE CONSTANT BARRAGE OF LIGHTNING AND thunder. Whatever he's doing to Maddy, he will pay for it. Rain starts to fall, and my insides twist in agony for her. I'm gonna spend eternity torturing him for this.

MJ, Alexander's voice says in my mind as he uses Cerebrallink. We've split up to cover a three-square-mile grid around her school. The storm is strongest here, but I can't pinpoint its eye to locate where Maddy is. *There's a terrified girl running toward me.*

Show me, I answer back. I close my eyes and reach out for Alexander's essence. My mind links with his. Through his eyes, I see a brown-haired girl running toward the bridge.

That's Maddy's sister! I close my eyes, step into the Veil of Shadows, and reappear beside Alexander.

Tears stream down her face as she runs for her life, though nothing is chasing her. I grab her by the arms, stare into her dark-brown eyes, and immediately get to work on calming her so she can focus and tell me what I need to know.

My essence flows into her and splits into three pieces. The first goes to her brain and stops its distress signals. The second flows through her veins to her heart and slows its beats. The third piece goes to her lungs to control her panicked breath.

"Hannah," I say in the soothing tone we use for compulsion. "It's me, MJ. Maddy's friend. Show me what happened to you."

Synapses fire across her mind as images play out:

It's dark outside. She's walking up a sidewalk to a two-story house. The paint is chipping. Loud noises come from inside—music of some kind with a pulsating beat.

She moves to knock on the door, but it opens before she touches it. Ben opened it. He smiles and ushers her in. The lights are off, but there's a strobe light hanging from the ceiling, flashing a blinding light. The room is filled with people dancing strangely. Their moves are slow, almost flowing, as they dance in unison. She scans them and recognizes Maddy's friends and many other students from Maddy's grade. She keeps searching, looking for Maddy, but doesn't find her.

Kelli grabs her hand and pulls her to dance with her, Kayla, and Maggie. The only ones not dancing are Ben and the man in the kitchen doorway. His black eyes look out over the crowd as he also watches the front door, as if he's waiting for someone to show up.

After a while, he looks down at something, then the music stops. Everyone turns to him. He smiles. "She's coming."

The music comes back on, and they drink and dance faster, crazier as they share in the good news.

"Who's coming?" Hannah asks Kelli.

"Maddy," she shouts over the noise.

Through the crowd, she notices Ben leave.

They dance to an unending song as they wait for Maddy to come.

Sometime later, Ben comes back. He looks nervous. He talks with the man in the kitchen. When the man looks up, his eyes are red. The music and lights stop.

He screams, "Get out!"

Everyone stands still in a daze. Then he kicks a hole in the TV. People push and shove as they race to get out. Behind her, the red-eyed man breaks more furniture in anger and shouts, "She's not coming. She's with *him*!"

A hand grabs her arm and pulls her. It's Ben.

"Come with me," he says.

She follows him to the kitchen, expecting him to show her another door out so she can leave too. Instead the red-eyed man is there. Ben blocks the kitchen doorway, trapping Hannah as the red-eyed man walks toward her.

"Hannah," he says. "Your sister has been a very naughty girl."

He reaches out for her.

Then everything falls dark.

The memory ends, and I blink as my essence cycles back to me. The party was last night and I stopped Maddy from going. Thank Father I did. But because of it, Hannah suffered. More had to have taken place there. That can't be all she knows. It's not enough. I need more. I have to see what he's done to Maddy.

I push my essence back into Hannah, searching her mind for more memories of Justin's house.

"Show me what happened when you woke up."

Everything is dark again. For a moment, I think the link isn't working, that she's too overwhelmed. But then a flash of lightning breaks through the darkness through a large window. It illuminates the room she had danced in. She's seated, facing a wall. She tries to move, but she can't. She's tied to a chair. There is tape over her mouth too.

I fight against my anger, pushing it down so I can concentrate on connecting to Hannah's memory.

Lightning flashes again. This time, Ben and Justin enter the room.

"What is it?" Ben asks.

"She's waking up from a nightmare about *him*," Justin says. "Won't be long now."

Thunder rumbles as someone screams. Justin disappears.

Knowing Maddy is also tied up somewhere, Hannah struggles to get free, but the ropes are too tight.

Justin reappears with a smirk on his face. "You didn't tell me she's an escape artist," he says to Ben.

"What do you mean?"

"She broke free from her restraints."

Lightning flashes and thunder shakes the walls.

Justin's smile widens. "I think she just found Mrs. Samuels in the bathtub. This is turning out to be more fun than I had anticipated."

Then blackness claims Hannah's mind again as the memory ends.

I pause to catch my breath and keep my emotions in check.

"Do you know where he's keeping her?" Alexander asks.

I recall the images. "It's a small, older two-story house. There's a large window in the front room."

"That could be any house over here."

I nod, hating that he's right. This is the older part of town. Nearly every house is the same. Alexander could go to Heaven and search for anyone recently deceased by the surname of Samuels, but that could take hours.

"It doesn't matter," I say. "I won't give up. I'll find her. Maddy's there, fighting against something she doesn't understand, because of me. If I had done what she asked and told her what I am, she would know what Justin is. She'd be more prepared to handle him."

"You can't be serious," he says. "You know the rules."

"The rules don't apply to her—"

A boom of thunder shakes the ground, and lightning strikes a lamppost near us. I close my eyes, counting to three to calm myself enough to continue searching Hannah's mind. She's my best shot at finding Maddy before it's too late.

"Once more," I say to Hannah. "And then you'll never have to think about this again."

I push my essence back into her. "Show me how you escaped."

For a moment, she hesitates, then blackness claims my vision once more. There's movement in the dark. A loud thud comes from the hallway ahead of her, as if something or someone has hit a wall. A minute later, a figure moves in the living room toward the door. The lights suddenly turn on and someone touches Hannah. She screams.

When Hannah opens her eyes, Maddy is there. Her mouth is red and swollen, likely from tape being ripped off. There are red marks on her wrists from whatever they had tied her up with.

She touches Hannah's cheek and says, "I'm going to get you out of here."

The memory ends again as Hannah starts to panic. She's feeling guilty for running away and leaving Maddy with them.

I need more, but that's all she can handle. I take a deep breath and take away her guilt. Then I focus on her own injuries, the rope markings on her wrists and ankles as well as the swelling and redness around her mouth. My essence pools in those places, healing her and erasing the physical reminders of the demon.

Now all that remains is to take away her memories. "Hannah, you didn't attend a party last night. Instead, you went to sleep shortly after dinner because you had a headache. When you woke up, your mother came in and told you your school had flooded. There was no school today, and there will be no school tomorrow either. You will have no memory of the red-eyed man or Ben's involvement or Maddy being in danger."

I lean back, releasing her fully from my compulsion. She sways under the weight of her trauma and new memories.

"Take her home," I say to Alexander.

A basic description of the house isn't nearly enough, but it's better than what I had. As much as I don't want to think it, the easiest way to find her would be for Maddy to get angry or scared enough to show me where she is. Until then, I'll keep searching. I will find her.

I'm coming, Maddy. Just hold on a little longer.

CHAPTER 55

Madely

M Y BREATH RACES AS I WRAP MY HEAD AROUND what just happened. "You … you killed him. You took him away from me. Why?"

Justin stands and shrugs. "I released him. I told you—I don't waste my time erasing memories unless I feel like it."

I glare up at him from the floor beside Ben. "He was your friend!"

Justin laughs. "If it weren't for you, I would have killed him the day we met."

My blood boils. Anger consumes me like wildfire. "You're going to pay for this."

Metal touches my bloody fingertips. I look down—it's the knitting needle.

I can do this. I can kill him. Ben, that old woman, Hannah, and everyone Justin manipulated to get to me—they need justice. *I* need justice.

I grab the needle and launch myself at him.

A second before I'm about to plunge it into his left eye, he disappears.

"You're so much fun!" Justin laughs, reappearing across the room. "We're going to have a great time together. Especially when I punish you for insubordination."

My lips twist in a victorious grin. I take slow steps toward him, my hand—coated with Ben's blood—still gripping the needle. "I haven't signed yet. And because you didn't let Ben go, I'm not going to."

Again I lunge at him, but again he moves through the room unseen.

He's now standing by the bar. "Oh, but I did let him go. He's moved on to the afterlife. Probably crossing over as we speak."

"I never took you for the religious type," I say before striking at him again.

Justin disappears and emerges in the kitchen doorway. "They say seeing is believing." He grins at the needle. "I can do this all day, Mads."

"So you expect me to believe you've seen Heaven, yet you still choose to be an asshole."

Justin smirks. "That's two times I get to reprimand you, now."

"How? You're already trying to force me to leave everyone I love. You've killed and hurt people I care about. There's nothing left you can do to me."

"Oh, I don't know about that. I thought of plenty while you were bound and gagged on my bed."

I stiffen.

"You denied me what I wanted at my party. I've never been denied before. As intriguing as that was, I've grown impatient. I possessed Ben for an afternoon and tried, but then MJ showed up and ruined everything. I'm done waiting."

"Possessed? What are you talking about?"

"Come on—you know what that means." He shakes his head as if he can't understand why I'm even asking him these questions. "He stopped here yesterday before you were done with school. That's when I entered his body. *I* picked you up. *I* held you. *I* kissed you. It was amazing to actually taste your lips and touch you." He shudders. "No one will ever be the same for me again."

I knew Ben was under Justin's control, but my stomach churns at the realization that Justin was somehow in Ben's body. Then it occurs to me: I've done that to Elizabeth all my life. But that's a dream—her memories. And I couldn't control her body. So how can Justin do it? How did he drive a car, hold me, and *kiss* me from inside Ben?

I try to slow my breaths. "Well, you enjoyed it much more than I did."

"I did enjoy it. You will too, eventually. We'll just have to practice." He steps toward me with a slanted grin on his lips and hunger in his eyes. "Once I'm through punishing you for this, we're going to do a little role playing in the hallway. This time when I tell you how you can make amends for all the trouble you've caused, I guarantee you won't laugh."

My body goes rigid. The last time we were in the hallway was the night of his party. I laughed at him when he said I should sleep with him to make amends for offending him. Is that what this whole "game" has really been about—because

I refused him? He lied earlier. He doesn't just want my supposed abilities—he wants *me*.

I close my eyes and fight against the fear building inside me. *My master. His pet. Be at his beck and call.* I can't do that. I can't give up hope yet.

Suddenly my feet feel warm and tingly for a moment—as if I stepped on a beach cooked by the sun. Then this hot, charged energy rushes up my legs to my torso. It pauses in my heart, placing itself there—filling every broken crack perfectly as if it's always belonged. Then the rest of it spreads throughout my body. I've felt this before—when I faced Justin and MJ and fought Ben.

My fear evaporates. My grief is gone. In their place is fury I've never felt before. Not even from Damien. It feels … good. Fantastic, actually. And somehow, even with what I've seen Justin do, I know I can fight. He will pay for what he's done and what he's trying to do to me.

This is what I need. One last push of adrenaline.

I open my eyes to glare at Justin, but I don't see him. He hasn't left—I know that. He must be using another of his abilities. I close my eyes and use my other senses to find him. A clock ticks in the kitchen. Pickles still cling to the air. A warm breath blows on my face.

Justin.

He's right in front of me.

Without opening my eyes, I shove the knitting needle in his ear, breaking through the cartilage and into his skull.

"Damn it!" He backhands me across the face.

The impossible force sends me flying through the room and into the wall.

As I lie balled up on the floor, my heart pounds like a jackhammer. My bones are heavy like cement. Pain drills into my wrist, shoulder, and ribs—every nerve ending. Everything screams in agony. But the worst part is, the rush of adrenaline is gone again, leaving me broken physically and emotionally.

It would be easy to give in to the pain and black out. But if I did, Justin would probably take me somewhere far away. I can't let that happen.

I blink up at him as he pulls the bloody needle from his ear and tosses it behind him. I shoved it in enough to hit his brain. I know I did. He should be paralyzed or twitching on the floor like a fish out of water—or better yet, dead. That's what I was aiming for.

"That actually hurt!" Justin says with a wince. He cracks his neck from side to side while the bleeding stops and the wound seals shut.

He laughs. "Nice try, Mads. But you can't kill someone who's already dead."

All I can do is gasp through the pain.

His laughter ends as he looks me over. "Hmm. You're hurt. Judging from the snaps I heard when you hit the wall and floor, I'm guessing your left wrist is broken. From your shallow, labored breathing, I'd say at least three of your ribs are cracked. And from the way your left arm is dangling, I'd bet your shoulder is dislocated. You must have a pretty high tolerance for pain." He pauses and nods to himself. "That's good. I don't want you being hysterical whenever things get a little rough."

"I'll try … not to disappoint you … asshole."

He smiles weakly. "There's my Mads."

In a blur, he's in front of me, crouching down. "You're no good to me like *this*. I wanted the first time I touched you to be ... a more satisfactory one. You have no idea the willpower it took to restrain myself. I'm stronger than I knew. But not strong enough to wait several weeks for you to heal on your own. I'm not sure if I can heal you, though. I've never bothered to fix anyone before. *They* do it all the time, so I suppose it should work for me. Lay still. This should only take a moment."

As he reaches for me I'm reminded of what Elizabeth said: "When they touch you, they can either heal you or harm you." I don't know what that means, but I'm not about to find out.

"Don't touch me!" I shout. I try to get away, but I crawl only a foot before I double over. I again fight against the tempting darkness.

Instead of shifting a few inches, Justin disappears and reappears next to me. "Again with this, Mads? There's nowhere you can go to escape me. I'm immortal. I've been dead for a long time. Not as long as MJ, but—" He looks at me and smiles when my eyes widen in shock. "He did tell you he's dead, right?"

No.

There's no way to deny it now. MJ. My hero. My love. Is dead. That dream ... *memory* ... was true.

"He didn't?" Justin asks in surprise. "Oh—so he's protecting you without their approval. Interesting ... They'll be angry when they find out. He's their poster boy, you know." He stares past me, thinking. "That means the *others* will come down for a big investigation. Everyone's minds will be erased. And you ... they'll—*no!*"

In a flash, he grabs me from the floor and pins me against a wall, ignoring my screams.

He's touching me.

The same static-charged rush of sensations from MJ's touch now springs to life from Justin's. But this time, it's stronger, faster, and nearly painful. It attaches itself to the agony ripping apart my ribs, shoulder, and wrist, fixing the damage he created.

He stares down at me so forcefully I can't look away, though I desperately want to.

My gasping breaths come faster, drawing in his scent. It flows through me. It's the same smoky aroma I smelled every night I spent as Elizabeth.

He smells exactly like Damien.

A fog swirls in my head. His horror house fades away. All that remains are his hollow black eyes.

"You have to trust me, Madison," he grits. "MJ will get you killed."

No. This is wrong. I don't want to hear this. MJ would never harm me—I know it. But I can't move. I can't speak. The fog envelops me.

"I can keep you safe. Spending eternity with me won't be as bad as you think. Whatever you want, it's yours. Name it and I'll do it."

I stare into his eyes while his essence inside me changes. My heart slows. My fears begin to lessen. Visions of new life play out against the black screen of his eyes. Us holding hands. Him gazing at me with love and tenderness. Me laughing and happy. We'll travel the world together. Forever.

My body becomes lighter as I let go of … I don't know what anymore. Things that existed before Justin. And because they came before him, they aren't important. He's important. Everything is perfect now.

I open my mouth to agree.

"O—"

A light breeze swirls between us, pushing strands of my hair across my face. It blocks his eyes. The image of our pristine future dissipates.

I want it back.

Something touches my shoulder, as if someone is leaning into me. A woman's voice whispers, *"MJ."*

MJ.

I know that name.

I try to place the name in the fog in my head, but I can't. My heart races again, thumping furiously, but I don't know why.

MJ. I let it echo inside me. It flows so easily, as if it's already familiar with the space. It stops in the hole in my heart, as if it has been there before.

Images flash so quickly in my mind of me and a brown-haired, hazel-eyed boy. He's mysterious. Complex. But he's more than that. He's passionate. Caring. He gives me hope. He gives me strength. He's my center. My other half. I think … I think I'm in love with him.

Yes.

I love MJ.

I want that life with MJ, not Justin.

The darkness evaporates. I blink, breaking his hold on me. But I can still feel his essence. It pools along my right side and left shoulder and wrist, dulling my pain.

My pain ...

Whenever I was hurt, MJ could feel my pain too when his essence traveled back into him. If I can somehow force Justin's essence to stop healing my pain and instead make it go back to him, I can hurt him too.

I close my eyes and imagine his essence is dark blue. I push against it. At first, nothing happens. I push harder and harder. And little by little, the massive blue blobs separate from my injuries.

I take a deep breath, then push with all my might, sending them speeding through my body and into Justin.

He cries out in agony and falls to his knees. "What are you doing?" he bellows.

I know I could run now, but it would sever the connection. He needs to hurt longer.

He continues to wither and wail while clinging to my legs. I don't know how long he's gone without having to feel any pain at all—let alone this much. But from how badly this is crippling him, I'd say it's been a while. Long enough that his body doesn't know how to handle it.

He deserves this, and more. But I can't keep this up forever. Eventually I'll have to stop. Not to free him from the pain, but to escape. I just don't know how yet—aside from running for the door. But Justin will catch me. Unless ... unless I keep pushing him. Maybe, just maybe, he'll black out.

But what if that doesn't work? He's strong. Far stronger than me.

Maybe I don't need to do this alone. What if Hannah reaches Duane? He could help. Or better yet, MJ. Justin's abilities don't work on him either.

Maybe I could get a message to MJ. Ask him to help.

I close my eyes and think of Hiniker Bridge and MJ. Wherever he is now, maybe I can transport him there to meet me. I've got to find him and tell him where I am.

The tightness of Justin's arms around my legs is gone. Instead, I feel the cold, hard wooden railings of Hiniker Bridge on my belly as I lean against it.

It worked. I'm here.

I open my eyes to millions of shining stars. With their light, I gaze around the pond.

It's frozen. The trees are bare. Empty branches sway slowly in the chilly air. I don't hear any bugs.

Maybe it isn't as welcoming as it was the other times, but I'd rather stay here forever than go back to that house.

I take a deep breath—feeling no pain from the movement—and inhale the strong scent of a campfire right next to me.

"*What are you?*" asks an awestruck voice.

It *really* worked. MJ's here too.

I turn and come face to face with Justin.

CHAPTER FIFTY-SIX

Maddy

STANDING AT THE OTHER RAILING, JUSTIN GAZES around, taking in as much of my safe haven as possible.

I stagger back on my bridge railing as my knees weaken. "You're not supposed to be here. It was supposed to be MJ. Get out!"

Faster than I'd thought possible, Justin is leaning over me, his hands gripping the railing behind me. I can't lunge at him or even try to escape without touching him—and being sent back to his horrible house.

His eyes search mine as he slowly leans forward. I tilt as far back as the railing will allow, but it's no use.

Justin's lips press against mine.

His kiss is such a shock, everything stops. It's delicate and strange, filled with anguish and remorse. His essence fills me again, becoming so strong it manifests outside our bodies and encases us in a bubble the same dark blue I pictured inside my body.

No. I don't care what emotions he puts behind it. As soon as we go back to his house I'm dead. Maybe not right away. But if I sign that paper, I might as well be. If that's not bad enough ... if Justin didn't take everything from me already ... now he's stolen my last kiss of what's left of my life. I hate him. I wish I'd never met him. I try to pull away, but it doesn't stop him.

Justin finally leans back.

Between the tightness of his arms around my legs, the pain in my body, and Ben lying still and bloody behind him, I know we're back in his house.

He lets go of my legs and slowly stands. He stares sorrowfully at me. "Even when I was alive, I never had a kiss as great as that. Whatever the reason you are the way you are, I'm grateful for it. I know you hate me—I could feel it. But in time, that will lessen. We will soon have eternity together."

His black eyes gleam as a wicked grin spreads across his face. Lightning and thunder crash as he digs his thighs into mine and presses his torso against me. It's impossible to move or kick him. His right hand grabs my broken wrist, and I yelp. His left hand grabs my right arm and holds it against the wall.

"Time to sign, Mads."

The feather pen appears, held between Justin's teeth. He shoves it into a vein in my forearm. My blood fans out along the feathers.

I scream and struggle as tears fall from my eyes, but Justin only holds me tighter. Outside a storm is blowing so forcefully, it might rip the siding from the house.

An explosion of thunder erupts. The front window bursts from the pressure, spraying shards of glass over Justin and me. Wetness slides down my face and arms. I don't know if it's blood, rain, or a mixture of both.

Lightning hits the gold couch, setting it on fire. Orange and amber flames climb the window curtains and spread out along the brown shag carpet.

Justin curses as he removes the pen from my arm.

"Justin—stop!" I cough as thick smoke chokes me.

My head feels dizzy and my vision blurs. If Justin weren't holding me, I'd fall to the floor.

He spins me around and pins me to the wall. There in front of me—looking just as magnificently terrifying as before—is the Binding Agreement.

Justin forces the pen into my hand. Ben's blood has changed to brown, reminding me he's gone forever.

"Sign it!" He glances back at the encroaching flames. "Hurry."

Unable to support itself, my head leans back against his neck. Thick smoke burns my throat and lungs with each breath. My hair sticks to my skin as beads of sweat fall down my face from the intense heat.

I could give in. I could die right here. MJ, Elizabeth, Damien, and Justin are all dead. They seem fine. If I were dead, Justin couldn't own my soul. I'd be free.

But if I died, I would give up everything—my life, my family, my friends, my dreams and ambitions—for Justin. No matter what choice I make—die or sign—he still takes everything from me. Death is pretty permanent; the contract is for eternity. Either way I lose.

I wish there was another option. Someway to still have a say in my life while protecting the people I love. Justin's not going to let me go, I know that, but maybe ... I can offer him something else. Something no one ever has before.

"If you *force* me to be with you ... I'll hate you forever. Deep down, you'd hate yourself for it too. You like that I'm different from everyone else. That I don't say or do what you expect me to. But if you give me a *choice*—the power to freely choose to be with you—" I stop and gasp for a clean breath of air.

The pressure of his body suddenly eases. I have enough room to turn and face him. I wobble and blink several times, trying to fight the darkness appearing at the edges of my vision.

"If you tear this up ... I'll go with you ... wherever you want ... But you have to promise ... to not hurt anyone ... ever again. That includes MJ."

His eyes flicker. A ring of light blue slowly forms around his pupils. Something is building inside them. Hope, maybe?

"You'd do that?"

I nod, my throat burning too much to speak now.

The pen falls to the ground. Slowly, a smile plays along his lips. It grows, parting to show some of his perfect teeth, and dimples form on his cheek. It looks ... natural on him. For the first time ever, I realize Justin is good looking.

"You've made me so happy, Mads. We'll travel the world. There are so many things I want to see and experience."

His hand strokes my cheek. I flinch.

His smile falls. "You're *lying*." Empty blackness reclaims his eyes. "You didn't mean any of it!" He grabs my hand,

and the pen leaps into my palm. He forces my fingers to close around it.

"*No!*" I shriek, though it's barely understandable.

He spins me around again and moves my hand toward the contract. It's barely visible from all the smoke. The flames reach for me. They're maybe three feet away now.

Blood drips from the pen tip as Justin forces my hand closer. I close my eyes, not wanting to watch my life get stolen from me.

Suddenly, he jerks me back. Then the pressure of his body is gone.

He screams.

My arms shield my face against the heat of the flames as I fall to the floor. I keep my eyes closed, trying to mentally escape and save myself from feeling the fire as it consumes me.

"Don't think," a panicked voice commands in my ear. "Stay with me."

The heat is gone. A new yet familiar sensation fills me—MJ's essence.

I blink up at him, then my eyes clamp shut again, too drained to stay open. Unable to fight it any longer, I finally fall into the darkness.

CHAPTER 57

MJ

"PLEASE WAKE UP," I WHISPER TO MADDY FOR THE THOU-sandth time as I sit beside her on her bed. As she does all the other times, she stays silent, sleeping and regaining her strength from the unspeakable things he did to her.

The demon disappeared right before hitting the flames. I let him go. I had to. I was alone—Alexander was taking Hannah home. If I had gone after Justin, Maddy would have died.

"She *will* wake, though. Won't she?" Alexander asks.

"Yes. When she does, I want you to give us some privacy. Do another sweep of the perimeter, then check in with the others. She's been through too much today. I'll wait a day or two before introducing you all to her."

"Will *you* be well enough to be on your own?"

"I'll be fine. I'll call you back when I want you to re-turn."

"Understood. Do you want me to get you anything before I leave? Another blanket for her … or perhaps a shirt for you?" He smirks.

I sigh as I look down at my bare chest. That's twice in one day I've been half-nude around her. This morning, I removed my shirt while she slept to heal the bruises I'd seen on her body the night before when she was in the bathroom. I think she may have even heard me gasp at them. Tonight, it's to heal all of her.

"No," I reply. "She heals faster this way."

I hold her closer, sending her more of my essence to heal her. One by one, I'm erasing the physical reminders—minus the two small holes on her forearm that refuse to fade. All I could do was stop the bleeding.

"What do you think the contract was?" he asks, following my gaze.

"I don't know. It vanished the second I arrived." I don't know if she signed it, and that thought terrifies me. If she did—if even a single drop of her blood touched that paper—her fate is sealed. She'll have to do whatever he wanted. No one can undo a signed contract.

"She's strong. I've never seen someone with two Featherling markings."

"Neither have I." I was shocked to find them when I cleaned the blood from her beautiful skin. The Featherling requires two pints of someone's blood to work. That monster stole four of hers. That's enough to kill a person. My essence is helping her body produce more blood. I've managed to replace one pint so far, and I'll continue holding her until the other three are accounted for. She will be weak when she wakes, but alive.

He must have held Hannah and Ben to force her into agreeing to sign. She must have stalled. And fought him.

"What are you going to do when you find him?"

"Make him wish he never left Hell."

"Is she worth it … all the trouble you're going to be in?"

I look at him and resist the urge to roll my eyes at his asinine question. "What do you think?"

"After meeting her, it's clear she's meant for a higher purpose." He looks from her to me. "I've stuck by your side for 205 years. I'm not about to leave now that it's finally getting interesting."

I snort. "Yeah, she definitely does make it that, doesn't she?"

"MJ?" His questioning tone makes me look up at him. "Something's been weighing on my mind since Friday… "

"Really? What is it?"

"It's about your Charge and the case. We know the demon is going after specific girls. But why them? What is it about these girls that makes them so special?"

"I don't know. They're basically the same. They're all brown-haired, green-eyed Caucasian females. Each of them is thought to be talented in a sport, music, or dance form of some type. All of them were born on October 31 seventeen years ago. And all of their parents died that same day. The odds that there are this many girls fitting that description is remarkable."

"That's what worries me. I mean, what if … the demon is looking for a specific girl, but only has that description to go off of? He'll keep killing anyone fitting the description until he finds the right one."

I shrug. "I suppose it's possible."

"What if a girl with this description knew something important? Or better yet, could do something that would shift power over to their side?"

"Like what?"

"I don't know." He pauses. "Maybe … make the dead feel?"

"No!" I growl. Maddy stirs, and I lower my voice again. "She's not one of the targets. She's not adopted. I've checked."

"That may be, but she's everything else in the description—and so much more. You have to consider that at some point in her life, another demon has either stumbled across her or heard of her. How many times did her family move before she was two years old? *Ten*? Each and every state she lived in is where a target lives."

"Not the state with the first two targets," I say as my chest heaves. He's not right. She's fine. I didn't save her today only to face losing her to another demon down the road.

"Maybe I'm wrong. I hope so. What she can do … it's bigger than all of us. In the wrong hands, she could be a very powerful weapon. We saw how difficult it was to find her today. If there is a next time, we may not be as lucky."

Maddy's hand tightens slightly on mine. "She's waking."

He disappears while I anxiously wait for her to come back to me. Whatever happens next, I will protect her.

Always.

CHAPTER 58

Maddy

SLOWLY, I PEEL MY EYES OPEN. MJ'S SMILING DOWN AT me. I'm home.

"Hey," I say, though it's barely audible.

He reaches behind me for something, and I notice he's not wearing a shirt. Before I can ask him why, he presses a glass to my lips. "Drink this," he says.

I part them, and cool water rushes down my throat. With each sip, I can feel my strength returning.

He takes the glass away. His hazel eyes rapidly move about as he searches every inch of my face. I'm not sure what he's looking for; I've never seen him act like this.

"Did you sign it?" he asks, his voice shaking.

I blink and try to focus on him again.

"Did you sign it?" he repeats. "The paper on the wall. Did any of your blood touch it?"

Memories of Justin's house come back. I shudder, thinking about those last foggy moments pinned to the wall while the house burned around us.

"I-I don't think so."

The fear and anguish leave MJ's eyes. For a moment, there is a spark of some new expression on his face, like raw pain mixed with sadness, guilt, and immense joy all at the same time.

But before I can do something to comfort him, his lips suddenly press to mine.

Neither of us moves. His eyes are clamped shut, but I'm too stunned to close mine. A rapid pulse of his essence emanates from our joined lips. It's so much better than when he kissed my hand. It's as if ... I'm absorbing him. Soaking in all his warmth, desires, relief, and pain.

Lines of strain and heartache begin to ease from his forehead and cheeks. I have wanted to kiss him for so long. Over and over, I have thought about this moment. But the circumstances leading up to that imagined first kiss were different than this. I sure as hell wasn't frozen in shock. I want to move. I want to touch him. Hold him. Comfort him. And I definitely want to kiss him back.

Before my lips can comply with my desires, MJ pulls away.

He rubs his lips together, then sighs. "I'm sorry. I know that was forward and ... after everything you just went through, I shouldn't have ... But while you were healing, I kept thinking about how we haven't even kissed yet ... And I wanted to kiss you and ... " He stops talking and runs his fingers through his hair.

My fingers twitch, aching to feel the texture for myself. Slowly I lift my hand and retrace the trail his fingers just made through his short brown hair. It's soft and thick. My palm tingles as the ends brush against it.

When I lower my gaze, his hazel eyes are wide and vibrant. It's as if someone turned a light on inside him.

Just like that, he's leaning into me. Everything moves in slow motion. His hand slides behind my neck into my hair. His breath rushes over my sensitive lips just before his lips press to mine again.

This time, I close my eyes and focus on him and me together. His lips are smooth and warm. I can smell a hint of crisp rainwater in his damp hair. His familiar essence races through me, being absorbed again. My whole body tingles, butterflies fill my stomach, and my head spins.

This is how I pictured kissing him.

His essence flows faster through this new form of contact. I'm still dizzy from the blood loss, but also from the incredible kiss. Once his essence has spread through me, it flows out to him, then back into me. It strengthens and moves beyond us. I open my eyes for a moment and see we're encased in a perfect silver bubble.

All too soon, I feel him pulling back from our intimate contact. He looks at me as if I am the best thing in this world or any other. His hand leaves the nape of my neck and caresses my cheek. A moment later, he softly kisses me again.

"*This feels amazing,*" MJ says. Our lips part only long enough for him to utter each word.

"*Shh.*" I don't want them to part at all. I learned what it would be like to lose him today. No matter what he is or what I am, being with him is all I want right now.

His lips are tender and soft; his kisses are slow, sweet, and intimate. My lips quiver in anticipation for more. I missed him. I love him.

A warm sensation, like flames deep in my belly, increases, and heat flows through me. Every inch of me yearns to feel him. He's familiar. He's safe. My arms curl around his back, feeling his bare skin as I pull him closer to me on my bed.

Our bodies press together, and he's the first to break for air. His lips move along my cheek, down my neck, and back up to my ear.

"I'm so happy I found you. Never do that to me again."

My body goes limp and the silver bubble dissipates as what happened at Justin's house comes barreling back to haunt me. Tears stream down my face. The sound of raindrops hitting the house fills the room.

MJ pulls me into his smooth chest, cradling me as I give into my grief for Ben and the old woman, my regret for Hannah's involvement, and the loss of my innocence. I'm no longer ignorant to the world around me. There are beings with abilities that shouldn't exist outside of science fiction stories. I fought one … and lived.

"Maddy?" MJ asks timidly after a few moments.

I sniffle and lean back to look at him. My heart breaks again. MJ's crying. Are the tears his, or are they mine? If they're from me—from him feeling how much I'm hurting through his essence coursing through me—his tears won't stop until mine do.

"I don't know what to do, Maddy," he says, his voice smaller than I've ever heard it. "With everyone else in the whole world, I have the power to simply erase their memories, make all their pain go away. Everything in me is screaming out to fix this and take your pain away, but I can't. I'm ... powerless. What should I do?"

I squeeze his hand intertwined in mine. "You're here with me—that's all I need."

We share a smile through our tears.

I find the strength to push away my pain, and my tears slow, then stop. I look at MJ, and no more fall from him either. MJ gazes to the window as the rain stops. He sighs in relief.

Why would he be relieved it's no longer raining? As I watch him, I remember what Justin said—it rains when I'm crying.

"You know?" I ask.

MJ's jaw clenches, and he lowers his head to look at me. "Yes, but I didn't know if you did."

"Justin told me." Seriously, how did I never notice?

"I'm sorry you had to find out that way."

"Do you know what I am?" I blurt.

"No, but I'll help you figure it out."

"You will?"

"Yes."

More memories of Justin's house stir, stopping on my final moment alone with Ben. I know he was under Justin's control, so I don't blame him for anything he said or did. But I can't help wondering if there was any truth to what he said about MJ—that he's only with me because I can make him feel.

I experienced firsthand what lengths Justin went to because of my … abilities. And as Ben said, at least Justin was honest about it. But what if Ben was also right about MJ? Is MJ being honest with me—and himself? Does he have feelings *for* me? Or does he just get "feelings" *from* me?

"Why are you with me, MJ?" Even though I don't really want to know the answer, I *need* to know.

"What do you mean?"

"Ben said the only reason you want me is because I make you feel."

He closes his eyes and presses his forehead to mine. "How can you still not know what you mean to me? *Minn eiga hjarta rót.*"

My heart flutters. "What does that mean?"

"It means, roughly, 'You who are at the very center of my heart.'"

"Is that Norwegian?"

A shy smile appears as he nods. "An old form of it."

"That's beautiful." Tears of joy threaten to stream down my face, but I hold them back, not wanting to flood the town.

"It's true. You are my everything. I spent most of the day and night thinking I'd lost you."

"How did you find me?"

"I followed your storm, but it was so massive, I couldn't find the starting point. I found Hannah, hoping she knew, but she was in shock. It took the largest bolt of lightning I've ever seen to fall from the sky and set fire to that house for me to know where you were."

"Is Hannah okay?" I ask, worried.

"She's sleeping. I—" He pauses and looks away. "Her memories had to be erased."

I'm glad that for Hannah the nightmare is over. "What about everyone else?" I ask.

He sighs. "There are … people coming here in the morning. They're going to wipe all traces of Justin from the whole town's minds. I'm in charge of your family's house, though."

I freeze, remembering Justin's panic over the "others" coming to do that. He acted as if I'd be in danger. "Why are they coming here? Why are you in charge of erasing my family's minds?"

"Because your memory can't be erased."

I stare at him, waiting for him to explain more, but he doesn't. Then I realize *that* is the answer. "You mean because if one of them tried to erase my memory and found out they couldn't, they'd kill me, right?"

He shivers. "No. Maddy, I'm … we're good. Justin's not. He and I are the same, but we're different. I know that's hard to understand, but please trust me on that."

"Justin said you'd get me killed," I press. "I'm pretty sure that's what he meant, that your side will kill me."

"No. Never," he says, though I don't know if he's trying to assure me or himself.

"*You* tried to kill me by the fountain."

MJ falls silent.

This talk about killing brings me back to Justin's house. It takes all my effort to not sob, thinking about Ben. "I'll have to call Ben's family. They need to know what happened so they can plan his funeral."

"We can worry about that after you've rested."

"But what about Justin? Where is he?"

"Gone. You're safe from him now. He's not allowed to come near you ever again. It's one of our rules."

I shake my head. "He won't follow it. You're not following the rules, either."

"Well," MJ says with a deep breath, "if he comes back, I'll be here to stop him."

"Really?"

"I'm yours now," he says, holding me tighter. "Always."

"Promise?"

He nods.

"You won't leave me?"

"Never."

I smile and rest my head on his broad shoulders. I run my fingers up his arm as he gazes down at me. "What happened to your shirt?" I decide to ask.

"Um ... " he begins, "you were bleeding a lot when I found you. I cleaned you up, but I couldn't leave you alone to fetch new clothes. Plus, the more contact I have with you, the faster you heal."

"Oh." I nuzzle closer to him and notice the scar, the one created when he died. I kiss it.

MJ stills.

I gaze into his vulnerable eyes. "This scar is the reason you and I are together."

"How do you know what my scar is from?"

I think back to my time with Elizabeth, grateful for her help tonight and wishing I knew where she was so I could thank her. Even though Elizabeth said MJ can't know about their involvement, I have to tell him something. Maybe I can just keep their names hidden, like she had? "Remember those dreams I have, that you learned about at school?"

"Kind of hard to forget learning that your girlfriend is psychic."

Girlfriend. My stomach flips, and I smile. I do want to be his girlfriend. I want to be more than his girlfriend, actually. I want the vision at Justin's house. I want to spend my life happy with MJ. I'm not scared by that revelation, merely excited. This is new for me. It's new for him too. In order for it to work, I have to start opening up to him.

I don't correct him about me not being psychic. It's too confusing right now. Instead, I focus on him.

"While I was unconscious, I dreamed of you. You were protecting a girl around my age from someone named Sigurdsson. I watched him kill you."

"I'm so sorry you had to see that," he says as he frowns. "I should have told you."

"I wouldn't have believed you."

He lifts my chin and places a quick kiss on my lips. "You're probably right. No more secrets," he commands. "From either of us."

I give a small smile, wishing it were that simple. It's not that I want to lie to him or keep secrets anymore. But I just know there are things he wouldn't understand. How could I tell him about Damien and Elizabeth?

"So ... your turn. What's a Protector?" I ask.

His jaw tightens, and he shakes his head. "Always so eager for information." He takes a breath then lets it out. "Given everything you experienced today, is it safe for me to assume you now believe in Heaven and Hell?"

I nod, afraid my voice will betray my nerves.

"*I'm an angel, Maddy.*"

My heart stalls. My lungs freeze. All thoughts vanish.

I've been demanding to know what he is since meeting him. I've made a list of all the "logical" things he could be, and it turns out he's the one thing I had said didn't exist.

I accepted that Elizabeth could be an angel; she looked the part. But MJ ... Where's the signature white gown Elizabeth wore? Why don't either of them have halos or wings? Why is he visible here when she wasn't? There are so many differences between them, but one thing is the same—their *essence*. I feel it each time I touch them.

After a moment, he continues, "There are many facets of Heaven and Hell people are allowed to be aware of. Spirits, ghosts, angels. More specifically, Archangels; Guardian Angels; Satan, or the Devil; and demons. They all exist."

I just stare absorbing it all and trying not to freak out.

"Archangels came before man. They're the Originals. When God created man, some Archangels became jealous. There was a great battle, and five of them fell from Heaven. One became the Devil, and the others serve him. The Archangels that remained in Heaven were given a new task. As man transcended into the afterlife, the Archangels watched over them and created new angels to help fight against their brothers in Hell."

I release my breath and brace myself for more—knowing he's not yet finished bringing to life beings I'd written off.

"Guardian Angels are each assigned to watch over one person, from birth all the way through to the afterlife. They can guide people and help them make good choices, but they can't actually interfere in their lives."

I think of Elizabeth again—wondering where she is and whether she's okay. Justin's words as he chased her ring out in my mind: *Guardians can't interfere.* MJ just said the same thing. So did Elizabeth break the rules to help me, or is she something other than my Guardian?

"Because Guardians can't interfere, that's where I come in. I am a Protector. I can do whatever I need to do in order to save someone from a demon."

MJ's brows furrow a bit before he caresses my cheek. "Demons are souls of men who have been sent to Hell. Like their ruler, the Devil, they don't like to play by the rules. Almost every crime and war is because of demonic influence. That's what Justin is. He's an Influencer. It's my job to stop him and other demons that pose a threat to people."

This is so far beyond anything I expected. First God, then angels, and now the Devil and demons. Justin is a demon. I fought a *demon*. I fought him for my soul.

"So, where do Binding Agreements come into play?"

A tremor runs through his body. "*What*? That's what that contract was?"

Crimson fills his eyes. I watch him as he breathes in quick pants, but I know he's not angry with me. He understands what that contract means—apparently even more than I do.

"You're absolutely positive none of your blood touched that paper while the pen was in your hand?"

"I'm pretty sure ... But everything happened so fast those last few moments." I pause. "I guess I don't really know."

MJ closes his eyes for a moment. When they reopen, the red is gone, but his eyes are distant.

"When I arrived, he had you pinned to the wall. I saw the contract, but it disappeared before I could read it. I threw Justin into the flames, then grabbed you before you got burnt." A smaller tremor shakes him again. "I can't believe it's a Binding Agreement. Demons like him aren't allowed to make that kind of deal. It's where the saying, 'sell your soul to the Devil' comes from. Only the Devil is allowed to possess souls for eternity. I have no idea how Justin managed to get that, but I'm going to find out."

"Oh," I say and swallow back my fears. I'm eternally grateful Elizabeth took that paper. She kept me from signing it more than once. It was also her when the wind blew my hair in front of my eyes. That's what broke the fog in my head from looking into Justin's eyes.

We're silent for a few moments before I ask, "What was your transfer?"

MJ's mouth twitches, and he lies back down next to me. "I was going to be reborn."

I inhale sharply. "You can do that?"

"Free will isn't just for the living. We can choose to remain in Heaven for eternity, serving as either Guardians or Protectors—if we qualify. Or we can be reborn as often as we'd like."

"So you'd be alive again if you did that?"

"I'm alive enough when I'm with you. You are what I've been waiting for."

I smile as my heart flutters, then I kiss his chest.

Lying next to him, feeling this way, it almost feels as if Justin's house didn't happen. It's just strange that something so good can happen on the same day of something so tragic.

"So ... what about Amber? You're supposed to be protecting her."

"She's fine. I called in my team when you disappeared. You'll meet them in a day or so, after you've rested."

"Your team?"

"Three angels I work with."

"They're Protectors like you?"

"Yes."

"Is ... is a *demon* after Amber?"

"Yes."

"How bad is it?"

"Bad enough to where your uncle is tracking him too."

"Duane? But he tracks serial killers."

"Exactly," he says matter-of-factly.

I frown. Why would Duane be tracking a serial killer who's actually a demon? It's not like he knows such things even exist. Or does he?

He warned me about MJ—forbid me from seeing him. Said MJ's not what I think and that he's a threat to me. He knew some of MJ's and Justin's abilities too. I guess maybe Duane does know then. Is he the only one with this knowledge, or is he part of some special branch of the FBI that handles cases outside of the norm?

"We know all the targets now, though," MJ says, disrupting my thoughts, "and each one has a Protector assigned to her."

"Her? They're all girls?"

"Yes."

"Like Amber?"

He nods.

"But … I'm not one?"

"No."

"You're sure?"

"Yes."

"How?"

MJ falls silent.

"Hey," I say and place my hand under his chin. "We said no secrets."

He lets out a long exhale. "It's a long, sad story. We've both had a horrendous day. I don't want to fill your head with this particular evil today. Let's get you rested, healed, and fed. Then I'll tell you all about Amber, the serial killer, and anything else you desire."

I nod, and his eyes soften. "Once you've rested, I'm taking you out on many, many dates. Real ones," he laughs. "There's so much I want to show you."

I smile. "I'd like that."

After a moment, I lie back down. His humming essence turns into pulses inside me. It's peaceful, like lying on a hammock in the yard and being rocked to sleep by a mild summer breeze. I yawn, and his fingertips brush along my temple. He's helping me relax so I'll fall asleep.

We should talk more, but I know this is just the beginning with Justin, the others coming to town, and the serial killer. Whatever I am, I'm still human. Still capable of dying and possibly losing whatever I do that allows MJ to feel. I trust him. I'm safe with him. I love him. Always.

In time, the rest of our secrets will come out, but right now, all I want to do is hold him close and relish that we are finally together.

CHAPTER 59

Justin

FIRE FLICKERS BRIGHTLY ALONG THE BASE OF THE STONE walls, in the massive fireplace, and high above on multiple candle chandeliers, illuminating the Acquisitioner's personal chambers. It almost resembles a luxury bachelor pad instead of the lodgings of the most sadistic demon to ever walk the earth. There's a bar beside the door, a table long enough to accommodate fifty people though there are only two chairs, and a seating area with leather couches and a massive TV. Off to my right is an alcove. I'm not sure what's in there, but after seeing the furnishings, I suspect it's his bedroom. I didn't think *they* slept.

I thought I would be quick. Just a quick peek into Mads's file, then I'd leave. But I searched through millions of files—every possible name combination and birth date—and Mads doesn't have one. This room holds a file on every single soul created since the beginning, and she isn't here. How could she not be here?

"What are you doing?" asks a gruff male voice.

Terror immobilizes me. No matter what punishment he chooses to inflict upon me, I'm going to suffer more greatly than I've ever suffered before. For the first time, I wish Mads hadn't given me the ability to feel.

I turn and drop my gaze to the floor, careful not to look him in the eyes. My body clenches as beads of sweat fall down my forehead and neck.

The black robed figure moves closer. The only sound is the light swishing of his robes along the ground. It didn't take long to pick that sound out above the screams when I first arrived here. It's the only warning we have when the Fallen are near. It's the most frightening sound in the universe.

"Forgive me, sir," I reply. "I was looking for something, but I can't find it."

The swishing of his robe stops as the leader of the Fallen comes to a halt in front of me. "And who was that?"

"The file for the girl I asked you to write the contract for, sir."

"I see." He walks to the stone slab that is his desk in the center of the room. "Did you succeed in getting her to sign it?"

Visions of myself tied to a stick, roasting in the massive fireplace, play out in my mind. I shiver. He's going to torture me for eternity for losing both Mads and the contract.

"There was a ... complication. Several, to be exact. Someone—a spirit of some kind—helped her. At first I thought it was her Guardian, but Guardians can't interfere."

"What did this *spirit* do?"

"It spoke to the girl, several times, strengthening her courage. The voice was female. It also tried to take the contract, but I handled it."

"*Did* you?"

"Yes. I got it back. Later a Protector showed up right before I could get her to sign."

"The girl. Where is she now?"

"With him."

"So not only did you fail to get her to sign the Binding Agreement, which you nearly lost to ... an *unknown* spirit, but you also left her in the hands of the Original?"

I swallow some of my fears. He already knows what happened, and so far he hasn't flayed me.

"No, not yet," the Acquisitioner says, responding to my thoughts, "but it is an intriguing idea."

A tremor runs through me, but I'm determined to not let him know just how much he terrifies me. "Why did you write that contract, sir?"

Even without looking up, I can feel his now-red eyes burning into me. "Are you questioning my judgment?"

"No, sir. It's just ... I know I'm not the first to ask you for a Binding Agreement, but I'm the first to be granted one."

It was the Protector who spurred me to come to the Acquisitioner Sunday night, when I thought Mads disappeared. My fear of losing her overshadowed my fear of him. That's why I thought of the Binding Agreement. That way, no matter what, I'd always know where she is.

As the Acquisitioner, he drafts all contracts in Hell for all demons. Each one is tailored to our rank and abilities. But his main job is to draft Binding Agreements to acquire souls for the Devil. I didn't expect him to actually agree to my plan, but he did instantly.

That night, he gave me powers outside of my rank. He strengthened me and allowed me to possess Ben and everyone else so I could get to Mads. All he said he wanted was a favor in return later. What he gets from the deal, I still don't know.

As soon as that thought forms in my head, I know he hears it. His pale fingers trace the edge of his desk as he moves for the first time in what feels like age. He creates a fine mist of powder as layers of stone crumble under the slightest pressure of his touch. "I get more than a weak demon like yourself."

Realization dawns. "Mads. You get my Mads."

"She is not *yours!*" he roars.

My feet leave the ground. Against my control, my arms and legs spread out like an X, stretching to the brink of dislocation. My body shakes. I clench my teeth to hold back my scream. I will not give him the satisfaction. I will not cry for him. I killed the last man who made me cry.

"You think just because you stumble upon something it belongs to you?" He's silent for a moment, then the hood of the black robe slowly turns from side to side, saying no. "Foolish boy. She is alive only because I have allowed it. I made it so the other side would not know about her. She was born with powers even I do not command."

My breath hitches. He's known about Mads her whole life?

"With her by my side, I will not only be the next ruler of Hell once Satan resigns next Hallows' Eve, but I will reign over Heaven as well. You will get her to sign the Binding Agreement. Then you will declare your allegiance to me. If you so much as think about double-crossing me, remember this: according to both Heaven and Hell, Madison does not exist. If she does not exist, neither side will claim her soul."

"No," I gasp. She's unclaimed. All the times I almost killed her, I would have lost her permanently. I'm such a fool.

"Once she signs the Binding Agreement, you can lay claim to her soul after she dies. You are her only hope for an afterlife."

My head hangs as guilt, shame, and hopelessness bear down on me. I can't be responsible for her like that. Only one person has ever depended on me, and I let her down. And this is so much bigger than that. I'm not worthy of her.

"Do you know what the other three members of the Fallen are doing?"

The muscles and tissues in my shoulders and hips tear as he pulls them farther from my body.

I scream.

"They are up there," he says, pointing to the ceiling, "on Mortal Ground, trying in vain to kill as many mortals as possible before Satan resigns without drawing the attention of the *others*. But even with their numbers combined, they do not come close to mine. I am the Devil's second in command—the rightful successor. I will be the next ruler—with or without the girl. When that day comes, you had better be on my side. You have until her seventeenth birthday to get her to sign. I do not care how you do it. Do not fail me again."

"But … " I struggle against the pain. "The contract … it vanished."

"Do you think I would be foolish enough to not have it safe-guarded? If a Protector gets too close to any of my contracts, they return here."

On the desk, he places two objects. One is a rolled scroll I assume is the Binding Agreement. The other is a gold ring with a black stone. I don't know what the ring is for, but he wouldn't be giving it to me if it didn't serve a purpose.

The Acquisitioner stills beside the desk with his back facing me. A long, pale finger taps the edge while he waits for only he knows what.

"She is strong and unique. But … broken. Things that are broken have weaknesses. Find hers. Succeed in that, and then she will sign the Binding Agreement."

I fall to the stone floor as the Acquisitioner disappears into the alcove. Even though I'm unable to move, my body already begins repairing the damage.

Her seventeenth birthday. I have less than ten days to find her weakness, get her alone—away from *him*—and get her to sign the contract.

We can't have the life I envisioned. Instead, we'll both be slaves. What have I done?

Forgive me, Mads.

Acknowledgments

THANK YOU SO MUCH, ALISHA BJORKLUND, ASTRID Bryce, Miriam Khan, Jennifer Noles, Sara Campbell, and Jamie Hostetler for putting up with all my rewrites, crazy emails, and quadruple-checks on my quest to ensure that Maddy and MJ's story is the best it could be. All of you amaze me with your knowledge, ideas, and patience.

I would also like to thank my family and coworkers for supporting me as I follow my dream. I appreciate your encouragement more than words can express.

Finally, I am so grateful to Amy Quale at Wise Ink. Thank you for working so hard behind the scenes; for pairing me with my fabulous editor, Angela Wiechmann, and brilliant designer, Tiffany Laschinger; and most of all, for making my dream a reality.

L AURIE WETZEL HAS always had a passion for writing, but it wasn't until a New Years Resolution in 2011 that she finally shared her lifelong dream of being an author with her husband. He read the very first draft of Unclaimed and gave her the words she needed to hear, "This is what you need to be doing." Three years later the first book in the Unclaimed series was published with the second book expected to be out in 2015. Laurie lives in Mankato, MN, with her husband and two young sons. When she's not writing, working, or spending time with her family, she's either reading, running, or catching up on her favorite shows on Netflix. For updates on the Unclaimed series as well as other works in progress, feel free to check her out online!

 http://www.facebook.com/LaurieRWetzel

 http://www.twitter.com/Laurie_Wetzel

 http://lauriewetzel.com